THE KIL

Kevin Sampson is the author of eight novels –
Awaydays, *Powder*, *Leisure*, *Outlaws*, *Clubland*,
Freshers, *Stars Are Stars* and *The Killing Pool* – and a
work of non-fiction, *Extra Time*. He lives and works
in Liverpool.

KEVIN SAMPSON

The Killing Pool

VINTAGE BOOKS
London

Published by Vintage 2014

2 4 6 8 10 9 7 5 3 1

First published in Great Britain in 2013 by
Jonathan Cape

Vintage
Random House, 20 Vauxhall Bridge Road,
London SW1V 2SA

www.vintage-books.co.uk

Addresses for companies within The Random House Group Limited
can be found at: www.randomhouse.co.uk/offices.htm

The Random House Group Limited Reg. No. 954009

A CIP catalogue record for this book
is available from the British Library

ISBN 9780099470267

The Random House Group Limited supports the Forest Stewardship
Council® (FSC®),the leading international forest-certification organisation.
Our books carrying the FSC label are printed on FSC®-certified paper. FSC
is the only forest-certification scheme supported by the leading environmental
organisations, including Greenpeace. Our paper procurement policy can be
found at www.randomhouse.co.uk/environment

Typeset in Perpetua by Palimpsest Book Production Limited,
Falkirk, Stirlingshire
Printed and bound by CPI Group (UK) Ltd, Croydon, CR0 4YY

To Dave Hughes and Charlie Galloway, my men of rock.

ACKNOWLEDGEMENTS

The input and advice of former DIs Billy Riley and Jim Fitzsimmons was invaluable. Huge thanks to both.

The insights and suggestions of Alison Hennessey at Harvill were inspirational. Huge thanks.

The keen eye and diligent work of Clare Bullock at Cape was indispensable. Thanks.

2012

Hodge

Calamity. Absolute disaster. Mere weeks from the long goodbye and the whole shebang blows up in my face. Not that one's retirement is the overriding concern in a situation like this, it goes without saying. Forget all that – the plaudits, the legacy, the feeling of immense and lasting satisfaction one might have anticipated, had this all gone to plan. Those are the trimmings – the aftertaste of a job well done. Appreciation would be welcome, no doubt, but above all one would simply have preferred to bid the job farewell on something akin to a positive note. It's not to be, now. The curtain call one had in mind is simply not to be.

From the moment Una Farlowe informed me of the girl's existence I've had a bad feeling as to how this might end up. That it's ended up like this with Kalan hacked and stabbed and slashed so badly that his body has basically drained flat – is a total and utter tragedy. Tragic for the boy, of course. Horrific. And for his girlfriend, too. Misha. But for all of us who've been running this job for all this time, it really is too awful to take on board. For myself, for Una and McCartney – McCartney, especially, will be distraught at this turn of events – Kalan Rozaki's demise is a devastating blow.

I glance over to check on Gilroy's progress, but I have to

look away. I heave out a weary-sick sigh of despair, asking myself all over again if there is more we could have done to protect the boy. The truth is there is *always* more one could have done. Always. But nobody could have predicted this; the savagery of it. I'm assuming this is a message from his brothers – a message to me, to the force, to everyone. Who else would deal with a snitch in this way? Anyone crosses the Rozaki brothers, they're saying – *this* is what happens to them, whoever they are. Even one of their own; a Rozaki brother in name and in blood.

I squeeze Mal Gilroy's arm and we give one another the look, the silent understanding that can only come from years of nights like this. 'Sordid world,' says the look. 'Sick place we live in.' Mally zips up his bag, gives the kid one last, sad glance, and he's off and back to his car, leaving me alone with the remains. Poor Kalan. I find myself poking at him with my toe, but the fact is he's gone now and it's what we do from this point on that counts. We cannot, we *dare* not, let this one slip. I look down on the boy's butchered torso and start to think damage limitation. I call McCartney. If anyone can save this cursed situation it's Billy McCartney.

McCartney

I take one last, loving toke on the carlota, flick it hard at the wall and enjoy the firespray, then I'm into the kart and off, gunning back into town, eyes left and right as you do. I take every which one-way, no-entry and backstreet I know, every second crucial as I race against time to get to Kalan before the uniform boys start making things worse than they already are. I try Una again. She's as good as given up. The trail has gone cold at the main park gates and she doesn't know whether to stick or twist, or if she's bust already.

'Just stay there, U. I'll be with you any minute.'

I've got 'Bright Eyes' on low to keep me calm as my brain races and races, trying to anticipate every twist and turn that's coming my way. *This is the first day of your life.* Yeah, right. I cut past the bombed-out church, and skirt Chinatown. All these years on, and I still grip the wheel and grit my teeth when I spy that neon strip. Maybe one day I can enjoy its sights and spices again. Maybe when I finally get that bastard put away.

1984

Hattie Vine

Here we go, then. This is it. Deep breath, Hattie – nice deep breath. This is what it's all been building up to: all the work, the sacrifice, the turning the other cheek. All the pain you've gone through has been leading up to the moment you walk through those doors as the cop who's going to make a difference. Who'd have thought it'd be Liverpool, though. Liverpool – of all places. Gotcha!

Hodge

She's a bright cookie, I'll give her that. Sharp as a tack. God alone knows how tough she is, but she's going to need to dig deep if this is going to work. I'll give her a few weeks, a month maybe, to find her feet and learn what's what up here, but I'll admit I'm excited about getting Vine started on the real stuff. With her degree and her background, she brings something completely new to our onslaught against drugs in this city – and make no mistake, this is a war zone. We may try to downplay the statistics but the heroin problem has gone beyond rife up here. It's a pandemic. Been creeping in and creeping up since the turn of the decade, but it's like sticking your thumb in the dam, now. One scarcely knows where or how to concentrate the resources. When she came in for interview, I asked her straight.

'What would *you* do, DS Vine? How would you focus your approach?'

She was impressive, if a little naive in the way she responded. She referenced the horribly voguish 'broken window' theory the Monday Club have cloned from the Yanks – but only to dispute it. In the States, the theory is that if we act early and decisively in relation to minor incidents, the bigger issues tend not to arise – hence the moniker. As soon as there's a broken window in a tenement, you fix it. Immediately. It deters the wreckers from smashing more windows, for starters; and it stops the vagrants breaking in, the squatters starting fires, the junkies using needles. It stops the rain getting in, too. If one mends the broken window then the framework doesn't rot. There's no rising damp. The apartments are decent. Tenants feel a sense of pride in their home. The alienation and exclusion driving the self-pity that fuels the antisocial behaviour and, ultimately, the crime are kept to a bare minimum. The city is a better place to live – for everyone. Vine's take on the notion is that the framework here in Liverpool is already beyond repair and one has to look at demolishing the building and starting again. In basic policing terms, she argues that we have to forget the minnows and the street dealers and start to target the major-level drug barons. I'm with her all the way on that one. I'll be plain, here; I have a very good feeling about the girl.

Manners

Tidy, very tidy, I'll give her that. Neat little arse jutting out from them slacks, nice perky tits, pretty in a Plain Jane way. Girl next door. She's in a suit and that, giving it all the 'treat me as a copper, not as a woman' thingio. Do us a favour, love.

Seen your CV – nice photo, by the way, before you went and got your hair cut. Harriet Vine, born Coalville, Leicestershire, 17 March 1960. Tell you what, girl, hope you're not a fucking Fenian with that birthday; we'd have you out of here faster than you can say Guildford fucking Four. But what gives, eh? When will these trumped-up civil servants down there take the hint? Cops are born, not taught. Either it's in you, or you're down the road, no back answers. One thing you cannot do is *learn* this job. Degree in Criminology! *I've* got a degree in fucking Criminology, but I never went to no fucking university to get it! She's a sergeant already too, by the way. Detective Sergeant Harriet Vine, after minutes in the job. Well, I'll tell you this for nothing, Miss Prim – you won't last two minutes in this city. Liverpool will find a phoney out in the blink of an eye, and you in your suit and your so-calm voice and your bored-of-it-all pretty little face are one bad phoney, girl. Criminology!

Hattie Vine

It seems the sinister, ever-smiling Yardley is the boss around here – another man's man with his winks and wisecracks with the lads. They're all nudges and snidey little in-comments, but if I say anything – and I'm definitely not rising to it – you just know how it'll play. They'll be all wide-eyed innocence, put it all down to 'banter' or claiming I'm oversensitive or whatever. I can handle it. It's not like I wasn't expecting a little locker-room tomfoolery, but this lot are the worst I have ever encountered – and that's after one morning. Half of me has been dreading Liverpool – obviously. The closer this day has loomed, the more I've felt I just won't be able to handle it. But the old man has been terrific; any doubts I've had, he's talked them through and talked the nonsense out of me. I'm here now, and I'm going to make my dad proud of me – with or without the help of my colleagues.

The main mouth, DC Manners, is sidling over now, and there's nothing less than unadulterated malice emanating from his twitchy, blinking face.

'Deeeeeee-vine!'

And what? I haven't had *that* one a thousand times before? Jesus wept. He looks to his mates for their tittering approval. I don't even bother looking up. I've survived Hendon and I'm all too wearily familiar with how this ritual plays. If I react, I'll get a row of blank expressions, all giving out that standard macho 'don't know what you're on about' look. He's like a bad comedian, Manners, the way he keeps turning to his pals for encouragement. And if I so much as look up from my newspaper, the other buffoon, Dooley, is running his tongue over his lips. It's laughable – these men are here to ensure the good folk of Liverpool sleep safe in their cots, God help us. DC Manners is breathing on me, now – *the* foulest breath I have *ever* encountered anywhere. Just in case I didn't get the brilliance of his gag, he translates it for me.

'Vine by name, divine by bloody looks!'

Turns to his mates. I ignore him. He claps his hands, then rubs them together in the seediest manner imaginable.

'How d'you fancy some action, Hattie?'

I want to pull him up, insist he calls me DS Vine – but there's already the incipient dread that I'm going to have to keep my powder dry for bigger battles ahead. His eyes are glimmering with ill intent, so I simply call his bluff.

'Sure. Let's go.'

He gives Yardley and the gurning DC Dooley his raised eyebrows and, with as much belligerence as three men can plausibly exude, they shuffle towards the door.

I grit my teeth and follow them, wondering how long this initiation idiocy can be expected to last. We pile into an unmarked Nova and Dooley forcibly yanks Manners out of the way so he can press up against me in the back. Yardley has started up the engine before we've even shut the doors. He grins and wheel-spins the car out on to Hope Street. Manners cranes round from the front seat, wiggling his eyebrows and putting on a dopey redneck accent.

'Let's go and roast us some coon!'

I'm appalled. I can't get close to explaining how hideous they are or how sickened I am by their proximity. They explode with laughter – quite honestly, they're almost hyperventilating, slapping the roof of the car and shrieking out these jackal howls as we tear through the streets. I'm trying to come up with a form of words that will register my absolute dismay in a succinct and authoritative manner, when there's Dooley squeezing my thigh, shouting: 'Eyes left! Eyes left! He'll do!'

The car screeches to a halt, cutting right across the path of a non-Caucasian male, age approx. mid-thirties. He's not exactly keeping himself to himself in his big flamboyant beret and those mustard-coloured strides, but since when was that a crime? Manners just flies out of the front seat, slams this guy against the wall – a church wall, incidentally – kicks his feet outwards and begins frisking him. It's not even a side street. We're on a major main road in full glare of the public and bypassing traffic. I'm rooted to my seat.

'Where's the drugs, Sambo? Where's the fucking drugs?!'

'I got no drugs,' he pants. He can barely get his words out – Manners has stuck his finger right under his chin. Next thing Dooley's there. With no announcement, no warning, he just cracks the guy across the face.

'Don't fuck about, dickhead! Where's your fucking gear?'

I get out, dazed. I walk towards the scene in nightmarish slow motion. DI Yardley – our *boss* – heads me off, grinning. He hands me a sap, hard rubber – non-standard issue. I stare

8

at it, numb. Yardley winks and presses the baton into my palm until my fingers grasp hold of it.

'Go on, Hattie – give him a dig, love. Just walk up and give him a fucking crack! Got to lose your virginity sometime . . .'

I look at Yardley and for a split second I force a panicked, fearful grin. This is not happening. I step back a pace and stand there, horrified, as Dooley and Manners continue to beat and kick the victim. I can feel DI Yardley's eyes boring into me. I pull myself together and head back to the car, as certain as anything that this is the first and last time I'll work with this team.

Manners

We've got the sooty bang to rights, just the tart we need to sort, now. Face on it, by the way! She's got a bad case of the toffee nose, this one, stood back all aloof and wincing with disgust at us. Fuck sake, girl, a collar is a collar is a collar – don't they teach that to you soft shites down there? Whining on about the nignog's fucking rights, if you will! Give her a week or two round here and she'll soon wake up. This is how it works, darling. Us, good guys; them, baddies. Might take you a week, might take you a fucking year, but sooner or later you'll get the picture, love. There's no such thing as a ordinary decent coon.

Evan Kavanagh for fuck's sake, put your shirt on it, every time. Bad nigger, la. Bad, bad nigger. Every time, man – every single time. Fella can't help himself. Quarter of Rocky on him, personal use, whatever, personal, business, little or large – doesn't make it fucking legal, does it? Don't give a fuck what the limbo-dancing lowlife says, if he's got gear then he's bought it or he's dealing it. Either way, he's got what we want. He's got Names. Let the Sambo sweat it in there a bit longer, he'll soon start singing. And if he don't – he knows what he's got coming.

Shakespeare

What they take me for? Seriously? That fool Manners really think ol' Shakespeare going to suddenly turn blackleg and sell my kith and kin down the river? Fella don't know a thing about me, if that what he thinking. Fella don't know about pride. Don't know about struggle. Don't know the first thing about how a man's dignity, his standards, his *story* play, if he thinks the world really that cheap. Captain Manners – don't make me laugh! They too stupid for words. They can take a brother in. They can break my back. But they can't have my heart and mind. Shame on them thinking any other thought about Evan Portius Kavanagh Esquire.

Hattie Vine

I'm sitting here staring at the wall, still don't quite know what's hit me. I know I've got to get this down, exactly as it happened. I know I've got to submit my report to Hodge – no omissions, pull no punches. But strike a light, what I also know is that, before I've even started, this is going to be the end of me. It's crushing, it really is a devastating kick in the teeth. You come into this with your hopes and aspirations. You get a dream transfer to a prime posting in one of *the* great capitals of crime – and *this*. Your colleagues are worse than the offenders. I'm building myself up to type the first words of my complaint when DI Yardley appears at the door, all smarmy-contrite, sympathetic smiles.

'Bit of a baptism of fire, eh?'

'I'll say.'

'Still. All done and dusted, now. The lads know you're one of us. They can trust you.'

'Is that what that was all about then, sir? A question of trust?'

He starts walking over, very deliberately, still the fixed smile on his face. He must have been quite a good-looking man once upon a time, DI Yardley. There's a bit of intelligence in his eyes, and the remnants of a decent physique, but he's let it all go. You can see the gradual dissipation, the putting it off until tomorrow, the night after night on the piss. His smile, which is designed to reassure, I find menacing. He's holding out his hand.

'Look. Let's start again . . .'

I realise he wants me to shake his hand. I do so.

'Doug. Yards. *Everyone* calls me Yards.'

I don't want to call him Yards. I merely nod my comprehension. He knee-squats so his head is level with mine. He, too, has revoltingly stale breath.

'Look. Alfie Manners is a fucking good cop. Yes, his methods can be a little direct at times. But sometimes needs must . . .'

I try to swallow it, but I just can't let it go. 'Sir, on any and every level, Manners assaulted that witness –'

'That witness is a time-served career offender, Hattie –'

'But, sir, what we've just seen is as clinical a violation –'

He claps his hands and springs up, talking over my protests.

'Come on! Come. They're about to start questioning him. Come and sit in, see how these things occur up here. See if Alfie gets the names he's looking for. I promise you, Hat – if you don't think the end result justifies his means once you've seen Alfie in action, then you're not the cop I think you are.'

He winks at me.

'Come on . . .'

I feel horribly sullied and compromised, yet off I trot after him like a good girl.

Manners

I'll be honest and that, I wouldn't normally have worked the prick over that bad, but what with the bint sitting there, all snooty-faced, looking right through us . . . I'm going to myself, you think you're Job, do you? I'll show you what this job is all about, you tart. Think you can mix it with the big boys? Well, this is a man's world, darling, get used to it – cos this is what it's all about. Welcome on board. Seeing her looking down on us like Holy Joe – I just wanted to get a rise out of her, if I'm being honest about it. I threw all sorts at him. Had him crying his eyes out, snot bubbles, blood, owning up to all kinds, he was. I still hit him again like, just to be sure. That new piece pure couldn't watch by the end. Job done.

Hattie Vine

I don't even have a chance to process the anger and revulsion coursing through me. DI Yardley is back, smiling. He puts an arm around me and walks me out of the interview room. Yes, I'm upset by what I've just seen but more than anything I feel disconnected, disembodied, like those moments of subconscious dream-voyaging just before you drift off to sleep.

'Brutal, eh?' smiles Yardley.

I don't answer.

'To an outsider, that probably looked like a bit too much force . . .'

'A bit?'

'Know what, though? It worked. You can question his use of gentle coercion as much as you like, but by God Alfie Manners gets results! That lowlife Kavanagh gave up the whole roadshow, there.'

'I must have missed that part, sir.'

He shakes his head, face slowly dissolving from radiant grin to benign frown.

'Hattie, love – you've got a lot to learn . . .'

I'm about to give him a smart-arse answer, but suddenly I see red.

'A lot to learn? What — about beating confessions out of innocent people?'

He looks down at his shoes, scuffs his foot at something, then looks up sharply to eyeball me.

'Look. Hat. I've got a good feeling about you. I think you're going to do all right here — I really do. But, love . . . you're going to have to do something about *that*.'

He jerks his head at something behind me. Pathetically, I turn to look.

'What?'

He's grinning again.

'That.'

'What?'

'That chip on your shoulder — it's weighing you down, love. It's holding you back!'

This is clearly intended to make us both chuckle over the absurdities of life — how easily these little misunderstandings can get blown out of all proportion. In reality, I feel faintly sick in Yardley's presence — which is why I say nothing in response. He's over again with his arm around me, ready to ram home his advantage.

'Look . . .'

His wallet is out now and he's counting out five, ten, fifteen, twenty, twenty-five, thirty quid in five-pound notes.

'What I want you to do, right?'

He presses the money into my hand.

'Is go in there and tell the lads you're taking them out tonight. Yeah? It's a tradition round here — the new lad gets the ale in and what have you. New lass, in your case. I think it'll do everyone the world of good, yeah? Clean sheet. Get a little feel for the city — how the lads see the job.'

He goes all Max Bygraves, sincere and serious and a little bit world-weary.

'They're not bad lads, Hattie.'

He pauses and bends his knees, tries to find my gaze with his suddenly moist eyes.

'They're just cops.'

He pats me on the side of my face.

'Will you do that for me? Make a fuss of them? For Yards?'

He hits me with the grin again and squeezes the hand with the money in. Before I can say anything he winks and turns sharply, and he's gone.

Manners

That's laughing, that is, man! The kipper on her when we walks in here – strippers on and everything, Joey Sad Kecks walking round with his pint pot collecting for the girls, that mad loon with the voice box singing 'Thriller' and doing all his crazy Michael Jackson moves, moonwalking backwards while he blasts it out. Laughing! Sounds like a Jewish harp, he does – like he's been put through a Moulinex blender. Fucking mad old gaff, the Carousel. Mental. There's smackheads selling batteries, socks, Duran Duran cassettes, you name it – not for long, by the way. Offski soon as the boys in blue walk in. I pulls the bint over and make sure she's copped for the respect we get.

'See that? That's fear, that is. That's knowing when you're beat.'

She just pulls one of her snotty faces and goes: 'What's everyone having?'

Dools stays with his pint but I'm on it now, aren't I? I've got the taste for it and it's shorts all the way for my good self from now on in.

'Go 'ead then, love, get us a large rum and black . . .'

She's taking her time, mind you. Dools is all 'we should give her a hand' but I won't have none of it. I'm – No, stay here. Bint half wants to be a fella, let her get her round in.

Hattie Vine

The night goes from bad to worse. I fully comprehend that this whole ordeal is some kind of a test but what I'm failing, utterly, to get to grips with is what pleasure these men can possibly derive from frequenting such unremittingly dull clubs. The music is dreadful. The decor has, at best, seen better days and in most cases has not seen a Spontex cloth in many a year. Every single place we've been in, establishments with names such as the Babaloo, the Gazebo and Ugly's, the clientele have stood back and glared at us, unflinchingly. Left to my own devices I'd have to leave, or nick someone. Manners and Dooley do neither. They laugh, loudly, at their own jokes.

'Doesn't that bother you?' I ask.

'What?'

'Those guys. The way they're looking over.'

Manners looks up, grins in the direction of a group of young lads with Charlie Nicholas haircuts.

'Them? Gang of little divvies them, love. Couldn't be arsed with them.'

Dooley joins in. 'Just nice to ruin their night, isn't it?'

'How come?'

'Just being here. Kills it for them, doesn't it?'

So the point of *our* big DS night out is not, after all, to bury our misgivings about one another and somehow try to forge some kind of common ground, some way of working together; it's to prevent the general public from enjoying theirs. Nice.

Manners and Dooley carry on supping without relish, chatting without engagement, laughing without mirth. I just lean back against the bar and take in the sideshow. Every now and then some Job groupie will totter over on glitter heels and try to be flirtatious. Our heroic duo barely even brush them off, these atrocities in lamé dresses; they ignore them, mainly, carry on talking, scanning the room constantly, never seeming to relax at all. The only time they're remotely engaged or animated comes whenever I ask a question that's deemed gauche, or make a fool of myself in some other way – suddenly they're cracking up with laughter, one or other of them putting their arm around me and giving it:

'You've got to love her, though, haven't you? Got to love the girl for trying!'

The ribaldry is cut short by the arrival of a group of hard-faced middle-aged men, accompanied by one or two younger guys. Manners straightens himself up, his face a mixture of fear and something approaching excitement. The men arrive at the bar, look me up and down briefly, then pretend I'm not there. They pull Manners and Dooley to the far end of the bar and go into a huddle of conspiracy. I try not to stare too much, but these fellas look *evil*. Even the least threatening of them, a diminutive, wiry, elfin man, has violence in his smile. His face twinkles, but his eyes remain dead. A guy I hadn't clocked sidles over from the other end of the bar, clears his throat and holds out his hand to shake.

'Roddy Dixon, *Liverpool Echo*.'

He stands back as though that's supposed to mean something to me, then inches even closer.

'So this is where the swine come for their pearls?'

He must think that's a good one, as he chuckles to himself, revealing horse-like gums and yellowing teeth. Acknowledging my utter lack of any response, he steps back and tries to start afresh.

'Sorry. Just that I couldn't help marvelling at how wholly out of your depth you look there. Here.'

Under the bar lighting, his badly dyed hair glows a vicious shade of orange.

'That so, Roddy? That makes us equal then, because I can't help marvelling at your exceptional toupee.'

To my surprise he roars with laughter and claps me on the back.

'Excellent, excellent! We're going to get along famously, you and I!'

Dixon's laughter makes the Diddyman look up. He says something to Manners who clocks me like he's seeing me for the very first time. He beckons me to join them. I try to take my time but the truth is I'm curious. I want to know who these hoodlums are. Roddy from the *Echo* whispers in my ear and squeezes my shoulder.

'Chop chop, precious. You've been summoned!'

I take a deep breath and head on over to their huddle. With a forced bonhomie, Alfie introduces me.

'Gentlemen, I'd like you to meet the latest whizz-kid on the block, Miss Hattie Wino! You'll be seeing and hearing a lot of this little loony!'

They all over-laugh hideously, and the dapper little death-smile, who looks like a racehorse owner in his tailored, felt-collared coat, holds out a hand and goes: 'All right, Hattie, love. Terry Connolly. Take no notice of these.'

I realise I'm looking down on him. He holds my hand a second too long for comfort, those deadly eyes raking over me, then that's it. He puts one arm around Manners, the other around a younger fat lad in a black satin shirt, and guides them a few yards further down the bar. They chat quietly and intently in hushed but urgent tones; they're within touching distance but just out of earshot. Every now and then the little one smiles over; he thinks he's a bit of a catch. Dixon appears at my side again.

'So? What exotic promises did Uncle Terry make?'

'Sorry?'

Again the sarcastic snort.

'Either you're very naive, my lovely, or you think I'm born yesterday . . .'

I eye the wig. 'Clearly not the latter.'

He seems hurt. He digs down inside his threadbare jacket and pulls out a biro.

'Listen. Sorry about the false start. Here's my number . . .'

He tears the picture off a beer mat and scribbles his number, thrusts it into my hand.

'I am actually an extremely nice chap . . .'

He hits me with the stale yellow gnashers again and gives a funny bow.

'. . . trying to do a not-very-nice job. And I'm always on the side of the good guys. So. Anything you think I need to know about Liverpool's colourful mafiosi . . .'

He enjoys the moment as I re-examine the clutch of whispering bruisers.

'*Them?*'

Dixon nods, leans right up close and whispers: 'If you're *extra* vigilant you'll see the sidekick slot Alfie his envelope . . .'

He nods at the younger guy in the shiny black blouse.

'The fat lad?'

'He'd probably prefer stocky, but yes. Kelly. Watch. Any second now Terry Connolly will toddle off to the loo and Bobby Kelly will take care of Alfredo's drink.'

'Drink?'

Dixon gets up, his face all grave with this sad, sloping smile. He shakes hands once more.

'On second thoughts, let's not, hey? Let's keep you pure. There has to be one good cop, after all . . .'

He bows again, gives it the theatrical flourish and backs away out of the club, leaving me perched at the bar.

Hodge

How far do we go to appease the new kid on the block? I can scarcely confide in her after a week in the city, can I? But the truth is, she's right: Alfie Manners and his ilk are animals. We tolerate them, however. We do so out of expediency in the main; one has learnt to pick one's fights. But with Manners, there's more. Give him enough rope and he'll hang himself, no doubt; but he'll lead us somewhere interesting first. We've got our eye on him all right. We know all about Alfie Manners and his associates.

Hattie Vine

I'm getting nowhere with the Chief. He's just humouring me.

'And you're suggesting they used excessive force to question this witness?'

'I'm not *suggesting* anything, sir. I saw it. That wasn't "questioning a witness". DS Manners beat him up!'

'Mmm. Well, if that actually is the case . . .'

'Sir, I assure you.'

I'm so demoralised by his utter lack of interest that I wonder whether I'll even bother bringing up the backhanders.

'And then there's the money he took. I'm certain his *associates* last night, sir, were hardly of the kind –'

Hodge holds one hand up to silence me.

'Vine, let's be under no illusions here – that's a very serious allegation to make against a colleague . . .'

He hits me with the sleepy eyes for a second, looks me up and down as though he's trying to assess how far he can go; whether he can trust me. His first few words are just one long sigh.

'Listen. Forget DS Manners. He's come to our attention before. We're keeping a very beady eye on him.'

He leans forward; rests his chin on his fingertips as he stares right into my eyes.

'What I want you to focus on is, I sincerely hope, a much more productive use of your talents . . .'

Hodge

That's stopped the carping all of a sudden. I continue.

'The heroin question, Vine.'

Ha! *Now* she's sitting up! Now I have her full and undivided attention.

'What I want to know is – given the usual restraints – what would your approach be? I'm interested.'

She looks me in the eye, says nothing for a moment, then lets go.

'Well, sir, we touched upon some of this during my interview, and if I was cautious then, then I'm even more so now that I've seen what we're faced with up here.'

'In what sense?'

'In every sense, sir, but particularly in terms of resources. Given the personnel we have at our disposal presently I don't know whether my approach could possibly work . . .'

Big pause – long, significant, searching look, then she's bang into academic mode.

'But all things being equal, sir, and given a degree of independence, I would be looking to gather intelligence from ground level. Street level. The lowest of the low. Every organisation has its weak spot. Every gang has a drunk or a junkie or a blabbermouth. It seldom takes too long to identify them. We put ourselves out on the street, we penetrate the organisation by stealth, we wait and we watch . . . I'm absolutely certain about this, sir. It's the way to go. Without doubt.'

I find myself becoming a tad excited as she drills me with

those keen eyes. Is this mere idealism or could the girl have something here? I chew it all over.

'Mmm. In terms of protocol, it's a tricky one. You'd need Yards's blessing . . . It's his budget and his overtime we'd be cannibalising, after all . . .'

'It is? I thought all such decisions ultimately came down to yourself, sir . . .'

She's good. I've got to give it to her, she's good, backing me against the ropes like that. Bottom line is that decision-makers survive by avoiding the making of decisions – but Vine has got me, here.

'Tell you what we'll do, Vine. Let's speak plainly, shall we?'

'I'd welcome that, sir.'

'We're not making much headway up there at Hope Street, are we? It's not exactly working out?'

'I'd have to say not, sir.'

'So. What we do is this. I tell DI Yardley I'm giving you compassionate leave. We can't prevent rumours from circulating – couldn't hack the job, et cetera, et cetera, too sensitive for such a big gig, bit of a southern pansy –'

She goes to complain. I hold up a hand, and smile her down.

'I'm just telling you what will undoubtedly be said in the canteen and so forth . . .'

She nods, once.

'But the good news is they'll think they've won. They'll think you've gone and, as such, hey presto! You're free of them. You will answer directly to myself – that shall be the sole chain of command. Other than that, you will be at liberty to operate, if you like, as a freelance. Just go in there and do the job you wish to do in the manner you wish to do it. I shall expect regular bulletins from you but, between you and me and these four walls, this is me playing with my train set. I'm having a stab at some progressive policing here – doing the job in the way I suspect it needs doing. Does that make *any* sense at all?'

From the wide open smile on her face, I'd say it does.

'Absolutely, sir. Can't say I'm thrilled at being the subject of locker-room speculation among Manners and co, but what the heck . . .'

Again the big smile. She's very . . . I don't want to say *pretty*, that would be to demean the girl. She has a very attractive brio about her, though – let's say that. Girl can't stop grinning, she's so gung-ho!

'I know exactly how to make this work, sir. I'm certain of it. Next time you see me, I guarantee you will not recognise me. You absolutely will not regret this.'

'Good. Good. And I sincerely hope *you* won't either!'

With that she's gone. I'll give her her due – she doesn't stand on ceremony, that one. Good cop. Very good cop.

Hattie Vine

One of the very few good things about heroin addicts is that the delusions run right to the core. They can make themselves believe absolutely anything it suits them to believe, so if Thommo wants to think I'm a posh girl from down south who may well be an easy touch for money that's fine by me. I haven't said as much, but I don't need to. We've got talking in the Oxford, I've given him an absolutely heart-rending sob story about dropping out of uni. All the pressure got to me, I've caved in, dropped out and, yes, shock-horror, I've tried this and that, here and there. Bit of whizz, bit of dope. Bit of H, at my lowest ebb. Nothing serious, but to my mum and dad I may as well be on the streets. So now they're refusing to speak to me; my brother and two sisters have cut me dead, all because I admitted to Amanda, my oldest sister, that I started dabbling. Just chasing; nothing regular. Just a bit of brown to counter the stress of exams. Thommo has lapped the whole thing up, of course. You could see his eyes going dizzy with the sudden anticipation of all the ways he could exploit this little innocent.

'All me mates are the same, Ginny . . .'

I've introduced myself as Ginny. Virginia. Mother's name. Always use that at times like this. I've pitched the accent as southern slumming-it, like I'm covering up a bit of posh.

'I've got boys and girls from all over come and stay at Uncle Thommo's. I consider every last one of them a personal friend. It's my sincere delight to be of some small comfort where possible, do you know? Bed for the night, little bit of dough to tide them over . . . what's mine is theirs. Do you know what I'm saying to you? Every one of them started out like you . . .'

I had to dig my fingernails into the palm of my hand, to stop myself wincing when he gave my arm a reassuring squeeze. This is a man who sweats deceit and what's worse is that he believes his own bullshit. Thommo sees himself as some Jesus figure walking the desolate backstreets in search of waifs and strays he can rescue – at a price. He smiles at me so long, without blinking, that I feel violated. I offer up a meek little grin. I try to transmit a kind of forlorn 'you seem nice' face, followed by a 'please don't let me down' look. I shrink my head meekly into my shoulders virtually asking him to abuse the situation, then I scurry off to the loo.

I stare at myself now in the Ladies mirror, hair lank and greasy, eyes dull and sunken from a self-imposed wake that would trouble the most disciplined method actor, satisfied with the start I've made. I splash water on my face and try to work out how I can fend off having to go back to Thommo's flat. Sooner or later, something like this must come to pass. If I want the basic inside track on what goes down and how it happens on the streets round here, it's not going to just come tumbling out after a glass of vodka and Ribena in the pub. I'm going to have to bite the bullet and get my face known and trusted round these parts. Just standing here envisaging the filth and degradation I expect to be their norm is starting to turn my stomach. Mother used to call me Florence Nightingale, so fastidious was I in airing my room and shaking down my bedclothes, but she was never one for housework. I couldn't abide one stray crumb or speck of wool on my sheets. Still, a grotty bedsit will come as nothing compared to the real big issues I'm going to have to face up to, sooner or later. If this pet scheme of mine is going to stand a chance, I'm going to have to dive in and join these wraiths in their habit. There really is no plan B.

I look at myself long and hard, and come to a decision. I'll chase, but that's all. For the cause, for the job, I will puff the magic dragon — but injecting is an absolute non-starter. Devotion to the cause only goes so far, and Aids is not a price I'm prepared to pay. I'll sow the seeds good and early; let it be known that I have a deep-seated phobia of needles, and from that point in I'll just have to work fast and hope for good luck and a decent wind. If I sell myself to them as a bit naive, spread a bit of money around, that should keep them zoned — for a while. They'll be more interested in conning me out of my loot than giving me the third degree. But one thing I know for a cast-iron fact from my Masters research is that misery loves a bedfellow. Any seasoned injector will be looking to 'convert' his innocents, and I shall be no exception. My best guess is that Thommo will leave me alone to toot for a week or two, so long as I carry on coming up with my fair share of wedge. He's not daft, Thommo; on the contrary, he seems a bit too bright for my liking. But a guy like him — an addict, after all — will always succumb. If it comes down to a choice between a nagging suspicion and a sure bag, he'll take the easy ride time after time. The day *will* come, though – it will surely come – when his need to possess me supersedes even his overpowering desire for blessed oblivion. After that, it's open season. He'll be wheedling and nagging and urging me to try the Real Thing. I've got two, maybe three weeks max to work out the lines of supply here – but if I can't do that then, frankly, I'm not Job.

Manners

What did I tell yous? Was I ever right about her or does Alfie Manners just know his fucking onions? I *knew* she'd never last, that one. Too fucking thingio, the tart – always getting her knickers in a twist over this, that and the other. Tell you one thing for nothing, though, kidda – tidy little hoop on it. I don't think I'm alone here in saying I would burst that tight arse of hers every day of the week. There's not much else about the snotty little mare I'll miss, though. Get back to school, love. Read all about it. Best place for you.

Hattie Vine

The flat is nowhere near as bad as I'd been preparing myself for; there's a cheese plant, its leaves a lustrous green, a scattering of Persian rugs, big beanbag cushions in the corners and huge framed cinema posters on the wall – *Apocalypse Now*, *The Tin Drum* and *Fritz the Cat*. Thommo's regulars don't seem so bad either. Compared to the skull-headed denizens I've studied and seen on the street, these are a somewhat more cultured bunch. They jack up and lie back and they just pontificate, on and on, about whatever seems to slide through their fuzzy minds. One minute it's exaggerated outrage at Eddie Shah's plans to take over the media, the next they're ardently debating whether Madonna is in fact a man.

Thatcher, Buddhism, the arcane meanings of 'Hand in Glove' by the Smiths . . . each and all are debated with a slovenly reverence. My problem is the jack-up part of the affair. Almost without exception they inject, seemingly relishing the communion of the ritual, helping each other through to the other side. I can feel it coming. It truly is just a matter of time before one of the girls drifts over and tries to tell me what I'm missing. I keep myself away from the spotlight, sifting through Thommo's LPs. There's an odd assortment here – Camel and Yes and Genesis records, King Crimson, the Grateful Dead. There's a whole slab of Bowie. I don't want to stick on something that's likely to draw attention to me, but even Bowie is bound to stimulate some kind of debate. I find a Doors compilation, blow off the dust and throw it on before they all start complaining there's no sounds.

I get through the afternoon pretending to be on the nod. I just lie there, no sense of time, of anything – only the occasional ring of the phone and crunch of a Zippo flint cutting through the languid torpor. Every now and then I hear Thommo talking in an animated whisper.

'Mikey lad, believe me, lad, I would . . . you know I would. Just . . . I got a roomful of them here need lining up, mate . . .'

Daylight starts to filter away and a weird and greenish twilight fills the room. I'm stiff on one side. I roll over, trying to work the circulation back into the arm I've been lying on. The phone goes again. Thommo is agitated, now.

'How long have we known each other, Mikey? How long? Can't you just send little Moz up here or something?'

One of the lads crawls over and lies next to me, starts stroking my tummy. I tense up. He rolls on to his side and starts pushing his crotch up against me. I have to fight myself not to overreact. Too frigid will find me out like a searchlight;

but no way in the world is this smacked-up rag-arse getting his yellowing fingertips under my clothes. He's still got his jeans and T-shirt on; that's something. He's very slowly gyrating against my hip, but his hand is moving under my top now. I have to act out this heavy-lidded, gradual awakening and roll myself over so it's not too abrupt. I come on like I'm just confused and foggy. It puts the focus on him, for trying it on while I was out of the game.

'All right, babe? Sweet dreams?' he drawls. He's not a bad-looking lad in this light. Naturally blond, thick, curly hair; lively eyes. The academic in me is drawn to him, fascinated at how a nice boy like this has ended up on the slow chute to hell.

'Yeah. Think so,' I ham.

I rub my eyes and start looking all around me, like I only vaguely recognise the place. He's getting the message. I smile at him.

'D'you come here often?'

That gets him laughing.

'Love it, man!' he goes, and does this funny clicking thing with his fingers.

Thommo comes over.

'Martin. Bit of privacy for a moment, lad, if you will . . .'

The craven, obliging smile on Martin and the haste with which he retreats says he's seen Thommo do bad things. Thommo gives it a moment, then he's crouching down on his haunches. I'm on my guard straight away.

'Ginny . . .'

For a split second, the name jars, but it's the only way I can countenance that she's out there somewhere.

'You want to earn a few *brownie* points?'

He grins at his own joke — one he's made a hundred times. I shrug.

'Sure.'

He checks behind – an affectation for my benefit.

'Don't you wanna know what I'm gonna ask you to do?'

I nod. He puts his lips right up against my ear, making me shudder. He's pressing an envelope into my hand.

'Corner of here and Prinny there's a call box, yeah? You know it?'

I don't know it – but I nod.

'Yep.'

'Take this. A gentleman of Afro-Caribbean appearance will arrive on a mountain bike at precisely 7 p.m. He'll be wearing a pale purple Ellesse zip-up top. You will merely say 'Hello'. That's all. If he replies 'Nice night', you pass him the envelope. He will give you a package, which you bring straight back here . . .'

All I can do is continue nodding, but inside I am shivering with the thrill of a sudden breakthrough. This is it. This could genuinely be The One.

'You hear me, Gin-Gin? You come right back with it, straight away. Yes? That sound doable?'

'Can't one of the others go?'

God, I'm clever. His eyes are all over me, but in a good way. If Thommo still harboured any doubts about me, they've just been put to rest. I'm shy. I'm reluctant. I truly don't want to go out there, and Thommo's main concern now is how he talks me into running this little message for him while he carries on dosing up his dependants.

'This lot? You seriously think I'd trust one of these with it?' He gives a good-natured guffaw. 'Look at 'em!'

He laughs again as his arm sweeps over his raggle-taggle commune of addicts and dossers. Brown stumps of teeth grin at me.

'Would *you* trust any of these with a monkey?'

I manage to convey the right amount of puzzlement. He pulls the money out of the envelope, sprays the wad with his thumb.

'No offence and that, Gin. I love the bones of them. But they'd kill themselves on this.'

He stuffs the cash back in the envelope and holds it out to me. I mug up the appropriate level of uncertainty, then I take the envelope.

'OK.'

I start for the door. He pulls me back, gives me a very funny look.

'Aren't you going ask what your reward shall be for granting me this simple favour?'

I shrug. 'It's no big thing, is it? Why would I want a reward?'

He leers horribly. 'Wrong. Mistake. Bad, bad mistake. Rule one – nothing is *ever* for nothing.'

He's crushing my wrist in his grip. I look him in the eye, try not to come across as scared as I'm feeling.

'OK. Sorry.'

The demonic leer softens into a smile. It's a twisted, knowing smile, but it tells me I'm off the hook. For now. He lets go of my wrist and looks at his watch.

'Good girl. Your next toot's on the house, yeah?'

He pats my bottom.

'Off you trot then. Pacey-pacey.'

I force a smile, and make for the door. Thommo's eyes are dead.

'Hurry home, sweet tits.'

I can't help feeling nauscous as I pad down the stairs. My two- to three-week estimate seems laughably generous all of a sudden. I'm going to have to get this right, and quickly – as in right now. I resist the urge to turn round and look up, but I know that, up on the top floor, Thommo is watching me like a hawk eagle.

Hodge

She's sitting there in silence as I read her report, hardly flexing a muscle – not a twitch. She's like a scholar who knows they've handed in excellent homework. She doesn't have to study my face for the nuances of approval – she knows it will be forthcoming. I carry on through to her concluding recommendations, but I'm already sold on this. One has to hand it to the girl – she's delivered precisely what she promised.

Hattie Vine

Step one was managing to follow Mikey, the lad in the mauve top, for long enough to make an educated guess where he was going for his gear. Chinatown. That was the easy part. Since that first handover, Thommo seems more inclined to trust me. I've seen Mikey, out on his BMX, half a dozen times. I've seen him when I haven't even been looking for him. He seems to pride himself on being a Face, always pedalling around the Triangle at menacing half-speed, staring people in the face until they look away. It's obvious the kid is craving notoriety. He wears that horrible tracksuit top every day, hardly inconspicuous. It's as though it's his calling card to customers and coppers alike. 'Here I am. Come and get me.'

The hard bit has been keeping all the variables going, trying to call their bluff without drawing too much attention to myself. Thommo has been easy enough – he's got too many victims to abuse to keep his beady eye solely on myself for any given time. I've managed to strike a note that's vulnerable enough to assure him that the best is yet to come from me, but not so far gone that he can't keep playing me as and when he needs. If he taps me up for a loan I'll usually come good, but not without a plaintive 'doesn't grow on trees, you know' or 'my giro isn't due'. It works in the sense that it gives me licence to get out

of the squat – trips to the bank, the social, cashing my giro –
but the price I have to pay is his Uncle Thommo routine, hugging
me from behind and kissing my neck, telling me everything
is going to be just fine. It's disgusting.

Mikey is a different proposition. He has a soft, girlish voice,
beautifully manicured hands and I have no doubt whatsoever
that he is a born killer. Seriously – if my academic life has taught
me anything about the make-up of most murderers, then Mikey
fits the profile. He may speak with that gentle lilt but there is
nothing, no humanity in his eyes. My blood runs cold whenever
I have to deal with him. You have a sickening and genuine dread
that this could be your last time breathing, every time he looks
you over and tosses his options in his mind. I've had to count
on his greed and his innate predator's instinct to keep him
interested – a tightrope balance on razor wire when it's your
own neck at stake. But as much as he'd love to just rob me and
trash me, the promise that I'll be back again with even more
dough is just too much for him to resist. This is where it was
critical that Hodge backed me. I had to show these guys I was
worth a second look – and that meant upping the level of deal
that Thommo was working with him. I'm going to say so myself
– I think I played my opening gambit pretty well. I was dopey
and ingratiating enough that the guy knew I was a smackhead.
But I still got it across to him that it wasn't worth having me
over – not yet, anyway. I all but told him that this was just an
entry-level sortie to see how things panned out. If all went nice
and smoothly, the clear inference was that I'm good for more
– much more. For now, though, I asked him for a five-ton deal,
same as Thommo's regular score.

'This is just you and me though, yeah? No one else has to
know . . .'

Straight away his eyes were all over me, probing for
weaknesses.

'Hardly worth my while, that, is it?'

'That's what I'm saying to you. This is just a taste . . .'

He held his hand out, looking the other way.

'Go 'ead then.'

I gave him my very best cackle with just enough strung-out madness to let him off his guard.

'Sweeties first,' I simpered.

He seemed to home right in on my mouth, as though my teeth were of special interest to him. He just sat there on his bike, one foot on the kerb, one on the pedal, staring at my smiling lips until I started trying to picture my own frozen face in my mind's eye. What was grabbing his attention? Were my teeth not brown enough for a baghead? He shook his head to himself and whispered in that eunuch's voice: 'Wait there. Hear me? Do not fucking move.'

He pushed himself off the pavement and rode away in the direction of town.

Hodge

One is already fearful of the level of manpower this is going to take to properly implement her suggestions. The downside of fast-tracking these intellectuals is that they approach crime-fighting as a case study – as theory. In an ideal world we would have limitless resources to lop off the mobsters' heads and apply weedkiller to root and branch. Meanwhile, back in real time, I have a finite budget and a limited amount of men. Beyond that, it's a case of joining the queue with begging bowl in hand. I'm keen to support DS Vine here, but I dread her answers to my questions. I look up, force a smile.

'So. Even if we were to stick with what we've got, there's enough there to put Greene away for a very long time . . .'

'There is, sir.'

'But?'

'Sir?'

'I'm sensing a "but" . . .'

She fires back a very patronising smile.

'With respect, sir . . . the likes of Mikey Greene and street dealers of his ilk are not exactly the level of target we discussed.'

'No. Of course not. I'm merely pointing out –'

'I hear that, sir – and appreciate it. And I'm not suggesting we go for the kill, so to speak, just yet –'

'No?'

'No, sir. There are bigger fish than Mikey Greene – but I'm putting my neck on the line, dealing with Greene directly. It's only a matter of time before he rats me out to Thompson.'

'Thompson?'

'Thommo. There in the file, sir. Can I take it I have your approval to take the next steps, sir?'

I pick up the last few pages of her report. I'm looking for figures. I don't recall her attaching a budget.

'Sir – just to clarify . . . if you go to pages 7 and 8 and reference various citations of "the Chinaman", reference a possible Chinatown connection . . . this is purely on the basis of conversations overheard and intelligence gleaned. Before considering any kind of a strategy for arrests and convictions, I recommend further operations to establish that connection beyond all reasonable doubt, sir.'

I'm feeling somewhat told off here, yet there's nothing – she's said nothing I can object to. I find the pages in question. I'm reading, without taking in the information.

'Sir. Dressed like this . . .'

She looks revolting. Shrunken, grubby T-shirt with, if I may say so, little left to the imagination vis-à-vis her nipple situation. She's wearing those skintight elasticated jeans they all wear, with little slits cut into the ankle cuffs so, one suspects, they don't have to bother taking their training shoes off. Her hair is dull, greasy, slapped tight to her pretty face. Very convincing, I have to say. Excellent show.

'So my suggestion – and it will take next to no manpower from your rotas, sir . . .'

Good grief. Girl's a mind-reader, now. She lets out a huge long sigh, an expiration, one surmises, of pent-up frustration. And I sympathise. I truly do. I want to help make this work. I start reading through from page 1 again. I very deliberately keep my eyes glued to her file as I speak.

'How would you wish to proceed? Assuming –'

'Assuming the necessary support were at our disposal? Next step is easy, sir. I hope. I scrub up, dress up and find myself a date in Chinatown . . .'

She stands up and leans over my desk, eyes shining. She's got this victorious, demented smile on her face. One finds oneself backing away in mild terror.

'Give me a pager and some backup and I'll give you your collar.'

Not for the first time, the sheer force of nature that is DS Harriet Vine's conviction to duty leaves me powerless.

'Very well, Vine. Let's do it. But be careful. Agreed? Softly bloody softly!'

Her smile lights up the room and chases my misgivings. One of the dwindling perks of this job is the frisson of unbridled joy one feels from a bright and committed young copper on the scent of a collar. Glad to have been of assistance, young lady. Now go and get the bad guys.

Hattie Vine

I succumb to the joyous bite of the hot, hot shower. I don't want to think how long it is since I had one. I've lived, more or less, round the clock at Thommo's in that time. As predicted, he has begun to turn the screw and, notch by notch, he's become more possessive, more suspicious, ever more alert to my every move. He can't quite pinpoint his unease where I'm concerned, but his animal wit is fine-tuned and, one way or the other, he's getting interference on his radar. His flat is far from being the worst shooting gallery I've encountered, but the last thing I would ever do in there is undress. If one or other of them didn't try to shag me or inculcate me into their soft-focus smack coven, they'd have had my jeans picked clean the moment the steam hit the mirror. Understandably, then, the sensation of scalding hot water stinging my scalp and shoulders and teeming down my spine is heavenly. I could stand here for hours – but a date with destiny awaits.

Although the Kowloon Kitchen is virtually empty as I come through its warped steel door, the elegant, unsmiling proprietor greets me with near disdain.

'Just you?'

I reach for a smart retort but think better of it. She leads me upstairs and into a small room panelled with teak-effect laminated board. Without any pretence of courtesy, she points at a table in the corner of the room.

'There.'

I ignore her and sit down at the window table. I can hear her sighing and tutting behind me as she snatches up a menu and slaps it down on the formica table-top. I have my back to the room – my window affords me a view of an empty Nelson Street and a leaden sky. She bullies me into ordering a Tsingtao and some crackers and, for now, leaves me in peace. All I know for certain about her place is that Mikey Greene has visited no fewer than nine times over the short period of my surveillance. Four of those occasions came directly after liaisons with myself, and immediately before returning to our meeting point with consignments of heroin – in exchange for which I have handed him sums of money varying between five and fifteen hundred pounds. We know – or we strongly suspect – that he accesses the restaurant via an alleyway to the back of Nelson Street and Cummings Street. Clearly I could only follow him so far on the days I gave him money, but I've backed that up with sufficient photographic and documentary evidence to make the assumption stand up that this place is central to Mikey Greene's activities.

The objective this evening is simply to take a look around the premises from the inside. Hodge and I have minimal expectations in terms of hard-and-fast evidence, but if I can get a sense of the layout and perhaps put faces to some of the personnel involved it's all grist to the mill; and to be perfectly honest it just feels good to be clean, to be out – to look like myself, again.

Mrs Happy returns with beer and, one has to give credit where it's due, prawn crackers whose freshness you can smell. I realise all of a sudden how hungry I am.

'Yiss?'

It still stands me up, hearing the Chinese speak in a local dialect. By her own brusque standards I infer muted content-ment at my order of a quarter crispy duck followed by a supposed house special of chicken in a honey, lemon and pineapple sauce with vegetable fried rice. She nods – once – and bustles off downstairs, shouting the order in jarring staccato. The beer is delicious, though. I sip it straight from the dew-cold bottle, relishing this sense of freedom.

I shift around as far as my chair will allow and crane my neck to check out this little nook of a room. Not much to see. No sign of any doors or other rooms leading off – yet, for the size of the building, there'd have to be more up here than this, surely? The chimes announce more arrivals down-stairs and there's an instantaneous buzz of noisy, welcoming voices. Gone is the hostess's curt tone; she's all tinkling cadence as her voice goes up and down the scales, merry and ingratiating all of a sudden. There's a quick conference about something or other – their chat goes all sotto voce for a second – then the next thing there are feet padding upstairs. I'm dying to see who it is that gets such a wondrous welcome, and I'm shifting my seat round to get a better view, when their voices start to become audible. Two of them I know – and my heart plunges at the recognition. The first of them is gruff and aggressive. I only heard it in short bursts that night, but he made his mark.

'*All right, Hattie, love. Terry Connolly. Take no notice of these.*'

My night out with the Lads. The old guy in the fitted overcoat. Him, alone, I could handle – just. But the other voice spells disaster. Jumpy and eager to please, its nervy stabs and cackles bring me out in a panic sweat. No. No, no, no, no, *no*! Let that not be Alfie Manners – *please*! But it is. It's him. I'd know his voice anywhere – the joker, the life and soul, twitching and blinking and cracking his gags. Alfie Manners is in the room with a consortium of gangsters, and my chances of surviving this are receding with each new step they take. It matters little in the grand scheme of things that Manners thinks I've fled back down south. But his flagging up my resurrection in front of a shady ensemble like these is only going to beg the question as to what I'm doing back in town; and why so hush-hush? My mind is racing – what, oh, what can I do? My one saving grace is that I have my back to the room.

Hodge. I must get word out to Hodge. I fish out my pager and tap out the message.

URGENT. MANNERS HERE. ADVICE?

Dammit! Won't send. Too many characters. My heart is pounding through my gullet as I crouch in close to the table, trying to work out what I can ditch.

ALF MANNERS HERE! HELP!

Thank God. I get that one away to him. Very quickly I bash out another, lest his reply alert their table to my presence.

DO NOT RESPOND!!

Good. I try to breathe, slowly. OK – sent. That will get the wheels in motion. One more.

T CONNOLLY ALSO PRESENT.

Right. Now I need to give him much clearer instructions before he comes charging in with the cavalry. I can hear the party behind me horsing around. Sooner or later one of them will become aware there's a single female within earshot, and he – or they – will go into overbearing compensation mode. They will apologise, loudly. They will upbraid one another for their coarse language in the company of a fair lady. Worst of all – they will insist, at the very least, upon sending me a drink, on the house. More likely, though – and this is the killer – one of them will come over to the table to apologise in person. He will smile and wince and try to insist that I come and join them, at their expense. At that point Manners will see me, and this entire house of cards will collapse in a fragment of a second. Catastrophe beckons – unless I can direct Hodge, precisely, intricately, to bring about the kind of distraction that will take Manners out of the building for long enough for me to make my escape. Shit. Shit, shit, shit, shit, *shit*! I *have* to word this right. *Breathe!* OK, twenty-five characters maximum . . .

ABSOLUTE IMPERATIVE . . .

Send. I can hear Manners imitating Hodge, and the mobsters laughing raucously. I really do hope my ears aren't radiating the sudden flush of fearful panic that's ripping through me right now. I try to keep my head down as I tap out another.

CONTACT DUTY SERGEANT.

Send.

BREAKIN AT DC MANNERS CAR

Done. Bang on twenty-five! Heartbeat slowly returning to something like normality.

UNIFORM ATTENDING.

Send. Deep breath. Nothing more to be done about it, except to wait for the chain reaction. I can still walk out of this restaurant without DC Alfred Manners ever knowing I was here – or not until it's too late anyway. I'll have him in the dock by then. Come on, come on, come on! Why isn't your pager bleeping, Alfie? Hope Street should have been on to you by now. Jesus. I switch mine off. I'm on my own now. It's just me, myself and I, hoping for deliverance from the Mob. Let it be, oh Lord. Let it be.

Jehovah isn't listening. They're on to me, now. They're talking about me. I know it from the way they've dropped their voices all of a sudden. I can tell from the variation in volume that one or two of them have turned to get a look at me – you can almost hear the gaps in their conversation. This is bad. I can feel it; I just know, now, that they're on to me. There's nothing from the outside world, either; nothing to say that Hodge is acting on my red alerts. He must, at the very least, have received my first SOS?

And then, suddenly, hallelujah! I didn't hear his bleeper go but Alfie Manners is standing up and telling the table he has to 'go on a little message'. I'm ready to collapse with relief as they take the rise out of him, ribbing him not to be too long, his dinner's going to go cold, et cetera, et cetera. It's their tone, their jollity, as much as Manners' imminent departure that's starting to persuade me I might just might pull this off. I tense myself, straining every sinew to keep my features pointed away from Manners' field of vision. There's manly cackling from the table as he makes his final departure. I hear his footfall on the staircase. The others return to their chit-chat and, once I've counted fifty to give Manners ample time to get back to his car, I'm up and out of my seat, head down and face turned away, and I've made it out of the room without TC and the gang even looking up. I'm off down the stairs, a ten-pound note ready to pay for the meal I haven't had, no questions asked. It takes a moment for me to realise that an immaculate Chinaman is blocking the doorway.

'No eat?' he smiles. 'Come.'

Only one other time in my life have I heard three words sound more chilling.

I have no way of knowing how long I've been down here. I can see very little. It is as much as I can do to counter the most hysterical excesses of my imagination. The Chinaman led me to a manhole in the Kowloon's storeroom. We descended an iron ladder so steep that I slipped twice, skinning my shins on its rungs. I made out a small, cellar-type room, but at that stage he tied me to a large iron ring set into the wall, blindfolded me, gagged me and left me here. The walls feel like sandstone, moist and rough. I can smell a tangy, ancient damp. I can hear – or I think I can hear – rats or mice scurrying, sending spasmodic shivers of revulsion down my spine. I'm scared – really scared. Even if Hodge has come piling in with the troops like some action hero, there is absolutely no trace of me whatsoever in that restaurant. I'm twenty, thirty feet underground here – sacks of flour and monosodium glutamate no doubt covering the manhole they shoved me down. Even if I were able to free myself of this gag, nobody would hear me shouting. If a rescue party is to come, they'll never guess I'm still here. The dapper little Chinaman can say whatever he wants to them. He'll smile and shrug and tell them I left some time ago. Didn't see which direction I went. Wasn't looking.

* * *

If I slept at all, it was for moments. My brain and my eyeballs ache as I am stirred by the crunch and scraping of the manhole cover coming off. Even through my blindfold I can sense an inlet of light – but there's no telling whether that's the strip light from the kitchens or any kind of natural daylight. My shoulders are caving in on themselves and my shin bones throb – the pain is extraordinary. Footsteps on the ladder. Laughter, and male voices – at least three of them. I try to stand up straight and tall. Show no fear. There's a torch or lamplight being shone, then, with no preamble, no warning, nothing to presage it, there's a blinding crack to my cheekbone and that's it. All my lights go out. Everything I feel, every sensation, is numb, dislocated. This is happening to someone else. I'm half awake but I don't have the strength or the focus to pull myself out of the flickering slideshow that plays inside my eyeballs. I squeeze my fists tight to banish this ghoulish, slow-motion reverie. I am aware of things happening without being able to process them. My jeans are being tugged down.

'Look at that little arse!'

Mean, coarse laughter. There is a sharp, stinging slap on my buttocks which jerks me out of my stupor, but still I am sluggish. A jagged pain in my anus. Someone is gripping me around my hips and entering me, thrusting roughly into my bottom, tugging my hair back, forcing me down lower and digging their knees into the backs of my thighs. The sounds, the voices, the laughter . . . it is all warped, disconnected white noise. I pass out.

A flood of light brings me round. It might be two minutes or two days later. I feel weak and heavy and sick. The moment I drag open my eyes, a brutal pain stabs through my skull, my neck, everywhere. My backside, my entire anal passage aches horribly. I try to focus, but I can't see at all. The voices are concerned; familiar. A WPC is wrapping a blanket around me as others debate the best way of getting me out of there. I see the iron ring set into the wall. I begin to gag. I vomit in powerful jets all over the cell walls. I feel myself being hoist up towards the manhole – a peculiar fairground sensation, giddy and disembodied. They transfer me to a stretcher and carry me out to the ambulance, and the slap of cold dawn air knocks me sideways. A huddle of coppers and colleagues stands there, heads bowed. The last face I see before I pass out is that of Hodge, solemn, his face etched with concern and regret.

1997

McCartney

As the train pulls in and the hordes spill off, I just sit there, unable or unwilling to move. Liverpool. Shit. I was back in Liverpool. I've been waiting so long for another crack at these people, yet, now the time has come, I'm blindsided with a deep and insatiable fear that this will all turn out badly. I have to keep telling myself, all over again, that if it goes wrong, it goes wrong. *C'est la vie.* What would be worse is to know that they're still out there, out here – and do nothing.

I wait for the last excitable backpackers to step off the train – don't they know what they're letting themselves in for, here in Beatle City? – before I shuffle out on to the platform. Even now, I can't be certain I'll be able to see this through. I breathe in the Lime Street smog and feel inside my jacket for a smoke. All they had at Euston was Hamlet. Better than nothing. I light up and drag down a whole whack of thick spicy cigar smoke and hold it in until my head goes dizzy. It's one of those where you become conscious of the space above you. I watch a pigeon up in the eaves of the station's big glass roof, flapping its wings in slow motion. The sound drops right out and everything starts spinning. Dislocated voices. Hodge, bereft, staring down at the stretcher.

So awful, what happened; so horribly, utterly avoidable. I

43

screw my eyes tight shut and dig my nails into the ball of my thumb, waiting for it to pass. The platform is near empty, now; the cleaners preparing the train for its journey back down south. I could easily, very easily, step right back on board – but I don't. I take another drag on the cigarillo and slowly, slowly, the good vibrations begin to return. I remind myself why I've sought this out, why I'm doing this, and I find myself strangely excited all of a sudden. This is what it must have been like to be a spy at the height of the Cold War – going into the heart of darkness with only yourself and your own abilities to see you through.

I finish off the smoke and start the short walk to HQ. I head out the back of the station, past the Empire Theatre's stage doors, across London Road and past the den of iniquity that is the Clock, past Pickwick's and over the dual carriageway to St Anne Street. I'll admit it, this new crack squad or whatever Hodge wants to call it is a major, major step forward for me at this point in my career. When I met with him for the preliminaries – Hodge was adamant these chats were not 'interviews' – he was at pains to stress he'd been tracking me for a while. Oh yes, the great Hubert Hodge reckons he's created his model for an elite, drug-busting 'cell' with myself and only me on his list to head it up. Gratifying. Highly gratifying, if true. I've worked hard for this. I deserve it. Billy McCartney is good at this shit. He's *very* good.

Got to say, though, even I am gobsmacked at the leaps and strides I've made since I was last up here. Since rejoining the Drug Squad, I've definitely found my vocation. My own role in the Ibiza tablet haul was, surprisingly, held up as a model for the efficacy of surveillance and I've gone on from there, really. It's not luck, either. It's instinct. Somehow, some way, it's turned out that my nose for this shit is among the very best around. I've been intimately involved in the seizure of over two hundred tonnes of class-A tartan, putting more than thirty lesser lights of the drug trade behind bars for sentences totalling nigh on five hundred years.

But these last few years, since I got made up to Inspector, I've upped my game another level, even if I say so myself. It was a baptism of fire, for sure – a case of welcome to the big league, Billy – but I played a massive part in the conviction of that Hackney slob Dougie Doughnuts. *The* fattest human being I have ever encountered, incidentally; monumentally obese. Lord alone knows how a big, slovenly knuckle-dragger like that ran an empire when he could hardly walk to the kitchen without having to stop for his ventilator, but there you go. Then I went straight from the Doughnut collar on to the successful recapture of Robbie Blake in Fuengirola, and *that's* when I reckon Hodge got on to me. The Blake thing was pretty high profile what with the red tops being so fixated on their Costa del Crime splashes. Hodge can't have failed to have seen the big *News of the Screws* lowdown on how I sunk myself in with the expat community in Torreblanca and, basically, flushed the laughable wide boy out. Hodge would have loved that – the bit where I took his last thousand pesetas at poker then told him:

'Oh, and Robbie – you're nicked.'

I'll be dead straight about it, those kind of collars have given me the taste back. As good as the game has been so far, it's the major players I'm interested in now. I want to bring down the big guns, and in this, I know for a fact, Hubert Hodge shares my ambition. Welcome to Liverpool, Billy. We've been expecting you.

I'm buzzing like an absolute beginner as I bound up those three steps into reception and take the lift to the sixth floor. The other two are already there, sat straight-backed in immaculately tailored suits. Wow! Cops in schmutter. I feel suddenly self-conscious in this bit-too-young-for-me Helmut Lang jacket. Note to self — you're a *boss* now, Billy. A more mature look is an *urgent* priority. Hodge gestures for me to sit down.

'Bill. Good to see you again. I'd like you to meet Rob Peters and Penelope Anderson. Rob and Penny will introduce themselves properly immediately this briefing is over and explain to you, in much greater detail than I could possibly *begin* to do justice to, what it is that they *do* . . .'

He breaks off and gives a mysterious little in-smile to Penny, who looks like one of those gamine supermodels from a Mario Testino shoot. Short hair. Perfect skin. Expressionless face. She just *is*.

'But this is the bit where I feel like Q in James Bond.'

Another little grin, this time bestowed upon us all. He lets out a long sigh.

'Where to begin? Maybe I should start by asking you three something . . . Where would you estimate the biggest headache in the country lies, vis-à-vis drug crime?'

I clear my throat, hoping one of the others will answer. No one does.

'Manchester?'

'Good shout. Wrong though. I have a little — I don't know — *observation* I quite rely upon when it comes to matters of resources and priorities, and it's this. If it's in the news, it ain't happening. Seriously. Manchester, with its gangs and gun wars, Cheetham Hillbillies fighting the Gooch and what have you . . . sure it's great copy for *Loaded* magazine and the *Daily Star*. *Gunchester*. Hah! I wish all our troubles could be so trite . . .'

We sit back and wait for him to deliver his words of wisdom.

'Ladies and gentlemen — you're sitting in the current world capital of the international drug trade. Not London. Not Medellin. Not even Amsterdam. Sadly, very sadly, it's happening right here. It's been happening for years. And it's reached insufferable levels.'

He takes a sip of water and focuses his eyes on each of us in turn.

'This is what we're here for – to return the good name of Liverpool to its citizens. To bring some semblance of law to what is, one has to admit, currently akin to Dodge City . . .'

He takes another gulp of water. Gives us each the eye again.

'If we're to do that, then we have to bring the dealers down. And let me be clear about this – I'm not talking about the pettifogging little runners and street dealers and toerags on the corners and council estates. I'm talking about the Big Boys. We're after the ringmasters, the moguls. The bubbas at the top of the barrel . . .'

He pauses and scans us to see if we're hooked. Oh yes. We're hooked, all right. Hodge suppresses his smirk before it even makes it to his face.

'Now, I don't want to describe this as a crusade or anything like that – it's not even a mission. But since I returned to this city last year . . .' He musters the appropriate level of bemused incomprehension, mixed with a tiny little sprinkle of weary resignation. 'Well – let me simply say that there exists here, has always existed, an endemic, almost an *institutional* culture of high-end criminality – and this displeases me. But since I've been back here what I've come to realise is that it's not just wide boys on the make. This is business. It's big, *big* business. Local hoodlums are making substantial fortunes, and they're ruining lives and families while they're at it. Now, as Detective Chief Inspector in charge of this little aspect of the city's netherworld, that doesn't just anger me. It saddens me. It *hurts* me.'

Hodge pauses and eyeballs each of us, individually, to ram his point home.

'It kills me that the lowlifes who thrive in Liverpool's murky waters seem to feel they can just . . . *do* that. They're untouchable. They think — no, let's be plain, here — they *know* that they can set up shop and do what they do and no one seems able to lay a finger on them. Well, I've got news for those gentlemen — and I've got news for you three. If my life in this job is to amount to anything, that culture is going to change. It's going to stop. That historic, ingrained, professional lawlessness . . . I want that extinguished from Liverpool's character.'

I smile to myself. That's not a crusade? Who's Hodge trying to kid! His eyes seek me out and he frowns, as though reading my thoughts. Like a vexed schoolmaster, he waits for me to stop thinking anything negative, then continues.

'I have thought about this and very little else since I returned to the city . . .'

Mission!

He places his fingertips together as he enunciates every syllable of his mission statement.

'And what I have come to believe is that if we bring down the paymasters then we bring down the entire mountain. Don't underestimate it for a moment. Liverpool is Drug Mountain. I cannot get close to imagining how grotesque is the wealth generated by this sordid empire . . . but it's something staggering. It's mind-boggling. And it's happening here, it's happening now, it's happening right under our very noses . . .'

Minimal nudge from Peters to Anderson. Flicker of a smile from her then she reverts to stony-face.

'You will, of course, all be familiar with the NCS?'

We all nod. Newly formulated National Crime Squad, elite super-force dedicated to combatting serious organised crime.

'Well, within that system we're a little bit of a rule unto ourselves — guinea pigs, if you like. It's all brand new, but the Chief Constable has given me something of a carte blanche to tackle one of *the* most active drug cartels in the city – the so-called Triangle Crew . . .'

He gets up and carefully hands each of us a dossier.

'This will give you something of a crash course . . .'

Don't need it, sir, I'm thinking, with mounting excitement. I already know this stuff. The riots. The entrenched no-go zones around Granby. The subtle shift in the balance of power between the historic white gangs and the up-and-coming black boys. I know exactly who he means by the Triangle and I'm on tenterhooks as I pull out the first few sheets and begin to speed-scan the literature for familiar names. Could this possibly be –

'So!'

He claps his hands once. I'm starting to shiver here, as I speed-read the file.

'To tackle this beast, I have instituted something of a cell system. Many of the dedicated officers and specialists I've detailed to the operation will not know of each other's involvement *at all*. I have put together several small, uniquely skilled and highly mobile outfits, each tasked with the investigation and disabling of one specific spoke of Lance Campion's drug cartwheel . . .'

Yes! That is precisely the name I wanted to hear. Fantastic! Oh my word, this is just brilliant news – we're going after Campion! Hodge just slides the name in there, but I'm on fire. This is a step up all right! This is as big as they come, right now. I've run across Lanky a couple of times on previous jobs, most recently the Robbie Blake collar on the Costa del Sol. They were all out there too, the Scousers – oh aye, proper rogues' gallery it was; Russians, Albanians, Colombians – every shade of criminality had their reps out on the sunshine coast. I hardly ventured outside of one little patch of Fuengirola on the Blake job, but even I could see that Lanky's mob were the real boys out there. The respect they garnered from all and sundry made you sick to the pits, but there was no doubting the pull they had. This is brilliant, though – a wonderful start. Lance Campion! I suddenly feel very good about being back in this bad, bad town.

I'm sat on the cathedral steps having a smoke and enjoying this moment of calm before it all kicks off. The lunch was good, and not just the food, either – though I have to admit I'm shocked that the shabby Hope Street town house that used to serve as a quasi after-hours club for coppers, hookers and likely lads is now a very fine restaurant indeed. Peters and Anderson were a little reserved – that's to be expected, all things considered – but the overall feeling is one of quiet confidence. We'll get these guys; I can feel it.

It's mad to think I'm sitting only a few hundred yards from Chinatown, down the hill, and Toxteth, up the road. Liverpool 8. Granby. Call it what you will but these very streets are my past, of sorts, and now my immediate future. Am I ready for this? Damn right I am! I stub out my pungent smoke (Note to Self 2: locate reliable source of finest carlotas as a matter of supreme urgency) and head off to meet the estate agent. I'm doing this for real; buying somewhere to live. I'm going to make it work, this time, and I can't help feeling good about the whole proposition. There's no getting away from it – I'm excited being back in this hopeless seething cauldron of criminality, and excited to be on the tail of such a major, major target as Lance Campion.

Against the estate agent's advice I've settled on this vast, slightly sloping, light-filled top floor of a creaking Gothic pile in Mossley Hill. She thinks the place will be impossible to sell on but forget all that. Let's talk about now. I can see myself, say it gently, *living* here. I can never love this tribe they call Scouse; even the honest Johns whose good name Hodge is fighting for are, in my own not impartial view, tainted by association. But in the interests of balance, and to my quite considerable surprise, the city *has* definitely come on a bit as this millennium spins out of all control towards inevitable and eternal damnation. For starters, you can get a coffee that doesn't have granules floating on the surface. All those rat-infested warehouses and after-hours clubs and drinking dens have been tarted up now, too – Liverpool embracing gentrification about twenty years after the rest of the civilised world but doing it 'differently', of course.

There *is* one thing Hodge has not allowed his romantic Damascene reframing to pervert, though; in one vibrant industry, the city of Liverpool *is* unquestionably leading the world by the nose. Literally. *The* big change I can feel and smell, the moment I walk into any one of these sleek new bars, is the ever-present thrum of gack. It's in the air, everywhere, the urgent menace of cocaine. Crowded bars throb with that horrible testosterone sweat of coke-addled aggression and anxiety. Girls with honed bodies come on to you the second you arrive at the bar. It's a clear and direct come-on, their zinc-sparkling eyes and those lurid, lancing smiles full of promise – provided you've got gear.

You can buzz off the depraved energy as you walk down any main road. Coke is king and everyone is on it; bankers, teachers, lorry drivers. Librarians, plumbers, nurses, students . . . everyone is pumped-up and wild-eyed and going somewhere, fast – even if it's only the toilet. The city I left behind is simply not there now. It's far, far worse. Liverpool is the coke capital of Europe and by God am I up for Hodge's master plan to save the world from its sins.

* * *

My new comrades from Customs are similarly zealous. What we discussed over grilled sea bass and chilled Sancerre were the practicalities of Hodge's theory. You can't fault his logic. For all that this caper starts out – in this country, anyway – as tightly pressed bars of near pristine flake cocaine, it ends up as bin liners full, packed to bursting, with used notes. Small fortunes in paper money is the endgame – fives and tens and twenties, *loads* of twenties, notes that themselves, more often than not, are contaminated with the residue of the cut and adulterated shite that passes for coke on the street and in the clubs. The money pile; *that* was where Hodge wanted us to dig.

Me, Peters and Anderson had to suss out the money trail and work out how all that physical mass of cash was 'disappeared' into assets. It wasn't as though we were talking about a paltry few grand being laundered, either – this was big, big money, and it had to end up somewhere, somehow. The old-time gangsters of yore had a hard enough time transforming a fifty-grand blag into legitimate bunce. They had salvage yards and taxi cabs and second-hand car showrooms to hide behind, but it was low-level, limited turnover, old-school cash and carry. With these boys today, you were looking at upwards of 100k per *night*, twice, three times that at weekends – and that was just one firm. Millions and millions and *millions* of pounds in hard cash money, vanishing into thin air. No wonder so many kids wanted to be gangsters these days. No wonder Hodge wanted Lance Campion caught, plucked and roasted.

Campion, let's face it, was already notorious when I had my first coming. A cherubic-looking, ginger-haired Afro-Irish buck from the lawless heartlands of Granby, Lanky was an unlikely Al Capone. That's because he *wasn't* Al Capone. Don't get me wrong, Lanky could have a fight all right, and being one of those benighted throwbacks who got the worst of all worlds — a ginger, a short-arse, a black, no dad and freckles all over to boot — believe you me, he *had* to handle himself on those vicious streets. He was very much known to the police and by the age of fourteen was one of the most nicked kids in town. It only took Lanky a few stints in DC to work out that a mixed-race lad with orange hair is an easy nick for PC Plod. If Lance Campion goes sauntering into Boodles and swipes a tray of rings, Old Bill knows where to come a-calling, time after time. It came as no surprise then when Lanky graduated, inevitably, to HMP that he razored his hair to a shiny bald dome. He gave up on the clobber too — the gaudy shirts and shoes that had been a part of his shtick. Once he was out of there, Lanky binned the labels and dressed down in the same sort of loose-fitting gym gear he'd worn inside — T-shirts, jogging pants tucked into thick athletics socks, and always the bright white training shoes. From the day he got out of Strangeways, Lance Campion was just another face in the crowd.

But under that smooth brown lid, Lanky had noodles too. He saw the bigger picture; the long game, call it what you will. When I was out in Spain on the Blake job, you could see how extremely and effectively Lance Campion had changed his game, and you could only surmise that Strangeways itself was his game-changer. That's where he rubbed shoulders with the A-team, the real heavy hitters of the crime world. And in particular, that's where I'm guessing he first met TC. As soon as he had his in to Top Cat, that was Lanky — up, up and away. From small-time hoister to big-time charlie baron, you'd have to allow that Lance Campion has brought a certain elan to the sordid world of drug-dealing, and his rise has been strat-ospheric. If he wasn't, at his height, the world's most wanted when it came to class As then I can't think of anyone else who was in any deeper. He's been shrewd enough to ease off, of late — younger, more ruthless gangs; the inevitable attention from the likes of my good self — but not so very long ago gangling Lance Campion, from Granby Street, Liverpool 8, was in my own humble opinion the biggest fish in the whole wide ocean. That's not to say there's anything approaching admiration here — let's just say that my close proximity to the man made me appreciate *some* of his methods. End of the day, though, Lance 'Lanky' Campion is one ruthless mother, and I'd have to admit a certain how-you-say frisson of anticipation as we three sleuths set off to plot his downfall.

The file is thin on any real detail, but there's enough. For an operation such as we're intending to mount, there is more than enough. There's an address, for starters, of a supposed counting house where Campion's network of pushers, dealers, runners and enforcers meet, plot and store unimaginable quantities of drugs — and drug money. For as long as it takes for something to happen, this is going to be a watching brief.

And we know from bitter previous that these Granby bucks are not daft. They're far from daft. They have that awesome, awful combination of wits, organisation and a shocking facility for violence allied to the pure animal instinct of time-served street nous. Lanky can smell a sting a mile away. Many is the time he's just left a consignment of drugs rotting on the quay-side or in a juggernaut on a lay-by miles from anywhere. I've developed a sixth sense myself over the years and I can only imagine he's the same. You just *know* sometimes, don't you? So if three newcomers suddenly appear in Granby, no matter how sure our patter or how kosher our guise, we won't get anywhere *near* Lance Campion. His stand-offs, the everyday scals and foot soldiers on the street will know straight away that five-o are having another little go — the latest laughable attempt in a lifetime of embarrassing own goals.

Legend has it that when Hodge first took up the reins after the riots, he targeted the Granby Triangle as a fulcrum that needed breaking. His hand-picked Drug Squad boys decided to set up shop in a derelict house right there in the heartland, Granby Street itself. So what did the deadheads do? They only went and poked a few loose bricks out and tried to install the crudest bloody surveillance camera known to man and beast: a full-sized Betamax recorder wired into a bloody TV set! It didn't last a night. Not only did the local hoodlums manage to nick the camera right from under my esteemed colleagues' noses, they weighed it in at the bric-a-brac shop on Lodge Lane and laughed when the boys in blue had to buy their own camera back next day. To add insult to injury they daubed the outside wall of the boarded-up house with the message: *Smile Your [sic] On Granby Camera*, with an arrow pointing up at the hole where the camera used to be. DS packed up and left that very same day.

We won't be making the same mistake on Tango. Uh-uh, no way. *Everything* new, anything that wasn't there yesterday – nothing but nothing goes unnoticed on Granby Street. We could try to park up a battered old transit van with slashed tyres and no tax disc but they'd still force the back doors open – and not because they'd expect to find hidden bounty. They'd expect to find bizzies with listening devices. These kids have got scanners, high-powered binoculars, walkie-talkies, everything. They guard the main arteries in and out, they hang on the corners, they sit on the steps. Nothing escapes their loving gaze. We may well have an address but we'll still need a way of monitoring the gaff. It's not going to be easy.

Our lettings team try everywhere in the vicinity. The closest we can viably get to Lanky's counting house without arousing any suspicions is a garret in the student stretch on Princes Avenue.

It's at the back of the building and gives a reasonable spec over Harrington Street as far as the corner of Jermyn Street. It's far from ideal, but it'll do. If nothing else, we'll get a close-up of *some* of the regular traffic in and out of the hood. There's nothing to say that any of those vehicles are in any way involved in the transportation of narcotics, but just as Lance Campion has a finely tuned nose for trouble, so do we. Something will turn up. If we sit it out long enough, something's got to give.

It gives sooner than we dared hope. Let's have it right about these wretched bloody stakeouts, by the way – they are *slow*. You can walk into a job on a Saturday teatime and literally not see the light of day for a fortnight. Longer. Even our own side forget we're stuck up here on jobs like this, and it's not as though we're overwhelmed with options to relieve the boredom. This is a touch-sensitive site – you can *feel* the tension every time there's a foot on the staircase or a ring on one of the bells. We hardly dare speak to one another, let alone risk a TV or cards or *any* form of whiling the time away. But after a particularly dull start to our first Saturday night in the flat, Anderson nudges me and hands me the gigs. She points and mouths 'white Golf' and I pick it up straight away, a sporty little GTi making no concessions to anonymity as it speeds along Granby Street. You can hear the screech of the right turn and another squeal again as it pulls up. I can only begin to imagine the roasting the jockey will get from Lanky's gang when he gets inside that counting house. A clip round the ear doesn't come into it – he'll be lucky not get clipped, end of.

The other two are both watching me keenly, wanting to know if I think this could be The One. I nod just the once as I hand back the bins, then jerk my head at the door. It's a gamble this, but to be honest, a lot of what we're going to have to do here, to make this fly, is pure gut. I'd say the odds on the Golf look middling-to-good. The beauty of these bastards doing what they do from within the supposed sanctity of the no-go Granby Triangle is that there are only so many ways in, and the same back out again. It makes life easy for the baddies, yes – but it can work very nicely for fellas in white too. If we stick a car halfway up Kingsley Road and another near the Princes Park gates there's a reasonable chance we'll eyeball this white Golf again before the night's out. Whether he's picking up, dropping off or none of the above, it's a start, an in, it's something to go on – and that's all we need right now. Quickly and quietly I run through the plan of action with Anderson and Peters and, one at a time, we let ourselves out of the flat and pad very carefully down the stairs and out on to the Avenue. I wave them off in the knowledge that, however this plays, I won't see them till tomorrow now. Radio silence is an absolute dead-on must if we're going to stay under Lanky's radar.

Peters and Anderson head off back to the old Volvo estate they've been using – fully loaded with gear but very possibly *the* least conspicuous car on the road after mine. For my sins I am in charge of a dull, grey Vauxhall Astra that, under its bonnet, is capable of a flat-out 155 mph on the wide-open, and can hit 60 in just over three seconds from standstill – not bad in a city-centre chase scenario. You wouldn't think so to look at it, mind you. No one would give it a second glance, and that's what you want around here. I sit off under the thinning trees of Devonshire Road, sensing in my guts that the show is about to start.

I'm not mistaken. I can hear the fool long before I see him, bombing down Kingsley Road and screeching right over the roundabout without slowing. Whatever they've said to the jockey in there, it hasn't sunk in. From the way he's driving, the only thing that's hit the mark is line after line of crazy marching powder, and that gives me confidence I can tail this on-one knob without too much trouble. It's a specialist sport by the way, putting a tail on a car. Forget the movies. Jesus – how no one ever gets on to those super-sleuths on the silver screen who just sit off ten foot down the road and pull out the second the perp makes off . . . Half the kids around here would suss them the minute they show up in the mirror; the other half would've had their wheels off before they got the chance. Tailing a car is a masterclass, an art, a game of patience, and I should know. I've been tailing bad guys for fifteen years now, here, there and every which where, and what I've learnt is that you have to trust yourself and back yourself, even if you lose sight of your target for a protracted length of time. So long as you've got a good idea where he's going, your mark will always show up again.

I don't go right after him, and that proves to be a good call. Twenty seconds later there's an outrider on a Suzuki watching his back, just making double sure there's no one on his tail looking to take liberties. The bike only stays with him to the bottom of Belvidere, then he banks into a U-turn by the school and razzes back up towards home base. I let him go, turn over and I'm off in hot pursuit. A white Golf with hot tyres shouldn't present too many problems. I'll pick him up, no trouble.

Having never shared my home or my life with anyone other than my beloved mater and pater, the stint outside the semi on Cuckoo Lane gives me no problems either. I'm more than used to biding my time. I'll sit, and sit, and sit until something happens – and something *will* happen. The jockey has left his Golf parked at a sixty-degree angle across the drive and unless I'm very much mistaken there's still a bag containing a substantial quantity of drug-stained cash in his boot. This loon was so far gone last night – this morning – that he honestly could not be bothered lugging his load indoors. Maybe he forgot he had it at all. Knowing this gives me an ultra-warm glow inside. The knowledge that, no matter how intricate, concise and brilliant Lance Campion's strategies are to flood this land with Bolivian marching dust, the moment he has to delegate he's in trouble. His very closest crew may be the finest, most solid and reliable in the world. He's got this far by leaving nothing to chance. But an empire like his runs on many pairs of feet, and not every foot soldier can be personally vetted and sent out to boot camp for intensive training. If Lanky could control every cog in his works, every link in the chain, I'm certain he'd be on it — chapter and verse — but he can't. And I am even more deadly dead certain that he hates having to accept that there are some things he just has to wing. Lance Campion is generating enormous amounts of money, yet so much of the actual graft consists of the everyday rigmarole of getting the gear in, getting it cut and getting it back out to the network, the ten-key men, the five-key men, right down to the little street teams who'll split a bar among five or six of them. But with so much activity and so many pieces to the jigsaw, it follows there are weak links in the chain. Lanky has no choice but to settle for jerks like this guy and hope he doesn't make too many waves — and knowing this makes McCartney a very happy cop.

Hello. Here we go. The door inches open and a grizzled face peers out. He's looking left and right not because he's cautious, not because he remotely expects there's a watchful lawman lurking out here, clocking his every move. It's because he's still done in, his head is throbbing like an outboard engine and he's having to summon up the vim just to step out to his car and bring in the laundry. He stretches hideously, and out he comes, dressed in boxer shorts, a grotty grey T-shirt and flip-flops. What is it with Scousers and summer gear? Are they in permanent bloody denial? We're still in February here and they're all smooching around like we're in Miami – which we are, I suppose, after a fashion.

He comes round the front of the car and points his zapper at the driver's door. He opens it, leans inside, ducks back out and shuffles round to the boot. Hello, hello, *hello*! Now then! This is interesting. This is very interesting indeed . . . for, yes – on closer inspection, the pallid, haggard-looking scruff currently rooting around in the boot of his badly parked Golf is none other than former LFC idol Georgie bloody Smallwood! OK, OK – idol is pushing it a bit. Georgie was one of half a dozen lads from the all-conquering Liverpool Youth team of a few years ago who made the step up to the big league. In Madrid, in Buenos Aires, in Amsterdam, that's the start of a fairytale career. In this depraved hellhole, though, fame writes its own horror story. The kids think they've made it. They're feted like Scouse royalty by the girls, the bouncers and the baddies. They're given a walkover into every club, every bar, every VIP room, plastic gangsters thinking they're superstars, shoving coke up the young players' noses and snapping themselves with their arms around today's Star of Tomorrow, gurning like goons. Sad. Sad, sad, sad. I have little time and even less love for the round-ball kicking game, but even I know Georgie Smallwood was a talent to behold. That's him now, hollow-cheeked, wasted, lugging a dirty big sackful of drug money into his mum's front room. I'd heard it on the grapevine he was in the game these days and there's the proof playing out in black and white. I fire up the Astra and crawl away, depressed, now, at my tawdry role in a soulless world.

'You're certain this guy's a player?'

I'm certain he's not. I know full well that Smallwood is a used-up nonentity. But I know with absolute cast-iron cop logic that he's going to lead us right to the players' front door, and maybe a way beyond. If Hodge will green-light this marvellous little sting Anderson's devised, it's going to cash us in big time.

'He is, sir. I assure you – there's no downside here.'

'Really? You're certain he's that thick?'

'It's better than that, sir. He's desperate.'

Hodge extinguishes his smile before it's crept halfway up his face. He turns to his window, nods.

'Very well. Let's do it.'

'Yes!'

Me, Peters and Anderson pump our fists at each other – we know we're on to something here and, in our world, that's one fantastic buzz.

'Thanks, sir. We'll get right on to it.'

'Just . . .'

He turns back round to give me the full theatrical glower.

'Make this work, McCartney. Make absolutely damned sure that every piece stacks up. Yes? And keep me informed.'

'Absolutely.'

'I mean it, McCartney. This *has* to work!'

'It will do, sir.'

We're out of there before he has time to change his mind.

The scam is this. Penny Anderson will bring about a mild-mannered crash with Georgie Smallwood. Smallwood will jump out of his newly pranged car and call her every bitch under the sun. She'll eat the abuse, come over all shook up and tell him her husband's got a body shop. She'll beg him not to call the cops – knowing that calling the cops is the last thing Georgie's going to do, even in the unlikely event he is actually insured – and she'll offer to get his whole car filled and resprayed and body beautiful at zero cost, good as new. He'll make a big thing of doing her a favour and he'll try to squeeze a ton out of her for loss of his car for the day . . . but by the time he gets the thing back it will look a million dollars – and his every word will come winging its way back to ourselves care of the listening device Peters will insert in his dashboard.

'If there's time, I'll try to get one of these little devils fitted, too . . .'

He holds up what looks like a hearing aid.

'What's that then, mate?'

'It's called a GPS.'

'George the Plank Smallwood?' I grin. 'Picks up his coke-crazed heartbeat . . .'

'Very close, actually,' he winks. 'If all goes well, it'll certainly pick up his whereabouts.'

'Go 'way!'

'Yup. Tell him, Pen . . .'

Anderson raises her eyebrows ever so slightly – I don't think she's sure about me yet – and goes into schoolteacher mode.

'It's a global positioning system . . . essentially a mini-satellite that, if you want it to, tells you where you are and where you're going. But if you don't know you've got one . . . it tells *us* where you are, too.'

'Wow.'

'Wow indeed. Accurate to a radius of about fifty miles. Should give us something extra, hey?'

'Not half. That's . . . super-wow! That really is something else, hey?'

'Could be, sir. It really could make a difference. Just the small matter of pranging his silly little stud-mobile first, now . . .'

And she does it. It goes like a dream. By the time we three meet up for a libation in their Wirral hotel, Penny's relaxed a thousandfold.

'Should have heard him! Any other time and I'd have been calling you to nick him for adopting an aggressive stance.'

Peters almost spits his wine all over the table.

'That doesn't exist! You can*not* get a pull for adopting an aggressive stance.'

'Tell him, sir.'

I confirm it, and regale them with sundry tales of sad cases who've repented such stances at their leisure. My first ever New Year's Eve on the Met I collared a kid in Cambridge Circus for this precise offence – in his case, removing his outer garments and approaching a constable with his fists up, inviting him to engage in fisticuffs. They hoot and giggle, but the subtext to all our merriment is a case that is up and running. In a few hours' time our wire goes live and I'll regale them with tall stories for a week if our little birdie starts to sing.

This is brilliant. It's just like being in a spy thriller – except the baddies in spy thrillers don't divulge the intimate details of their sexual exploits over a wiretap. Georgie Smallwood may well be all washed up as a footballer but if his macho bragging is anything to go by he still has a line for the ladies.

'This one last night, lad. Telling you. Little shorts on, long brown legs, little ankle boots –'

'Go 'way!'

'Telling you, kidda, stretched out on the dashboard, just looking at us and she's, like –'

'Fucking stop it, you!'

'Not getting thingio there, are you, Mick?'

Wild, high-pitched laughter from Mick. He laughs like a girl.

'Fuck off, you! Sex case . . .'

More laughter. Penny registers bemused resignation with the arch of an eyebrow. Peters mugs back at her. 'I know', sort of thing. Tell you what, they're very politically correct, these two. Wouldn't last a day in the real job, some of the stuff they'd have to swallow. I give Peters the basic sign language – 'Where is he?' Peters twiddles some knobs and zooms in on this little yellow line on his screen. He keeps on zooming in until we can see landmarks and names we know. The tracking device in Smallwood's car has just vicariously taken us past Hunt's Cross station. The Ford plant is showing up to his left, but he peels right. Looks like he might be headed for the airport. I wink at Peters, genuinely excited at what's going down here.

The wire crackles as Georgie's pal giggles at yet another pearl of wisdom. The audio is far from perfect with all the engine noise and gear changes as he razzes through the south end, but you can still hear everything well enough. The other guy's tone changes, his effeminate voice taking on a harder edge.

'So. That jaborge . . .'

Here we go with the back slang. Honestly. These south-enders think they're in their own secret garden talking in tongues that no outsider could ever begin to comprehend. They make me laugh. All they do is they add an extra syllable halfway through a key word, or tag something on the end for good measure, and they think it'll take a Russian code-cracker to work out what they're on about. *Jaborge*. George. George Raft equals graft, job; illegal enterprise. Thanks, guys – you had me going there.

'Yiss?'

'You on it?'

'Am on it, lad.'

'Is right, lad.'

Ith wite, lad.

Almost sounds camp. I *know* that voice. I do, I'm sure
of it . . .

'And your lad. Is he proper, lad?'

'Oh yiss. Telling you, lad . . .'

Lad, lad, lad — what about some names, you pair of
no-marks? Say something incriminating!

'Is right.'

'Wanna know why this is so fuckin' beautiful?'

'Go 'ead.'

'Cos my lad's a bird.'

'Go 'way.'

'Innit.'

'Fuckin' case, you.'

'Oh yiss!'

More laughter.

'Who is she?'

'Told you, lad. Little crop top . . .'

Sudden change of atmosphere; even down the line you can
feel it.

'Whoa, whoa, whoa, Georgie! What have I said, lad? What
have I always said?'

'I know, I know — 'kinell, man! You think I'm a dickhead
or something?'

You can actually hear Smallwood regulate his breathing out
there. His coke-fuelled engine is overheating and it's an effort
for him to stay calm.

'Fuck's sake, Mikey —'

'*Names*, you quilt!'

'Sorry, lad —'

'What have I told you about that?'

Mikey! Of course! Mikey Greene! How could I not have
picked up on that? Well, well, well, our old quarry rears his
head again. This is getting *very* interesting!

'I said I'm sorry . . .'

'Jesus Christ, lad . . . go 'ead, then . . .'

Big long pause. Georgie composing himself.

'The bird's uncle, right . . .'

'Go 'ead . . .'

'Got a travel agent's, innit? Brum.'

'Go 'ead . . .'

'He does all the trips back home and that. Middle East, Bangladesh, wherever . . . there's all sorts in and out of there. Big money. So it's her uncle's gaff, but the lad what's running it day-to-day and that, he's pure gone on little Melanie. Telling you, lad, he'll do whatever – all she's got to do is ask. We give him a drink and he'll carve the bread however we want.'

'Serious?'

Thee-wee-yuth? It's definitely Mikey Greene.

'Proper, lad.'

'What sort of drink?'

'You know the score, lad. A drink.'

'Go 'ead then . . . what's he saying? What can he do?'

'Whatever we want. Dollars. Deutschmarks. Gregories . . .'

'Birmingham?'

'Yiss.'

'Love it, lad. Proper. What size?'

'Small-small for starters, hey, lad? See how we go from there . . .'

'Small-small? How come, Jabba?'

'That's how the L man likes it, innit?'

Light though his alto is, we can hear the sudden menace in Mikey's voice.

'Well, Lanky's not here, is he, man? – so you better square it with myself!'

We wink at one another. I swear you can hear Smallwood choking back the urge to shout 'names'.

'All right, all right, M. You're the boss end of the day, lad. Say medium, then. How's that with you? See how they get on with that?'

'Is right.'

'Told you.'

Mikey Greene is all smiles again.

'You did, lad. You fuckin' did tell me, didn't you?'

The pair of them crack up laughing again and I can see it from here, the two of them high-fiving, thinking they're way, way above and beyond the Law. Well, they better enjoy the moment because this is going to be among their last of leisure for a long time. They go over the where and when, and that's that. Game on.

I'm there on the walkway by Runcorn station good and early. They've said 12.25, and they seem so complacent I doubt it's even entered their orbit that anyone could be on their case . . . but you leave nothing to chance where Lance Campion's firm is concerned. If I work on the basis that every single thing I do is known in advance, in triplicate, by Lanky and co, then there's at least an outside chance I might be able to steal this on them. I'm scoping the car parks, two small ones on the entrance side of the station and the big one to the rear. There's half a chance they'll turn up on the bus or by taxi – it's just a case of keeping my eyes open and looking for a long-legged schoolgirl with a suitcase or similar. There won't be many that fit the bill travelling to Birmingham on the 12.25.

I see him before I see her, and it's a huge shock to the system. Evan Kavanagh. Shakespeare. He's aged quite a bit since last I clapped eyes on him, but he's still one natty old dread, I have to say – jade-green homburg hat with a bottle-green side feather, picking out an outrageous pair of green velvet troos. Long Edwardian jacket, mustard-coloured waistcoat and a cotton shirt done up to the collar with a single-link golden neck chain just below. He still has the funny little Guy Fawkes beard and, of course, the deep warrior's scar from his right earlobe to just above his chin, but there's no denying it – even at fifty-odd, Evan Kavanagh's a good-looking dude. With his cane and his highly polished ox-blood shoes, I can't help chuckling to myself at the sight of Shakespeare going incognito. Lord alone knows what he'd do if he had to stand out in a crowd. I shake my head as I go bounding down to the platform. No way in hell is he going to recognise me after all this time away.

They're so casual, it beggars belief. By my reckoning there's anything up to a quarter of a million pounds in each holdall and, for most of the journey, they've got them stowed right out of sight, in the alcove between theirs and the seat behind them. I'm in the next carriage along, but they're right in my eyeline, larking about, not a care in the great wide world. Evan is literally old enough to be her grandad, but he's trying it on with the girl, oblivious. A fortune big enough to retire on in his care, and he's stroking her thigh with his thumb, whispering sweet nothings into her ear.

But they're not completely daft. The train pulls in at Wolverhampton. Almost without warning, and at the last possible second, they stand up, dig out their bags and hop off. If I jump up now, right after them, I'll be goosed. As casual and slapdash as they are, even these two will be on to me if I stand up now. Sickener. I'm going to have to let them go. The train trundles interminably on to Birmingham, where I hop off and find a call box. I'm straight on to Penny. Somehow the idea of Peters' reedy voice with all its pent-up sarcasm is not something I can deal with right now.

'Pen? Are you on the doodah?'

'The copse?'

68

'Him.'

'No. Why?'

'Blurred vision.'

'Crap.'

'I know.'

'Give me a minute.'

'Let me know.'

Nothing comes of it. She gets right on Georgie Smallwood, but there's no dice. He just blethers on about the 'specials' in some new massage parlour that's opened, doesn't mention today at all. I ask her to get me a list of travel agents in Wolverhampton and curse myself as I wait at New Street for a train back there. If the ticket inspector gets smart I'll roast him, I swear.

It's a mixed bag to be honest, but compared to how things were looking at two o'clock I'll take it, thank you very much. I was back in Wolverhampton within the half-hour. I thought about calling up two excellent comrades I worked with in the aftermath of the Ibiza case. Even there we only really got the grafters and the middlemen. Davey Lane and Randy John vanished into thin air – literally. The guys in The Hague picked them up landing a Cessna Skyhawk on a private strip, but they had nothing on them – not even currency. Gary Havers and Tim Miller came to me from the Special Operations Unit to help with the search for Heidi. Two great guys, especially Tim, whose mordant humour was only enhanced by that deadpan Black Country accent – but I quell the urge to get in touch and carry on square-bashing through my list of Wolverhampton's travel agencies.

I'm just starting to get irate about the length of Compton Road when my heart almost vaults through my gullet. Two, three hundred yards up the road, hand raised defiantly as he flags down non-existent taxis, is the unmistakable spectacle of Shakespeare's bright green garb and, yes! He's standing right outside a travel agency. You old beauty, Evan Kay! I find myself muttering his nickname in Granby slang: 'Shay-gake-speare . . .'

I smile to myself. Never imagined I could be this pleased to see the old rascal. I'll just keep ambling on by, I think – head down, no reason for anyone to give me a second glance. I'll clock the travel agent's shopfront; might even take a little gander inside, memorise all the pertinent details before I swoop back to the train station myself. Actually, no – even with these two, suffused as they are with self-satisfaction at a job done adequately well, there's the chance that, on some submerged, subconscious level, they may twig that they've seen my dial somewhere else today. That's the last thing we need, what remains of my cover blown before we've even got going on this. I can easily radio them in and have someone jump on at Crewe to tail them, though we pretty well know where they're domiciled. I'll take my time, have a little shufti round here. For now, this is a not-bad result; not bad at all.

We step up the watch on three fronts. The girl is the most difficult because of her age. We've had to bring the Child Support Agency in on this one, though the notion that Melanie is anything other than a knowing, cool and ruthless young woman is laughable. She's only fifteen but she's hard-faced and calculating, and she knows exactly what she's doing. No one is forcing Melanie into this; there are no bribes, blackmail or threats, no major drug story that we know of. She's doing it because she wants to – end of bloody story. She's known around town as Mello Pop and she is absolutely drop-dead beautiful. I've had to walk away blushing after looking at her file. Cypriot father, Scouse mother and a serial truant since the age of twelve, Melanie Papadopoulos has been a veteran of the Liverpool club scene for a couple of years now. Like so many of those long-limbed beauties her age, she's got the idea into her head that it's clever and sophisticated to frequent doormen – but this one has long since moved on from the free entry and a line of gack for a blow-job game. She's caught the eye of some serious players and, while we can't exactly do her for going to gangsters' parties, it seems young Mello Pop has been KTP for a while. It's tragic. You can see it in the eyes; there's an intelligence there, a sensitivity; she's well groomed and she's been well brought up. You don't get hair that lustrous and skin that flawless if your mum and dad don't give a toss. This one's come off the rails because she's chosen to. It beats school, hands down. It's a laugh, a trip. It's bloody exciting. We'll try to nip her quick, before the real rot sets in.

Our second mark is dear old Evan Kavanagh. I feel guilty, grubby even, putting through the paperwork to get after him, but the truth is that Shakey's going down. Again. May take a month or two, may take longer this time, but Shakespeare can't keep his nose out of trouble. God alone knows why I should feel any kind of sympathy for the dippy old crook, he's a serial jailbird. Three weeks ago, he got out from his latest stint at Hotel Paradiso. *Three weeks!* What gets into them? Seriously? They must jump off the bus, have a pint, check whether they've still got somewhere to live, then get straight on to Crime Incorporated.

'Hello? Is this the Bad Guys speaking? Anything doing?'

It beggars belief, it really does, but nick him I must.

And while it's fair to say it hasn't quite been rubber-stamped at Home Office level yet, it's a nailed-on certainty we'll be running a wire on the travel agency too. Even preliminary checks show it's likely being used as a major, major wash-house. Sol Travel, behind a clean but unprepossessing facade, specialises in bespoke trips to far-flung places. It's also doing a roaring sideline in currency fraud. We get some taps in there and who knows what leaks might come gushing springlike into our ever-welcoming pails.

While in Wolverhampton the other day I availed myself of a batch of gear and some new works to boot. Once you're on the firm and in the system, so to speak, you can pick up gear pretty well anywhere. I can, anyway. You just have to know who to phone. There's nothing quite like a hit with a pristine new needle and, after today's exertions, I'm gagging for it. Just as I've stripped down to my vest and shorts and I'm settling down to fix myself up, the buzzer goes, loud and angry. The phone is the same; when you don't want it or least expect the call, it sounds threatening, somehow. Accusatory. Right now it's a nuisance for two reasons: one is that no one really knows I live here yet, so it can only be kids, canvassers or clowns, meaning I'm going to have to chase them or else they'll keep on buzzing. Two is that I've already stripped down for this fix. I've been flailing since Birmingham, truth be told, but the day has just been too full on for me to find a quiet moment to myself. I've lit the candles and got the *Nocturnes* on low and mellow, ready to sort myself big time – and now this. I lunge for the intercom. The wall still smells of paint.

'Yes!' I snap.

'Sorry for the late hour, Billy . . .'

Hodge. Jesus wept.

'No problem, sir. Come on up. Just give me a moment while I get dressed.'

I find myself laughing at the absurdity of the situation – me about to crank and the boss at the door. I stow the doings, slip on a shirt and a pair of jeans, check myself out in the mirror, cough two or three times to get the larynx functioning and wait for the knock from my lord and master. He takes ages. Yes, fine, it's five and a half flights, but come on – even the top brass have to conform to certain physical standards.

He leans on the door jamb a moment, breathless; realises he's embarrassing himself and makes a big thing of smiling and trying to look like he isn't completely knackered. Pats the door and jerks his head back towards the staircase.

'Keep you fit!'

'I'll say.'

'Wouldn't want to try *that* after a session . . .'

My questions: Why are you here? Why are you being coltish and matey? Why do you look so uneasy? Come to the point if you will, sir, then kindly get lost and let me get back to business. Hodge gives that perfunctory scope round the room that we all do, second nature, the moment we step into somewhere new.

'Nice place. You starting to feel at home yet?'

'Getting there, sir. Got my eye on some bits and pieces . . .'

'Good, good. We're incredibly pleased to have you with us . . .'

He just stands there looking simple. I do my best to lead him to his mission by the hand.

'Thanks. It seems to be going well. Peters and Anderson are terrific . . .'

'Good.'

Long pause. Steely eye contact.

'Good.'

He turns away from me and strolls across to the big sash window, runs his fingertip along the sill. Among every tell we've come to rely upon, the fingertip run is up there with the best. This is the bit where he comes to the point. He turns to face me – more of the eye-to-eye ritual.

'The girl, Billy . . .'

I know exactly who he means, but have no intention of making this easy for Hodge.

'Penny?'

'No! The girl . . . the one you've been . . .'

I wait. Purely a matter of procedure, but under the terms of my 'cell' assignment, I can't disclose any information to anybody without the express permission of Hodge himself. Technically, he hasn't given me said permission. He gives it his trademark deep, despondent sigh.

'The Papadopoulos girl, Bill. You need to tread carefully there . . .'

'In what way, sir?'

He stands there screwing his face up all agonised like he's preparing himself for one almighty dump.

'Is this a warning, sir?'

'No, no . . . nothing like that.'

Another big sigh.

'I can't go into it in too much detail. Just . . . trust me. Yes? I want you to be extremely vigilant and exercise extreme caution . . .'

'That sounds very much like a warning to me, sir.'

More facial gymnastics from Hodge.

'Take it how you will, Billy . . .'

'Can you be any more specific, sir?'

'For crying out loud, McCartney! Just . . . *be careful.*'

My dial must betray mild shock at this because Hodge goes all humble and contrite in his mannerisms. He steps up and gives me that funny little squeeze on the shoulder that he does, mugs up a smile that's intended to communicate a hint of reluctance, a bit of regret, a suggestion that he finds himself compromised, even sorry to have to ask these things. The only thing he handles at all well is his exit, and that's because he does it so swiftly. He's barely got his message out to me than he's gone. I shake my head, double-lock the door, flop down and crank up.

I'm sitting in the back of the Volvo trying to take it all in. Anderson is trying to soothe me with her 'reasonable' voice, but I am not liking the sound of this one little bit.

'Peters . . . just so I'm absolutely clear here. You're telling me Evan Kavanagh is planning to abscond with the Papadopoulos girl?'

Nervous glances between them.

'In essence, and cutting to the heart of it, we've intercepted conversations between the girl and Kavanagh . . . suggesting that may very well be the case . . .'

Now I know why Hodge felt compelled to pay his late-night visit. For some reason Peters is beaming madly.

'What's for certain, though, is they're definitely making a swoop for the cash . . .'

'. . . and quite possibly a dash *with* the cash. The point being –'

'The point being she's a minor,' I snap. 'Forget how this development may or may not impact upon our case. There's no debate in the matter. Hodge has been warning me the girl's age might become an issue. We have to nick Kavanagh now.'

'But, sir –'

'Did I not make myself clear?'

Awkward, uncomfortable silence. Penny takes a deep breath.

'Sir. Melanie is a willing participant in this affair. From what we can discern, she's the *instigator* –'

'Penny . . . whether or not the tail is wagging the dog is immaterial in this instance. It's *wrong* . . . you know? The thing we're supposed to be against?' They exchange looks. They think I've lost the plot. I continue. 'And besides, there's no way CPS will let us go after a minor. It'll never stand up in court.'

Peters interjects. 'Sir. Melanie Papadapoulus is *not* a minor. She's sixteen.'

'She's sixteen?'

'Yes. Melanie turned sixteen on Valentine's Day . . .'

Peters hands me Mello Pop's file. I start flicking through it again, but I know from his triumphal tone they've got their facts right.

'We're good to go here, sir.'

I nod my head, slowly. I feel exposed, embarrassed and very, very foolish indeed. Peters and Anderson are absolute sticklers for detail – I should have known that. I try to inject some brio into my voice.

'Well, *OK* then! Why didn't you just tell me that from the outset? So – what have we got?'

And what we've got is dynamite.

I wish it weren't Shakespeare. Anyone but him. I go through his files and case notes again and, I don't know, seems like a crazy thing to say about an incurable career criminal, but there's something innocent about Evan Kavanagh, some childlike belief in his statements that what he's doing isn't actually *wrong*. It ill behoves a cop to start dwelling on the background, the mitigating circumstances, but, with Shakespeare, so many of his offences have been trivial; poor decisions he's made when drunk or when desperate, or both. And I shouldn't be saying this, but, looking at his file in detail, he hasn't half had the rough end of the sentencing spectrum. The judges clearly don't take kindly to a foppish black guy who talks like a Jacobean earl. If the guideline for a sentence is between three and five, he'll get the five, poor Shakespeare. He's born unlucky, but on this one he can have no complaints.

We've got him every which way. For Shakespeare it's going to come as a shock and a real bitter sting having come within touching distance of the score of his life. But when we bring him in and show him how he has zero choice in the matter – either he works alongside us or we let Lanky's crew know what we know – he's going to feel like crying.

Sad thing is, old Shakey is just the stooge in all this. The entire magnificent scheme is all Melanie's brainchild. How it's going down is like this: Srinath, the cashier at the travel agent's, the guy who's been changing all the currency for them, is sweet on our caramel-limbed temptress. Aren't we all, by the way? – now I know she's sixteen, I may just ease up the portcullis, if only a chink, on those thoughts that batter away in the middle of the night. Poor Srinath, though – he's lost the plot completely. He's gone, he is, bedazzled by those long brown legs and her little bum which she no doubt displays to perfection for him like she doesn't know he's looking. Poor boy – she's got him wound up so tight around her little finger that he'll do whatever she asks him.

As per our ever more addictive listening-in, what she's asked of Srinath are three things. One: passports for herself and Evan Kavanagh – bogus names *naturellement*, and Mello will provide the photos. Thing two: flights to Port of Spain. Wow! Trinidad. Shakespeare's mother country. Now I have to say that this one surprises me. I'm reserving judgement on this whole 'having an affair with Shakespeare' thing – maybe I simply do not want it to be so, but I have to say I just can't see it. I can't *feel* it. Occasional shag, maybe. They're horny at that age, they want it when they want it, and they're curious too. They'll experiment. They think it's cool to go with older guys, baddies, lads that slap them around. I myself had a fascination with the bony and domineering Becci Hyman, twenty years my senior and a skilled and sometimes brutal dominatrix, yet – beyond compare – the ride of my life. The love of my life. I get how that works for an impressionable kid, but Mello Pop running away to start a new life with Evan Kavanagh? I don't think so. If she ever gets on that plane at all, it'll be a staging post for some bigger scheme she's scammed up.

She's a live one, Mello Pop, and on this point Hodge is right, again; we're going to have to handle her carefully – especially as prong three of her triangle of deception is a proposition so barefaced in its audacity that it made me laugh out loud. The kid knows no fear. I really want to shake her hand and sit her down and ask where she's got this madness from, because from where I'm sitting, her dad's just a hard-working restaurant owner and his wife's a devoted mother to young Melanie. Criminal tendency doesn't *have* to run in the genes, of course not, but this one makes very little sense to me. What the nubile Melanie has done here is, she's talked Srinath into a double switch. She and Shakespeare take, we think, two bags to Wolverhampton, each containing a few hundred grand to be changed into crispy US greenbacks. We can't be certain exactly how much until we nick them and count it out – it's another one that Mikey and Smallwood are calling 'medium'. Peters plays me the wiretap in its entirety. I show myself up, again, with my evident amazement at his playing back the feed through a little hearing-aid-sized gadget he shoves into his mobile phone, but the recording lays out the proposition fairly crudely. It's Melanie's voice, all bubbly and full of charm and seductive promise.

'That's what I'm saying to you, sweetheart. That'll be bag three . . .'

Her voice takes on an extra level of crooning persuasion for that last line, like she's talking her grandmother into a place in an old people's home. There's a long pause while

Srinath, presumably, weighs up common sense against raging lust.

'You just want the extra bag?'

'With what we said.'

A long pause, then a big fat smile in his reply. I can hear it all in his voice – greed, thrill, fear and a great big dollop of indulgent love for mellow Mello.

'OK. I'm gonna say yes. Seein' as it's you, yeah? Don't you forget that!'

'Ah, you're the best, kid! I won't forget –'

'But it comes on top –'

'It won't –'

'I don't know nothing about this. OK? Everything I given you clean cash –'

There follows a prolonged chuckle from Srinath that is just besotted – but maybe that's the money he's about to make too. If Peters and Anderson have got this right, then Shakespeare and Melanie will travel to Sol Travel, as per last time, and hand over the two holdalls of cash. Srinath will oversee the transubstantiation before sending them merrily back to Liverpool with not two, but three holdalls, each chock-a-block with currency – and there's the rub, the sting, the beauty of Melanie's little plan. One of the holdalls – the one that shall remain in the care of Evan and Mello – will be stuffed with the major part of the take; Srinath will take his cut but Shakespeare and Melanie will leave Wolverhampton with most of the money they transported to Sol Travel to be laundered. The other two bags will contain dollars; thousands and thousands of crisply minted dollars in high-denomination bills, as commissioned and as expected by Mikey Greene. Except that it's not. In his attempts to win Mello's respect, if not her love, Srinath has been boasting about his sideline in fake notes. By the time Lanky's money men suss this latest bagwash is counterfeit, Evan and Mello Pop will have slipped out of the country, with a couple of hundred grand to blow in paradise. Was I ever right about Campion's misfiring foot soldiers? You just can't get the people these days. Suddenly I don't feel quite so sorry for old Shakespeare.

'What d'you think?'

What do I think? I think we've just stumbled upon real cop gold dust. As much as this is going to slay poor Shakespeare when it comes home to roost, I am now more certain than ever before that we can penetrate Lance Campion's counting house and bring him down once and for all.

'It's brilliant, Rob. Absolutely superb . . .'

'Not so good for the old guy, hey?'

We all make the wincing face. What we've just heard is the playback of a conversation between the effervescent Melanie Papadopoulos and her lover, Mr George 'Georgie' Smallwood. The conversation was short and sour, outlining what must now be, at a conservative estimate, a triple-cross. Shakespeare and Mello will come trundling back from Wolverhampton, full of beans after successfully switching a bumper load of drug lolly. While Melanie stays on the train with the kosher cash, Shakespeare will hop off at Runcorn with the jarg notes. He'll make his way to the rendezvous, happy in the knowledge that in a few hours' time he and Mello will pass through Manchester airport on brand-new passports whence they shall hightail it to London's Gatwick aerodrome and onwards to Trinidad, sunshine, anonymity and a life of ease. Melanie will blow kisses through the window as Shakey gets into a waiting cab with two bagfuls of counterfeit bunce, love-struck as he fast-forwards to their moonlight flit. But that's the last he'll see of her; poor Shakey will more than likely never see his lithe young companion again. While he waits in vain at

Lime Street station, Melanie will be riding the wild wind down the A55 with her paramour George Smallwood, a former footballer, laughing as they congratulate one another on the brilliance of their scam. At Holyhead they will, if we're filling in the gaps correctly here, take the night crossing to Dun Laoghaire – still giggling and pinching themselves, no doubt. From Dublin we can only surmise there will be onward travel to destinations unknown but, not to put too fine a point on it, old Shakespeare's been shafted, whichever way you cut it up.

'Not good for the old boy at all. Still – what doesn't kill him will only make us stronger. Here's what we do . . .'

The train begins to slow into Runcorn. With something approaching a world-weary *tristesse*, I give the signal to the team. From seats fore and aft we rise and make our way down the carriage. I clear my throat to alert Evan and Melanie to the presence of myself and several arresting officers. I crouch and lean in nice and close, flash the badge and semi-whisper the standard introduction. Not only do they not have anything they may wish to say, they are in complete and utter shock. Melanie looks at Shakespeare. Kavanagh looks at the floor, shaking his head slowly as the promise of another stint beckons.

'Nice and quiet, hey? No need to upset the other passengers. We'll be taking you off at Runcorn and transporting you directly to police HQ for further questioning. If you wish to make a telephone call, we can arrange that once we've booked you in. If you could just hand me your phones now, please . . .'

Shakespeare's all indignant, claiming he doesn't have a mobile. This necessitates an undignified body search in the passageway between carriages. The pat-down unearths no weapons, no phone and no other incriminating evidence; it does, however, tend to support the urban legend that Evan Kavanagh is packing some meat on him. We get the miscreants off the train and into the sleek Volvo they've sent. Nice. We glide over the bridge and a sad winter sun glints off the Mersey, flitting in and out of the car through the slats of the bridge. I've got to admit it — it's beautiful. I can say that today. I can feel it in my bones — that thing every born cop knows. We've got them. We've got the big boys. They don't know it yet as they sit there in their Granby counting house and plot and connive and peddle their filth, but we're right on their case now. The good guys are coming over the hill.

For all the usual reasons, I check left and right before I secrete myself in the Disabled and tease out my needle from its protective sheath. Lord above knows what I would've done in the days before these capacious, little-used conveniences became mandatory. If I was how I am now when I first started off on this thankless calling, I'd have been sussed within days. God, but I need this now, though. I do what I have to do as quickly and efficiently as possible and exit the cubicle. On my way out I snatch a quick look at myself in the mirror, more nervous than I've been in ages, and swallow back the fear that's ripping through me. I don't know why I feel this way. It's weird. It's chemical — a sort of bile-stoked dread that this is not going to end well. That's nonsense, of course. It's bloody madness. This entire roadshow is wrapped up tight and ready to bring home now — and what's more, from start to finish this operation has been Hodge's masterstroke. Why would he be anything other than cock-a-hoop at our progress, and our plan? Of *course* he's going to love it.

And he does. He loves it so much that, for a second there,

I think old Hodge is going to cuss. His eyes beam a radiant delight but he clamps down on his facial smile, gritting his teeth and gripping his fists tight.

'This is . . . *marvellous*, McCartney! Utterly superb work . . .'

I, too, try to ignore the strum of self-satisfaction that's tinkling the keys of my spine. There's one big stupid grin drilling its way out of me and I have to strain every sinew not to break down giggling like a tart. I double-breathe and suck the merriment up, exhaling hard and using the expulsion to push forth the big question.

'And the wire, sir? You're OK about that?'

'The wire?'

Uh-oh. Thought so. I *knew* there'd be something. I show no emotion. Not a twitch. Nothing.

'Kavanagh, sir. We want to send him right into the hornet's nest, so to speak . . . there's a slight debate ongoing as to what extent wiretap evidence is admissible as evidence . . .'

He wafts a dismissive hand at it.

'Climb that one as and when. I'm more concerned about the cash . . .'

'Yes, sir.'

I've asked him to make real currency available for Shakespeare's plant. Hodge flicks through the file.

'It's a lot of money.'

It is. It's three hundred grand in dollars. But it gives us a whole new hand in this crazy game of canasta. It sends currency into their system that we control. Traceable serial numbers. Hard evidence. It also allows us to plant a listening device right in the heart of their empire. It's beautiful. Priceless. A one-off opportunity to get our ears right inside their Granby HQ. I drive home my advantage.

'There's twice that amount passes through Campion's hands every week, sir. We'll get that money back – and more . . .'

'Yes. Yes.'

He's holding his head in his hands now. He wouldn't. He *wouldn't*. He's not going to kill this now – just as we've made our breakthrough. If there's one bitter lesson I've learnt about police life, though, it's that nothing is ever black and white. I started into this adventure as a kid, believing with all my heart that I existed solely and utterly to stop the bad guys; to prevent those moments happening when everything changes. Those days that start in docile tame normality – and end up in carnage. Your life has changed, for ever – all down to you coming between bad men and the things they want. I exist to stop those people – that's what I've given myself to believing. I want to use every day of my life trying my best to make sure that other people don't have to know those agonies. Much of the time, most of the time, the public won't know what I've done for them – because I've stopped the man in the balaclava from crashing through their patio doors or waking them up with a hand over their mouth and a hammer to their head. I despise those people. I want them off our streets. Hodge does, too. I know this. I *have* to believe this. He paces away from me, stroking his chin like a comic baddie, searching for inspiration in the near-distant vista of our drizzle-slick car park. He turns back to me.

'You're aware, of course, of the sensitivities in Liverpool 8?'

'I am, sir. Acutely aware. However –'

He eyes me sharply. I don't care.

'– I've never subscribed to the idea of no-go areas, as you know, sir.'

'No. No. Still . . .'

He's back to staring out of the window, thinking it all out, thinking it through. The possible repercussions. His career.

'How many personnel?'

'Nothing has changed, sir. It's just the three of us . . .'

'Really? Mmm. Mmm.'

He seems frustrated that he can't use numbers and budget as a reason to back off. He's facing me, now. He looks sad. Weary.

'We still have the um . . . um . . .' He wafts his hand as he seeks the *mot juste*. '. . . the listening post?'

'Of course. Peters and Anderson have barely left their positions at all these last weeks.'

'Good, good. That makes things . . .'

He doesn't tell me what that 'makes things', but it still doesn't sound good.

'And the girl?'

I run it by him. Again. We have Melanie in custody. We're awaiting the necessary documentation for her to be moved to a young persons' remand centre while we assess what charges she can expect to face. What charges she can expect to face depend, to a large extent, on how well her jilted admirer performs for us. Shakespeare was, by anyone's standards, crushed when we played him the tape. I'll admit it – I didn't enjoy putting him through it; poor fella tried to keep his head up in front of PC Plod but there were times you could see he was fighting back the tears. At one point Melanie referred to him as 'soft shite' and broke off laughing, hysterically, breathlessly, endlessly, until her cackling rasped out into vicious, silent hiccuping. Smallwood too – the pair of them cracking up over how brilliantly they'd duped the besotted Shakespeare. I had no choice, though. I had to play it back to him to show Shakespeare that Lance Campion's outfit were laughing at him, and here was his chance to show them who the real mugs were.

'And Kavanagh's having that? He'll do what you're asking him to?'

'It seems that way, sir. Yes.'

There's more heavy breathing and shaking of the head as Hodge stares on and on, out of his window. Just as I'm bracing myself for him to throw his spanner in the works, tell us we can't use Shakespeare for whatever trumped-up reason, he turns to face me. He doesn't look like Hubert Hodge at all. He shoots me his funny, worried smile and goes: 'Very well. Let's do it. I can't sanction the currency at this short notice. Impossible. But our man says these are excellent forgeries. I can OK the wire but that's as far as we go. Yes?'

I nod. It's not ideal but it will have to do. Peters has assured me he can wire the bags with these mega-sensitive pin microphones. He'd better be right. I nod to Hodge.

'Yes, sir. Thanks. We'll get them, sir. We'll bring Lance Campion in . . .'

I turn to leave.

'Billy . . .'

What now? Let me *get* these guys, will you?! Hodge gives me the most heartfelt once-over; eyes burning right into me, like I'm going off to war. And I suppose that is precisely what I am doing.

'I've said it once and I'll say it again. The girl. She *will* remain in custody. Until this is over. Yes?'

I smile back at him, once again squashing back a wave of nauseous euphoria.

'Of course, sir.'

And I'm out of there before he can lay down any more conditions. Here we go, then. This is it.

This is killing Shakespeare. It goes against every particle of his psyche to cooperate with the Law, but in spite of everything his only concern is Melanie.

'She safe?'

'Perfectly safe. She's in custody.'

'I do this, some bad men want to get to she . . .'

'You do this, and the bad men won't be *able* to get to she . . .'

Shakespeare runs all the equations round his agile mind, his eyes regaining their sparkle.

'Smallwood?'

'He's at large.'

'But you bring him in, yeah?'

'We have a warrant for his arrest.'

He grunts and snorts and shakes his head, but he's in.

'OK. OK. I'm gonna do it, yeah? But small-small. Talkin' bare minimum, in and out. Anything else them boy gonna smell. You hear me?'

And as much as it galls me to have a perp laying down terms and conditions – a perp we have wrapped up so tight his balls are squeaking, at that – I have to concede that there's sense in what he's saying here. Shakespeare may not like to admit it to us Babylon, but he's far from stupid; he's got a good idea how he's perceived among the Granby bucks. The truth is that Shakespeare's a bit of a joke figure among the brutal young homeboys who rule the hood today. He doesn't own houses. He doesn't fraternise with footballers, glamour models, C-list soap-opera nonentities. There's no Merc or BMW with tinted windows. He can't even drive, old Shakey. He's just a relic from the old days; a vagabond in fancy clothes who tries to use long words. The idea of him strolling into the counting house and instantly engaging Lanky's firm about their comings and goings is a tad fanciful, even for an ever-hopeful cop. If Shakespeare can just get the bags into Lanky's office, Peters' wire will do the rest. I find myself about to give his shoulder a squeeze, and have to pull back.

'Fair enough, Evan. You play it straight with us and we'll be straight with you. Deal?'

'What sort of deal?'

'You know the score, Evan. You know there are no guarantees. You'll just have to trust me, hey?'

He laughs. He's got a fantastic chuckle, old Shakespeare.

'Now I heard it all, brethren! Evan Kay, trust a cop . . .?'

He laughs again. He looks me all over with those clever, narrow eyes. There must have been Chinese in the Kavanagh mix somewhere down the line; he's a great-looking bloke, no doubt about it. We eye-lock for a few seconds then he looks away; snorts and shakes his head, half smiling, now.

'OK. Fair enough. Deal. I'll do it . . .'

A big moody sigh from him and he lays his head down on his arms, splayed out on the interview table. I'm elated here. We've got him. Shakespeare's in.

As soon as I tiptoe through the door, Peters beckons me over, hands me the cans without ever once taking his eye off the monitor. He's sat there, straight back, crisp white cotton shirt. Zero expression on his face as we listen in. I have to say Shakespeare has done us proud here. He could very easily have just dumped the holdall wherever, told us he'd done his best, et cetera, et cetera. But whether by design or default, he's plugged us right into them, loud and crystal clear. The quality is unbelievable – it's like we are quite literally in the same room. And it's the main men we're getting here, too. I'm actually shaking with excitement – maybe, if I'm honest, a touch of fear too, being so near to the man himself you feel he might look up at any moment. That's definitely Lance Campion there. Wherever he's been, he's back – and there's no doubting who's the boss. Lanky is instructing Mikey, the pair of them talking in riddles as ever.

'The G fella . . .'

'Corky?'

'Him.'

'Go 'ead . . .'

''kinell, lad . . .'

'Go 'ead . . .'

'He'll do the Druid thing when we said.'

'Sound.'

'It's not gonna be the full thingio though, kidda.'

Pause from Mikey.

'Torpedoes, still?'

'What?'

'Barracudas?'

'Should be.'

'What?'

'What about the road trip?'

'Just be four of the little ones.'

'Sound, lad. Even if they're only Bedfords. Four's still four.'

'Four's still four.'

'Innit.'

Mikey starts into his nervous giggling. I can just picture them clicking their fingers, thinking they're fucking brilliant. I take the earphones off – a funny, not unpleasant suck on your ear as the leather cups come away. Penny is scribbling on her notepad. I grimace at Peters.

'I'm going to be dead honest here, Rob. I haven't got a Scooby what they're talking about . . . Torpedoes? They moving into the arms trade?'

Peters flashes me a smile – an event in and of itself.

'Funnily enough . . .' He stands up, cracks his knuckles, stretches and body-yawns. 'They may well have an interest in hardware. All the evidence would suggest they do. And, perhaps coincidentally, those are Irish connections they're talking about. "Corky", we think, is none other than Conn Gilligan – no introduction necessary, I take it?'

I nod and make the appropriate grimace. Gilligan is well known in paramilitary circles and has been no stranger and no little menace to ourselves, over the years. It's no surprise that he and Campion have teamed up for the common bad. Peters acknowledges the gravity of this with a cheek smile and continues.

'That said, weaponry is not something we're expecting on this particular shipment. No . . . by our reckoning . . .'

He glances over at Penny, who looks up briefly and nods.

'We're pretty sure from the context and the regularity of that usage that the torpedoes he refers to are marine craft of some sort.' He pauses for dramatic effect. 'Possibly submarines.'

I laugh hard – maybe because I know that, with Campion, anything is possible. I pause to make sure that this really is no joke but, embarrassed now, I laugh some more then wipe my eyes and apologise.

'Sorry, sorry . . . but that is just too silly for words! Who does he think he is? Captain Nemo?'

Neither of them is laughing.

'Serious? They'll go to those lengths?'

Peters shrugs. 'Who knows? We'd be mad *not* to treat it seriously, though . . .'

Now Penny is up on her feet. 'Of course . . .' She, too, is enjoying the drama. The performance. '. . . it does slightly alter the dynamic of the project if they *are* thinking of bringing military craft into British naval space . . .'

Oh. Oh dear me. I get it straight away. I see what they're doing here. I shouldn't take it personally – we all jostle for supremacy, for credit – but I was starting to think there was an element of respect between us three after all this time cooped up together, fighting the baddies.

'Does it really, though?'

Peters takes over. 'Well, yes. Obviously. It becomes at the very least a matter for Special Branch, posing, as it does, a clear and present threat to national security. Especially with there being this new element of the Irish involvement . . .'

'Yeah, but there's no suggestion of any real and present threat to —'

He talks right over me.

'It's an issue for Border Patrol and it's a military issue now, too. Technically, this is an invasion . . .'

I feel sick here. I get up out of my chair but my head is spinning and I sit straight back down again. I feel hopelessly done up, and done in. They've had me. No wonder they're in here all hours, using my leads, my intincts, my *time*, for God's sake! Her Majesty's Customs have had us good style this time . . . I feel like punching him. Peters must see what's coming. The flat of his palm is up, begging clemency.

'That's *if, if* — and at this stage it is a huge unsubstantiated if — we're certain they're bringing the gear in that way.'

I pull all my loosening threads together, haul my guts back in and try to remind myself we're on the same side here. It's not a case of our lot getting the kudos for the bust or them going back to Customs HQ with their chests puffed out. It's a case of taking drugs, maybe weapons and some very bad men indeed off our streets. I blow my cheeks out and forcibly calm myself.

'Wow. OK. So, given all that, you guys are going to know better than me how we go from here on in . . .'

They exchange looks. So clean and programmed. I sincerely doubt they're banging each other. There's nothing — not a glimmer — between them. I mean it — they turn me on. Not like that, obviously. But that clinical, metronomic subservience to the job . . . I love it. It's Penny who speaks first.

'What we've got so far is a pattern emerging. Same words,

same phrases. But we're not certain when they aim to do this. And we're not sure where –'

Peters jumps in. 'Well, come on . . . "the Druid place"? That's *got* to be Anglesey, no?'

She rolls her eyes. 'We've been through this, Rob. I'm sure Billy will agree with me – "the Druid place" could cover a multitude of sins. Could be a pub, for God's sake!'

Terrific! They're human, after all. They're tired, they're irritable, they feel the strains we all feel.

'Guys? Suggestion. Just an old cop's intuition but my gut says that if this is happening at all, it's happening now. As in soon. Shall we just get our heads down for a bit? God knows when we'll get a chance if I'm right about this.'

I'm right about this. Penny Anderson shakes me awake. For a second I don't know where I am, then the stale musty stench of the stakeout invades my nostrils and I'm back in the saddle.

'Sir? Come and listen to this. I think we're good to go . . .'

Peters and Anderson may well be trying to snaffle the case away from yours truly, but as the Big One has moved ever closer, their sheer coltish excitement has been a joyful reminder of what this is all about – getting the bad guys. I'm a tad jealous. They've never done this before – certainly they won't have come this close to reeling in a major league player like Lance Campion before. I wish I could feel that thrill again – the sheer frisson of hauling in a big-game shark. Penny hands me the cans, grinning from ear to ear.

'You get that?'

'Oh yes!'

Micky Flynn, eh? I get it all right. I get it loud and clear. Peters is over, eyes gleaming.

'Do you know him?'

'Know him? Micky Flynn? Only a little bit! Jockey to the underworld is Micky . . .'

'And you think he's linked?'

I enlighten them as to Micky Flynn and my assumptions as regards his presence on the Isle of Anglesey.

'Linked? This is *the* missing link, boys and girls! This is the final piece in the jigsaw.'

'Great,' says Anderson. 'Then what are we waiting for?'

'Time for action,' says Peters. 'Yes?'

And it's a Yes from McCartney too.

'Let me speak to Hodge.'

I ring Hodge on the direct number he's given me for emergencies like this. We reckon we've cracked Lanky's plan and we need Hodge's green light to go-go-go on this one, *now*. The basics are as follows. Shipment goes from Caracas to Cork, and from Cork to a point off the west coast of Anglesey. The vessel will drop anchor, whereupon a fleet of super-fast rubber dinghies – torpedoes – will head out to ferry the drugs back to dry land.

Dry land, we reckon, is Newborough Warren, out on the south-western tip of Anglesey – the Druid place. As a drop-off point, it's genius. Remote as it is, Newborough is fifteen minutes tops from the A55, and all routes north and south – yet it's as secluded a spot as you could possibly land that level of shipment. Once again I find myself the reluctant admirer of Lanky's fine-print planning. I can hear him in my sleep-starved subconscious, running over the detail with Mikey Greene.

'Even if they're just Bedfords . . .'

'Four's still four . . .'

There's no answer from Hodge. This private number really *does* bypass the system if the trusty Diana isn't picking up. I'm bouncing all over the place like a jumping bean, unable to think straight such is my nervous excitement. Flynn has been picked up just outside Valley on the isle of Anglesey – lunatic was trying to ram the police's Eye in the Sky in a stolen car. Taken in isolation, it's just another nutter from Liverpool, out of his head on beak, trying to make a name for himself. Billy McCartney knows different, though. Flynn trying a stunt like that in the wee small hours of this morning can only mean one thing: he was trying to disable what may well be Newborough's sole means of pursuit. If I didn't know it already, I'm certain now. The shipment is on its way. This is happening now, and we have to act on it right now. We have to get out there, before the Campion crew bring in their flotilla of dinghies. Get in early is the mantra they rammed down our throats at training college; get there first. I'll be damned if we're going to get caught with our trousers down on *this* one.

I phone again – still no answer. Crap! Gently, oh-so gently, I let myself out of the flat. No one will be up in this dosshouse, anyway, but at this critical stage of the operation one can take no chances. I creep down the main stairs, let myself out on to the Boulevard, jog back into town. I flash my pass at the car park, hop in and razz off to St Anne Street. I have to get to Hodge. For this to turn out as the mega-touch we all know it's going to be, now, we're going to need serious manpower, and quick-quick. Four juggernauts, a *massive* haul of drugs by anyone's standards, anywhere in the world – we're going to need the heavy artillery; camera teams to log it all in real time, as the action unfolds; sniffer dogs and handlers; at least twenty arresting officers to nab these drug-dealing scumbags, and two or three meat wagons plus guards to cart them all off to the nick. I vault the stairs three at a time, stupidly, madly in love with the moment – in love with this crazy,

94

topsy-turvy job. Hodge isn't there. After not too much pleading and stressing the impact on Western civilisation if I don't see him, Diana tells me the boss won't be in this morning. Further pleading reveals that, this morning of all bloody mornings, His Royal Hodgeness is off playing golf! I raise an eyebrow at her, still too high on adrenalin to feel piqued.

'It better be promotion . . .'

'I got the impression it was perhaps even more important than that . . .'

I smile at her. Worth her weight in gold, Di is.

'Birkdale?'

'The Royal Liverpool.'

'Who's he playing with?'

She just smiles to herself in that way she does, and returns to her typing. I thank my Lord for small mercies — at least I don't have to get out to Southport — and leg it back to the car. I'll make it over to Hoylake in no time at all.

I'm there in twenty minutes, but finding Hodge is a different proposition altogether. The jobsworth in the car park takes one look at the cruddy Astra and he's on his way over, all puffed up with a dozen questions. In his quotidian existence, these next five minutes are going to be like sex to him. He'll have licence to quiz me, look down at me, satisfy himself — a nobody — that I have legitimate business there at the venerable and ancient Royal Liverpool Golf Club. Then he will, with excessive politeness, request that I go back out again and park in the registered guests' area over by the main road. Sorry, but no. Not today. Much as I would love to drag that odious no-mark over the bonnet and humiliate him with a body search in front of his peanuts-paying bosses, time is flying here and I'm a cop on a mission. I have to find Hodge, tell him about Lanky's crude attempts to take the coast patrol's helicopter out and beg him to wave his wand now, get the necessary authorisation for us to join forces with our sheep-shagging comrades on the wild west isle of Anglesey and nick these cowboys, once and for all. And with that comes the dazzling flash of reality that the only way I'm finding Hodge is in person, out on those verdant fairways.

I send the gravel flying in the car-park fella's face as I screech into a U-turn and belt off out of there, hard left on to the Meols Stretch and left again into King's Gap. Pulling over halfway up Stanley Road, I train my binoculars on the golf links. Not too many out on this raw and salty morning. I scan left and right before picking out a tall and wiry figure, awkward in his own skin as he thrashes and hacks, bent into avid conversation with a thickset guy. I stow the bins, wait impatiently for Hodge and his playing partner to get parallel with me then clear the little wire fence in one neatly gymnastic push-and-leap manoeuvre.

He's sizing up a putt when the penny drops that the hollering fool he's been trying to ignore is none other than my good self. I've been shouting into the wind, waving and gesticulating to get his attention as I encroach ever closer, but he hasn't looked up until now. He comes marching towards me, fists screwed tight but, ever the professional, strangling my name in his larynx. I'm impressed by his devout application of the no-names rule, but I have to say his golfing partner wouldn't have known me from Adam even if Hodge had cussed me out loud. He gets right up to me before he hisses in my ear.

'For fuck's sake, McCartney! What are you playing at?'

It's the first time I have ever heard Hubert Hodge swear. I don't have to wait long for my second helping.

'This is fucked up, you halfwit. Fuck off out of here, as fast as you like!'

'Sir –'

'Stow it, Billy!'

His eyes glower at me, jugular tense.

'I mean it. Walk!'

I'm momentarily stunned. I run the equation through my computer at high speed. No. Once he knows what this is all about, he'll thank me. I've come too far and got too close to let this slip away over a miscommunication. I find myself gabbling out the info so fast I can hardly understand what I'm saying myself.

'Sir, if you'll approve the movement order – give me ten men and full support team for twelve hours tonight and I will hand you Lance Campion's entire operation.'

For all the world it looks as though Hodge is tilting his head back and counting to ten before answering. He looks me directly in the eye, chews on it and softens his tone.

'Billy, you're bang out of order freelancing it like this. Well out of line. Just understand this – as of now, Operation Tango is no longer live.'

I go to speak, but the words get stuck in my throat. All I am conscious of is a chunk of bile-soaked potato coming up, and my chewing it momentarily, rather than spitting it right out on the Royal Liverpool Golf Club's springy fairways.

'What . . .?'

He's fully composed himself again by now. The ire is replaced by a semblance of contrition. His golfing companion comes over. He's a dark-skinned, dark-haired guy but his face is drained and pinched with dread.

'Should I just . . .?'

'No. No . . .'

He smiles at his mate, makes that little face you do when you're only going to be a minute. Hodge puts an arm around me and starts walking me back across the fairway towards where I'm parked.

'Billy, this is brand new, OK? As in last few minutes. I'm sorry. OK? I've only just . . . this is a completely new development — literally news just in. I truly am sorry. I was going to call you —'

'As soon as you finished your game of golf?'

'I wasn't *playing* golf!'

The absurdity of the comment is not lost on him. He follows my eyeline down to his driver.

'I was literally just about to call you . . .'

His words just fade out into white noise. I feel faint. Pathetic, I know. I've tasted some ups and downs in my life as a copper up until this point — but this is a low worse than any I've ever known, and I just can't take it. I shrug his arm off me like an angry kid. I turn to give him a mouthful. I can't speak. All I know for sure is that if I don't turn and get right out of there, I am going to break down crying. I can feel it coming, this monstrous wave of grief about to submerge me. I must have started shaking, or maybe my lips have started trembling — some sissy tell has given me away, because Hodge is crouching down now, trying to look me in the eye. His voice has gone all soft and sincere and concerned.

'Billy? Trust me on this one. Please. I promise I'll explain it all as soon as I'm able. Yes?'

I nod, glare at him and begin to walk away.

'Take a couple of days off!' he shouts after me. 'On me.'

I turn back towards him. I want to run up and drive my nut right into his face. That'll show him. That'll tell him what he needs to be told. We face one another down, like we're about to have a duel.

'Fuck off, sir,' I say.

That would have been the first time he heard me swear, too.

* * *

I'm sitting in the Astra and I'm staring out at a pale sky that seems to shelve away, but I'm seeing nothing. I'm feeling nothing. I have shut down. No sadness; no anger; no sickness; no despair. Nothing. Everything was pointing towards this. Hodge's confirmation of his duplicity should not have winded me the way it did ten minutes ago. I cast my eyes left to the golf course and even now I can see him, with his arm around the swarthy guy's shoulders. I try, as I do at times like this, to place myself in the other guy's shoes. What must it take to just switch off like that? Experience, I suppose. He's not a bad man, Hubert Hodge. I believe this still. I have to believe this.

I can only think in terms of the next five minutes of my life. I truly do not know what I'm going to do after this. I start the car and trundle at very slow pace all the way down Stanley Road to the dead end by the beach. I leave the engine running and look out past the little rocky islands to the distant Irish Sea. I teleport myself like Superman across the ocean, swooping only a few feet above the sea's surface and flying at the speed of sound right across to Cork, where the shipment is being prepared, right now. Why, Hodge – why? What changed?

I unwind the window and suck down a big salty gulp of fresh sea air. This city and the sea – it's a never-ending story. In the early hours of this morning a young Scouse tearaway by the name of Micky Flynn – known to police – was apprehended in a stolen Subaru after a high-speed chase along the A5 in Anglesey. Half an hour earlier Flynn had been picked up on CCTV using the car as a battering ram – repeatedly driving it at HM Border Patrol's helicopter stationed at RAF Valley on the west coast of the island. I checked it out on the map immediately Anderson alerted me to Flynn's arrest. Valley. Right on the coast where Lance Campion's flotilla of super-fast dinghies awaits. Why is a known jockey to the underworld ramming Anglesey's sole aerial surveillance into scrappage? Why is my boss, formerly so hawkishly keen, suddenly so disinterested? A melange of twisted thoughts slews through my mind's eye, and its inner ear.

'*The Papadopoulos girl, Bill. You need to tread carefully there . . .*'

Damn right it was a warning. I feel sick — but in spite of everything, this is nothing like the debilitating nausea of disappointment; of defeat. What courses through me is the kind of hideous tummy ache that presages life's big moments. Eleven-plus. First scrap. First kiss. I'm swooning at how close we are to the biggest bleeding result of my career. Hodge has just given me compassionate leave — but he hasn't taken my badge. I'm going to be there tonight, come what may. I shall be there when that shipment lands. I may not get the collar but I'm bloody well going to be there to see it happen. I pull over at the phone box by the roundabout and, bizarrely, I find myself having to use all my might to heave open the heavy red door. I slip twenty pence in and call Roddy Dixon.

Peters and Anderson will have been briefed by now that I'm off the case, but I would have liked the chance to say goodbye to them, nonetheless. They were good kids, those two. I don't care if they *have* pulled a few strokes here — their priority has always been the catch. Mine too. The priority now is getting myself *in situ* in good time and in a manner that will not jeopardise the operation in any way, shape or form.

In that respect it's imperative that I get in early and brace myself for a long, long wait. I'm guessing Peters, Anderson and their arrests and seizures team will have teamed up with North Wales Police and based themselves at Caernarfon — possibly even Holyhead. That's fine. They won't make their move until their ground team have given the nod that all the little duckies are lined up in a row for them. This gives me literally all day to get myself within striking distance, find the right plot – and wait it out. Once again, the cut and thrust of this operation is the waiting game.

I pick up a hire car in Chester, stick to the A-roads and stop off at an outdoor leisure shop in Mold. I pick out a beautiful, polished walnut hiking stick, a decent waterproof and one of those waxed Barbour-type hats. I smile at my new image in the mirror, every inch the retired bank manager from Altrincham out for a day's walking in the Cambrian Hills. I cross the Menai Straits via the old bridge and follow the National Trust road signs to Plas Newydd. I park up, stretch and stand back to admire the serene and magnificent ancestral home of the Marquess of Anglesey. I exchange pleasantries with the old history buff on the till and spend a fascinating hour or so on the official tour of the house itself, marvelling at the Bunteresque enormity of a former earl's pantaloons; but when it comes to the guided walk around the grounds and gardens, I slip away to the riverfront path and, I don't mind admitting it, thoroughly enjoy my extensive ramble right along the western straits, almost as far as Newborough Warren itself. I cut inland, swinging my hiking staff as I go – to all intents and purposes a birdwatcher or a nature lover out walking, but I'm extra careful to keep my collar up and my head down, the closer I get to the car park by the beach.

It's become a well-worn cliché that coppers can smell trouble, smell danger – but it's here all right. There's a hint of something fresh and perfumed every time the wind rustles the bushy headland, but it's followed immediately by the sub-notes of some strange menace in the air. I can feel it – like I'm in a Western, and the hills have eyes. All around me is thorny scrubland – gorse and brush and stumpy trees bent double by the fierce winds piling in off Caernarfon Bay. I imagine spies camping out in those very bushes right now, alerting their co-conspirators to my presence via secret codes. But there's no one; not a sound. I use my binoculars to follow the progress of an osprey and, long after it's dropped like a stone through the twilight sky and emerged from the sea with a slick and wriggling mackerel in its talons, I'm still scanning the coast and around and about. Everything tells me I'm alone, still – and I should use this chance to dig myself in somewhere safe.

It's already starting to go dark when I stumble upon a birdwatchers' hide. It's dilapidated, but it'll do. The windows, such as they are, are far from ideal – they're the long, letter-box type, cut specifically for twitchers; fine for silently observing the birdlife directly ahead, but hopeless for anything other than tunnel vision. If anyone were to creep up on me from behind, I'd be done for. Still, the little hut is so well camouflaged I literally fell into it, and although the smell of damp and rot and various types of animal shit is overpowering, it's going to have to suffice. So this is going to be it for the next few hours; this is base camp for however long it takes for this panto to play out. I reach for a carlota; quell the urge.

There are distant engines and the possible signs of an operation cranking to life. It's weird being here, like this; I feel oddly dislocated. There's no sense of fear, or anticipation or anything to connect me emotionally with this bust. It's academic. It's nothing to do with me now. There's only my curiosity keeping me here to see how it goes.

If that's my feeling for the four and a half hours I sit and wait from just before six to well after ten o'clock, I'm yanked violently back into the full-tilt adrenalin of the operation by a menacing and ever-building rumble from the road beyond. There's no mistaking the chunky thrum of their engines – these are lorries, big ones, too. There's no mistaking the frantic lurch of my heart, either. This is real drama thundering out before my wide and frightened eyes. I turn, slowly, painstakingly quiet. It's absurd to think they'll hear a thing above the noise of their motors and their gigantic tyres scrambling down the unmade road, but I'm terrified here. Even with the consolation that no one need ever know I'm here — was there — this is as anxious as I've known myself in years. I catch the tang of fear-sweat from my armpits as the trucks slow down below me. Down there, thirty or forty feet away — a stone's throw away — four heavy-goods vehicles park up, shut down and wait. I shall be waiting with them. Waiting for the strangulated roar of high-performance outboard motors cutting through the waves and the wind; waiting for the dot-dash signal of torches on the beach; waiting for their awful, their awesome burden to be unloaded and swiftly, efficiently stacked, pack by poly-wrapped pack, into the eager jaws of the mule train. And I'll be waiting for Rob Peters and Penny Anderson to come charging out of the brush, dazzling spotlights sending the foot soldiers scattering as more and more police appear on the scene, rugby-tackling the fleeing vermin, pinning them to the deck, driving their faces into the grit as they read them their rights — their last rites.

I don't even want to move now. Any little creak or glint could give me away. Softly, softly, I take my body weight on my palms and lower myself down to the floor. I'm just going to lie here now, until the action starts. I hear a lorry door open, then close. A muttered consultation. There's the click of a lighter and the waft of nicotine. The crunch of gravel underfoot. One of them tramps into the scrub to piss — probably nowhere near, but it sounds so close he could be slashing right against the hide. The giddy terror of his proximity makes me want to go myself. A different, distant throb is getting nearer now — another engine. It comes closer and gets louder – the confident thrum of a high-performance vehicle. It cuts into the car park and the engine stops. A succession of doors opening and closing, and footfall on the gravel, low voices. They seem calm, precise and orderly as they make their way down to the shore to light the torpedoes' way to the drop point. I can hear the whine of the boats' motors now, one long and strangely discordant note, straining against the elements. I can hear the thrash and slam of the dinghies' rubberised bottoms as they slap against the waves. They're getting close now – very close. Through this narrow slit hole, I can see the boats' silhouettes ricochet in choppy motion, one rising up as another ducks down. They're almost here. Where are the Law, for crying out loud! Dare I step out of here? Can I get closer without giving myself away?

I'm dying to sneak down there, but I know it's no good. Five more minutes won't make a difference. Give them five, and I'll start scrambling my way down there. The dinghies' engines are slowing right down to neutral now, then cutting out altogether. Strident shouts; hissed commands, dying on the wind. I strain through the peephole to try to make out the water's edge. There is definite activity down there. Figures wading into the sea towards the dark blimps bobbing up and down, moored and silent, now. Come on, Peters! If you're going to get them, get the whole gang, now – couriers and all. They're there, for fuck's sake! The whole fucking gang is right *there*, bang at it! Go, go, go, Peters! GO! And as though hearing my command through whatever cerebral transmitters those boffins have devised, the mother of all hullabaloos suddenly kicks off below. There are three, four, five shrill blasts of a whistle – how brilliantly retro – and a madding cacophony of shouting and stampeding feet. I step out of my hut to witness the show in all its rampant glory, aching with hurt at my exile from the kill.

It's not Peters leading the sortie – he stands coolly to one side, pointing and speaking into a mouthpiece – but what a team! What a squad they've put together . . . there must be getting on for thirty bobbies down there, ready for the gang of miscreants they're expecting. On that score, the potential nab looks disappointing at first glance . . . There are one, two, three . . . six black rubber dinghies, admittedly stacked high with what look like white polystyrene crates, and Old Bill have rounded up every last one of the pilots. The mystery at the moment is where all the Scousers have gone. There are four times one hundredweight trucks awaiting drug bounty – yet they've only arrested two of the drivers. There must be at least four of the bastards, and others too, to help them load up the haul – so by my count a good few have absconded. If this was my collar I'd have every one of my team radio back to me: 'Suspect detained! Crime scene secured!' et cetera, et cetera . . . but this is not my show. I should get down there, warn Peters and co there may be gunmen in the scrubland, on the loose – but before I can get even halfway down the little pathway, the lorries themselves are lit up by bright white headlights. Parked behind the trucks, set back among gorse bushes, is a pristine silver-grey Jaguar, its elegant curves resembling a beached yet still beautiful space capsule. The Jag's lights are trained full beam on the four lorries, and after momentary confusion among the arresting officers, a fleshy inspector with an impressive walrus moustache warily approaches the car. Before he gets there, a slender black man steps out of the front passenger seat and heads him off. It is Lance Campion.

'Is there some problem here, officer?'

I have to smile. The Taffy bridles at being called 'officer' and, predictably, overreacts. He shoves Lanky against the car's bonnet.

'Right, you uppity fucking coon, don't be thinking you can

breeze into my fucking yard, looking the likes of myself in the eye. You do not. Look. Me. In the eye. Hear? Look at the floor . . .'

Lance Campion smiles.

'Look at the fucking floor!'

Lanky begins tutting slowly, and winces briefly as the Welshie cracks him one with the side of his hand. At this point a bespectacled man in a suit announces himself to all and sundry. My heart sinks and my stomach churns horribly – as always happens, reflexively, whenever and wherever I lay eyes on him. Striding into the limelight, voice recorder in his left hand, is John Oliver Prendergast, legal counsel to the underworld.

'Good evening . . .'

Prendergast – who I consider to be a crook worse than just about any scumbag operational in Liverpool right now – gently drains the rouge from the Taffy Inspector's face as he advises him that his conduct and choice of verbiage is all on record, and he should expect a diligent and punitive lawsuit to follow. I can see the copper's thought processes churn their way round his lazy, old-establishment mind. He's trying to work out whether he can still outmanoeuvre Lanky's mob. Maybe he can pen them in and, in so doing, seize any evidence the brief might have on him. It'd be a risk. In his shoes, I'd go for damage limitation. I'd have smelt the coffee big time by now. Prendergast gets to the end of his obviously pre-prepared speech.

'. . . and I'd appreciate it if you would now accompany me to my client's business interest and advise definitively upon the nature and substance of his transgression . . .'

He pauses for added impact like the ham we all know he is and beckons a lad with a camera forward; one of those nuclear-strength jobs with a lens as big as a cricket bat.

'Our photographer will document your findings, for the avoidance of any further doubt in this matter.'

Oh dear. This is all beginning to make horrible sense now. A sudden surge of inexplicable hilarity and appreciable nausea assaults my guts. Lanky *knew* this op was coming off! He knew it. He's brought his brief, he's brought photographers and he's about to make a holy show of our entire team. Except it's not our team. I belatedly remember we're off the hook on this one, and simultaneously wonder just how deeply Hodge's shit runs. All I can vaguely compute is that Hodge had the nod that the Triangle were on to us — how and why doesn't even bear thinking about. The full team plods down to the stack of white polystyrene cases now stacked in piles where the beach meets the path to the car park. I can't hear them properly, so I edge myself just that little bit closer. John Prendergast is supervising the careful removal of the lid of one of the poly cases. His photographer snaps away. One of the Welsh bobbies goes to close him down but the Big Chief gives him the signal to step back. He knows his goose is cooked here.

The lid comes off. I can't see what's inside there, but I can hear everything, loud and clear. This time I really am laughing and, yes, I concede, there's one last flake of desperate, begrudging admiration at this hugely audacious two fingers from Lanky Campion to the Law. The crates contain oysters. He has all the necessary paperwork to demonstrate a legitimate purchaser-supplier relationship with a Cork-based fishery. And at this exact moment the gleaming pate of Roddy Dixon steps into the fray, notebook in one hand and a miniature recorder in the other.

'Inspector . . . Roddy Dixon, Chief Crime Reporter, *Liverpool Echo*. If I could just have a moment of your time . . .'

Once again I stifle laughter as the harried Big Chief shoulder-charges past him, sending Dixon sprawling into a stack of crates. He buttonholes Prendergast and gives him a half-hearted sermon about the legality of their moonlit landing arrangements in Welsh coastal waters, but the smarmy brief just bats it off and invites the Taff to bring it up at his arraignment for racial harassment. Dixon makes a pew of two oyster crates and scribbles the highlights down. The Welsh lot just melt into the night with the same stealth as they arrived.

I have not seen Peters since his whistle called the operation on – what? – twenty-seven minutes ago. I wait another twenty after the last of the engines has faded out into the middle distance before I break my cover and begin the long walk back to Plas Newydd.

I run it all round my head on the drive back to Chester. I'm no student of the classics but even I understand the basic grammar of subterfuge. Somehow, at some point since dawn, we've been rumbled; Campion has ratted us out. But how? When? Who? I try to trace things back and trace them further back again, up till the last time things were normal. This time last night a fearless serial car thief from Liverpool was well on his way to the Isle of Anglesey with the singular brief of bringing down the force's sole surveillance helicopter. At that stage, Lance Campion's plan to bring in a significant haul of cocaine was very much on – I have utterly no doubt whatsoever about that. There's no way even he would sent Micky Flynn into the fray purely out of mischief, and neither could he have had the time to arrange a dummy flotilla of high-speed dinghies and sturdy transportation trucks at the eleventh hour just to make fools of us. We have to assume that the drug run from Cork was, at that stage, all too live and real. Therefore, it's whatever happened next that provides the key to all this.

What, though? What *happened*? All I know for sure is that as I hurtled my way to the Royal Liverpool Golf Club for Hodge's official blessing to press Go on his own pet project, the boss had already moved on to another page. Who got at him? It doesn't add up; it just doesn't make sense at all. Somewhere along the line, though, Lance Campion got wind of the operation in time to switch the coke for fucking cockles. Hodge was so keen to distance himself from a collar that would have made him, made his name, that he hid out on the golf course till it all blew over. Lanky knew. Hodge knew. The only jerk who knew nothing whatsoever was myself.

Well, that's the last time. Fuck it. Fuck them. I can't trust any of them. It's dog eat dog in this job – and this dog just grew teeth. If I ever come back to this job and right now, that is the very last thing my numb and beaten ego will countenance – there will be no more fucking around from me; no toeing the line, waiting for the supposed supercops to have me over. This sorts out the men from the boys, this does – and Billy McCartney isn't taking any more shit from any of them.

2012

Hodge

Calamity. Absolute disaster. Mere weeks from the long goodbye and the whole shebang blows up in my face. Not that one's retirement is the overriding concern in a situation like this, it goes without saying. Forget all that – the plaudits, the legacy, the feeling of immense and lasting satisfaction one might have anticipated, had this all gone to plan. Those are the trimmings – the aftertaste of a job well done. Appreciation would be welcome, no doubt, but above all one would simply have preferred to bid the job farewell on something akin to a positive note. It's not to be, now. The curtain call one had in mind is simply not to be.

From the moment Una Farlowe informed me of the girl's existence I've had a bad feeling as to how this might end up. That it's ended up like this – with Kalan hacked and stabbed and slashed so badly that his body has basically drained flat – is a total and utter tragedy. Tragic for the boy, of course. Horrific. And for his girlfriend, too. Misha. But for all of us who've been running this job for all this time, it really is too awful to take on board. For myself, Una and McCartney – McCartney, especially, will be distraught at this turn of events – Kalan Rozaki's demise is a devastating blow.

I glance over to check on Gilroy's progress, but I have to

look away. I heave out a weary-sick sigh of despair, asking myself all over again if there is more we could have done to protect the boy. The truth is there is *always* more one could have done. Always. But nobody could have predicted this; the savagery of it. I'm assuming this is a message from his brothers – a message to me, to the force, to everyone. Who else would deal with a snitch in this way? Anyone crosses the Rozaki brothers, they're saying – *this* is what happens to them, whoever they are. Even one of their own; a Rozaki brother in name and in blood.

I squeeze Mal Gilroy's arm and we give one another the look, the silent understanding that can only come from years of nights like this. 'Sordid world,' says the look. 'Sick place we live in.' Mally zips up his bag, gives the kid one last, sad glance, and he's off and back to his car, leaving me alone with the remains. Poor Kalan. I find myself poking at him with my toe, but the fact is he's gone now and it's what we do from this point on that counts. We cannot, we *dare* not, let this one slip. I look down on the boy's butchered torso and start to think damage limitation. I call McCartney. If anyone can save this cursed situation it's Billy McCartney.

McCartney

I can feel the BlackBerry buzzing in my pocket. Won't be a job. Not on a Tuesday. Can't remember when I last had a shout on a Tuesday. Weekends are bad – obviously. Sundays have always been the worst, weirdly, and those ones often drag on into the Monday. But Tuesday? Nope. Not that I can think of. I love my Tuesdays, I do. Not because they're slow – or not *just* because they're slow. No siree. Since the night it opened, Tuesday nights have seen Detective Chief Inspector William A. McCartney down the Golden Nugget, shimmying my snakelike hips to those fine, fine country sounds. For those few hours

I'm me. I'm anyone. I'm not the filth they take me for in this godforsaken city. I'm not McCartney. In the Nugget on Country Night, I'm whoever I want to be. I'm with people I want to be with, holding off the world outside as we lose ourselves to those songs of joy and pain.

When Tuesday comes, people I want to be with means one big personality in the diminutive form of Kylene Kelly. Since I first clapped eyes on our little Dolly Parton-lite, I have dreamed of little else but she. She's in my heart, she's in my head from the moment I wake up on a Tuesday morning till, feet heavy but light-hearted, I drag myself back up those stairs and succumb to my needy dreams. She'll stay there, sadly; for McCartney, it's always just a dream.

I'm watching Kylene, hands on her hips, as she hops, skips and jumps to Garth Brooks and Shania Twain. Left to my own devices I'm more an aficionado of how-you-say Alt Country. I can veer left towards Americana, or right for a little folk crossover, too — those Unthank girls being a particular soul-love for YT. The Unthanks, a bit of Calexico, the Low Anthem, Deer Tick, the Felice Brothers, Brandi Carlile, Phosphorescent, the Decemberists, Lykke Li, Lucinda Williams — they're all ever-presents on the McCartney shuffle; them and, day in, day out, the divine and peerless Shelby Lynne are the soundtrack to my sometime life. She breaks my heart, Shelby Lynne. She tears me to shreds, and then she puts me back together again.

I delve for my phone as I sit and watch lil' KK strut her stuff on the floor. Boy, but I'd love to dance with her! Would I get sparks flying from those little built-up cowboy boots! Must be a size nothing, those boots; a kid has bigger feet, which only makes me ache for her more. I just want to hold her in my arms. Nothing has to happen — not if she didn't want it to; I'd just stroke her hair and rock her till she fell fast asleep, then I'd watch over her, all night long. In your dreams, McCartney; only in your sweetest dreams. In real time, in Liverpool, you go with a copper and that's you finished. I'm fine just sitting here, thanks – smiling and clapping and watching little Miss Kylene dance.

I fish the BB out of my jacket. I see the name on my phone and my heart drops stone dead. I know straight away what this is going to be. These past few days, I've been walking on eggshells, willing the days away so we can wrap the Rozaki job up and turn off the lights, once and for all. I should know better, shouldn't I? There's always something in this job, and as soon as Kalan dropped the bombshell about his new squeeze, I was praying against this call coming – but knowing, deep down, it would only be a matter of time. Kalan knew it too. He knew full well how that would play – a Kurdish lad loving a Somali girl. Even though they're both good Muslim kids, even in this day and age, Kalan and Misha was always going to end in tears. But young love will – and this is where it's brought us. Another number in the debit column. Another wrong we have to make right. I spark up one of my little helpers as I step outside to speak to the boss.

Hodge
There's zero satisfaction in handling this the way one must, but really, there's no choice, either. There is *no* other way. McCartney will understand. When all's said and done, he'd do exactly the same himself. As soon as the haul is landed, the drugs impounded and the brothers brought into custody, I'll be able to sit McCartney down and talk him through exactly what, why and when. For now, though, one merely sticks to the principles one has always held dear, and which have, by and large, served this copper well. Need to know is

the motto. Need to know. Above and beyond that you close your eyes and, when it all comes down to it, you hope for the best.

McCartney

I press green to answer, and we're off. How bad is this going to be? Hodge hesitates, clears his throat, then goes for it.

'Billy? It's not good, I'm afraid . . .'

He doesn't have to tell me the rest. I know. I'm already on to the next stage, plea-bargaining now, hoping against hope that this isn't the worst. I'll settle for the Rozakis sussing their kid as the leak, but he's managed to talk his way out of it. So long as Kalan and Misha are OK, I'm not bothered about the bust. If the whole operation goes up in flames I'll take that, any day – just so long as the kids are OK. He quickly puts me right on that score, though – the kids are not OK. Far from it. All we really know is that Misha called Una in a blind panic. A gang has found the love nest and kicked down the door and come at the pair of them with blades. Misha's managed to get away – we think – but from what little she has been able to say, Kalan is hurt. Badly hurt. He got out of the flat through the back window, but he is out there, some- where in the park, losing a lot of blood, and some bad, angry men are on his trail. Now, of all times; this week, of all weeks. I'm scared, big time, for Kalan and Misha, but I've got to be honest – I'm crushed at the sheer injustice of it all, too. *Months* we've spent on the Rozaki job – near enough a year. For it to go belly up like this, at this late stage, is bad enough – but if we lose Kalan and Misha too, it's going to break my heart. The boss seems to agree.

'Call Una now, establish Misha's location and get to Kalan as soon as you humanly can . . .'

I hear him perfectly well but all I can do is just stand there.

A gentle zephyr breezes through me. Everything slows down. I can hear, I can *feel* my heart beating.

'Billy! You *must* find Kalan before these bastards get to him . . .'

I'm back. It's fine.

'Roger that, sir. Over.'

This is bad. The more it starts to penetrate, in all its implications, this is just horrible. I get on to Una – for so long the cool negotiator at the heart of this op – but she's beside herself. She's gone. I can hear her heavy breath and the laboured footfall as she runs along a gravel path.

'Billy. They've gone back for her. They're after Misha now!'

'Una! Stop! Just stop right where you are, will you –'

'I can't, Billy. This is down to me. I've *got* to find Misha before these animals get hold of her!'

'Una! *Listen* to me, will you? Please. Where's Kalan?'

'I . . .'

'We need to get Kalan safe and we need to get him to hospital . . .'

But that's it. All I'm getting is the stolid grind of her feet, running.

'Una! *Speak* to me, will you . . .?'

I can hear her panting like mad and then the phone's gone dead. Shit. *Shit!* What the hell is happening all of a sudden? Is that it? Ten months down the drain then, just like that? Jesus! Why couldn't Kalan just keep to the script? Why go falling in love anyway, when he had the rest of his life ahead of him for all that?

Soon as we found out there was a girlfriend on the scene – or, should I say, soon as we found out who the girlfriend *was*, we knew there could be trouble. With a whistle-blower the basic thing is, you just want time to fast-forward to the wrap. Roll credits. Cue baddies being taken off and taken down. Up until that point there is *so much* that can go wobbly, and from the moment Kalan coughed about Misha things have gone from bad to worse. Even last week, when she hit us with the news about the guy flying in from Somalia, we offered to get the pair of them out of harm's way till it all blew over, but oh no, not those two. They had their studies and their prayers and whatever else going on that was so damn important to the two of them. I'm on the floor here – you just can't help some people. You despair of them – you really do. I try to switch my focus to the nuts and bolts of how we're going to firefight this one. I call Hodge back for any detail on where Una might be searching for Misha, my mind racing ahead all the time.

'Is Gilroy on standby?'

'Gilroy? Why Gilroy?'

'Just anticipating the worst, boss.'

'I hear you, dammit!'

What the hell? Not like Hodge, that. Perfectly reasonable observation from myself. If we need to hide Kalan's identity – even if it's only for a day or two while we buy time – then Malcolm Gilroy's our first port of call. Mally is our man in the morgue, last man standing from the days when we were all on the same side. The rest of them, these days, I don't know what job they think they signed up for. They want everything in writing, in triplicate, with a Home Office stamp, the pansies. Gilroy's not like that. He knows how this works.

'Sir?'

Lengthy silence from the Hodge.

'If it transpires we need him, Malcolm will do whatever we ask.'

'Are you absolutely certain of that, sir?'

'Yes, McCartney. Absolutely certain.'

Hodge

High time I beat my retreat. The kid's in safe hands with Billy McCartney. If there's a way of sorting this thing out, Billy is the man to find it. I find myself saying a little prayer – something I haven't done in a very long time. I bow my head and close my eyes for a moment. I can see Kalan, clearly, the day Una first brought him in to see us. Very good-looking boy. Not as dark as his brothers, Kalan – more of a caramel colouring where the other two Rozaki scum are dirty brown. If push came to shove you'd place Kalan as Hispanic in appearance, more than Persian. Not that that's evident now – with his body brutalised beyond all recognition, Kalan Rozaki looks nothing but grey. Such a clever kid, too. Grade-A law student, definitely going places. Clearly he saw the family business as an impediment to his ambitions in the legal profession, yet one always had the sense with Kalan that his stance was rooted morally. Very, very bright boy, Kalan Rozaki; very sure in his beliefs and wholly intent on clearing the decks and doing what's right. What *was* right.

And yet, and yet . . . I had such mixed feelings about his shopping the brothers. Insane, but true. After all this time tracking them, watching them, orchestrating the downfall of the pernicious drug-dealing Rozaki clan, there was of course a degree of euphoria when their own kith and kin walked in to blow the whistle on the family firm. But to have them gift-wrapped like that; their heads quite simply handed to us on a platter, after all the minutely plotted hours, weeks, months and years on their case. I don't know. It was a let-down, if I'm honest about it. Awful thing to say when your key witness lies butchered at your feet, but there it is. One would have felt a much greater satisfaction cracking this through our own best endeavours.

The sound of a distant siren brings me back round. Time to

go, Hubert. High time you were away from here. I take the little cut-through to Ibbotson's Lane and call Una from the car. She says there's still no sign of Misha. The girl has quite seriously vanished into thin air.

'Una? Billy McCartney is on his way. Can you . . .' How do you put this into words, for God's sake? 'The boy . . .' Silence from Una. Damm it! Does she mean to force it out of me?

'I think I understand, sir.'

Her voice is sapped of all life. She knows. Girl isn't stupid – she's guessed. For crying out loud – anyone would think that I myself am somehow responsible. I try again.

'Una, it is critically important that you and McCartney . . .'

'We'll take care of it, sir.'

'Before the fuzz get down there, please. Can't have fuzz making things worse than they already are, hey?'

This fails to elicit the hoped-for levity.

'I understand the situation, sir.'

The girl sounds wretched. Cut your losses, Hubert. Over and out.

'I know you do. Thank you.'

I kill the call, compose myself and start up the engine. All I can think is that two hours ago none of this had happened. Oh, to be back there, enjoying my own company and a medium-rare *filet mignon* at the Athenaeum! Two hours ago, life's major quandary was a question of whether to order a second bottle of Pomerol, when Una's call came in. A shade after eight, it was. At that precise moment, Operation Samsun was alive and kicking – kicking the Rozaki brothers all the way to Clink Street. Up until Una's call, their little brother had ratted them out and the net was closing in. Any day now, any moment, and we'd have the pair of them and half their shabby empire cuffed and neutered, snivelling for their briefs.

It's nothing more than a moment in time now, the death knell on my grand farewell. BUC, Hubert – Before Una's Call. Perhaps if I'd adhered to club protocol and left the damned phone at reception . . .

The essence of her message was that a terrified and largely incoherent Misha had phoned her, almost too scared to speak. Misha had managed to tell Una that men with machetes had broken down the door to their flat. They attacked Kalan – who had thrown himself through a window and fled – and now they were coming after her. At 8.21 p.m. Una had a text from Misha telling her she was hiding out, begging her to send in the cavalry. That was the last Una heard from Misha. Her phone is dead now. One hopes and prays that she herself is not.

Shakespeare

It not so often a young girl comes in this old place unaccompanied, so old Evan would notice she, come what may. We haven't had more than two-three payin' customer in all night but this lady stand out in a multitude, so help me. She stagger in through the door just as I'm thinking I might as well close up for the night, take myself upstairs and listen to the *Book at Bedtime* or some such. She some sight, man, eye swollen, lip bleeding and this wild, scared look all over her, dress torn at the shoulder, and the one thing that goes through my head is: Jesus Christ. She is beautiful. She's deranged like she seen a ghost she is, or she been hit by a car; but if I'm honest about it all I'm thinking is that in spite of the wild eyes and the near-frothing at the mouth, she is one exceptional-looking lady. She fine, but – like Andromeda come to bewitch ol' Shakespeare. Abyssinian, if I'm to hazard a educated guess – most likely Somali or Yem, round Liverpool 8 – but whatever she be, she a princess, man. She a lady. Even in distress, she got refinement. Old Evan has known them high and he's known them low; I've known them good and bad in my time and this troubled soul got a elegance and intelligence that shine through.

'Hello,' I smiles. No reply. Nothing. 'May I be of assistance?' She just look right past me. Maybe not so refined after all.

McCartney

I take one last, loving toke on the carlota, flick it hard at the wall and enjoy the firespray, then I'm into the kart and off, gunning back into town, eyes left and right as you do. I take every which one-way, no-entry and backstreet I know, every second crucial as I race against time to get to Kalan before the uniform boys start making things worse than they already are. I try Una again. She's as good as given up. The trail has gone cold at the main park gates and she doesn't know whether to stick or twist, or if she's bust already.

'Just stay there, U. I'll be with you any minute.'

I've got 'Bright Eyes' on low to keep me calm as my brain races and races, trying to anticipate every twist and turn that's coming my way. *This is the first day of your life.* Yeah, right. I cut past the bombed-out church, and skirt Chinatown. All these years on, and I still grip the wheel and grit my teeth when I spy that neon strip. Maybe one day I can enjoy its sights and spices again. Maybe when I finally get that bastard put away.

Town is alive with all the new students pissing it up. I'll be fair – the city's come on leaps and bounds since the likes of myself pitched up here way back when. There's thousands more students these days and for all the new bars and the round-the-clock drinking I've got to doff my cap; there's much less trouble all round. I head down Princes Ave and I feel like Batman. Here I am once again, with grim inevitability, riding out along this lawless artery that bisects Toxteth, ready to take on its worst. Wherever this city throws me, I always seem to end up back here. Granby. The Triangle. Liverpool 8. Call it what you will, but to me this is gangsterland. That's where Mikey Greene's phone box used to be. Rest in torment, Mikey, you out-and-out villain. There on the left — there's the stakeout where I virtually lived with those two mannequins from Customs all those years ago, tuned in to the pulse of the UK cocaine trade. And there's the old Greek church, where we had Big Jim Mulcahy surrounded at the so-called 'cocaine christening' a few years back. Canvey Jim. How the fuck did he ever slip *that* net? One that got away, Canvey Jim — and there haven't been too many of them. There was him. There was Lanky, for a while. And there was Hamilton. The mere thought of that sleaze gets me thinking to Millie again. But it doesn't take much. Barely a day goes by when I *don't* think of DS Camilla Baker. Another that got away. Rest in peace, Millie.

Packed with clubs this stretch, when I first came to town. Seething with lowlife, all hours of the day and night. Clubs named for the nations that thronged the quayside. The Sierra Leone. The Ibo. The Somali. But you won't catch McCartney going all *Liverpool Echo*, trying to make out the city's a cultural this or a cosmopolitan that, just because some Scouser's put a chess table in his cafe. Let's have this right. This is Liverpool we're talking about, one of the great, dirty knocking shops of the world. And just like all those other mongrel cesspits — your New Orleans, your Marseilles, the utter shit heap that is Naples, dare I say — it's centuries of runaways and ship-jumpers that have dragged the place down to the lowest dregs of criminality. Capital of Culture? Liverpool is one of *the* great capitals of criminality. Forget all this groovy bohemian melting pot the academics and all the professional bleeding-heart Scousers would have us believe. Merchant seamen bringing back a bit of this, a bit of that; all the diaspora adding their spice to the recipe. No. Forget it. Three and a bit centuries of racial indiscrimination means one thing, and one thing only. Crime. Baddies. Ports means wrong 'uns, and Liverpool's been a love shack to the lot of them since I don't know when. But I'll call an amnesty, for now. Tonight the sky is all pinks and oranges and there's some strange electricity in the air as the students stagger down the boulevard, not a care in the world.

The phone goes again. Even that delicate refrain gives me a jolt. I've looped an Erik Satie nocturne for my call alert. *The* nocturne – Gnossienne No. 1. The elegant score to Rebecca Hyman, my bony siren, luring me into her world. It's the sound of McCartney's liberation, that piano riff, but it still makes me jump now and then, piping up like that, out of the blower. It's Una again. I tell her I'm just passing the Croxteth Gate and I'll be with her any minute.

'Too late,' she says.

Una is standing in the lay-by just past the park's main roundabout. She waves me over. She doesn't look good. It strikes me, all over again, how much I've come to like this woman, and it hits me again, too, that I know absolutely nothing about her. I don't even know who she works for. All we've been told officially is that Una Farlowe is Kalan Rozaki's negotiator, his handler. As Kalan talked us through the intimate details of his brothers' drug-smuggling operation, Una would work in tandem with us and departments unknown, advising on what's admissible, what's relevant, what needs fleshing out and standing up on our side. Between us all, we've been compiling a case against the Rozaki brothers so indestructible that not even silk-to-the-scum John Prendergast himself would dream of entering a plea for them.

Most of what we know, we know courtesy of Una's patient assembly of Kalan's inside track, and what we know is this: the Rozakis bring in monster loads of smack and weed. They use their extensive family network to source it and sort it – there are Rozakis in Iran, Afghanistan, Turkey, Syria, Iraq, Armenia,

Georgia. They are all over that lawless back of beyond – the so-called Kurdistan. But Kurdistan doesn't exist, does it? – a state of play the Rozaki clan has been milking and squeezing until the pips squeak. This is where Una's work has been so painstaking and ultimately so horribly illuminating. Kalan has told her that the family has been abusing the Kurds' relative immunity as a 'stateless' nation for years now   dealing with the Taliban, the mujahedin or whichever particular lunatic fringe are controlling supply in a particular territory at any given time. The Rozakis purchase enormous quantities of near-pure narcotics and they literally pump the shit into Liverpool. That's where you half have to marvel at the cheek of the bastards. Even I have got to acknowledge the genius and the sheer scale and audacity of the operation. The Rozakis used the fallout from the upheavals of the nineties to set up a bona fide – seemingly – petrochemical company, Puroil. Puroil may or may not be concerned in the location, exploration, drilling, extraction and export of crude oil, as their distinctly cruddy website claims (you would expect an outfit like theirs to invest a few bob in a convincing web page – decent graphics at the very least). But what we *do* know – and again we thank Kalan and Una for giving substance to our suspicions here – is that Puroil *is* concerned in the transportation and supply of the Taliban's most lucrative crop. I know I shouldn't be as impressed as I am, but come on! They're sending the gear over in *oil* tankers, customised so their middle section is one enormous chamber filled to capacity with lethal, lucrative, unprocessed opium, ready for Merlin and co to transform it into diacetylmorphine. Smack, to you, me and that young hooker on Everton Brow. The Rozaki crew drive that shit right across Europe and, three days later, they're pumping it into the bowels of the petrol station on the Dock Road that's been their base since they set up shop there ten years ago.

This latest shipment is something else again though, and the cop in me thanks Our Lord that Kalan was able to draw us the picture – literally – before the bad guys caught up with him. This one is a shipment in every sense – a gigantic ocean-going Aframax tanker capable of carrying 100,000 tonnes of crude oil, yes; but whose inner chamber holds, not oil, but dizzying quantities of high-grade heroin. The ship set sail from Turkey yesterday, if Kalan's info is on the money, though he'll never again offer up a progress report. Poor lad. All he wanted was to study in peace and be able to hold his head up and live his life the way he wanted – as an honest and honourable man. Too sad. Too, too sad. I know we could've done more.

I pull over and Una jumps in. She's ashen and I know, now, that I should extinguish all hope of any kind of happy ending.

'About a hundred yards down here,' she points.

'Dead?'

Slight nod of the head.

'Definitely?'

She flashes a grim smile.

'Beyond all reasonable doubt.'

She turns to me.

'What's he told you?'

'Hodge? Nothing. As per.'

She points to a lay-by just past the cave.

'Here'll do.'

I pull up opposite the allotments, step out of the kart, automatically zap the locks even though there's no one – not a soul – around. Una half opens her door but stays seated. I go round to her side, unlock and open her door.

'Show me.'

I search her face for clues. I like Una, but I know she keeps things from me. The Hodge I'm used to but I like to think Una and I are on the same side. She drops her head, chews on her bottom lip.

'Una?'

'Just . . .'

Out of nothing, she slumps back in her car scat and starts crying. Not just crying – sobbing, hardly any noise at first, then this convulsive and ever building crescendo of juddering sobs.

''Those poor k-k-k-kids!' she's howling. 'What have we *done* to them?'

'Hey, hey . . .' I murmur, but I really don't know what to say. I'm the worst at times like this – truly, I am hopeless. I crouch down, lean into the car and hold her, shushing her into her ear. There's a faint floral tang from her neck.

'Come on,' I say. I pull away, indicating that the human moment is over. 'Fuzz'll be here soon.'

That brings a smile, of sorts. 'Fuzz' has been a little in-joke of ours. She can't tell us who she is, exactly – as in who she's working for. We know she's in touch with the Borders Agency and SOCA, but Hodge thinks the Home Office is Una's uberboss. I should talk. I'm a department within a department who's been given special dispensation to target one major crime family, namely the Liverpool-Kurdish Rozaki clan, and apart from Hodge I answer to no one. Billy McCartney's the last fella should gripe about secrecy. For the best part of a year it's been me, Hodge and now Una. Everyone else is the Fuzz.

'Over there?'

Una nods, once. She pulls out a tissue and dries her face, blows her nose hard and stifles a nervous laugh as I pull a Scooby-Doo face for her.

'Wish me luck,' I grimace.

I make my way into the thicket.

'Warning you, Billy,' she shouts after me. 'It's bad.'

'Bad-bad? Or just bad?'

She trains her eyes on me.

'Bad.'

I nod my thanks and turn, stumbling over a low wire fence that delineates the allotments. I put out my hand to prevent myself falling, and as I grasp the sturdy furze of a rhubarb leaf, I see him. See it.

I can't say what I'd been expecting now. The grusome reality of the scene has blasted all and any preconceptions from my psyche. Everything I'd anticipated has been supplanted by this grotesque tableau – right here, right now. I'm in shock – truly. I can't think. I can only stand here, and stare at this monstrosity. The only notions I can process are the basics I've been able glean from Una. A masked gang charged down Kalan's front door. They had blades – blades big enough to hack great holes through that door. After that, the sequence of events is vague. Whatever took place, this is the aftermath. Other than that, it's educated guesswork. I've done what I always do at this juncture. I shut myself off and try to place myself there, in the moment. I try to *see* it. I've been visualising the kid tearing pell-mell through the woodland, a gang on his tail, screaming and slashing at him. Somehow, though, none of it has even remotely prepared me for what now lies within touching distance: a flaccid, decapitated torso, whose hands and feet have been hacked off too. That's all that is left of him – a hideous lump of hacked flesh. I feel nothing; no shock, no fear, nothing. I have never seen anything, *anything* like this and I cannot tear my eyes away. For a long time, I do not move. It is obscene, yet you carry on staring. I kneel in close and there's something strangely serene about a horror scene like this – the awesome and brutal finality of it all; the fuzzy, outsized rhubarb leaves half covering the near-naked stiff. He's lying chest down, his back and sides sliced wide open with a series of deep, slanted cuts. Machete wounds, those. He's puckered with a dozen more punctures to his backside and thighs too, smaller these ones, stiletto-type knife. The lad is dressed only in boxer shorts, soaked through with blood where they've slashed and stabbed at his fleeing backside. I have a quick look-see but my head's already whizzing with the whys and wherefores. How do we handle this? What do we *do*? One thing we do above all else, is we find Misha as quick as we can – alive still, hopefully – and we get her somewhere safe. At some point Una appears by my side.

'What do we do, Billy? How do we fix this?'

'How can we be sure it's Kalan?'

Whoever has done this has taken his head, his hands, his feet as trophies of war; a message to someone – or perhaps just as evidence of a job well executed. Her raincoat rustles as she flaps her hands in exasperation.

'It's him,' she says. 'I know it is.'

A headless torso, bled dry and hewn of its hands and feet – yet I know it's Kalan too.

'What do we tell Hodge?'

She squeezes my shoulder.

'I really do not know.'

She turns to look me directly in the eyes. For the first time, I register her shock, her complete horror at what is going on around us. I haven't known her long, Una, but I've come to rely on her big, positive personality. Una Farlowe is one of those people of whom we say they light up a room; a tremendously attractive woman whose abundant confidence rubs off on you – sometimes to a fault.

'Look, I . . .'

She sighs out loud and shakes her head in despair. She chews her lip then hits me with it.

'Billy, Hodge wants us to get him out of here before uniform arrive . . .'

'He *what*?'

She's crestfallen. Her head hangs limp as she just stares at the ground.

'Una . . .'

I'm speechless. I can't make out whether I'm angry, or shocked, or even how-you-say *amused* in some awful way I cannot control.

'Listen. Hodge is bang out of order. He can't –'

She jerks her head up, hits me with those clever, questioning eyes.

'Billy, I know, right? I know. But if the Rozakis find out what's happened to their black sheep we can wave goodbye to ever wrapping this thing up. Ever.'

'What if the Rozakis *did* it?'

'No. I don't know . . . I don't think it's them.'

'No?'

She's back looking at the floor again. 'No.'

I chew it over, think it through. 'Who, then?'

Una shrugs. 'Could be fucking kids from Norris Green for all we know, thinking they're it, trying to make a statement. The main thing is to make sure that Moz and Dara Rozaki do not find out what's happened . . .'

Execution. Mutilation. I still think Kalan's brothers have sussed him as a grass and dealt with him in the way these things are dealt with. The way I'm looking at it, this kid has been hacked up. It's not a hit – it's a message. I put my arm around her and pull her close.

'Look. Let me deal with Hodge. Yes? Leave him to me. We have to find Misha.'

She's all steely pro, all of a sudden.

'We do. But we have to take care of Kalan first.'

'Kalan's dead, Una. Misha is still out there, scared out of her wits.'

'She is. And we'll find her. But in terms of this case, Billy . . . *the* moment Moz and Dara Rozaki get wind of what's happened to their baby brother, you know it's going to be open season. Literally. It'll be war. And we can forget the op. Seriously. If this gets out about Kalan, it's game over.'

I hate what I'm hearing, the more so because I know she's right. Operation Samsun is hanging by a slender thread now, and if the Kurds aren't behind this then we have to make sure we keep Kalan's murder under wraps. They get wind of it and there'll be reprisals all over the city – and we can forget about the Big One. We've got to get Kalan – or what's left of him – out of here, out of sight, and out of their minds. I don't say anything. I just nod.

'Thanks, Billy. I mean it.'

Una hands me surgical gloves and overshoes. I peel the slimy latex gauntlets over my fingers – I hate, have always hated, the smell of these things. She crouches down, tries to get a grip-hold on Kalan's truncated wrists.

'Come on,' she spits. 'Only so much a girl can do on her own.'

I stoop to the task. I hesitate at the sight, close up, of his splintered ankle bone sticking out through the knotted gristle of muscle and blood. I close my eyes and steady myself, rocking at the flashback. Dad, eyes gaping; pelvis – it would've been his pelvis – protruding. I drag myself back, brace myself and take a manly hold on Kalan's calves but it's hopeless. My grip slithers as I try to lift him, and no sooner do we get him off the ground than we have to drop him. I dig my hands and arms under the body, changing my position twice, three times, as I realise there is nothing to cling on to. Una gets hold of the gusset of Kalan's boxer shorts, doubling them over and twisting the elastic in her hands but she cannot move him an inch now.

'Jesus! How the fuck . . .' She makes a guttural growl and starts dragging at him madly.

'Hey! Nice and easy does it, tiger . . .'

She snorts and digs underneath him again. We get him about a yard off the ground, using our thighs to get purchase as we stagger forward one, two, three paces before we feel him rolling away and out of our grip once more. A sleek black kidney slides with awful grace from a deep slice under his ribcage as the torso hits the ground, and that's it — Una is gone. She's crying and screaming and shaking, absolutely gone to pieces. I put my arms around her and start to guide her away from this mess.

'Come on. Let me call Hodge. You shouldn't have to be dealing with this . . .'

But before I can even get my phone out of my pocket, that distant siren has got louder and closer still — so near that there can be no doubt. It has a sobering effect on Una. She visibly pulls herself back, tries to breathe regular, rocking on the balls of her feet, eyes screwed tight shut.

'That's coming here,' I say.

She opens her eyes.

'Yep,' she winces.

'Come on, U. We need to get gone.'

'Yes. That we do . . .' She hesitates. 'Will you . . .?' She shakes her head, dismissing the thought before it even has chance to take wing.

'What?'

She snorts, looks me right in the eye now.

'Want to come back to the hotel? I need whisky. I — I don't know if I can be on my own right now.'

She folds her arms and turns away, but she's back again

in no time, covering her tracks, retracting all and any vulnerability.

'You're right. Bad idea.'

'No, U, it's not that . . . I just . . . As long as Misha's out there . . .' Una nods. I try for the right type of regretful smile. 'And I'll be called in to oversee this. Here . . .'

Her eyes burn into me with a fierce desperation. We've worked closely on this, Una and I, and we've built up a really great rapport. There's an instinctual trust, but it goes beyond that. We're close. All the same, I find myself taken aback by her offer: the look in her eye; what she's saying to me here; and my realisation of how much I really do want that too. Yet in that same instant, I'm taken by surprise, also, at how crushed I am, knowing I just can't. At my feet are the remains of a key witness in a major and ongoing drugs case – and my head is all over the place. There are sirens blaring from all directions now. They'll be here any minute. I give her the rueful smile.

'I would love to, Una. Honest to God – I mean it.'

I hold her gaze for as long as I can. She just stares at me until I look away.

'You know the score, comrade. I cannot do *anything* until I speak with Hodge. This thing has just gone mega-nightmare.'

She nods, takes it on the chin. 'You do that,' she smiles. 'Go and be a policeman.'

She draws her raincoat up round her shoulders, gives a little shiver and heads off into the night. I head back to the eyrie to clean up, speed-dialling Hodge as I walk.

Shakespeare

She just stand there by the door, staring dead ahead. She only young – eighteen, nineteen? Hard to say, she so very thin. Not thin-thin, hear – she like they want to call 'toned' today.

It's clear as can be that all is not well but, even from here, old Shakespeare can see this girl got something about her. Remind me of little Melanie in that way, God bless — she radiating some keen intelligence, cut and confused as she be.

I take a step toward she, but the girl recoil. It all there in the traumas of her face, horror and haunting in them slim brown eyes — whatever happen, it some bad shit gone down. She just standing there, like she seen the Furies descend upon she. I go and take her hand, gentle as can be, try to communicate that she with friend now. She seems to comprehend and she lets me lead her through back, take she upstairs to lay down and rest. I know that once she back with us, once I've calmed her down and cleaned her up this little lady will flee like the winds from my humble home-from-home here in the Corona — and so she should. I shall accept the burden of a sister in distress, yet shall I seek nothing in return. For Evan, the joy shall be in the solution and the salvation. Don't mind admitting it — I am intrigued. Sir Shakespeare going to find out what's went on with this princess and shall not rest till she put back together again.

McCartney

One of the major advantages to having the *capo di tutti capi* onside is he's answerable to nobody — not on a local level, he isn't. So if he wants to hand me the mystery slaying to the exclusion of all others, no questions asked, that's exactly what he'll do. He's told me I've got to make this look good. I've got to seal off the crime scene within the bounds of normality and, by the same principles, get Kalan bagged and filed and out of sight. Once we've got him off to Gilroy no one's going to be any the wiser who he is or how he died. Then, and only then, can we retrain our eyes on the main prize — his big, bad brothers, Dara and Moz Rozaki.

'Any news on Misha?' sighs Hodge.

'Not a dicky bird . . .'

'One can only hope and pray . . .'

'She's my number-one priority, sir. I *will* find her . . .'

'I know you will, Billy. I know you will . . .'

Hodge has stood FMIT down for the time being, no questions asked, and given me Tony Soprano for appearances' sake. Could have been worse. He's OK, Tony. Forensics are here now too in their spacesuits, sizing the kid up, measuring his lacerations, doing what they do. I hand Tony latex gloves and overshoes. He crouches down to fit the plastic bags over his feet.

'Tony?'

He stops what he's doing, cranes his face up at me.

'Just – it's bad, OK? What you're about to see – it's pretty fucking horrible. Yeah?'

He nods. 'Nothing we haven't seen before, right?'

'Like I say – steady yourself.'

I hold his stare until he looks away. He finishes fitting the overshoes, ducks under the tape and shuffles towards the body, but he doesn't even get close.

'Jesus Christ . . .'

His voice is even squeakier than usual. He's seen a lot, DS Anthony Gorton, been around almost as long as I have, but you can see the shock tear right through him when he gets his first gander at Kalan's massacred remains. I tried, but nothing I could have told Tony would have prepared him for the horrible ultra-graphics of this butchered torso laid bare on that scabby rhubarb patch, even from this distance. I give him a reassuring pat on the side of the face and leave him to his horrors.

Incident Support are on their hands and knees, carrying out their fingertip. There are specks of blood here and there,

zigzagging from the path to the roadway and into the under-
growth, but until they bring in the arc lamps and their UV
lightsabres they're going to find it hard picking up any kind
of meaningful trail. I already know more just from what Misha's
told Una. Starting to drizzle now, too. We're going to need
to get the canopy up pronto – at least preserve the spot where
we've found the poor bastard. I call Tony over.

'Make sure they get a move on with that tent, will you,
Tone?'

He nods, still a little disconnected after the shock of the
headless corpse.

'And keep people away from the crime scene, yes?'

He nods, face blank. I button my Crombie at the neck – not
a good look, but who's counting.

'Tony? Chop-chop, mate. Starting to rain.'

This brings Soprano out of his trance. He blows out his
cheeks and seems to steady himself.

'Someone wanted this kid gone for good, hey?'

I give his shoulder a little squeeze.

'Didn't they? Let's make sure we catch whichever bastard's
done this . . .'

He nods and heads across to supervise the placing of the
canopy that's now going up. The snapper is flashing away with
her camera. I wander over, ask her if she's done yet.

'Yeah. For now. Until we can get a good look at him. Any
idea who it is?'

'Not a clue,' I lie.

She's shaking her head in sad disbelief.

'Horrible. Just – awful.'

'Isn't it?'

Tony has got his second wind now. He slopes back over to
us and crouches down next to the butchered trunk, his face
a picture of world-weary resignation.

'Got to be drugs, hey?'

I give one, slight, non-committal nod. The snapper makes the appropriate 'life's fucked up' face and packs up her gear.

'Bet you a pound to a penny this kid's one or the other,' Soprano opines. He's a good cop, Tony Gorton, but it's no accident his career path has stalled the way it has. He's a bit of a tart when push comes to shove, and you get the sense with him that he'll be happy enough sticking with what he's got and playing out what's left of his career as someone's sidekick. One thing I'm certain about Tony Soprano is he isn't leadership material. The way he still bullies and banters the younger bobbies; the way he has to think every last little thought out loud, showing everyone he's giving the matter the benefit of his incisive mind. He's doing that 'mark my words' look he does, eyes all wide and serious like he's unlocked the mystery that has continued to elude the rest of us.

'User or dealer. Pound to a penny.'

I nod again. 'Wouldn't surprise me, Toe.'

The meat wagon arrives and the guys bring out their gear. I nod to them and hold up one hand – five minutes. I squat down for one last look before they cart him off to the slab.

Shakespeare

Can't get no sense out of the girl. She's been flat out on the couch in some kind of dread limbo, neither awake nor asleep. Just staring straight up at the ceiling like there's some ghoulish monster coming down through the damp patch to eat her alive. I'm not going to rush her. She'll say something when she's good and ready. Evan more than happy to sit back in his cranky old rocking chair, feet on the bed, listen to the wireless and watch her breast rise and fall. Lord, but she is fine. This late-night Agatha Christie tale being narrated by the great Mr Clive Anderson, QC. Hah! Imagine if you had *him* step in to bat, some of these cases. Happen Old Evan seen a little more daylight in his life if Mr Clive Anderson pleading his case.

'Your Honour, and with the greatest of respect – Shakespeare never done it!'

Still, no use crying now over spilt milk. Spilt blood, more like.

McCartney

The *Echo* are here in the form of the odious Barnaby Giles. Maybe he can't help himself but I cannot abide the way this one starts *smirking* the second he opens his mouth. You could be at the scene of a born-again loon-ball's machine-gun massacre of a playground full of toddlers but Giles's farting little voice recorder would be out along with that weird, droopy smile as he tries to put words into your mouth. 'So what you're saying is . . .' At least the toerag knows better than to try saying *that* to me any more.

'Barney,' I nod.

'Looks bad . . .'

I wish I could be more respectful. I know these guys are only doing their job, but this one just invites disdain. The old-school journos, the likes of Roddy Dixon and Mick Parnell, would sit around in the Print Club buying your Hodges and your Doug Yardleys round after round in the hope of getting a sniff, but this little twerp just exudes entitlement. I treat him with the contempt he deserves.

'All murders are bad, Barney.'

'So you're saying that it *is* definitely a homicide?'

I don't know whether to laugh out loud or nut him. His notepad's out and I already know from the way he's looking at the floor that he's going to get smart.

'Which leaves me wondering, Inspector . . .'

I swallow it, nod for him to continue. He smirks back.

'Well, I'm asking myself why *you're* here?'

'Oh?'

'Come, come, Mr McCartney. You're Drug Squad. What has a murder like this to do with you?'

I force myself to relax my tight fist in my pocket and smile. Years of bitter experience have taught me that it's better to try to roll with the local media, feed them what little bits you're able to rather than trying to keep a lid on the whole roadshow.

'Barney – look, mate. I understand you have a duty to your readers. I appreciate that. Just as you'll appreciate that *we* have a duty to try to keep these streets safe, yeah? These next hours are going to be critical on this one. What I'll say to you, Barney, is that if you can keep this out of the public domain for just this next twenty-four hours, I will speak to nobody before I've spoken to you. Deal?'

'Twenty-four hours?'

'Twenty-four hours.'

'We get a proper window on it?'

'Absolutely.'

Sticks his bottom lip out.

'Fair dos.'

He holds out his slithery hand and we shake.

'Twenty-four hours. Starting now.'

I experience a strange desire to crush his hand to powder as he smirks into my face one last time.

They bag the stiff for transport. *Now* then! As the doors swing open and they haul him into the back, I get the briefest glimpse of Mal Gilroy himself, ashen-faced. Maybe I'm mistaken; can't say I've *ever* known the coroner to come out to a job – certainly not on a night like this. Maybe Hodge has had a word, after all? But the doors are slammed shut again before I have chance to double-check, and they're off, with Kalan, into the night. Can't have been him. Move on.

I can see Tony Soprano winking at the local bobbies, puffing himself up ready to make the young girl ride shotgun with the body or whatever side-splitting ruse he's lined up to try to spook her out. For God's sake – these macho men really do love their stupid initiation rituals, don't they? Well, not tonight, they don't. No way. I'm back over the rhubarb patch and under the tape like a shot.

'Hello. Constable . . .?'

Redhead. Big green eyes, she has.

'Smithson, sir.'

'Smithson.'

I nod to Gorton that this is all in hand and place one gentle hand on Smithson's shoulder and jerk my head towards a little gaggle of druggies who've assembled on the periphery of the crime scene.

'I wonder if you could do me a huge favour and have a word with those friendly neighbourhood smackheads who've just rolled up for a nosy?'

That cracks a smile from her. I smile back.

'They'll feed you a load of bull, but with heroin addicts and the like you just never know. There's times they think they're reaming you and they're actually telling you what's really gone down . . .'

She stays exactly where she is, looking over at the bagheads. I try to inject an extra level of encouragement into my voice.

'Just – anything they may or may not have seen.'

She jumps to. 'Sir.'

Gorton slopes away, thwarted. Smithson goes off to quiz the dossers. I observe her carefully – erect and purposeful in her stride. Another one I've rescued. For now.

* * *

We weren't done until gone midnight but I'm up with the larks all the same — or the rain on my garret's slates, in this case. I do some half-hearted push-ups, and eat a breakfast of Bran Flakes and pumpkin seeds off my lap while I watch the Ron Sexsmith show I Sky-Plussed on Friday night.

The rain has been steady all night, quite soothing when you live on the top floor, but the moment I step out of the front door is the cue for the downpour to up the ante. It is absolutely lashing down now. I bung last night's shop-soiled clobber in at Doreen's. She wouldn't raise an eyebrow if I gave her a set of bed sheets smeared in Nutella, Doreen. Her stance is — you make a mess, I clean it up. It's business. All the same I give her my own little 'all in a day's work' grimace, take the ticket and I'm on my way.

I decide I'll head in to work via the park, see if there's anything doing in daylight that I missed last night. I pass the mortuary — such a tranquil location for such barbaric labour. Mally lives somewhere round here too so, even with him working late last night, I should catch him in one or the other. I try his mobile.

'Gilroy.'

'Mally. Not letting on these days, then?'

'What?'

'Last night. In the park . . .'

'Billy. I'm *extremely* busy . . .'

He's never the most how-you-say *effusive* of dudes, Mal Gilroy, but there's always a certain bleak humour in the way he goes about that rotten job of his. Right now, he's just plain ratty. I abandon thoughts of going to see him here and now, and try to appeal to his gallows side instead.

'Just — we need to talk about Kalan.'

He's not exactly pissing himself.

'Yes. I'm well aware . . .'

'Mal?'

'Look. It'll be done. Yes? I'll get the damned thing done!'

'Scuse *me*! I get the message. Best all round if we leave this one till later.

'Fair enough, Mal. Sorry to trouble you.'

'Billy . . .'

'If you could – I mean, obviously once you've bagged him and tagged him . . .'

What we're asking here is not so damned unusual! Nothing he hasn't done a dozen times before. He has to come up with a new identity for the deceased, plain and simple – or rebrand him, shall we say, for as long as we need to buy ourselves a little time. What's with all the self-righteous huffing and puffing from him?

'Yes, yes . . . this we know, Billy. This we already know . . .'

Heavy, heavy sighs from the other end. Leave him be, Billy. Stick to what we absolutely need right now.

'If you could fax his new name, his . . . whatever you decide for him. If you could fax it for my own attention at this number . . .'

I read out the number for the incident room, knowing full well that Manners will be prowling the corridors, then cut and run before Mal's misery engulfs me.

One suit down and my best Golden Nugget shirt with it, it's imperative that I make my fitting at Gieves & Hawkes. I've chosen a single-breasted coronet-blue mohair suit, with flat-front trousers. In times gone by I wouldn't even entertain the thought of mohair past August, but we had sunshine in December last year, it was snowing into April, I love the suit and that's that. In times gone by the idea of Gieves & Hawkes setting up shop in Liverpool would have had you committed anyway, so what's not to like? While I'm there I pick up a couple of double-cuff, ice-white herringbone cotton shirts, a pair of robust, almost manically pristine black Gibson brogues, a cute blue tie with microscopic anchor detail and on my way to pay I try on this dirty sand-coloured raincoat that pure slays me. Could have done with something *just* like this last night — buttoning up my Crombie to the throat, for Christ's sake! All I need now is a homburg hat and I'm Dick Tracy. Even without the balancing payment on the whistle it's almost a grand, but what else am I going to spend the money on? I slot the plastic, bang in the PIN and rebuff three attempts at chit-chat from the nancy boy on the till.

I'm running through the door-to-doors with Gorton when there's a chaste tap on the window and blow me down if it isn't Alfie Manners, gurning at me through the glass partition. What took you so long, Alfie? Not as well connected as you like to make out? I let it be known I'm non-chuffed as I shuffle to the door and haul it wide open so's Tony can hear everything. Manners does that obnoxious 'can we get privacy' thing he does with his eyes and I hate it that I can't exactly say no to him.

'Billy . . .' He's looking this way and that, like the Stasi are listening in. 'Look . . .'

I know what's coming, but I stand back and make him say it anyway. He finally looks me in the eye.

'Word is you're on the thingio from last night?'

I shrug and nod, as blasé as I can manage.

'How come, like?'

'Just the way it fell, Alf.'

This seems to satisfy him. Once again he's scanning left and right, alert to eavesdroppers. He lowers his voice.

'Any ID on the stiff as yet?'

He thinks I'm thick, Alfie Manners — has always thought me gauche and gullible. He knows he has no right to be asking these questions but, because it's me, he asks. I shake my head. That's why I was so specific Gilroy had to fax his findings through. Human nature being what it is, it'll be all round the gaff without me having to lift a finger to help plant the seed. In the meantime, under no circumstances can Detective Inspector Alfred Manners of the Matrix Squad come to know the true identity of our frozen soul.

'Bit early, Alf. He had nothing on him. Good as naked . . .'

'No distinguishing marks, like? Tats?'

I give it the 'I'm a bit distracted' voice, looking over his shoulder as I speak.

'Like I say, Alfie, bit early. Soon as I know . . .'

He counters me with another of his looking left and right and lowering his voice things.

'Look . . .'

Big, dramatic sigh. He dips into his pocket, whips out pad and pen, scribbles something down. Tears off the notelet and holds it in front of my eyes for less than a second before he whips it away again.

'Has this name come up at all?'

I see and read it perfectly – *Kalan Rozaki* – but I hold out my hand for another look. He makes a big thing of handing over the notelet, checking all around us to make sure no one witnessed this highly secretive act. I wait for his loving gaze to settle on mine again and I completely fudge it – bottom lip jutting out, little shrug, the lot.

'No. Why?'

'Ah, nothing. You know how it goes, kidda.' He puts on a jovial PC Plod voice. 'Following all lines of inquiry.'

He stands there, grinning at me, like I'm expected to be in bulk at his rapier wit. He's getting nothing back from Billy McCartney, so it's back to the ever-watchful, reticent gumshoe routine.

'Nah. The lad in question missed a bit of a family get-together yesterday. Unlike him, that's all. Hasn't been seen in a day or two . . .'

And what's *your* interest? I want to ask him. Why should *you* care about the whereabouts of the youngest sibling of the smack-dealing Rozaki clan? But I just look at the name again, repeat the shrug of ignorance and hand the notelet back to him. 'Sorry, Alf. Heard nothing.' I'll admit it. I buzz off his ignorance. He just nods once. Hard to tell if this is what he wants to hear or not. His eyes slither all over me.

'You know the way rumours get around in this fucking city, eh, Bill? I'd be grateful anyway. If you hear this name . . .'

For fuck's sake. '*Hear this name.*' You don't even have to be a copper to know who the fucking Rozakis are. Jesus. Listen to any teenage wannabe in the Triangle and they'll be giving it Dara Rozaki this, Moz Rozaki that, in that dopey put-on voice they all have, lionising those drug-dealing Kurdish rats. Gangsters is what the Rozakis are. Baddies, plain and simple. Liverpool's biggest smack barons. *If you hear this name!* I should just say nothing, but I can't let Manners talk to me like that.

'Kalan's the kid brother, isn't he? The nice one . . .'

'The black sheep, yeah,' smiles Manners with those spiky, rat-like teeth of his.

'Thought he was at the university or something?'

His tongue dips out and his eyes dart in opposite directions. 'That right?'

Shit! Bastard didn't know.

'Yep. At the uni, so I believe . . .'

'Right.' Manners starts backing away. 'Look. It's nothing. I'm just asking around for one of the lads. Forget it, yeah? Forget I even asked you.'

'One of the lads.' That insidious catch-all that you and your kind always use. Anything and everything is up for negotiation if it's for 'one of the lads'. No one ever knows who 'the lads' are. Cops? Robbers? To the Alfie Manners of this world there isn't any difference. Oh Alfie, Alfie. What's it all about? Even now, even you, I don't quite see it. I know you've never been a Good Cop. But you've never been the sharpest tool in the shed either. Are you clever enough to handle this? Do these guys *really* place their not inconsiderable livelihoods in your lazy hands? I don't buy it. Everything we know tells us you're at it, but I'm sorry, Alf – I cannot see those people taking you seriously. I have zero respect whatsoever for those Rozaki bastards, but no one can say that they're not clever. They have that mix of charm and intelligence and innate animal cunning that all successful baddies have, and I plain cannot see how you slot into their world. Maybe I've just got you wrong, Alfie – but I sincerely doubt you're at that level.

I remember you on my very first day here, long before you were a leading light in the Matrix. You were exactly then as you present yourself to me now. Jumpy. Calculating. On the make. I was the new kid on day one of front-line duty and you looked at me – looked *through* me – just precisely the way you're looking at me now.

'What's this divvy worth to me? What can I get?'

Shame on you, Alfie Manners. Woe betide you for letting yourself get like that.

He takes a step back, places one hand on my shoulder and gives me the big, staring, oh-so-significant look.

'. . . it'd be useful to know if he comes to your attention, Bill. More than useful. Yeah?'

I meet his beamers full on, and offer up the reaction he's looking for.

'Got you, Alfie. I'm on it.'

'Thanks, lad.'

Lad! As he heads off back down the corridor I notice he folds the paper over several times and tucks it deep inside his hip pocket.

Shakespeare

Can tell from the swelling that this lady been hit hard, real hard, and been hit more than once. One or two these lumps are nasty fresh, yet the bruising round her wrists and arms a good few days old. Whoever's done her has had more than one go at it. Not nice. Not nice at all. I pretty sure without her having to say so that she won't want the hospital; but if she don't come to, and soon, I might just have to. As lovely as she be, that biggest swelling don't look good. Right on the forehead going all round to the temple itself, this poor damsel has taken one wicked blow to the bonce. I woke up with one like that last time I was inside. It was the hiding of a lifetime – the one that made me knock that life on the head, for better or for worse. It woke me up, that hiding – for real. Kids, stamping on my head, getting up on the wall and jumping right down on my chest, proper trying to kill me, a old man. And for what? For respect. That what they was saying afterwards. Respect. Serious. I owe a kid for some ganja and I should know better, but come on, man, does that add up to you got to kill a chap?

I thought I'd seen it all, so I did. I get myself on a ship from Port of Spain in 1975, didn't even know where it going, man. Out, was all I care about. Destination elsewhere, hah! And I'm fighting all the way, fighting knives, fighting serious, man, just to stay alive – just to stay on the boat. When I get to Liverpool it's fighting, fighting, fighting. Please don't misunderstand old Evan here. I haven't exactly been a angel myself. During the entirety of my allocated time thus on God's hallowed turf, I'll be the first to allow that my judgement has, at times, been wanting. But by God Liverpool got some answerin' for that! That first night in Dutch's place shown me everything I need to know as to how it's going to be if I want to make anything of myself whatsoever in glorious Technicolor

Liverpool. Hah-hah, it the world in one city *that* night, all right! A win at the rummy. A bit of a dance. A bee-jay. A punch in the head. An empty pocket. I mean, don't get the boy wrong, I *love* this place, love it at first sight. It's ladies, clubs, blues, shebeens, all night long, night into day. It's Pool of Life, man. It's what I come for. But Evan a lover, not a fighter. Anything I done, I can't say I regret it. I done what I had to do. If there was another way, serious – I would've done it. But I would never done what them kids done to me. Never. *Respect?* Get thee gone!

I go to check on her breathing, feel her pulse. She going to be fine. I pick up my book. I'll keep going with it, but if you really want my opinion, it all over the goddam place. I truly don't know what all the fuss is about.

McCartney

Soprano's all red with excitement. The young redhead from last night, Smithson, has got something. It's c/o one of the dossers, fair enough, but Tony reckons it sounds like it could be kosher. We bring her in. You can feel the buzz off her as she walks into the incident room, her first time I'll wager. Her eyes widen as she takes in the layout of the room, her face flushed with that lovely self-satisfaction the newbies have when they know they've done something well. If that'd been me back in the day, they'd have roasted me, and taken my info and dressed it up as their own good work. We don't do that now. PACE works just as well for the bobbies as it's meant to for Joe Public. I have my feet up on the desk, admiring the stitchcraft on the heel of my Weejuns.

'So . . .'

'Sir . . .'

She's still eyeing the whiteboards. I smile, faintly but not unkindly. She flips out her notebook.

'Can't pin them down absolutely precisely as to time, sir . . .'

Welsh. Didn't quite pick up on that last night.

'But the least . . . well – the most reliable of the three gentlemen . . .'

I close my eyes and enjoy that lilting cadence on 'reliable'.

'Go on . . .'

I try for a reassuring smile. Not a natural fit with my good self, but she seems to appreciate the effort.

'The main, er . . .'

'Smackhead?'

I smile again. She looks uncomfortable.

'The witness you'd perhaps be tempted to trust, sir, alleges he saw the deceased being . . . I'm not sure what the terminology is, sir, but he thinks he saw the victim being dumped.'

Smithson gulps and looks a little foolish. My feet are right off the table as I sit bolt upright. I'm trying to look excited but there's a horrific dread coursing through me.

'He *what?*'

'Sir . . .'

I'm up and over to the window, trying to keep my face turned away from them like I'm searching for answers in the sky. Shit. *Shit!* Somebody's seen Una and me, in flagrante, last night. I would swear on my father's life that there wasn't a soul around, not even a passing jogger. The rain saw to that, but – bloody hell! Ten minutes we were there, if that. Eventually I have to turn and face them, praying the furnace of guilt that smoulders within me hasn't made its way to my face. I needn't have worried. Tony Gorton wouldn't notice if I'd had a butterfly tattooed on my forehead in the last thirty seconds – he just sits there, all expectant, as though words of incisive brilliance are mere moments away. I manage to hit a tone of controlled excitement.

'He's saying the victim was killed elsewhere?'

'Well, I don't . . . clearly he can't know that. But the suggestion is that –' She breaks off and consults her notebook. '– two, possibly even three men carried the victim to the, erm, the . . .'

'The spot where we found him? The allotments?'

'That's what he seems to be saying, sir.'

She folds up her notebook, bolder now, keeping up the eye contact. I turn away from her again like I'm tossing this radical new information in my mind. I spin back round, shaking my head all solemn and dejected.

'Do you think so? Nah . . .'

'He does seem somewhat adamant . . .'

'Can't see it. They hack the kid to bits then they drag what's left of him off and hide him? Can't see that at all. Why are they going to do that?'

I turn back round and face them both.

'Can you see that, Toe?'

Smithson searches Soprano's face for support, and the pussycat melts.

'Dunno, boss. I mean . . . wouldn't hurt to check it out, would it?'

She lets the slightest little smile of relief crack through. You little shit, Tony. You plodding, workaday, jobbing bobby. I nod.

'OK.'

I clap my hands once.

'Let's go and toss us some winos.'

Tony's up on his feet now, too, clapping *his* hands.

'Changes the whole landscape if this fella's right though, hey, boss?'

'Doesn't it?'

I turn to Smithson, solicitous in my attempts to make her feel a part of all this.

'I don't suppose you got an address for this . . .'

Out comes the pad again.

'Lambert, sir. Derek Lambert. No fixed abode, no . . .'

I strive for a consoling grimace, but before I can even congratulate her for what she's given us anyway, our little Welsh tiger is smiling her own self-congrats.

'But he *did* tell me where I can find him most days . . .'

I point at her, Kitchener-style.

'You're good. Don't suppose you could come with us, could you? Help break the ice, seeing as you've already spoken to him . . .'

She's blushing with pride.

'I'd have to . . . someone would need to . . .'

'Great. Tony – can you put a call in, see if Allerton can spare PC Smithson a bit longer?'

His face is a picture as he tries to let it be known to her that it's his support that's got her this gig. In truth, he's gutted that the uniform has turned something up, whereas he himself has remained clueless, without a single lead. Whatever. I tell them I'll meet them out front in five. In the meantime I have a small and not indelicate telephone call of my own to make.

Shakespeare

Hallelujah! She lives. She been sat up a good while now, let me wash away some of that mess with a gentle lukewarm sponge, and she sip a few spoonfuls of corn-pepper soup before she wince away in pain, say how her jaw is tender. But she smiling, trying to; trying to thank me.

'You take your time, honey,' I go. 'Just, whatever you want, yes? Whenever you're ready . . .'

She smile again and what a smile, man! You could do *anything* for this lady.

'I don't suppose . . .'

She make a face – ouch!

'Yes?'

I smiling like a fool here but she need to know she can trust old Evan. Trust him with her life.

'Do you happen to have a charger for a Nokia?'

I laugh out loud.

'Now then, madam, I don't avail myself of no cellphone, sorry to say, irrespective of flavour . . .'

She look a bit downcast, but she trying not to show it. She indicates that Evan can take the bowl from her, which I do, and place it out of harm's way on the floor. Can take it through to kitchen all in good time. I don't have to open up down there till eleven anyways, and if we have one single face in before midday I'll eat my hat, so help me. It makes me smile even though it's myself has said it, calling that little scullery a kitchen, even in my head. For all that this place is in a part of town where no one goes no more, for me this little belt has always been home. It used to be hoppin' down here in the day, but for all the money they've pumped into the so-called Georgian Quarter and for all they cooked up that World in One City scam, Stanhope Street was never a part of the master plan for our esteemed city fathers. From where I stand now you would have seen the Rialto's dome; you would have felt the shake and shudder of good times. The Real Thing come from these streets, man. *Can you feel the force?* We did, brother – we felt them good. Felt them truncheon; felt them boot up our backsides.

Good times died round these streets with the last burning embers of the riots. Stanhope, Windsor Street, this side of Parliament Street – you could spit into the cathedral graveyard from here, but we may as well be in Speke or Huyton for all that City Hall throw any breadcrumbs our way. Far as town is concerned, we gone, man. Finished. All the old alehouses long gone, only a hardy few of us hanging on in. There used to be music and good-time girls and muscle and money down here; all the seafarers gambling their pay away, ne'er-do-wells coming in with untold goodies, girls keen to meet them. Back then we were the other side of the tracks in a good way, this bit of town. Punters thought they had had a adventure, coming down here. Half-mile from the Philharmonic we are, and it's a expedition for them, so help me! Nowadays we been sealed off by speed bumps and dead ends and concrete bollards. We'll get a bit of passing trade from the Norwegians and the Irish when Liverpool are playing, the odd crackpot from the hostels, a stag crew gone astray. But John who owns the gaff hasn't been seen or heard of in months, since he upped and went to España. The flat comes with the job, but old Evan has long been readying himself and steadying himself for the day the knock comes and it's some young buck wants you out. It could happen today; could happen tomorrow. For now, I'm going to save her soul. Evan Kavanagh is going to put this young damsel back together if it damn well kills him.

McCartney

'Una? Slight issue. Witness has turned up, claiming to have seen persons unidentified hauling the deceased to its resting place. You recall seeing anyone around?'

Bit of a silence from U, then:

'No.'

Another long pause.

'Not that I can think of.'

She sounds wretched.

'You OK?'

'Fine.'

'Don't sound it.'

'Haven't slept.'

'No word from Misha?'

'Nothing.'

'Look –'

'I know. I know. Not our fault. But it *is*, isn't it?'

I find myself lost for words.

'Yeah. Yes. I suppose it is.'

More silence. Phone starts vibrating. Call waiting. Hodge.

'Look – do you fancy . . . do you want to go for that drink?'

'I don't know, Billy. Let me think about it. Yes?'

'Make sure you do, then.'

'Mmm?'

'Think about it. Don't fret about this witness thing. Lad with the supposed info was out of the game. Smackhead. Ciao.'

I end the call and let Chief Superintendent Hodge in.

'Anything?'

'Usual complications, sir. Nothing that can't be finessed.'

That's one of his favourite words, finessed. Hodge is all for lieutenants who can make stains vanish with a minimum of fuss.

'Good. See to it.'

'I shall do, sir.'

'Good man. Wouldn't want this . . .'

I can hear his laboured breath getting louder at the very thought of a spoke in the wheels at this late stage. On the telly or in the movies it's almost de rigueur for your career cop to rope in one last biggie before retirement, but here's old Hodge doing it for real. He's got less than a month to go and in all good conscience I can affirm the old contemptible has devoted a lifetime's work and pain to stymieing the drug barons of this city. Feels like a mad carousel, this job. I was here, just, when Hodge decided enough was enough and made his first incursions into the organised smack trades in Liverpool – and let's be perfectly upfront here and now, shall we? Smack is back with a vengeance. Heroin was my first taste of action when I came here in '84, and here I am back in the saddle and out on the trail of the dragon once again.

Must be weird for Hodge. It's like one long game of musical chairs – the dealer's excuse-me. He'll lock someone up, and no sooner has he got the bastard off the streets than another craven scumbag springs up overnight to take their place. This Rozaki job is an absolutely top-drawer collar if we *do* finally pull it off but we know in our heart of hearts there'll be a new firm along soon enough, eager to take their place. That's why it was always the Hodge's plan to get at the top rank. The schemers. The planners. The financiers. The bosses behind the scenes who run the show from top to bottom. It's been sad, really, watching the fight go out of Hodge. He may well have his eyes trained firmly on the Rozaki brothers for his last hurrah, but we all know who's behind the whole network. As soon as this one is nailed, I'll be back on the trail of the Terence Connollys of this world – the Untouchables.

Make no mistake, the big players now are *exactly* the same brazen scallies as we've been after since the eighties – just richer. Hard men and door firms may come and go, but the fellas at the very top just get older, further removed from the action, further removed from culpability – or so they like to think. They're borderline local establishment, these rats. Restaurants make a fuss of them. Charities are falling over each other to get their WAGs on their committees. They put their kids through the best schools and live in select residential postcodes. They socialise with posh-knobs and soap stars and footballers. They play golf and dress up in absurd suits for Aintree. Well, they can wipe down their dabs and cover their tracks as much as they want, but we all know and they all know they're just scallies. They always were and they always will be – and they hate that. They hate the thought that we know who they are; we know they're scum. And of all those old-school, born-again blaggers who've 'gone legit' and crave respectability, my public enemy number one is that callous old bastard Connolly. TC. Top Cat. Call him what you will, but Terry Connolly is the monster who rules drug mountain – and has done so since time immemorial. I'll allow that my desire to nail this monster to the cross borders on the obsessional. Today it feels delusional – but I myself will not rest until Connolly resides at Her Majesty's pleasure, for ever, amen. For now, though, I'll put him to one side as we endeavour to edge old Hodge over the line.

'Should we . . . later this afternoon?'

'By all means, sir.'

'Athenaeum? Say 5 p.m.?'

'Absolutely.'

'Good.'

I'm unthrilled at the prospect of another turgid session with the Hodge, but the Athenaeum is not without its consolations. A splendid menu is part of its offer, but I'd also have to admit a certain reverence for its *maleness*, if I may. The Ath, for all that it has long since admitted lady members, is a heavenly refuge of tweed and porter wine. I relish my invitations care of our retiring Chief, and it's for such august occasions that my new whistle is, how-you-say, tailor-made. I've already forgotten this glitch with Smithson's witness and am vacillating over which pods to pair with the new suit as I bid the boss adieu. The new brogues, or these trusty Bass Weejuns? I stow my phone and stride round the corner to the car park.

Soprano and Smithson – now *there's* a bespoke tailor's in the making – are a-waiting by the kart, standing back a yard as though their breath might trigger the alarm. OK, fair dinkum, even at my rank and service the lads don't tend to drive a vintage Merc to work but, honestly, it didn't cost anything like most people assume – plus a rake like McCartney has certain standards not to say an image to live up to. Until the day I finally carry my own little Kylene Kelly over the threshold, it's tangible items of restrained good taste all the way for my good self, thank you very much.

I'll admit to a little frisson of self-regard as Smithson sinks into the back seat and registers the sheer luxury of the worn-supple leather. We shoot across town to the soup kitchen. I kid. One is tediously well aware of the diligent and effective work the outreach teams do, seducing our forgotten and forsaken to these drop-in centres, dusting them down and putting them back on track so they can fuck it all up, all over again. Whichever charity or philanthropist is behind the Bedford Centre has done a cracking job converting another abandoned church into a funky little hostel; but let's face it – the place is a soup kitchen with bells on.

I take satisfaction in the resonant thud of the big iron door knocker, even though there's a variety of buzzers for our delectation. A social worker opens up (is it mandatory for them to have beards?), makes a big thing of examining our ID and reluctantly beckons us inside. Derek Lambert could be twenty, could be thirty – he has one of those ravaged faces with big, staring, childishly blue eyes. A smackhead's face, if ever I saw one, though he's well enough turned out, in the street style of these Liverpool lads. Brown, booze, rocks, whatever his poison is, Lambert is all we've got at the moment, so we're extra jaunty with our thanks and our 'Dereks'. Gordon, his case worker, is automatically belligerent, continually reminding his 'client' that he doesn't have to say a thing if he doesn't want to. Amusingly, Lambert is not only more than willing to wax lyrical, he prefers to do it away from the lefty's loving gaze.

'Don't worry, Gordy,' he winks. 'I'm sure these fine upstanding gentlemen – and women – mean me no ill.'

Uh-oh. We've got a live one, here. Everything I've learnt about body language and psychological profiling in thirty years of policing tells me that this lad is spinning us a line. He's just, I don't know . . . he's *enjoying* this a tad too much. Left to my own devices I'd no doubt pat him on the head and be off on my way, soon as you like – yet you just never know. Smithson seems convinced the wraith has seen something, and that's a possibility I simply cannot leave to chance. The social worker strokes his chin – as lefties will – subconsciously groping for a crumb of hashish, no doubt. Probably tells his clients he's an 'occasional toker' to earn their devotion and trust.

'Well, OK. If you're absolutely sure. But I'm here if you need me, yeah?'

Lambert nods, leads us outside and straight away taps up Tony Soprano.

'Would you happen to be in possession of the evil cheroot?'

One thing I cannot abide is articulate fucking smackheads. In that animal-clever way they have, they've worked out that people cross the street to avoid them. Ordinary decent folk have a perception of heroin addicts that generally amounts to this: saucer-eyed, hollow-faced, emaciated wretch with brown teeth and extremely tight jeans (why, smackhead? Why do you wear such tight jeans?), coming up with outlandish pretexts to ask for money. They'll invent curious sums of cash that, in their addled minds, they believe will deflect suspicion. They won't step up, hand outstretched and say: 'I'm clucking here, mate. Can you slot us a fiver for a bag of brown?' No, no, no – because that would be the truth, wouldn't it? Instead, it'll be: 'Can you lend me eighty-one pence to get home, please?' or 'I just need one pound twenty-three and that's me sorted for a hostel, sir.' Always over-polite. Eyes always averted. In short, nobody trusts a smackhead, so the brighter ones try to counter that perception by giving off an air of lively self-awareness and unexpected bonhomie.

'Good afternoon, sir. I'm cognisant of the fact I'm invading your personal space here . . . your "me" time as it were . . .'

Come to the point, you think. Ask for money. It's like that with Derek now, wheedling and conniving, trying to get us all onside while he senses out the sweet spot.

'And could I further press you for man's red fire, officer?'

'Not too backwards in coming forward you, are you?' squeaks Soprano in that eternally plaintive voice of his. Even sobbing his gratitude for an unexpected jump, one imagines an element of anguish in Gorton's timbre. He sparks up the baghead's fag. 'I hope you're not making a living from it?'

I get his drift, obviously. He's letting the lad know there's no dropsy in it for him, no matter how good his info may turn out to be. Still, it's v clumsy of Tony – way too early in our repartee to be tightening the thumbscrews on our prize witness. I step into the breach, bringing Smithson with me.

'So, Derek – thanks. I'm Detective Chief Inspector McCartney.' I love saying that. Love it. 'You've already spoken to PC Smithson, I believe . . .?'

The notebook's out and she clears her throat, eager to impress.

'Yes, sir, I –'

I talk over her, smiling my thanks just to let her know that all is well.

'Can you – Derek . . . sorry, mate . . .' – he winces at 'mate'. I continue, undeterred. '. . . just so I can get a clear mental picture, can you just run everything by me one more time? Everything you told PC Smithson?'

So he tells me. I have to endure more of his digressions and irritating facial tics, but we get there; eventually we get his shaggy-dog story out of him. There was him and two other dropouts sat back against the old tree trunk in the copse they frequent, having a few cans, he says. Digging smack, more like. They hear a car engine, think nothing of it. Hear a bit of an argument – not so much an argument as a discussion, a difference of opinion. Derek's two mates have been down this road before – more often than not voices in the park at night mean there's a kicking round the corner. They gather up their druggies' paraphernalia and amble off into the woods. Derek hesitates a moment longer and he's ready to swear he saw two, maybe three silhouettes bent almost double carrying, more or less *dragging* something towards the allotments. I'm curious now. An altercation; two or three people; I'm as good as certain this isn't me and Una he's describing.

'Can you give any detail, Derek? Anything you remember about them at all?'

Lambert looks at Soprano and I can see it in his eyes; he's thinking of making something up. Then he catches my sarcastic smile and opts for the truth.

'Nah. Too dark. Too far away. Never got that good a look, being completely honest with you.'

I nod, grip his shoulder.

'That's OK. Don't worry. This is all priceless stuff, Derek. Priceless. But, tell me . . . you say you might have heard these people arguing. Can you remember – did you *hear* anything in particular?'

Derek looks me in the eye.

'I think so.'

I eye him back. I need to know what he heard; whether there was a female voice.

'You'd need to be pretty sure, mate.'

His eyes flicker madly. Note to self. Don't call him 'mate' again. He lets out a long, pensive sigh and looks off to the middle distance, before coming back to meet my gaze again.

'I mean, it's nothing, really . . . don't see how it'll help yous at all . . . I'm bang into all me TV cops, man. I'm all over them. Love it. And, like, I'll watch them, yeah, and it's like . . .' He does a strange piano-tinkling motion with his fingers, opens his eyes all wide. '. . . I'm right inside their head, la. I get it. And this one last night and what have you . . . I can't see it . . .'

'Try us.'

He milks it. Either he's hamming it up or he's still hoping the elusive tenner of TV detective myth will materialise in front of his nose, only to be held out of reach until he spills the beans.

'All's it was, right, is the perps . . . the gentlemen in question . . . like I'm telling yous, they was having what I'd describe as a minor altercation, if you will. A slight difference of opinion . . .'

'In what way, Derek?'

'Just . . . one of them was getting angry, saying "What's wrong with here?" – I think he said that . . . "What's wrong with here like?"'

I try to keep Derek in the zone.

'Derek. Again thanks. Really. But before we go . . . if you could. Was there anything distinctive about the voice, or voices, you heard?'

'How d'you mean?'

'You described one of them as sounding angry. Did he . . . was there anything about what he said that stood out for you in some way?'

Smithson takes it upon herself to impress me as she enlightens a witness she considers her own.

'Did he have a local accent? Anything you'd recognise or remember if you heard him again?'

Derek closes his eyes and makes a big thing of shaking his head.

'No, no . . . that's what I'm saying. He defo weren't from round here. I wouldn't say so.'

'Did he have *any* kind of accent at all, Derek? Anything distinctive whatsoever?'

'I wouldn't call it an accent, as such . . .' He chews on it some more, enjoying the drama. 'He had, like . . . a military sort of voice, I'd say . . . authoritative.'

Thank Our Lord above. Definitely not me then – my vocal pitch has been known to fluctuate but I doubt my brand of gentle persuasion could ever be interpreted as military. No mention of any female voice, either.

'What makes you think military, Derek? Was he bullying in tone? Commanding?'

'I suppose, like, yeah. Impatient.'

Soprano scribbles away, darts Derek a look.

'Would you say he was well spoken?'

'Posh? Yeah. A bit.'

So he's making it up then. Nice try, Derek Lambert. He's a self-confessed fan of your cop procedurals, and he's thought it might be a fun way to pass an hour or two – bring a real-life investigation into his own little world, maybe make a bob or two while he's at it. Fair enough. But my take on this is that he caught a distant glimpse of Una and me starting to move Kalan's corpse and that's as far as it goes. He was too far away, too out of the game to take any great detail in. As soon as the sirens started getting closer and the Fuzz were on the scene, he's scattered. For now, at least, nobody knows what went on – or why. For now, our secret is safe; but the clock is ticking.

Shakespeare

Following my hunch that the young lady a Somali sister, it follows that Evan's first port of call should be Mohammed's place. Now, as much as our Somali brethren may like to call this establishment a social club, the Boubou far from being the most sociable nook in the neighbourhood. Unless you be from the old country more or less, or unless you got good cause to be there, the Boubou scoring pretty high tens on old Evan's to-don't list. Very easy to get looked at the wrong way if you amble in there thinking the Boubou same as old Somali Club. Uh-uh. Different times, different place. The old place back in the day, broad church for every kind of people. All types up all night, back then, dancing and drinking like there no tomorrow. Wonderful establishment, so help me. But most people stumble on the Boubou today, well, they better want to keep on walking. That's most people by the by, and suffice ye to say old Evan isn't most people round these parts. Isn't nobody who's anybody round Liverpool 8 don't know Shakespeare to say hello to.

I've taken the courtesy to call Momo first anyway and he's said sure, come on round – but he's giving me the old dead bat. Lance Pierre himself would find it tough to break through Mohammed's guard when he's in his I-don't-know mood – and Momo, lest we forget, is a uncommunicative soul even when he being chatty. Nonetheless, Evan is acutely aware that Mohammed Ibrahim is the first port of call if we want to do things as they should be done, and in this brotherly barrio that's the way it got to be.

I go up to his office on the second floor and we chew a little khat, sip an apple tea while Momo go through the motions of asking a little bit more about this girl I've taken in; but no sooner do I start telling him than he's shaking his head again – no, no, don't think there's anyone like that around here. Red hijab, you say? *Red*? A little immodest wouldn't you say? No. I'd know if there was anyone like *that* in the community. So that's that. Not sure Evan believe the old rascal by the way.

He one of those that like a pound note just for telling you what day it be. Still, if Momo not for telling then he not for telling.

On my way down the stairs and out of there, a few young lads stand back to let me pass but half jostle me anyway. Give me the look. With their long heads and their pipe-cleaner limbs, I always thought the Somali boys looked weak – but that was before I know Somalis. These are some mad, mad dervishes if you cross them, these boys. You don't want to get caught up in something with these cats. They will cut you to bits as soon as look at you. I mean it. Fight one of them and you're fighting the whole brotherhood, for real. I don't want to leave the young princess too long anyway. I more than happy to let their jostling go, keep on walking, make like I didn't even notice the little digs and what have you. Couple of them try to catch my eye but I keep my head down and get on out of there, start a gentle canter back towards the Corona.

McCartney

From the Hodge's complexion, he's been here an hour or two already. His nose is positively glowing, and his dial is streaked with purplish-red thread veins. I'm gratified to note the near-full decanter, however, and I'm already speculating what treat lies within. As he's whittled away at his last twelve months of service, Chief Superintendent Hodge has abandoned all and any moderation in his drinking. He's turned into a full-on sackhead with his fancy clarets. Oh aye, none of your muck for the *capo di capi*, and in the interests of full and frank disclosure, he's been good enough to let me wet my beak, too. Margaux, St Julien, even the occasional cheeky Pomerol, we've supped the very finest in the Ath as we plot the downfall of the vile Scouse villains right here on our doorstep who happen to be some of Europe's most wanted men. Hodge has promised we'll come in here the day after we finally nab them and gently toast our success with a bottle of Cheval Blanc they offer in here at a pert £1,800. 'A steal,' he's said, a dozen times or more, laughing voraciously every time. His tab anyway, so who's counting? All in the line of duty.

Whatever Hodge has ordered up from the club's cellars has been deemed worthy of pouring off into one of those funny lopsided decanters that looks like a blown-glass bedpan. He waves away the fusspot who tries to pour for us, fills my glass with a big, hearty glug, topping up his own. As ever, in his presence, I wince at his wire-brush eyebrows and whirl through a mental image of myself dough-tily paring them back with some sharp barber's shears. He reclines in the padded Queen Anne armchair (I have one just like it in the eyrie), rakes me with those rheumy eyes and clears his throat to no avail. His voice is near hoarse with phlegm.

'So. Make it simple for me, can you? Where are we with all this?'

I take a sip – by God, that is good fucking wine – and nod my approval as I set the glass down.

'OK. This is what we know . . .'

I offer a small, slightly awkward smile, merely to acknowledge the sensitivity of all this.

'A non-Caucasian body was found shortly before midnight in the Merebank allotments. When I say body, this is barely the case . . .'

Hodge screws his eyes tight shut. His shoulders heave.

'What we discovered was a torso. Its hands, feet and its head had been severed. The victim had sustained a prolonged and vicious attack with a variety of blades. Specifically –'

'Mac, for God's sake, man . . .' He shakes his head at me. 'Get to it, will you?'

I roll my eyes when he's not looking. It's your call, Chief Super. What the boss wants, the boss gets.

'The body has been transported to the mortuary, where we have . . . where I have arranged for its identity and precise location to be kept incognito for the time being. For reasons of discretion, in reference to matters of a locally, possibly racially sensitive nature, and particularly in reference to ongoing investigations, sir, we have requested a new identity for the deceased and a brand-new, ah, story . . .'

Hodge blazes a madder shade of red.

'For crying out loud, McCartney! This is *me* you're talking to! Does *anybody* else know who the stiff is?'

I look around and behind me, just to show Hodge that my diplomatic tone serves a purpose here; that walls have ears.

'Just us, sir.'

He grumbles something into his bowl-sized glass, but he seems placated. He takes a sip, swirls the wine around his glass then all of a sudden looks up.

'Do you need me to speak with Gilroy?'

Gilroy has done everything I've asked of him, so far. I wouldn't rule out playing the Hodge card further down the line if necessary, but for now I'm thinking I'll keep my *soi-disant* powder dry.

'The appropriate fax ought to be sitting on my desk right now, sir. I asked him to send it as I was leaving the building . . . nice and handy for prying eyes.'

This actually raises a smile – or something of an amiable grunt, at least.

'You're good, McCartney. Don't let anyone tell you other-wise, yes? You're good . . .'

He grunts again, hawks up, swallows it. He gives his wine another swirl and farts without acknowledgement. He's a class act, Hodge — God help his poor lady wife when he's home twenty-four/seven in a few weeks' time. Belatedly, Hodge checks his rancour and lowers his voice as he leans forward.

'You're sure Gilroy's onside? He's cooperating?'

'I won't try to pretend he's happy about all this, sir. But he'll do the right thing. Yes.'

'Mmm . . .'

He closes his eyes again, shakes his head slowly. I sympathise, absolutely. This is make or break for us. Eyes open. Right on me.

'Do we know if the fuel is still on schedule for delivery?'

A little discretion from the old bugger at last! Wonders will never cease.

'We have no intelligence to suggest anything to the contrary, sir.'

'Excellent. Excellent.' He actually looks up and cracks a smile. 'Bloody hell, eh?'

I know exactly what he means. This job.

'Manners shown his face as yet?'

I strive to sound as neutral as I'm able.

'DI Manners attended the incident room this morning, sir. Just some routine enquiries . . .'

'What sort of enquiries?'

I pause for as long as I can stand it, for impact.

'He's looking for Kalan Rozaki, sir.'

Hodge merely nods. He takes another sip of his wine and holds his glass up to the dim sepia light before returning it to the table. His phone vibrates and spins slightly, clinking the glass. He gives it a quick glance.

'It's the handler.'

'Una was with me when we discovered . . .'

'Yes. She told me.'

I'm starting to feel like I'm in trouble, here. It's me who's managing this whole nightmare. It's me who's kept a lid on it all so far. Yet I'm reddening, as though there are things I should have covered – things I'm letting slip.

'Will she be staying on the case? Now Kalan has –'

He glares at me.

'Out of my hands that, Billy. But I'm given to understand they've asked her to concentrate her efforts on finding the girl.'

Hodge's mobile winks on and off. He snatches it up with a sigh, listens to a message, eyes still boring into mine.

'This witness?'

'Yes. One Derek Lambert – no fixed address. I don't see him stacking up, sir.'

'Do we care?'

'Well . . . there was the matter of Una and myself, sir.'

'Mmm?'

His eyeballs seem to slide, very slowly, up and down my face as he queries me. This aspect of Hodge's persona riles me like anything. He knows full well it's himself who called me in – asked me to see to whatever needed doing. I would have been more than happy just staying put in the Nugget until his SOS came and burst my bubble. He knows damned well what he asked of me, and now here he is asking me to spell it out. Well, he can eff right off, the old bugger!

'You think Lambert might have witnessed yourself and Una interfering with the body?'

Says it as though it was not, indeed, a direct order from His Worshipful Hodgeness.

'I sincerely doubt it, sir. But one has to eliminate the possibility.'

Hodge's slovenly eyes cease roving. He's sat back like a walrus, sluicing his wine around and holding the glass up to the light.

'Why so, out of interest?'

'He's an addict. He can't be sure what he saw. Can't say whether there were two or three perps. He didn't get *that* good a look . . .' I pause for gravitas. 'And he intimated he'd be requiring payment, sir – if he were to come forward and testify.'

Hodge stares at his phone's screen, shaking his head. He snaps it off, puts it back down next to his glass.

'So you'd say that, in spite of a very close call, there's nothing to make us change direction?'

'I'd say not, sir. Clearly the Kalan Rozaki angle has to remain submerged for as long –'

'Of course it does, dammit!!'

His whole body jerks forward, face livid. I don't know what to say. I just sit there, waiting for whatever's coming. Hodge speaks through his teeth – pure venom.

'Which is why I find myself wondering why Evan blasted Kavanagh is poking round the Somalis, asking all sorts of questions about Kalan Rozaki's blasted girlfriend!'

It takes a second for the name to compute.

'Shakespeare?'

Hodge slumps back in his seat, exasperated.

'Shakespeare.'

Shakespeare

Girl looking a whole lot better by the time I get back from the Boubou. She's tidied the flat from top to bottom – my lady visitors always say the place lack a woman's touch – and she's sat up on the couch reading my book. She look me up and down as I come through the door, holds up *Freedom* like it's something a Trinidadian gentleman of a certain age ought not to be reading.

'Didn't have you down as the big reader . . .'

'I read, madam. 'Tis true.'

'Huh. Get *you* . . .'

She looking from myself, to the book, back to me.

'Any good?'

'Not as good as his *Corrections*, I'd vouchsafe. But I'll stick with it.'

She smiles at me like I got my zip down and don't know it. Little shake of the head.

She looks at the book's jacket again.

'I can't be doing with that "give it time" thing,' she say. She posh. Not posh-posh, but pleasant, if you will. Refined. It sound weird to me, coming from she, this beautiful, high-tone voice. She still studying the book cover with all the suspicion in the world.

'If they don't grab me in the first ten, twenty, pages I dump them . . .'

'And what d'you think? Are you hooked?'

She lets the book fall on to the sofa.

'Nah. Not for me.'

'Oh?'

'That's it.'

'That is the sum of your critique?'

'Sum of my critique? What a funny old dude you are!'

I tip my head back and laugh. I think I'm in love.

'You swallowed a dictionary or something?'

I don't know whether I should be flattered or not. From she, I shall take it as a compliment.

'One could posit there's a certain elegance to my syntax . . .'

She smiles again. I return it with my best Shakespearean

bow – often like to imagine this what the Bard mean in his stage directions when he indicate a cat going about his business with a flourish. I like to think old Evan do things with a bit of a flourish, no? I offer my hand.

'Evan. Evan Kavanagh. But you can call me Shakespeare.'

This sets her off laughing again, and she puts her hand to her jawbone.

'Ow! Don't make me laugh!'

'Sorry. And you arc?'

She places her delicate little hand in mine, squeezes gently.

'Misha.'

'Beautiful name, Misha. Suits you.'

'Aren't *you* the old player!'

She thinks she's offended me; corrects herself.

'Thanks for taking me in. Shakespeare.'

I wonder whether now is the time. Now is *always* the time.

'What *happened*, Misha? Can you remember at all?'

From the pain in hcr eyes, she remembers all too well. But she shakes her head; once this way, once t'other.

'You come running in here with the fear of God in your cyes, like the Devil himself is coming aftcr you. I went outside for a look-see, rcady to give whoever it was what for – but no one there. Not sight nor sound of anybody out there at all . . .'

She just close hcr eyes tight like she's shutting it all out, whatever it be. I crouch on the floor in front of her, try to make eye contact. She's looking straight at the rug behind me, all troubled again. I try changing tack with her.

'I'm guessing, like . . . I mean to say . . . can I take it you from the Somali side?'

Eyes back into me. *So* bloody fine. Slight nod of the head. 'That's kind of the problem here.'

I try to project my understanding in the form of a meek smile. Evan know how it can be with the Somali community. The traditions. I take her little hand, and tell her.

'I went to see Mohammed . . . see if he could put a name to the description.'

And that's it. She snatch her hand right back. Whatever the little round dance we been having, it gone. Finito. Over. Gone in a flash. What we got now is pure sudden shock on her face; this blind, naked fear – and Misha angry too. Turns away from Shakespeare, trembling little bit as she speaks.

'You know Mohammed?'

'I know everyone, dear Misha. A little bit.'

She looking this way, looking that way, like she want to jump out the window. She stands up, troubled like mad, pacing to and fro, staring out on to the street below. She turn sharpish at me.

'Is there a phone, at all?'

'We don't have no dedicated landline, per se . . .'

She's looking desperate now.

'. . . but you're welcome to use the coin box by the dartboard downstairs . . .'

She's off out the door and down the stairs. I shout after her.

'6op, Misha! Help yourself from the till . . .' I smile to myself and mutter, 'If there *be* 6op in the till!'

Evan don't care if the girl be calling Somalia. That her business. Ask no questions, you'll get no lies back at you. I sit in silence, hoping I'll catch a drift of the intrigue, whatever's going on. And after a minute it hits me like a big, stupid thud. Not a sound from down there. She hasn't made no call to nowhere. Misha not coming back.

Hodge

Manners, as ever, leaks mendacity from his every pore. He'd have made a frightful crook. One knows, one has always known, when Alfie Manners is lying, or is merely telling half the story – which is most of the time. I give him another second to slurp his tea. One of the many things I shall not mourn when I exit this building once and for all is the way Alfie Manners blows and slurps his tea. As thick as he is, it dawns on Manners that I await his full and unblinking attention. He looks up.

'So. What do they know?'

'Very little. Just that the kid brother missed a big family thing, which is unlike him . . .'

'And?'

'And that's about it. They've asked myself to ask around.'

I look him up and down. Let him know who's boss.

'In essence, Kalan Rozaki has done a runner and his family expect you to find him. Is that a fair assessment of the situation as things stand?'

'That's . . . yes. Yeah. That's about it, sir.'

'Very well.'

I begin busying myself with paperwork to let him know his time is up. He doesn't move. I look up.

'Yes?'

Manners makes a big thing of snapping out of a reverie, but for that split second his eyes were trained on my desk. He attempts an apologetic smile, as though he hadn't realised he'd been dismissed, but as he closes the door behind him my eyes rest upon the object of his interest. I curse myself. In the act of shuffling that stack of paperwork to bid Manners farewell, a page from my own Moleskine has dropped on to the desk. It reads as follows.

'*Shakespeare???*'

I have drawn a box around the word, tracing over it several times. I really could kick myself.

McCartney

I've got to say it – I like Shakespeare. Of all the mad bastards I've had to deal with in this rat run of devotional lawlessness, Evan Kavanagh is, how-you-say, a law unto himself. Funny, mannered old lag, he is. Beau Brummel meets Willy Wonka, with his lurid Edwardian coats and his cravats and canes and his crazy array of trilbies and top hats. Proper dandy, old Evan, walking the streets with his shoulders back and head held high like he's on the King's Road, not Princes Avenue. He's spent more time inside than out, old Evan. Longtime crook; up to this and that at all hours of the day and night. He can handle himself, too, for an old guy. Must be mid-sixties now, Shakespeare. Older, possibly – he's had a hard life.

I've had plenty of run-ins with Shakespeare in my time up here. I know he can't stand me. Hates my living guts, to be fair. He's got every right to. He's had a bad deal from the boys in blue, especially in the aftermath of the riots. When I got my first gig here, the Black Caucus was still very much running Liverpool 8. Running town. They were the untouchables, and Kavanagh was in with them up to his eyeballs – so everyone told me, anyway. The word on the wing was that Evan Kavanagh was a heavy hitter with the Liverpool 8 drug firms; approach with caution. Back in those dog days of Doug Yardley's regime, Alfie Manners, Kieran Dooley and all those other young coppers on the Drug Squad would say anything – *do* anything – to make that stick. Literally. Small wonder the likes of Shakespeare tar us all with the same brush.

Still – there's something about Shakespeare you just can't help liking. He's a charmer, Evan, a rogue – the last of the Ordinary Decent Criminals. I'd go as far as to say he just can't help himself, but in Evan's case he's far too clever to put his incorrigible criminality down to bad luck or bad choices. The crying shame about Evan Kavanagh is that he's brighter than a button, and he's lived his life of badness with his eyes wide open. He's sharp enough to have gone down a different route, but the truth is that he's weak to a life of ease. He wants things handed to him, Evan – other people's things, in the main. Saying that, it's never been a happy collar when we've had to nick him. I've had him on a dozen different counts, bang to rights every time. He thinks I've got a thing for him – I haven't. It's just that, time and time and time again, it's always him. It. Is. *Always* him. Some chancer from North Wales or somewhere turns up in the hood wanting an in and ends up out for the count, minus his start-up capital, I've got to be honest about it . . . Shakespeare's the first name springs to mind. Maybe I *have* got a thing about him. Still, it's weird to hear his name come up now in the context of the Rozaki case. If ever there was a case of never the twain, it's old-school Evan and those hi-tech, ruthless Rozaki animals. Just doesn't add up at all. Guess I'll be paying a visit to the Corona, then.

Shakespeare
Well, if it isn't my delightful old oppo McCartney. Without exception *the* worst copper in Liverpool. The others, man, they don't make no bones about the way they be; the way they think. They thuggish. Corrupt. Conniving. Racist. Mac-See, though, he act like he different. Act like he do his work with a heavy heart. He's always tried to cultivate this thing that he only going about his business, man – just doing the bare minimum that he really have to do. Never call you a nigger to your face. Never. The PC PC. Ha! I don't think so, somehow. Ol' Evan been round the block and then some, and I here to tell you I can smell a rotter a hundred yards

away. Terrible man, Mac-See. Terrible. Worse than the very worst. He turn up in the bar smiling that smile – he got a tart's smile, McCartney. Teeth so white. Face nary a wrinkle. He *got* to be fifty or thereabout, but he got the face of a young boy. Me tink 'im be a gelding or a mare. Chap scare me, he so false. Here he come again, walking into my bar, smiling – always the weary smile. Things must be getting desperate in their War on Crime. I smile back.

'Shakespeare.'

'Mac-See.'

He forgotten I call him that. He don't know what to say. He hesitant, if not downright nervous, here.

'I may as well come straight to the point . . .'

'That's most unlike yourself, Mr McCartney. Why not beat around the bush a little first?'

I've got to say it – the boy looks hurt. There's something in his eyes and, I don't know. A more sensitive observer than Shakespeare would say they something akin to regret, there. He lets out a long, long breath and stares at the floor, shaking his head.

'I'm wasting my time, aren't I? You've done nothing wrong. I'm not interviewing you. It's just . . . I could really do with some help.'

'And why would I, of all people, be willing to offer said help to you, of all people, Mac-See?'

There he go again with the prolonged, dramatic, head-shaking thing.

'No reason. I'm looking for a missing person. Young student. I grow more worried about her well-being by the hour . . .'

I feel wretched bad, but I just can't trust the man. Sorry, Misha. Sorry.

'And there's a suggestion you might know something of her whereabouts . . .'

Why they talk like this? Even when he here on bended knee, asking Evan for a favour, why he axing like I'm a suspect, like he's on to me, looking deep inside my black soul and shuddering to the bone at the evil he see? Talk to me like a equal, Mac-See. Talk to me like a man.

'Funny, that. There's always a *suggestion*, isn't there? Never anything hard and fast.'

'Shakespeare . . .'

I shrug and snort and wait it out. He struggling here. He holding my stare long and hard for all the added sincerity he can wring out of the moment. Makes me laugh the way police think they the only ones can see through what people mean by what they do.

'I truly have nothing of relevance to report, sir.'

He nods.

'Fair enough.'

He not going anywhere, though. He not moving.

'Evan, I know we always say it . . .'

I just stare at him, cool. Give nothing away. Nothing.

'If you should remember anything . . . if you change your mind . . .'

He goes to leave me a calling card, changes *his* mind. Holds on to it 'twixt finger and thumb. His face, for all its youth and blandness, is clouded over with troubles. He gives it one last shot.

'She's a beautiful, intelligent girl, Misha. One of the brightest kids at the Law School. She's got everything to live for. Her whole brilliant life ahead of her. But I'm worried for her. I'm worried she'll never see those days . . .'

Nice try, Mac-See. And thanks for the added information about my little princess. I should have guessed she be a scholar! Well, worry not, she'll see her best days all right, my Misha will. But no thanks to you, McCartney. All the policing in the world isn't worth a good ear to the ground. Let's see who gets there first, you rat. It like he could read my mind. He turn and go but, force of habit, no doubt, he leaves his damn card on the bartop anyways.

McCartney

Well, that seemed to go well. And as if the sesh with Shakespeare wasn't grim enough, the kart's been keyed outside the Corona — specialist bodywork job, that. Looking at a monkey, minimum. And now Tony Soprano is on the phone.

'Boss . . .'

It's going to be bad, this, whatever it is. His voice is almost falsetto.

'Go on, Toe . . .'

'Think you better get down here . . .'

'I'm on my way.'

The look Smithson gives me as I sweep into the incident room is heartbreaking. There's a red rim around her eyes, and I doubt Tony Gorton's consoling words have made things much better.

'Here y'are, girl,' he'll have said. 'Don't be getting all tearful . . .'

Probably tried to hug her while he was at it, Tony — the groping grief counsellor. He gives me a bit of a triumphant look; as though he's saying: 'See? Told you the greenhorn would only get in the way.'

Tony reads me quickly, though, his cop's intuition telling him I'm on Smithson's side here. He quickly becomes Smithson's apologist.

'You know what Alfie's like, boss. He had the fax out the machine before young Smudge here even knew he'd come in . . .'

He winks and tries to throw Smithson a grin. She blanks

him. I crouch down and modulate my voice to let her know she's not in trouble.

'OK, OK. Smithson. Lucy?'

'Lucinda, sir . . .'

'The facsimile DI Manners took . . . did you get chance to see it, at all? Before he took it away?'

She shakes her head. 'No, sir . . .'

She flushes a sudden pink, one angry streak gouging each cheek. I can see it all in a flash; the embarrassment, then an almost instantaneous self-defence mechanism kicking in, a defiant refusal to accept she got this wrong. She's resentful of the system — a system that allows a superior officer to flout the rules; to walk in there and do whatever he wants to, simply because he's a boss. She's resentful that the system can make a young newbie like herself look stupid, when she's not. She hates it that the job can allow her to feel as bad as she's feeling right now. I know this, because once upon a time I was her. I made much worse errors of judgement and I lived to tell the tale. We all do. It's how we move on that counts. If only she knew she'd done us all a favour here. If only I could tell her!

'I didn't see the fax itself . . .'

'No problem. Honestly, Lucy, it really is no big deal . . .'

She offers up a faint smile.

'But I did get a printout of the sender's number, sir.'

She does love her sucker punches, this girl. I can't give you Häagen-Dazs, but will Ben & Jerry's suffice? I like her. She hands me one of those tiny little notelets with the faint chequered grid, no bigger than a Christmas stamp — I used to love the big, decorative Christmas stamps with robins on, or snow scenes with a holly sprig in each corner. Do they still issue them, Christmas stamps? I can't say I've noticed. I peruse the number. Gilroy. Excellent.

'Lucinda . . .'

'Smithson, Sir.'

'Thanks for this . . .'

'I'm sorry again for the mistake, sir.'

'There's absolutely nothing for you to be sorry about. Really. You're hardly going to refuse a superior officer, are you?'

'Thank you, sir.'

'OK. Chin up. Now, let's go and get the bad guys!'

She forces a laugh. I hold up the little note and proceed to go through the motions, even though I know the number inside out. Three rings and he picks up.

'Mal. Sorry, mate, it's your favourite pain in the arse. Machine ran out of toner this end. Can you resend please, mate? Yep . . .'

I mug up a reassuring smile for young Smithson, let her know that all is well.

'No, honestly, Malcolm, that'll be just fine. Much appreciated. Ciao.'

Moments later the fax whirrs into action and I nod to PC Smithson. She grabs the pages as the machine spits them out. My heart twangs again at the sight of her, head bent to the task in hand, eyes averted lest she see anything she wasn't meant to. I speed-read the details, impressed as never before at what Mal Gilroy can pull off when he wants to. When he has to. He's surpassed himself here. The kite has been well and truly flown. As of now, DI Alfred Manners, noting the deceased is one Raul Rodellega, known to police in three cities and found to have traces of heroin in his system, will have dismissed the always-unlikely theory that the stiff may have been Kalan Rozaki. Satisfied in this knowledge, Manners can now redouble his efforts to locate said runaway. He'll have gobbled that up, Alfie, only too delighted to be able to give his paymasters the good news; he hasn't found Kalan yet, but the boy is definitely still alive. I try to stifle the satisfaction starting to radiate from within, and turn back to Smithson and Soprano.

'Did DI Manners mention anything else?'

'No, sir,' young Smithson gushes, hugely relieved.

'Well, I dunno if it's important . . .' squeaks Tony Soprano.

Somehow I know this is going to be awful. The bile spews up through my oesophagus as my heart plummets the other way, down, down, down through my solar plexus. I try to keep a lid on it. I make the face for Tony to elucidate.

'He did ask *me* if I knew where Evan Kavanagh hangs out these days.'

Yes, Tony. He *did* ask you. He asked you because he knew that if anyone would spill the beans at first time of asking it'd be *you*, you nervous little castrato. Dear God above – have mercy, please. That's the sunbeam back in its box for today then.

'Evan Kavanagh?' I mug.

Tony's triumphant 'I am a cop' face is back.

'You know? Shakespeare!'

Try as I might, I just cannot prevent myself muttering the words 'fucking hell' under my breath.

Shakespeare

Upon my soul, whatever next? It never rain but it pour. The animal Manners is here, talking to me like a copper should.

'I can very easily come back here with a warrant, Kavanagh. Believe me, you won't know this place after we've torn it apart. If that lad has been here –'

'What lad?'

I can look him straight in the eye and say that. Mac-See is sly and sinister – but this guy Manners make no pretence who he be. He's a monster, man. He evil. His thin weasel face is all over me, up and down, bristling.

'You know who I'm on about, Kavanagh . . .'

In point of fact I don't, Bad Manners. But I keen to find out. Something afoot here – most definitely something big going down. All the top-gun Bad Lieutenants out left, right and centre swinging punches. Something going down, and Evan going to get to the bottom of it. Manners steps right up into my face, puts his nose against mine.

'Listen, you piece of shit. I know that you know where he is. You fucking know that I know that. If I tell the Rozaki boys you've been hiding their brother . . .'

Interesting. He stupid as hell, Manners, but even he can see the surprise on mine dial.

'I can assure thee I have not the faintest idea what you refer to, Mr Manners.'

I hold his crazy boggle-eye look. He takes a step back, points at myself.

'Cross the Rozakis, and . . . I think you're more than well aware how that's gonna play, aren't you, Evan?'

I nod, but hold down the smile I feel surging through me. Rozakis, is it? Curiouser and curiouser. Well thank you, Lieutenant Bad, for handing me that one in a heart-shaped box. I trying to keep the sparkle out my eyes as I address him.

'Will that be all, officer?'

You can see it. You can feel it. He wants to work me over, like the good old days. As much as I'm submerging my smiles and laughter, he's fighting to keep a lid on his rage.

'I'll be back,' he growls.

'Hasta la vista, baby,' Evan right back at him.

I wait till his car gone and I lock up. Time scarce. I've got to find my girl before these yard dogs get to she.

McCartney

Nine times out of ten I'd ignore a number I don't recognise, let it go on to answer. On pure gut instinct I pick up, though – and instantly wish I'd left it.

'Is this the good Inspector?'

Lambert. His strung-out drawl more ingratiating and twice as aggravating as ever.

'Detective Chief Inspector McCartney speaking, yes . . .'

'Derek Lambert at your service.'

'Derek. What gives?'

'Well . . .'

Here we go, I'm thinking. He's given us the introductory rate. This is where he starts hitting us up for real, now.

'Go on.'

'Whereas I'd never be so precious as to start thinking my information was critical in any way, shape or form, I do belatedly realise two things . . .'

Oh dear. He's clucking like a strung-out battery hen. I sigh hard and steady myself for a long ride.

'Thing one?'

He gives out a nervous little chuckle.

'Well, see, now I'm on my feet so to speak, with the benefit of a good night's sleep I've got a much sharper perspective on the comings and goings of yesterday evening . . .'

I can see him doing that weaving action with his hands as he drones on and on, wiggling his eyebrows up and down. Jesus. The face that danced. I touch the desk with my forehead, take a deep breath and slowly, slowly let it out.

'Derek? Do us a favour, can you, mate? Can you talk plain English?'

He digests this.

'Is my information worth money?'

'Possibly.'

'It come back to me. Just now.'

'What did?'

'Last night. I think I heard a bird's voice, you know . . .'

Time slows to a standstill. I can hear my pulse throbbing faster than the wall clock.

'Where are you right now, Derek?'

'I'm at the place.' His voice tails off, drowsy.

'The Bedford?'

'The very same.'

'I'll be along momentarily.'

I kill the call and sit there, dead still, thinking it through. I decide there and then that I will not be following up Lambert's call. I do half feel sorry for the skag-bandit, but as sure as night follows day that lad will be attending to himself as we speak. He can't help himself. It's a kind of death wish, as good as. I mean that most sincerely too – the Derek Lamberts of this world cannot get themselves away from this shit. By the time he comes round he'll have forgotten speaking to me, and any belated rumbling of myself and Ms Farlowe will fade away on memory's bliss. But Lambert's call tells me, as if I needed reminding, that time is showing us its arse. Somewhere out there is a slowboat to Liverpool, loaded to the brim with pure-as-poison opiate. Somewhere out there is a still-clean kid too. The next Derek Lambert, if we don't keep that shit off the streets. It's time for action, Billy. Time you upped your game.

Manners

I half wish I'd never got wrapped up with these two. There's no pleasing them. Proper. Especially fucking Moz – the kite on the little twat! Narky, suspicious, growling face, like I'm making the whole thing up. You'd think they'd be pleased with what I'm telling them, but no.

'This is the actual coroner's report, Moz – rubber-stamped and everything. Cause of death, time of death, stiff's ID, the full monty. Reasons to be cheerful, part four, boys – it's not your Kalan!'

Moz's scowl gives birth to a whole new clan of frowns.

'Doesn't bring us no closer to knowing where he is though, does it?'

Dara touches his brother on the wrist. 'Least he's still out there somewhere, though, hey?'

Moz shakes his head. 'He's gone, man. I know he's gone. Can just feel it . . .'

Dara puts his arm around his brother, pulls him in close and touches his forehead with his own. 'He's going to be fine, kid. *I* can feel it . . .'

To be fair, it's always been Dara I've got along with. Got his head screwed on, that lad. Knows how this city works. Always did. His brother I can't be doing with. Whereas Dara is a bit of a face around town – not in a flash way, but he's one of them that's welcome wherever he goes – Moz is just a surly cunt. Hardly ever out, never cracks a smile, looks at all hands like they're trying to have him over. Got to ask yourself, end of the day – what's the point? Where's the joy in having all that dough if you're just going to sit around scowling at every cunt? But it's always been Moz that weighs me in, too, and it's him I've got to feed back to – even when there's fuck all to say. With this one, it's been blind alleys and cul-de-sacs all the way. Their kid's done a runner, end of story. Who wouldn't with fucking Moz looking over your shoulder, day in, day out, telling you what you can and can't do? He's been on my case every two, three hours since the lad disappeared, asking me what I've heard, what I know, anything afoot in Copland.

'What did his teacher have to say? At the university?'

Now I know I'm for the chop.

'I've been following different leads, boys. Come on, Moz . . .' I've got my arms spread out, appealing for a penalty. 'You know the score. I *had* to eliminate the possibility that . . .'

I wait for them to fill in the blanks. Dara nods. I nod back, all my pent-up pressure snorting out through my nose in one gust.

'The Law School was already closed by the time I got there. I'll go again first thing, no worries.'

'Make sure you do.'

I nod keenly, eager to move on. I whip open my notebook.

'Shakespeare knows nothing, either.'

I look up, meet Moz's stare and look away to Dara.

'Seriously, man. Whatever he's done, it's nothing to do with Kalan. Daft old loon didn't have a Scooby what I was on about. Proper. I know soon as he opens his mouth when that soft twat's lying. Swear to you. He never even knew who Kalan was . . .'

Dara holds his hand up, signalling all is well.

'Anything else?'

'Not so far.'

'OK. Grab yours on your way out.'

There's a little worktop where they make the tea and what have you. Every time I've been here, which is dozens if not hundreds of times, there's those plastic filing crates, full of cash — and I mean thousands and thousands of pounds, every time. Swear blind, talking brewsters here, stacks and stacks of cellophane-wrapped bunce, all in thousand-pound wads. I'm that relieved to be out of here, I ream them with a bit of the old Scouse humour.

'Double time by the way, boys.'

Neither of them laughs. I slot a grand and do one.

McCartney

I'm idly surfing channels when *Top Trucks* pops up. Jesus! Haven't seen this in *years*! The jangly, cod-C&W guitars and banjos, the voiceover — which I now realise is overtly and ironically gay — along with, naturally, loads and loads and loads of heavy machinery. I feel weird. It's a *good* weird, though, a nice, nostalgic sort of swooning that takes me all the way back. When I was little that's all we used to do, me and Dad. I was *obsessed* with trucks and diggers. Any building site or roadworks, he'd have to pull over while I stood there, goggle-eyed, watching in silence while the excavators scooped and scraped and dumped. I could name every one of them; backhoe loaders, excavators, chippers, low loaders, cherry pickers, bucket cranes, impact pulverisers, booms and de-limbers. Prince of them all were the snowploughs I ogled in books and magazines, but we never got to see one up close in Swanage. Kids at school wanted Stylo Matchmaker football boots, Adidas kit and a Gola bag to carry it all in. I wanted John Deere and Caterpillar and JCB.

Missing him hugely, all of a sudden, I reach for my BlackBerry to give Dad a tinkle. Three missed calls. Barnaby Giles. Shit! Forgot about him. I'm about to call him back to buy more time when the buzzer goes. Who the fuck? I haul myself up with a big sigh. I'll call Dad later, tell him I'll drive down to see him soon as this is all over. I press on the intercom.

'Yep?'

'Hi, Billy. It's me. We still on for that drink?'

Una. Jesus. It's Una Farlowe at my own front door.

'You betcha!'

I'm striving for jaunty swagger, but I can hear the little squeal of terror in my voice. Fight it, Billy. Drive it back! You want this. You want her, and here she is. Flatten out that tremble from your vox, you milksop!

'Enter! Take the stairs all the way up to the top.'

I buzz her up, as nervous as hell. Since last night I've been bracing myself for the inevitable news that Una's being taken off the case. With Kalan gone, there's nothing keeping her in Liverpool anyway, plus she'll have the inquest, the internal inquiry and all the finger-pointing from her bosses to endure. I know I'm going to miss her when she's gone, yet, now she's here, plodding up that staircase, I'm petrified. I've got a strong sense my feelings for Una are reciprocated and I don't want that put to the test. I'm just not ready for anything like that — like this — yet. That's all.

Una taps on the door and I do my Sir Walter Raleigh bow as I usher her in.

'Come into my eyrie . . .'

'Thanks . . .'

She looks different. She's straightened her hair, and that's a new shade of lipstick — a deep, rich red. She looks good. She's voluptuous, Una — big, full hips and a big arse — but then again, she's got big full everything. The curves, the flesh, the smile, it's all Una and I wouldn't have her any other way. I realise too late that she's waiting for me to help her out of her coat. She holds out a bottle of wine for me to take from her, so she can shrug her arm free. She eyes my face fearfully.

'Like the beard,' she twinkles.

It's not a beard. Not *meant* to be a beard. Just haven't had chance to shave with all of this kicking off.

'The chin-rug stays until we wrap this job,' I smile.

Una looks haunted, but if anything her vulnerability turns me on. I should stop this, right now. I'm going to get myself in trouble. I should be businesslike, cut myself off from any hint of intimacy — but I like her so much. Knowing how this will play out, how it always plays out, I could pull back, ignore the signs, save us both the pain; yet I know with horrible certainty I'll do no such thing. Excuses I can use, obstacles I can throw in the way — I'll utilise none of them. I will play and play until it's way too late, and by then all that's left is the aftertaste. The humiliation. I beckon for her to sit while

I go through to open the wine. From the kitchen I can see her eyeing everything up — but we all do that, don't we?

I pop two glasses down and sit myself next to her. I find myself aroused by the dimples on her thighs, close enough to stroke. I lean forward and pour.

'So,' I go, trying to keep things on message, 'what do we know?'

And that's it — her face begins to quiver, her lips tremble and she collapses under another hideous sobbing fit.

'Oh, Billy, Billy — what have we done? Those kids! Those poor kids . . .'

'Hey! Come on! Shhhhh . . .'

I hold her close and, I have to admit, the intimacy is beautiful. I cradle her head and stroke her hair, gently kissing the top of her scalp.

'Come on now. It wasn't your fault . . .'

She breaks loose from me, comes up for air.

'We weren't to know what would happen . . .'

She shudders. Wipes her eyes with the back of her hand.

'What happened was an absolutely tragedy — a barbarity. But, Una . . .'

I look deep into her eyes, wide open and wanting to believe.

'. . . we will *find* Misha!'

She's following my lips as I talk. I'm looking directly into her eyes, but she's just staring at my mouth then she's leaning in and she's kissing me, and my God! It's the most gorgeous, languorous, deep kiss, going on and on, and my head is spinning. I'm undoing her blouse and she's whispering to me, urging me on. Is that what you want, Billy? she's saying, and she lifts her hips where her skirt is trapped beneath her and I can hear the blood thumping in my eardrums and I know it's now or never and I just pull back and jump to my feet. I'm panting for breath and we just look at each other. Una doesn't get it. I start shaking my head.

'I'm sorry, Una. Honestly . . .'

'What's the matter?'

'I just. I . . .' I get my breath and hold up two flat palms. 'Just . . . not while we're working, yeah?'

She straightens her skirt and, very matter-of-fact, hooks her bra straps back over her shoulders and buttons up her blouse.

'Whatever . . .' She gives one sharp stab of a laugh and shakes her head. 'If that's what you want . . .'

My God, girl. If only you knew.

'It's not what I want. Not what I want at all . . .'

'So?'

'So trust me. I've been here before. It never has a happy ending . . .'

She digests that, nods slowly.

'Fair enough.'

She gets up. She only has one shoe on; makes a thing of being not-that-bothered, already engrossed in looking for her missing shoe.

'Some other time, hey?'

I spot the shoe, pass it to her, trying to make eye contact. 'Definitely.' She takes the shoe. I grab her by the wrist. 'Una? Definitely.'

She forces a smile. Looks me in the eye now.

'OK.'

She gives me a sad little look, fishes up her coat and walks to the door. Long after she's gone, I'm sat where she was on the couch and her perfume is still there, enticing me. I can't get her off my mind – her lips seeking mine, the brief yet heavenly yield of her breasts. I go to the cabinet, slide the top drawer open, take out my zip pouch and line up the works. Methodically, ritualistically, I tap up a vein and shoot, instantly reeling from the pulsating zest of the hit. I slide down low on the couch where we were and get myself off, thinking of her.

Shakespeare

It not so long after Bad Manners gone, and the thud hits the little window at the back. I take it to be the local rapscallions having their fun, as they will, and I take not a blind bit of notice. They want to launch cobbles at ol' Evan's window they going to get bored quick-quick. Not even a window so's you'd notice, more a little hatch to let some of the smells out from old Evan's bijou kitchenette. Smells? Fie-fie! Cooking aroma I should say. Evan Portius Kavanagh Esquire some top culinary master chef when he put his mind to it, from time to times. Oh yes, long as you giving me basic good ingredient, plenty limes, plenty spice and them hot, hot chillies, then Shakespeare going to cook you up a storm.

Another thud. That glass so thick, window so small it going to take a cricket ball at high velocity to break it. Muffled shout. Hard to tell it clear in the wind, but suddenly my heart lurch. Misha! That's who it be! My little Misha is down below trying to get old Shakespeare to open up. I near race down them stairs but by the time I get to the big front door I back to acting cautious, as per norm. I open a little fraction. Nothing to see. I should close back up, double-lock, slot the chunky old safety chain that been there since as long as the pub, I guessing, but just then there's a beep from over the way. I narrow mine eyes against the glare of the headlight. I can see now it one of those sleek Land Cruiser type of vehicles, pulled over just by the betties. Another little parp of the horn. The beamers blink on, off, on, off, indicating that I should venture forth. Every little voice in my head telling me to go back, go in, lock up, sit tight but then a cheery voice shouts, 'Evan!' Even if he don't call me 'Shakespeare' it someone knows myself, so I trot across to see what's what. I stop a pace or two away from the vehicle. The back window glides down and hang me if it isn't Momo looking gradely serious.

'Evan,' he go again, beckoning myself with cupped fingers to intimate I should step closer. 'Why he calling me Evan all formal-like?' I'm thinking, when wham! One wild flash of bright white light then it all goes dark and dead.

When I come to I'm laid out on a bare floor and there all these boys stood over me, snarling, glowering, rattling sabre. For real, man, they half of them waving machetes around, shouting themselves into a frenzy, 'cut him!', 'kill him!', all of this. I try to sit up, put my hand to the side of my head where it tender and this kid jump in and kicks me hard in the ribs, kicks me again, and again, until a older boy pull him back. It's the prison yard all over again, but all of these boys are tall and thin and black.

'Leave him!'

Momo appears from behind them, again the sour face, the frowning brow.

'Sit up, Evan.'

I can say for positive I'm in some grade of trouble if he persisting with calling me that. He crouch down right in my face.

'Where is she?'

I should twig, but I'm still half stunned. Mad, rabid screaming from one of the boys, 'where my sister?', 'where the fuck is she?', 'where my fucking sister?' . . . but it all woozy and disembodied like it just background noise. Momo jab his finger in my cheek.

'Where *is* she, Kavanagh?'

'Who?'

Crack! No backlift. No warning. Just smacks me with the back of his hand.

'You know who! The girl you come in here asking about is who. Red hijab. Misha. My niece . . .'

Oh dear. Oh dear, oh dear, oh dear . . . Shakespeare, you

fool. What you gone and done? I try to emit some kind of credible ignoramus vibe, hope they'll find some sympathy for a brother caught out of his depth.

'Momo, I had no idea, man . . . no idea. But honestly, honestly . . . this the God's honest truth, Momo. She turn up on my doorstep half dead and I give her shelter and clean her up then the next thing she gone. That's it, man! I got no clue at all where your girl be –'

Whack! Boot come in from the side. Bang! Another boot, the other side. Whack! Bang! Whack! All the shouting and hollering again. I go down and curl up in a ball.

'Cut him! Cut him!'

Crazy sounds of hate and lust for the kill. Feet shuffling and stamping, all these Somali boys closing in and bearing down on me, their eyes all wild and white. Misha's brother is right up at me, eyes open wide and mad, jabbering and poking me. I getting myself ready for my final curtains when Momo step in, one hand raised high like he some regal chief.

'Enough! Stand back!'

The lad stands back as Momo comes forward.

'When did you last see her?'

'Yesterday. When I come back from you . . .'

More muttering and arguing in the crowd. Some of the Somali boys pushing one another, flaring up in each other's faces. Momo shout something in Somali tongue and they shut up quick-quick. Misha's wild-eye brother step back all hangdog and told off. Momo back into my face.

'And? After you got back?'

'I tell her I been to see you, ask for help and that's it.'

'What happened?'

'She axed to use the phone, went down into the saloon and I ain't seen her since . . .'

Momo stands up, steps back, sucking his teeth and shaking

his head. The brother comes back with pure murder in his eyes – comes right up to me, puts the flat of his machete against my cheek. And woe betide me but I suddenly realise this is it. Old Evan going, here. I'm getting the chop. What a way to go. Slain. Bled to death on a lonely floor some place. No one to know. No one to mourn mine soul. I start to shake and I fight tight to stop myself whimpering. Dignity, Evan. Forbearance. They know not what they do.

Momo touches the boy's wrist and shakes his head.

'No.'

The lad is horrified like his dinner been taken away. Big, wild, scary eyes questioning Momo – why can't he chop me here and now?

'The police know he's been here.'

He carry on shaking his head, slowly, slowly, and I am doing all I can just to hang on to my load here.

'Mohammed, I didn't even know her *name* . . .'

Nothing back from him. Not even a glint of hope. As long as Momo got that solemn look and he shaking his head like that I'm thinking he'll just go – know what? Kill him anyway. But he doesn't. He walks away, still shaking his head, walks out the room. Shouts back.

'Throw him out.'

The sound of furious hissing as the room slowly comprehend there be no slaying today. They pull me up and they drag me down them stair – bump-bump-bump and I purely do not care. Bang! I'm out. Punch in the side, kick in back of leg, but I'm out, man. Fresh, wet, cold night air. I'm near to hysteria with joy and laughter. I swear to God I am sat there on the cold, damp pavement and I am crying tears of sheer relief and happiness. I gets up now and hauls myself away and out on to the Avenue, out of harm's way. I limp and stagger on a hundred yards and I collapse with the delayed shock of what has just occurred. I curl up outside a boarded-up house at the end of Beaconsfield and there's the statue right in front of me and I swear by Our Lord before me I have never been so pleased to drag myself back along the Boulevard, hurting every step, bruise all over. Never. But I still going to find that girl. Even if it *do* kill me.

McCartney

I wake up with a stone in my soul. Is this how it is going to be for me? In my professional life I'm admired, revered even, by some. I put myself on the line time and again. I have awards for valour, but away from the fray, I'm pathetic. Needs are submerged. Ignored. Left to my own devices I duck out, hide away and blow myself to oblivion, time after time. Last night, once again, walking the tightrope for a nanosecond, looking reality in the eye before falling, feebly, into fantasy's safety net. Another empty night, seeing to myself. Una. Kylene Kelly. Dreams, dreams, dreams. I haul myself out of bed. I look at myself a full long minute in the mirror. Why, McCartney? Why did you put yourself through that? Why do it to Una? You *knew* how it'd go. You knew. I decide there and then that, before I take a single step further on this case, the stubble is going to have to go.

I'm there in my usual chair at Alternatives, watching the rain drizzle down the big plate window, mulling on Derek Lambert's call last night. Should I go see him — just to make sure? No. What's he going to do? I'm his one port of call at the station. He's hardly going to go marching into the waiting room to stage a sit-in protest because I ignored his evidence, is he? As I acquiesce to the bite of the hot towel, I feel the vibration in my pocket. I'm into minute six of a full Dermalogica Skin Specific Facial with wet shave. This is where I do my strategic thinking, time away from the frenzy of the hub as I try to steer a course through this critical period ahead. I fear more for Misha every hour she is gone. The shipment is on its way, Una's heading off in the other direction, and the one sure thing I know is that, now more than ever before, Operation Samsun needs a lucky break.

My BlackBerry trembles again. I want to ignore it but, once you know there are messages pending, emails a-waiting, you may as well give up as gracefully as you can. I mug up an apologetic face for Natalie. She strips back the towel, gives me the sculptured eyebrow and beats a tactful retreat as I whip out the BB and scan the alert.

It's icliverpool. The *Echo*, one of my regular feeds. My stomach cramps as I compute the byline, and his story. Shit! Shit-shit-shit! Barnaby Giles. I was meant to call him back last night. My fault, completely – Una called and that was that – but the toerag has stiffed me big time. Under the banner headline of CITY SLAYING MYSTERY he's got a subheader reading: *Confusion over identity of cabbage-patch corpse* and goes on to say that although 'police sources' have ID'd the deceased as a nineteen-year-old Colombian national with links to Cali and Amsterdam, databases in neither city, nor here in Liverpool, have come up with any trace of a Raul Rodellega. I make my apologies to Natalie and step into the salon's little reception area. Giles isn't picking up. Surprise. I try Gilroy.

'Mal. It's McCartney. Jesus, mate! What the fuck happened there?'

'Billy. This has already gone way beyond the pale as it is. Please don't come wading in here with your language, throwing punches willy-nilly!'

'Mally – you saw through stiffs from gullet to arsehole each and every day, surely a little light banter –'

'Seriously. Enough. I'm in this way, *way* deep enough already without you turning gangster on me –'

'Deep enough? I'll say it's deep enough, mate! What happened with Raul Rodellega?'

'There was absolutely nobody on the database.'

'What? You're telling me you couldn't find *one* stiff with a drug conviction?'

'No! Not of the right age . . .'

'So you just invented someone. You made Rodellega up . . .'

'For crying out loud, Billy! What else *could* I do? You boys drag me out of bed at all hours of the night, compromise me in the most deplorable manner . . .'

His voice tails off. He takes a moment, then lightens his tone.

'Billy. Listen to me. I know this job stinks. I *know* you and the Hodge have to bend things this way and that to get the right result. But come on, fella – be reasonable! Have you even stepped back to think about what you asked me to do back there?'

I know. I know. He's right. We ask and we ask and we ask. Mal is a man of ethics – we shouldn't be putting him in this position. This is a rare sensation for yours truly. I am experiencing something not dissimilar to the thing they call guilt. Or, if not your actual heavy burden of conscience then I'm certainly more than a tad contrite. Sorry, Mal. I mean it, man. I'm dead, dead sorry about this – all of it. We asked you to 'hide' the body for us in the mortuary. We asked you to create a false identity for Kalan. I, for my part, asked you to disseminate that information in a manner that could only ever be distasteful and compromising, even for an old-stager like yourself. What we asked you to do for us was, as ever, beyond the call of duty. I can see that now. We've leant on you and leant on you and now you've snapped. And if the same set of circumstances came up all over again right this minute, I'd do the very same thing. Sorry, Mally – we're cops. We do what we have to do to stick the bad guys behind bars.

Damage limitation, McCartney. Damage limitation, then back to your blessed shave.

'Mal, you're right, you're right. Forgive me. I . . . I don't know what to say. I hope I'll be able to crack open a bottle with you next week and I'll tell you how this whole thing has panned out and how your own excellent work played such a massive part in nailing the bastards we're after. But one last thing, if I may . . .'

You can hear his sigh of despair from here to Lourdes Hospital.

'Go on . . .'

'If Alfie Manners or anybody else comes back to you on this issue, just insist you were right, will you? Tell them his student union card gave his name as Raul Rodellega. You can't say any more now because the last you heard Interpol were on their way to take up the reins. That's all you know, yes? That's the whole top and bottom of it as far as you're concerned. Can you do that for us, Mally?'

Silence.

'Mal?'

'Very well.'

'You're only a good 'un, mate.'

'If you say so.'

'I'll see you very soon.'

I hang up and make my excuses to Natalie and tell her I'll rebook the second my schedule allows. I bung her a score for her trouble.

Shakespeare

Big swollen lump under my eye socket as I look myself hard in the mirror, trying to ponder this thing through. I been mulling and looking at this from every possible side, and it comes down to this: from my very earliest days going in the Somali Club back in days of yore, I always thought of those boys as very particular people. Me, I always like the Somali lads a lot and I like their Somali Social Club even more. Looking at it now, opening up the club to all-hands was a pretty risky risk, but boy – it did work well! That whole thing of welcoming in the university students, the middle classes, the want-to-be free-thinking, hippy-type, left-wing Liverpool longhairs was something I loved to bits about the Somali. For those few years it was truly a special place to be, and Evan for one have some wonderful times there.

Here's the thing, though. I see plenty enough white girls there; young, pretty art students, studious ladies with spectacles, even punk-rocker girls when the seventies was on they last legs – but I can't say there was ever that many sisters there. Not Somali girl, uh-uh. So my point is this: while all the menfolk are taking care of business entertaining student and making beardy professors so homely there they stay late and spend big, where do we think the womenfolk be? I don't mean to say they sitting on the steps with a rolling pin or what have you, but it not unfair to surmise the ladies of the family stick together while the men out making bread, no? There going to be a real solid bond among those women and whatever been going on with my Misha, her mummy don't want to see her little girl wind up dead. Her sister, her lady cousin, her auntie, they going to be looking out for Misha, whatever been going down – and that's something I can work with. Give me a lachrymose aunt or a careworn sis and I swear old Evan can get a tune out of she. If I can bide my time and pick my moment to introduce myself in the right way, to the right lady, maybe but maybe she will throw me a line as to Misha's whereabouts and well-being. All I needs do now is find where such femme fatale reside.

Hodge

It's less than a month till my swansong in this hallowed profession, yet the wonders the job throws up never cease to amaze. This is just such a moment; among the most unsettling in recent memory. Five minutes ago I ended the call from Connolly's unctuous attorney John Prendergast and I realise now that I still have the receiver in my hand. I am sitting here perfectly erect, staring out of the window, shocked to the core. 'McCartney?' I ask myself as I belatedly replace the receiver. '*Et tu*, Billy? Surely, surely not.' In his call, Prendergast let it be known to myself that Mr Connolly is desirous of a meeting. Such a meeting, he assured me, will, if acted upon, reverberate upon the international drug trade on a scale seldom seen. The repercussions will be enormous – an exponential house of cards collapsing from Aberdeen to Amsterdam to Afghanistan is what he hinted at – yet it's the McCartney intrigue that has stunned me. I snap out of it, but still I find myself shaking my head in wonderment.

Terry Connolly. Well I never. I put it to Prendergast that, should this tête-à-tête take place, then its contents must be placed transparently on the record.

'As you wish,' said Prendergast with his customary reptilian disdain. Not for nothing is he known far and wide as Prenderghastly. 'But be aware that, should that record of the meeting become widely accessible, its impact will be nullified.'

'How so?' said I.

'Because you may well be shocked by some of the names my client brings to the table,' said he. 'Some of your own may very well be among them. Some of your finest.'

Tell me something I don't know, I smiled to myself.

'Noted. But I have to insist on one colleague being in attendance.'

'Namely?'

'Detective Chief Inspector William McCartney.'

A pause that narrators more skilled than I would describe as being 'pregnant'. One could feel the particles of each second tread glue before Ghastly came back to me.

'Him least of all.'

'I beg your pardon?'

'Mr Connolly respectfully suggests that the meeting could be compromised by that particular officer's attendance.'

'I'm sorry . . . your client specifically referenced DI McCartney?'

'That's my understanding.'

Which is why I sit here in silence, long after the call has ended and arrangements been made. *McCartney*? No. Never. I could name a hundred cops who've been at it, more or less, before Billy McCartney's name came up. A *thousand*. Without exception, those boys – and one or two young ladies, as well – have hit what we used to call their waterline back then. Something one was schooled to look out for as you made your way through the ranks, the waterline; that moment of disappointment or disillusionment that deviates an individual's career away from the straight and narrow, and off in a dangerous direction. The tipping point would be the expression today, but the principle is the same. A thwarted promotion. An illness or accident. Sometimes just an awful job experience can leave the best of coppers searching their souls and asking what it's all about. Very, very often in those circumstances the cop will be found with his hand out; sometimes even going over to the other side. McCartney, though? Bent? I genuinely, severely doubt it. We've had our moments, Billy and I, especially after that business with Operation Tango – but we soldiered on. Without making a big thing of it, McCartney and I put our differences to bed long, long ago. At least I thought we had.

McCartney

Well, that was a complete waste of time, wasn't it? One thing I cannot abide about this job is all the lefties and intellectuals you have to deal with who think they're better than everyone else. It's written all over their superior, smug faces – these wankers think they are literally, by virtue of their supreme fucking intellect, above and beyond the law. They think they can see through us; see past. They think they know it all. Some strung-out baghead comes smashing through their conservatory, though, and who they gonna call? Yep siree. 999. Emergency. What took you so long? I'm a taxpayer! This Peter Williamson phoney, Misha and Kalan's lecturer or professor or whatever he wants to call himself – he thinks he's striking a blow for the liberal world the way he looks down his nose at me. He stops about a millimetre short of outright belligerence, but it's obvious he thinks helping the police with their inquiries is some latent expression of fascism. I'm half amused by him, blinking rapidly as he tries to think up his smart answers, but after a while I'm just plain bored of his oh-so-predictable obstructions.

'To sum up then, sir, there is nothing whatsoever you're able to tell me that might help me locate your missing student Misha Ibrahima . . .'

He twitched when I said '*your* missing student' and he's straight back on the defensive.

'That's if Misha is, indeed, missing. Something we have yet to establish, I understand . . .'

I've got half a mind to give him a light grilling. I could turn that back on him and give it: 'Oh? So you *have* had information . . .?' But in the real world my time is precious and the truth is I can only start living again the moment I leave this chippy academic in my wake.

'Thank you for your time, Professor Williamson.'

'Not at all,' he snaps. He spins on his heel and strides off. I shake my head. Funny old world.

On my way out of the lecture theatre, my eye is taken by a girl sat reading. Headscarf. Full outfit. When I say my eye is taken by her, it goes further and deeper than that. What I mean is that my second sense, my inner-vision, my instinct – whatever you want to call that innate scanning device that comes as standard with all born cops – picks up a reading from her as I pass. This kid has something to tell me. She *wants* me to engage with her.

As I get closer I can see – along with the fact she wears steel-rimmed spectacles and suffers from medium-to severe-level acne – that the poor kid is hunched defensively and looks absolutely terrified. I stand over her.

'Hello.'

I can give good smile when I need to. On some base level I'm predisposed towards good humour – just that I never get chance to express myself. The Muslim girl tries to force a smile back.

'I'm Detective Chief Inspector Billy McCartney. Can I sit down?'

'Fatima.'

She keeps her eyes glued to the floor but indicates I can sit. From the corner of my peripheral vision I can see Williamson at the end of the corridor. He jerks his head in pique and stalks away.

'Fatima. Thanks. So . . .'

She shakes her head very slowly. I can see a build-up of tears under her specs. Instinctively, I want to put my arm around her.

'Was there something you wanted to tell me?'

She nods. More tears. I'm acutely aware I'm supposed to proffer a starched white handkerchief at moments like this, but preferring to keep my red Lanvin equivalent purely for decorative purposes I find myself subconsciously fingering it deeper down into my breast pocket.

'Take your time, Fatima. There's absolutely no hurry. No pressure at all . . .'

She sighs out loud and, still slowly shaking her head from left to right, left to right, she addresses the floor.

'There's nothing much. I knew . . .'

She realises what she's said. Her eyes spike up with yet more tears. She removes her specs, wipes the tears away, composes herself.

'I know Misha pretty well. Haven't spent so much time with her since she met Kalan, but . . . we've been in all the same classes since we started . . .'

'And when was that?'

'Just over a year ago.'

'Thanks, Fatima. That's great . . .'

I just sit there, the patron saint of patience. The sheer physicality of the silence drives her on. She takes a deep breath, holds it, thinks about what she's saying.

'It's nothing really. Well – it may be. But it's just . . . she's an old-fashioned girl, Misha. She used to tell me all about Kalan, their meetings, the way they fell in love . . . They weren't in a . . . physical relationship. Yet.'

'They weren't?'

Somehow that kills me. I don't want to believe Kalan's had his life snuffed out before he's tasted its delights.

'What about the flat? What was that for, if not . . .'

'They just wanted somewhere they could go. They both knew their families would never . . .' She chews on her lip, looks up to the ceiling for strength. The tears are flowing freely again. 'I'm sorry . . .' She stifles a sob, and fixes her eyes on me. 'Kalan and Misha had both become converts to Sufism. They needed a place . . .' She shakes her head.

'Take your time. You're doing very well . . .'

Fatima shrugs and tries to steel herself.

'Most of what I know, I only know from Misha trying to turn me on to it. Sufism embraces a form of asceticism. Followers are encouraged to simplify their lives and purify their souls . . .'

I know, or I knew, a little of Sufism from my first sessions with Rebecca, long, long ago. But that was more of a psychiatrist's view of the faith — a shrink's organic approach to coaxing me out of the shell whence I lurked. I nod for Fatima to continue.

'The purification aspect is open to interpretation. The common understanding of it is this notion of the whirling dervish, spinning himself to a state of higher consciousness as a means of cleansing his soul. I'm not saying that's incorrect, but it's a very crude representation. There's variance among practitioners but, in essence, the idea is that one cannot love fully if one is harbouring sin . . .'

That might throw some light on Kalan's seeming need to confess the sins of his family, I'm thinking to myself — but other than that I'm struggling to see where this is taking us.

'And of course two nations where Sufism still has a strong following are Somalia . . .' She eyes me with all the gravitas she can summon. '. . . and the former Persia.'

'Of which Kurdistan, spiritually and historically, forms a part. Fascinating. Thank you, Fatima. This is tremendous . . .'

'I hope it helps,' she mumbles, all shy and resentful again.

'It will do. I'm certain of it. Thanks.'

As soon as I'm out in the car park I call Smithson.

'Lucy . . .'

Slight hesitation from her, then: 'It's Lucinda, sir. Or Smithson. I –'

I over-chuckle to let her know I understand.

'No problem. I know where you're coming from. Really . . . I've been there.'

'Thank you, sir.'

'So. I'm wondering if you'll do something absolutely confidential for me?'

A worried laugh back from Smithson. 'So long as it's not illegal . . .'

'Far from it – though its efficacy would be diluted if *anybody* were to know your business. Do we understand one another?'

'I think so, sir.'

'Just work on the basis that only you and I are to know, for now, and you won't go far wrong.'

'Very well, sir.'

'Good. Good. OK. What I need you to do is check out the entire region for Sufi centres. S-U-F-I, as in the religion . . .'

'It's more of a faith, sir . . .'

Although she can't see me, I'm smiling here. She's good, this kid; she reminds me of me. If I ever get one of the top, top jobs I'll be taking her with me.

'Excellent. *Mea culpa.*'

'How far afield would you have me look, sir?'

'Far and wide, if you will, Lucinda. Smithson. Manchester. Leeds. Maybe as far as Birmingham . . .'

'Am I looking for anything specific, sir?'

I'd love to tell her. I know she wouldn't let me down. Need to know, though. Need to know.

'Just the contact names and telephone numbers for now please, Smithson.'

'I'm on it, sir.'

Once again I experience that delicious frisson that emanates from Smithson's excitement at doing this, and doing it well. I wish her luck and return to the kart. I fire her up and begin to edge out of the packed-tight car park. As I'm waiting to turn right into Myrtle Street my heart drops stone dead as one Alfred Manners passes, turning left into the university car park. I curse myself that, although I've left Fatima with my card, I don't have her own number to call her and warn her. I've made the most basic error of all here. I've under-estimated the opposition. If it wasn't already, finding Misha is now a matter of life and death. Hers.

Shakespeare

Well, that turn out easy as cake, man. I dress me down in my least eye-catching of outfits and I bide my time and wait it out. They spill out from the centre, fighting one another, joshin' one another, messin' around this and that, and not one of them look up to see Shakespeare Private Eye on them tail. It not as though I have to wear any exquisite disguise or something; they never so much as turn round once. I follow them along Jermyn Street and across Kingsley Road towards the new estate. New estate! Thirty years or more been here now — near as long as Shakespeare. They start into one last mock-fight as they commence splitting up and filtering off left and right into their side streets, but my boy, the one who said 'Where my sister?' accompanied by the flat of a blade on my querulous cheek — he weaves through the estate and out on to the Lane itself and in through the door of one of the shops by the bus stop. I give it a second then carry on right past and check through the window — and the boy is jostling with a girl at the counter. Happy days. If Shakespeare get his act together this going to be one easy piece.

I wait a few minutes more, check back through the window

and gratify myself that the coast be clear before I pop my head through the door.

'Miss . . .'

My jaw still tender when I speak. I checking behind me and all over the place, make sure no crazed dervish going to come running at me again.

'Miss . . . Please . . .'

I jerking my head for she to come out from behind the counter, join ol' Evan outside. I know, I know – stupidity and naivety in the extreme. How long I live here? Indeed. And here's me on one of the livelier streets in one of the livelier barrios in town, jerking my head like a rude boy, inviting the proprietor of a grocer's store to kindly step out into the road while I quickly ransack her shop. *Evan!*

I step inside, try to look as simpatico as I can muster so as to get my message across as succinct and appealing I can.

'OK. Listen,' I whisper at her. Girl just stare at me, dumbfounded. 'I here to help, hear me? I trying to help your sister. Misha.'

The girl hand shoot to her mouth. I take one step closer, but I don't want to scare the little lady. I'm holding both hands up, palms out to her like one of those police negotiators want a nutter put their gun down.

'It's OK. It's fine. Misha stayed at mine . . .'

Can't stop myself. I'm glancing left, right and all around, all over again. I soften my voice even quieter yet.

'The other night. When it all happened? Yes?'

Breakthrough. The girl nodding. Hallelujah!

'Good. OK. So now you know who you dealing with. I'm the one who took her in and dressed her cuts.'

She give me one long solemn look then bow her head oh-so slightly.

'Thank you.'

Voice so quiet you could hardly hear the girl. But she speaking to me. She speaking.

'The very least old Evan could do in the circumstances. But look. We got to work together. And we got to work quick-quick. They some real bad pennies on her case, seen? And we can't let them get to she . . .'

Girl seem to think on it then she nod once, decisive, and usher me outside. We walk briskly up Lodge Lane, but she suddenly take me by the wrist and pull me back. There's a couple of boys coming up towards us, too busy in their dispute to even look up, but she frightened just the same. We turn left at the old library then right again and out on to Parly, girl face stricken the whole time. It's only when we past the Baby Hospital that she comes back to life, so to speak. She stops, eyes darting this way, that way, then settle upon myself.

'OK. You've got one minute. Shoot.'

She posher even than her Misha. These girls getting brought up *good*! The sister's name Sagal and once I tell her what I tell her, the relief comes pouring out of her, just to be able to put two and two together.

'Right,' she snaps. 'They'll be looking for me by now anyway. In for a penny, in for a pound.'

She no fool. She tell me she can make no promises, other than that she gonna try speak to her sister and check me out with she. If Misha want to see me, so be it. She looking all around now, like someone about to pounce. She whispers to me that I should meet her outside the main entrance to the Belvedere Girls' School at 5 p.m. If Misha amenable to a powwow, Sagal going to be there at the school gates to give me further details. If not, then not. She hesitates a second and I swear she was going to kiss me, but she turn and start running along down Parliament Street and out of sight. I walk on down the same direction and look up at the great hulking mass of the cathedral and I pray to God they sisters going to be all right.

McCartney

I realise I've already lost this one the moment I drive on past the Boubou. All the way there I've been trying to rationalise it – trying to *visualise* how, in practical terms, I'll go about the business of stepping up to Misha's family and asking them: 'When did you last see your daughter?'

And it's one of those – you get so far and then your head closes down on you. I can't visualise this one because there's nothing *real* to go on. When push comes to shove, I have no grounds whatsoever for questioning anyone. In everyday detective work, you have to have the courage of your convictions. Even when you harbour doubt, you have to proceed as though your assumptions are rock solid and it's only a question of time before your suspect caves in and confirms what your instincts told you.

And what if Misha is tucked away somewhere, anyway – safe and sound and out of harm's way? What happens if I go blundering into the Ibrahim family and alert them to a situation they may know nothing about? Kalan, the flat, their Sufi faith, their plans together . . . what if they knew nothing at all of this and decide to go after the Rozakis themselves? When it all comes down to it, I don't know what I stand to gain from any confrontation with the Somalis. I don't know what I want from it – so I carry on driving and, purely on autopilot, turn left into Sefton Park Road and on into Lodge Lane.

I cruise past the shop – Closed sign is up – and head on towards the Boundary (never a name more apt) when the phone goes. It's Smithson.

'Don't suppose you're anywhere near Edge Lane, are you, sir?'

'Round the corner. Why?'

I can hear the gush of excitement in her voice.

'Bit of a result on the Sufi front, sir . . .'

'Go on . . .'

'OK, so, listen to this . . . the Nur Ashki Jerrahi Order is *the* up-and-coming branch of the Sufi faith . . .'

'How on earth . . .'

I'd swear she shushed me there, the insubordinate wretch!

'The order has communities all over North America, all over the world, practically, yet there's only one branch here in the UK. Guess where?'

'My word, Smithson, I'm getting the strangest sensation . . . it wouldn't happen to be here in sunny Liverpool, would it?'

'That it would, sir!'

'And I may well be running away with myself here, but . . . I can't escape this wild supposition that they base themselves somewhere around Edge Lane?'

'In one.'

She gives me the address.

'Sir . . . I was wondering . . .'

'Yes?'

'Apologies, sir. Nothing.'

'You want to know what this is all about, don't you?'

'I do, sir. Yes. If that's . . .'

I think about it. I really could do with the extra pair of hands. But, no – Manners wheedled that fax away from her without having to move into second gear. Only Hodge and myself know anything about Misha in all this – best it stays that way. What Lucinda Smithson doesn't know can't harm her.

'I'll fill you in as soon as I'm able, Smithson. But thanks for your help with this. Really.'

I end the call and head for Edge Lane.

Hodge

So. On the same day we had the nightmare regarding one promising law student, it seems Cambridge CID was doing everything possible – everything *legal* – to hush up another. The coroner's report confirmed that Emma Connolly, a final-year law student at Trinity College, had self-injected heroin of a purity that could have felled an elephant. Initial inquiries suggest that Emma left her room in Great Court at 8.35 a.m., ostensibly heading out to a lecture at the Law Faculty, a mere stroll away out through the Backs. She deviated from that route, though, turning right instead of left on to Queen's Road. The cleaner at the Punter public house saw a woman matching her description pass by around that time, certainly before 9 a.m., probably en route to her dealer's flat in Honey Hill. Said dealer is now being questioned in Cambridge where one hopes, for the chap's own safety, he is swiftly charged and incarcerated. Even within those walls, one suspects he will not last long.

The next sighting of Emma Connolly came at 10.10 a.m. when she was found dead. Emma overdosed and died quickly and alone in the alleyway behind her dealer's flat. Her father, Terence 'Top Cat' Connolly, a successful businessman, drove down from Liverpool to identify the body. He was, and is, inconsolable at the loss of his youngest child – the apple of his eye. He has sworn to Emma's mother, his third wife, Patricia, that he will hunt down the bastards who have been selling Emma that shit. This is why we fear for the dropout from Honey Hill. What the elegant Trish may not be aware of is that 'that shit' will have Scouse thumbprints all over it, even in sleepy Cambridge. And 'those bastards' will be, directly or indirectly, part of her Terry's extensive network of wrong 'uns, wretches and drug-dealing scoundrels. As she sobs forlornly in her Formby mansion, Patricia *must* surely wonder whether Emma's own father has played some part in her downfall. And while denial is the default setting for so many of these affluent career criminals, one assumes that Connolly himself understands his own complicity in his daughter's death. Why else would he be here?

Regardless, I can't claim our meeting was anything other than difficult. Physically, morally, emotionally, it's tough watching any man drown   even when that man is as evil as Terry Connolly. He sits there in his golfing attire, head bowed, and it's hard to reconcile this baffled, beaten, heartbroken bag of bones with one of Interpol's Most Wanted. Yet one gets the distinct impression this has done for Terry Connolly. He wants to spill the beans. He wants to claw something back from the abyss; try belatedly to make at least one tiny part of the world he's destroyed right again. I've done that dance a thousand times, and I genuinely believe he's for real here. Poor old, washed-out, used-up Top Cat Terry has had his day.

'I mean it, Hubert. That's me. Finished.'

I find it unsettling having to deal with Connolly at the best – the worst – of times. It has been a noisome accident of the job that one occasionally encounters TC at functions and, embarrassingly, on the fairways of Birkdale and the Royal Liverpool. I prefer my villains to talk tough. Broken noses. Scars. Silly nicknames. He's supplied the latter, but he's long since affected the tone and timbre of a mid-ranking barrister, over-enunciating his words and accompanying every other observation with a florid hand gesture and a roll of the eyes, like he's some sage, some intellectual powerhouse. Worst of all his trying affectations, I gravely resent his calling me by my first name – in any circumstances. Implicit in that is a suggestion that, for all that we've ploughed different furrows on opposing sides of the fence, we've grown up together. We're not so dissimilar after all. There's respect. Let me be abundantly clear. I have utterly no respect whatsoever for Terence Connolly and his ilk. I despise him. Despise *them*. Connolly has been a serious, consistent threat to public safety for at least fifty of his near-seventy years preying on society – and I would dearly love, even at this late stage of his life, to detain him at Her Majesty's pleasure for the rest of his days. He's a wrong 'un, Connolly, and *no* mistake. That said, there's no denying his proposition is enticing.

'I'll hand them to you, Hubert. I'll gift-wrap them. But you have to do right by me too.'

'In what way should I "do right" by you, Terry?'

I'll be honest here – TC does *not* look well. What he says comes as slim surprise to me.

'Let me live my days out. I haven't got long . . .'

'You know I can't make assurances of that nature.'

'It's my understanding you can.'

He's right, of course. I can cut a deal. The reason I have insisted on this initial exploratory conversation being informal, without the presence of his odious lawyer, is that I have no wish to cut him any kind of deal at all. My plan was to coax Connolly into a state of contrition; let him acknowledge and own the misery he has wreaked, culminating in the demise of his gifted and beautiful daughter. Acceptance is the first step to acquiescence and, once I have him where I want him, the theory is that he will voluntarily and substantially cough up the whole parcel. Get them singing at all, we're told, and you'll get them singing beautifully. I should have known better with Terry Connolly. He studies his fingernails casually.

'Let's not play games here, Hubert. Your side is in dear and desperate need of information. My side may potentially be able to supply some of the detail you're lacking.'

Now he jerks his head up to face me and it all becomes horribly clear. His expression is cold, deathly. There isn't a shred of regret behind this approach. Quite simply, he wants no-strings revenge on the Rozakis. He's blaming them for Emma's death, he wants them gone and he'll no doubt do very nicely out of the situation once they're removed from the equation. I lean forward and speak quietly.

'Then your side, so to speak, is going to have to be good. It's going to have to be *very* good.'

And it was. It is. His information is fascinating. Woefully misguided in some of the detail yet dynamite in its implications nonetheless. One could best summarise as follows. The Rozakis know, have known for some time, that their operation has been breached. They don't yet know who, but someone has been feeding us the inside track on their operation. By a process of elimination, they've narrowed down their prime suspects to three potential snitches – one of whom is a high-ranking police officer. But rather than weed out the rat and eliminate him, they've used the mole to their own advantage. They've been feeding their whole operation a line, knowing it'll end up back in our laps. The Puroil delivery we've been pinning all our hopes upon is a ghost run. It's bullshit. It'll come up duff. We'll have eighty men surrounding the Rozakis' petrol station and we'll give it the full pantomime:

'On the floor! On the floor! Face down! Put your hands where I can see them, NOW!'

Everything – handcuffs, searchlights, oxyacetylene cutters, sniffer dogs, cameras, perhaps even a cameo from our man at the *Echo* Barnaby Giles . . . and there'll be nothing. Nothing but a big fat grin from that hideous playboy Dara Rozaki and a dirty great claim for compensation from his brother. Just as happened with another enormous drugs haul that came to a sticky end, years ago. McCartney did the surveillance on that one too.

Connolly is relishing every moment of this, and who can

blame him? The operation we've spent so long – and so much money – putting together, layer by layer, stitch by stitch, is about to come apart at the seams. But just as I'm about to scream out loud and smash my fist into the wall, Connolly's calculating eyes glitter again. He holds up the palm of one hand.

'However. Before we all don sackcloth and head for the wilderness in despair, let us not forget the nature of the beast . . .'

'Speak plainly, if you will, Terry,' I sigh.

He's beaming at me, the bastard. He thinks he's got me.

'Well, it's nothing revolutionary, Hubert . . .'

Every time he says my name, I shudder. God speed me through this – please.

'. . . they're drug dealers. Plain and simple. Pure and evil. That's what they do. Just because they've rumbled your – forgive me for saying so – slightly amateurish attempts to spring a surprise on them doesn't mean they're going to leave a shipload of grade A rotting on the quayside. No, no, NO, Hubert! This ain't Lance Campion you're dealing with. Perish the thought!'

I experience something akin to a flash of glee.

'The drugs are still coming?'

He comes over all affronted – so much so he's almost camp. His eyes are wide and, one feels compelled to say, somewhat crazed. He tilts his head back and gives me what is intended to be, I am certain, a very serious stare.

'Shall we talk terms, Hubert?'

If only to cease the flow of loaded 'Huberts' from his lips, I indicate a willingness to hear him out. He says he'll give us the precise location, timing and method of the imminent delivery upon receipt of written confirmation of our '*entente*', as he insists upon calling this tawdry conspiracy. Furthermore, he undertakes to cooperate in the handing over of every last shekel he's made from his septic trade, even though he knows and I know there'll be tens of millions salted away and he'll live like a king for however long his medics can keep him hanging on. He says he'd like the sequestered money to go into a major drug rehabilitation programme in his daughter's name, but acknowledges he'll have no input into the destination of that portion of his millions he allows us to discover.

'Pleased you came?' he smiles, his ludicrous pink Lyle & Scott jumper giving me hot flushes.

'I wouldn't state it so strongly, Terry, no. But it's certainly not nothing.'

If only you knew who the snitch was, I muse to myself. He thinks about lighting a fag, remembers he's supposed to be dying. I get up to go and, in finest Columbo style, hit him with my most earnest stare.

'One final thing, before I go away to give your proposal serious consideration, Terry. Given how few people were in possession of any precise detail of our operation against the Rozakis, I see utterly no potential for any leaks at our end. Are you absolutely certain there's a mole?'

'*Hubert!*' He's enjoying his moment in the sun. He's laughing in my face. 'I'm surprised at you!'

'Don't be. Enlighten me, instead. Show me I should I take you seriously . . .'

That wipes the smile off the bastard's face. He tries to come over all reasonable now.

'*Think* about it . . .'

I give the matter due pause.

'Manners.'

He's shaking his head, tut-tut-tutting as he looks gravely at the floor.

'Alfie Manners is strictly small time, Hubert. Always has been. Always will be.'

This comes as no surprise, but no small relief either, I don't mind admitting. The Manners question is one I must address emphatically before my curtain call.

'So what's his interest in all of this?'

'Same as it ever was for Alfie Manners. He's moonlighting, isn't he, for a few dollars more. Told you. He's fuck all. Alfie's job is to reunite Kalan Rozaki with his ever-loving family, end of story.'

I chance my arm.

'I don't believe he's known to us. Which one is Kalan?'

'Their kid brother. The straight one.'

'He's gone missing, has he?'

TC shrugs and hold his palms outwards and upwards.

'So they say. Probably off on a dirty weekend somewhere, hey?'

'Don't see why that's a matter for Alfie Manners . . .'

'Like I say, Hubert. Who knows how the Rozakis think. No doubt they have high hopes the kid brother will see the error of his ways and put his legal expertise to the benefit of the family business one day?'

Good, excellent – at least we have that one in the bank for the time being. The Rozakis don't know what's happened, do they? They think Kalan's done a runner, plain and simple – and by God we have to keep it that way. Connolly brings his arms back down theatrically, and seeks out my gaze.

'But not if I have my way he won't, eh? There'll be no family business left for Kalan Rozaki to preside over by the time we're all done and dusted here.'

So they still believe Kalan's alive. Good. One needs to think and act decisively here. If and when the Rozakis find out how their little brother was chased down like game and butchered in the shadows of Sefton Park, there will be reprisals on a murderous scale. There'll be all-out war. I really do not have any choice but to deal with Terry Connolly – and quickly.

'Terry. Let's not play games here. This has to work . . . for both of us. I'll do my very best for you – but you have to give me a little more.'

I fix my eyes upon him – a small, wiry, bird-like man. A fixer for the international drug trade. A baddie, all his life.

'How did the Rozakis find out we were on to them?'

His beady eyes bore into me. There's an intelligence there, an animal cunning. What a waste – he could have been a captain of industry. I dare say he *was*, in his chosen field. He lowers his eyeline, drops his head down, clasps his hands between his knees and shakes his head again before coming back up, smiling sadly.

'Human error. It's the cause of over ninety per cent of all accidents.'

'Connolly . . .'

He looks wounded at the sudden formality, the reminder that he's a crook, going down.

'Think about it, Hubert. Apart from yourself, who else knew about the Puroil tanker shipment?'

'Hardly anyone. The team at the CPS. And DCI McCartney.'

'See what I mean?'

'*McCartney?*'

He shrugs and looks away. I'm not so sure my ailing ticker can take many more of these jolts to the system.

McCartney

I'm sat in silence in the kart, drumming my fingers on the wheel, unsure whether to spark her up or go back in for another pop at the delightful Hari from Finland. Five minutes after leaving the centre I can't make my mind up about the beatific Hari. On the face of things he was so open and affable that we already know where he's from (Tampere), why he's here (chose Liverpool University through his dual love of music and football) and what brought him to Sufism (a growing disillusionment with said superpowers of music and football). He freely admitted that Misha and Kalan were regulars there at the House. My clumsy references to 'church' and 'worship' were the only words that, albeit briefly, wiped that smile off Hari's face – along with 'thanks, but no' when I declined the meditation CD he offered at the special introductory rate of £15.99 – but he was resolute in his assertion that he had seen neither kid since the weekend.

I check my phone. Missed calls from Smithson. No message. I edge out into the new dual carriageway and make an illegal U-turn back on to Edge Lane and hard left into Botanic Road for a short cut back to base. An autumnal gust sends golden and yellow-brown leaves all over the windscreen and suddenly I'm wanting. I can go for hours on end, hardly give it a thought, then something will drag me back to the crashing reality of who I am and what I need just to get me through the day.

I pull over in the furthest corner of the overflow car park. I retrieve my pouch from the glove compartment, unzip it all the way round and flip it open on my lap. I ease out the works I prepared earlier, slide back the seat and take care of myself. Had I glanced up at HQ, I might have seen a silhouette in the window. Possibly. Had I waited a little longer, I'd have seen that selfsame figure emerge from the main car-park entrance. Definitely. I would have seen her wait impatiently until it was safe to cross. And I would have spied Police Constable Lucinda Smithson approaching the kart, a combination of anxiety and excitement on her face. Had I looked up I would have seen that look die with her spirits as Smithson witnessed my ritual – but I sat back, instead, as the hit rushed through me, and I didn't see her slope away, crushed.

Shakespeare

Sagal there at the school gates, like she said. She look me up and down.

'I see you went for the inconspicuous approach . . .'

Make Evan smile to hear a little thing like she, only from the Lane but, good girl, she talk like she to the manor born. I go to her, big smile to show all is well.

'One try one's best, my dear . . .'

I hold out my hand to Sagal, but she don't shake it, steps back a pace instead.

'How do I know I can trust you?'

I blow out the bridge of all sighs and shake my head at the girl. Honesty is the best policy, I thinking here.

'Truth is you don't, I guess. But I want to help you. I want to help Misha.'

'Why?'

Good question. That's a very good question indeed. Why I want to help she? Is it solely and only because she so easy on the eye? No. Little bit of that, course it is. Shakespeare not Shakespeare if he stop seeing the beauty all around him. But happen the truth be more than that; the more I gettin' old, the more I try to do the right thing. I close my eyes tight but it don't keep the recollection from seeping back in. Last time I had a chance to help save a young beauty, look what took place. Shame on you, Evan Kavanagh. It's one thing to say you will never help the police. One thing to pledge they will never, never, never make you bow down. But what if that pledge become the cause of ruining a young girl's life . . . shame on you, Evan Kavanagh. Never again. I open up my eyes and Sagal still there.

'Because I can. I can help she . . .'

She don't look no happier. I take a step closer.

'You just going to have to make your mind up on that one,

219

Sagal. All I can tell you is what I already told you. I'm worried for your sister. I think I can help she – and I *want* to help.'

She stare me out – beautiful cow's eyes, she got, never blink once – then slowly start to nod her head.

'OK. Fair enough . . .' She power-breathing through the emotions, steadies herself and pushes back the tears. 'Suppose I don't have any choice.'

She jerks her head for myself to follow she, and start off walking at a real pace.

McCartney

The blower tinkles the ivories. It's Lambert.

'Ah! The good Inspector himself. How goes it?'

'Satisfactory thank you, Derek. Was there something?'

'I'd be glad of a meeting with yourself, if at all possible.'

'Is a meeting really necessary? Just tell me what it is, and –'

'I think it does justify a PA from your good self, all things considered . . .'

I try to smooth the irritation out of my voice.

'OK, Derek. Tell me why?'

'Because I've gone to some lengths and some trouble to identify and download a particular sound for you . . .'

He sounds a bit slurred. That self-conscious verve he's striving for is already slipping away.

'It'd be rude in my humble opinion, if you was to merely ignore what I've gone and done for you after the troubles I've been to –'

'OK, OK, OK. I apologise. And I do appreciate the call –'

'Good. Because this noise, right . . .'

The last bit is just one long slurring noise, like he's fallen asleep in mid-sentence.

'Noise, Derek? Can you give me little bit more to go on?'

'That's what I'm trying to do!'

He sounds alert again, angry.

'When I was walking through the park, isn't it? I heard our good friends the thingio doctors . . . tree surgeons!'

He breaks off into this hideous cackling fit.

'Ha-ha-ha! Wonder if they put on them green outfits and give the tree a nice hit of morphine and that, ha-ha-ha! A nice analgesic and what have you — anaesthetic to put the old silver birch off to sleep before they lop its arms and legs off.'

He sounds as though he is seriously going to piss himself laughing, then, just like that, as if he's just a jobbing actor playing several roles he's suddenly serious again.

'Yeah, so like I'm saying to you, that's what thingio'd me — that's the noise what I heard on the night in question . . .'

'What are you saying, Derek? You heard a tree-saw?'

'Nah, nah, *listen*, will you? It weren't that. Not exactly. That's why I've done what I've done for you, see?'

I don't see. I want this loon off the phone, pronto.

'Derek, mate . . .'

'I've been right through them all, haven't I? All the sound effects libraries, your Sounddogs.com, Loopmasters, every audio file known to man and boy for all the *comparable* sounds . . .'

Oh dear me. I can just *see* his eyelids fluttering madly, his wiry hands dipping and diving.

'OK. Appreciate it, Derek, really. I'm pretty mad busy at the minute, yeah? But I promise I'll get to you as soon as I get a second. You still at the Bedford?'

Hesitation.

'No. No, I'm elsewhere as of this . . . as of now . . .'

He's been kicked out. It's a nap. Found using on the premises. The Bedford, for all its hippy tomfoolery and bearded care workers operates a one-strike policy. They'll have found Lambert at it — nailed on — and given him his marching orders.

'Fair enough. Where will I find you then, Derek?'

'I'm at Barton tonight. Just tonight, mind you . . . sort meself out tomorrow with a proper . . .'

'Where's Barton, Derek?'

'Barton Lodge. Just off of Parliament Street . . .'

I resent his dozy voice; his lazy, voguish 'off of' and the fact that he seems to think I'm at his beck and call, but I note the address and reassure him I'm on my way. It's a moment of supreme joy to me when I'm finally able to get him off the phone.

Manners

Same old, same old. Moz Rozaki looking at me like I'm pigeon shit on his Hugo Boss lapel. Like I've been holding back information.

'And this girl . . . how long?'

I just stare at him for clues. Dara gets up off the table he's been perched on, his toes pointing down and resting on the tiles. He ambles across, gives my arm a little squeeze.

'How long is our Kalan meant to have been seeing this Misha one, Alfie?'

'Dunno. Not long, like. The bird . . . her mate at the college, like – kept bursting out crying and that. But definitely not long. She reckoned they just went to church and that together . . .'

Moz gives me his worst scowl.

'Church . . .'

Dara talks right over him.

'But she was with Kalan last time this girl saw him?'

'That's what I'm saying, Dara. This . . .' I flicks a quick look at my notes. 'This Fatima, yeah? She seen the pair of them getting on the 86 right after class.'

'Which was?'

'Which was about a quarter past five.'

'On Tuesday?'

At last! A bit of appreciation from the hard-faced pair of so-and-sos.

'Exactly. Five fifteen on Tuesday, boarding a bus in the direction of Mossley Hill. We find the bird, we find Kalan!'

I snap my notebook shut for effect and stand there, dead straight, a fella who delivers what he says he's going to. Dara looks at Moz. Moz pulls his usual deadpan face. He gets up from behind his desk.

'Do it,' he goes. That's it. Just walks out without another word. Dara's stood there, little bit awkward. Gives us a little playful jab.

'You heard the man, Alfie. Go find that lady . . .'

I give him my best, can-do front, but fuck that, I'm fucked now, aren't I? What I haven't told the brothers is that this Misha piece is a Somali chick. Precisely. The one firm who has never had, *will* never have, anything to do with the boys in blue is your Somali clan. How the fuck am I expected to find her? Walk down Granby Street like Bruce Willis in that *Die Hard*, placard tied around me saying: *Lost. Cooness. Any idea, lad?*

I don't think so. I grabs my bunce and get on out of there. I think it's time to call it a day with this little firm. Judging the exit moment is a proper fucking skill of its own in this game and the heat is getting way too hot for this boy's liking. The Rozaki lads want to track that Misha down, they're welcome to try. Alfie's out. Over.

Shakespeare

We right across Aigburth Road and weaving down the little side streets towards St Michael's. I speed-walking here, just to keep up.

'Whoa-whoa, slow it down, sister! Make allowance for the youth-challenged!'

That brings a smile to her little face. Skin so tight and beautiful. Ol' Evan would have them like that all day long, once upon a time. She slow her step some del.

'Where we headed?' I gasp.

'Why? So you can tell your mafia friends?'

I just laugh. No one says 'mafia'.

'I wish I could pick an' choose,' I say. 'But I haven't got no friends mafia or otherwise . . . only people want to beat old Shakespeare and tie me up . . .'

She smiling again.

'I can see the appeal in that . . .'

Good. Good! We finally breaking the ice.

'I'll just shut up and do what I'm told then, shall I?'

'You're learning.'

We get down to St Michael's train station, and after waiting no time at all, along come the loud yellow Merseyrail trolley and we on it and away. Crazy to say, looking out the window over the slow-pulling river, but I never been on the local trains even once since I come to Liverpool – not one time. It pretty enough, too. The train scoot right by all the fancy old houses and the new yuppie estates, out through the old Garden Festival part of the riverfront. I'm just settling down looking out over Otterspool fields, away to the oil terminals and what have you on the other banks of the river, when she up and saying this us. This where we getting off. Pity. Was enjoying the ride and the education.

Cressington is another big surprise. Two mile if that from Liverpool 8, but I never even hear of this place. It hardly a place at all from what I can see. The station so to speak is just a ornate old sandstone folly – nothing much more than a platform, a hollow old waiting room and a little bowed bridge like something from the Father Brown mysteries. I lapped those up when I had time on my hands – read every last one of them. When I look at Cressington, it puts me in mind of Father Brown's England. Like, there no duck pond or village green; no pub even, or grocery store with a comely lady, hair in a bun. But it so *quiet*, man! It serene. You could hear a pin drop it so tranquil.

Following Sagal down this one straight road, I could imagine very fine gentlemen in their coach and horses trotting down to look the view. The houses set back, very grand in that way they had back in them days – little bit spooky, Gothic one might say. The road buckles into a little rise halfway down, like a steep bump, then seem to drop away towards the river.

'Come on!' she hissing.

I'm going as fast as I can. Well – not full tilt so to speak, but I'm enjoying the stroll, taking it all in. Never knew this little backwater was here at all. Never knew.

'Here,' she beckon me.

The avenue, Salisbury Road as I now see, just suddenly ends, peters out into a very narrow, very pretty drive called The Esplanade. It hardly a drive, more a riverside walkway, and I want nothing more than to just stop here and lean over the railing and take it all in, you know . . . think back on the times I first come here, just a boy, no more, fresh off the boat. Sagal having none of that. She waving me on like mad, want me to get to where she be, right at the end of the promenade. There's a big old wall where the railings end, all sealed off with those crazy bent-back security spikes to make sure nobody climb past. Nothing like that stopping my girl here.

'Follow me,' she whispering, and she just squeeze down through the railing then hold the bottom bar as she drop down on to the beach. Even in this light it suddenly not so idyllic. Everything from burst plastic footballs to a lonely old

Domestos bottle is ran aground in this little gulley, but she's over it in a trice and scrambling up this sloping, moss-covered wall; big sandstone wedge, it is – like a dock wall, but shallow, slanting down to the water's edge. There's this scummy foam lapping the bottom and you don't even want to put your foot in that, case it come out bones. Sagal holding out her hand like I need a bit of help but I'm over and up with her like a mountain goat, just to make my point that old Shakey not quite done for, yet. I catch my breath as we crouch here on the lip of a big, crumbling, derelict docks.

'Where are we, little miss? Where you taking me?'

She jerk her head over past rusting cranes and skips. Just ahead there's a deep still inlet and, behind it, what's left of a huge iron landing shed.

'We used to play here when we were kids.'

'Here?'

'Yep. Came down here with our dad and our uncles when they were bulk-buying. Papaya, guava, sweet potato, you name it . . . you'd get it all down here.'

'You joking me! Here?'

'No joke.'

'Guava? Man, what I wouldn't give!'

She shushes me, signals me to follow. She keep she head ducked down and breaks into this funny run, knees all bent, shoulders shrunk, right past the dock that the wind has whipped to ripples, and over behind the big landing shed. I follow. Ahead there's nothing but stacks and stacks of cargo containers, bright blue ones, yellow ones, red ones, some with company names and insignia. There's a red one bit further back, isolated from the stacks. Sagal check all around then tap firmly on the side of this big steel crate. She gives one last check behind and around her and nods for me to help shove this big arm lever up and try to haul the heavy big door open. We heave it and we heave it, but it one dead weight.

We pull and drag at the big steel door until it gives a bit, then a little bit more.

'Say-gah?' a voice echo from inside. Misha. She must put her shoulder into the door from the inside because now it creak open a foot. Inside I see a mattress, books, this and that. Then Misha come out, holding a torch. Her face still got the bumps and cuts, but nothing like how she was, man. You can see the person now – and she tense with anger when she clocks little me.

'What's *he* doing here?' she hiss at her sister. Sagal looks like she going to burst out crying for a second, then her face all warm and loving and she places her hands on Misha's shoulders.

'I told you, Mimi –'

'Didn't say you were bringing him here –'

'We need *help*, honey.'

She gives her a long, strong hug and Misha squeezes her back. She gives me a very wary look, goes back inside and indicates we to follow.

Hodge

I'll be absolutely straight about this – I don't even *want* to know. There is so much one has to decipher and digest, so many key decisions, so little margin for error as one tries to steer the good ship home to harbour that, frankly, whatever misdemeanor he's committed I'm tempted to say McCartney is welcome to it. Turning a blind eye has never been my way, however – and after Connolly's bombshell one has to, with faint heart and weary spirit, begin facing up to reality. Smithson continues to stare at the desk. I clear my throat.

'PC Smithson, I don't need to remind you –'

'I know, sir. I'll accept the consequences.'

For crying out loud! Girl breaks all protocol. Insists upon seeing me in person. All she's prepared to say at this point is that it's in reference to the work she's been doing with DCI McCartney and that it's highly sensitive, et cetera, et cetera, absolutely critical she is able to see me, it cannot wait, life and death, the full works. I've got a bloody function to go to but I clear a space in the damned diary for her and what does she do? She clams up. She says she has observed behaviour likely to compromise the integrity of the operation, doesn't wish to say more without a union representative present but wants her complaint on record, and requests an immediate transfer back to regular constabulary duties.

'Smithson?'

'Sir?'

'This is completely unacceptable conduct.'

'Sir.'

'You are absolutely *obliged* to divulge *any* information which may materially aid — or, indeed, hamper — the smooth conclusion of any ongoing operation. I shouldn't even be having this conversation with you, I —'

I don't get a chance to finish the sentence. Girl starts with the waterworks, completely caves in. One wouldn't be able to comprehend her at all now, even she *did* decide to change her tune.

'I used my initiative, sir. More fool me . . .' She tails off again. 'He . . . I went to deliver a message to DCI McCartney in person, sir . . .'

'Good grief! Chap hasn't molested you, has he?'

It's hard to tell whether she's laughing or crying. Her face is all crumpled and snot-streaked. I have little time for Smithson's waterworks and her will she, won't she revelations. I begin to shuffle the papers on my desk and eye my watch once, twice, then a third time to make sure she gets the message.

'If you should reconsider, Smithson . . .'

I start scribbling notes on a report. For ten seconds I forget that she's there at all, then it penetrates my subconscious that the girl hasn't moved. I look up. She stares directly into my face, bites her lip as though she's trying to summon up the courage. She stands up, her eyes never once blinking or looking away, and draws back her shoulders.

'It's my opinion, sir, that DCI McCartney is a drug user. As such, I feel . . . well, it's irrelevant what I think. Should disciplinary action follow, I shall expand upon my statement as required. For now, as requested, I would be appreciative of a return to Allerton Road with immediate effect.'

There's something about the way she serves up her message, without sentiment, that lilting accent of hers somehow making her sound strident as opposed to girlish that, amid the madness, slows me right down, as though I'm witnessing all this from the outside, looking in. It takes me a moment to digest what she's saying here. At my tender time of life, after all one has seen and done, all the jobs and atrocities that have come and gone, for the very first time I come as close as dammit to the sensation that one's eyes are popping out of one's skull.

McCartney

I call the Hodge straight back.

'Sorry, boss. Just trying to get bloody Lambert off the phone —'

'Lambert? Thought we'd ruled him out?'

'We have. Well, we *had* . . .'

'Yes?'

Small, short word — loaded with vexation.

'Just . . . I'm sure it's a case of convenient amnesia in Lambert's case, sir . . .'

'Go on . . .'

It's remarkable what the phone betrays, that you miss in a live situation. There's an almost tangible irritation in Hodge's voice; perhaps a touch of fear, too. Interesting.

'Ah, I don't know. Probably nothing, but his memory keeps coming back to him in fits and starts. And he called me just now to tell me he's been recording sound effects for me —'

'Speak plainly, will you, man?'

I love it when they say that. I bite my lip, and stick to the script.

'Derek Lambert reckons he heard some kind of a chainsaw going off the other night. Now, if a chainsaw had been used in the mutilation of Kalan Rozaki, I'm pretty certain Mally Gilroy would have mentioned that little detail, no?'

'One would assume there'd be burns. Abrasions . . .'

'Precisely. Still, the loon's been downloading electric saw noises off the Internet, trying to get an exact match with whatever he's hearing in his head. Anything for a payday, eh?'

'I'd steer clear if I were you, McCartney. Character like that could cause a lot of trouble for us . . .'

'Yeah, worry not on that score. I'm more than wise to the wiles of your common or garden baghead, sir . . .'

Hodge mutters something — just wet noise, this end.

'Anyway — while the possibility endures that Lambert may just have something locked away in that smack-addled bonce of his, it's got to be worth a quick chat, hasn't it?'

'I need you here, Billy. Sorry . . .'

'He's only up the road, sir . . .'

'Where's up the road?'

'Barton Lodge, sir. Upper Parliament Street.'

'Mmm. Well. Like I say. After you and I have discussed what we need to discuss.'

'Sir?'

Another silence. A deep, despondent sigh from Hodge.

'I need to see you. Now please, Billy . . .'

I check the time on my phone. Quarter to six.

'Literally right away, sir?'

Another big gust of despair as he speaks.

'It shouldn't take long, all things being equal. I have a function this evening in town. Be here for six, please.'

I want to ask him what this is about. I want to ask him lots of things. But I know my place. I know I'll have to wait. I'll speak when I'm spoken to.

'On my way, sir.'

'Good man. Until then, then.'

Once again I gun the kart back towards HQ. Another day, another mystery date with Hubert Hodge.

Hodge

'Alfie?'

'Speaking. Hello, gaffer.'

'You well?'

'Can't complain.'

'Good. Good . . .'

One ponders how best to phrase this. Manners will understand, though. He'll know what's required.

'Alf. Bit short notice, I confess . . . bit short-staffed at the minute. Wonder if you can drop by Barton Lodge. You know it? . . . Good . . . Yes. Only if you've time, mind you. Lad by the name of Derek Lambert. Need you to bring him in . . .'

'Am I to book him?'

'No. No. Just need him out of the way for a day or so. You know the sort of thing. Yes?'

'Of course, sir.'

'Thanks, Alfie. Over.'

Shakespeare

So now I know. Now Shakespeare know what gone down, and for all that I have, I confess, been no stranger to the dark side myself, this is some of the most harrowing shit I ever hear. Most of the tale Misha tell me herself — Sagal filling in the bits she forget, or don't want to say. The girl in love. Lucky boy. And she know her family won't have that. Even though her beau a good Muslim boy himself, her people traditional. Like I been saying, old Evan familiar with Somali people. They wonderful folk, don't get me wrong. Loyal. Respectful. Honourable. Just like old Evan, them been through a lot of challenges, man — lot of trial an' tribulation and a whole lot of horror, by and large. They take the exodus, these people, and they dust theyself down and start a whole new life way, way, way afar and in spite of all the trial an' tribulation, they do their very best and they come out smiling. But nevertheless I say unto thee that the Somali boys I come to know can be ruthless, man — and I do mean clinical in the extreme when it come to dealing with some matter that really cross them. Daughter marrying a foreign boy is pretty high on the hit list when it come to offend the Somali sensibility, and for all that Kalan Rozaki a good Muslim with honourable intentions and impeccable credentials, he hooking up with Misha just carnage waiting to happen.

She and he meet at the college, and they stealing off to this flat he renting on the side. They head over heels. They so certain, these kids, that they want to live out their every born day in each other's loving arms that they start to making plans for the future. Misha still not sure entirely what or why, but her beau keep telling she there things he need to finesse with the police before they take the first giant steps on love's great adventure. But they promise themselves to one another. They taken. All peaches and cream until her daddy sit her down and tell Misha that the man she going to marry coming over from Mogadishu to meet she and make of her his wife. Serious. Misha tell me the man is a good enough fellow, but the inescapable truth is he ain't the man she loves. Misha breaks down in paroxysm of grief and tells her daddy no way in the world will she be wed to this alien husband. At this point Misha get too upset and there are tears and huggings between both sisters, and Misha have to leave it to Sagal to finish up the story.

'Asad — that's the man my father wishes Misha to marry — arrived in Liverpool last week. Misha refused to meet him. It was very embarrassing for my parents. My father whipped Misha and beat her until, in despair, she confessed. She told our father all about the man she was in love with. Kalan. My father locked Misha in her room and informed Asad of the disgrace Misha had brought upon us. He gave Asad permission to kill Misha . . .'

'A honour killing?'

Sagal drop her head down low.

'There was no honour involved.'

She sigh hard and shake her head and, once again, the tears coming.

'Asad had already fallen in love with Misha. Who wouldn't? He knew what tradition expected of him, but he couldn't bring himself to do the killing. He tried to flee. Our brothers caught him and brought him back. The community — the men, that is — all my cousins and Asad's family, were insistent that he had to do what was required of a man of honour, there was no choice in the matter. He accepted. He said he would take care of it that same night . . .'

'That would be Tuesday?'

She nod. Yes. Tuesday. Only two nights ago, but already for ever.

'I helped Misha break out of her room. She fled to Kalan and they hid out in the flat . . .'

Misha bursts out sobbing, sobbing, sobbing – it pitiful, man. I so want to help her here but what can I do? I hold her hand tight, shushing her. I think on it. I think hard. It don't come easy to old Evan to say it, but I tell them I think they need to go to police.

'We did,' glares Misha. 'They were supposed to be protecting us.'

I look at Sagal. She nods.

'They had a handler. Una Farlowe. And this one cop, designated to look after my sister and Kalan.'

I have an uneasy feeling I know who this going to be, before they say.

'Who was your point of contact? With the police?'

Misha hang her head low between her knees, shaking her head.

'His name's McCartney.'

Manners

I don't even have to get shown up to his room. Soon as I tell the girl who I'm here to see, she gives us the untidy tidings. The kid's gone. Brown bread. Fuck knows what's went down with old Hodge and this Lambert lad, but what I do know is the story's best kept off the airwaves. News like this can only be delivered the old-fashioned way. I hot-step it back to the Danny before the circus pulls into town. I'm on my way down there to give Hodge the old face-to-face when the moby goes. Dara. Fuck. Not picking up. No way, la — not doing it. Whatever he wants, I pure am not going there. Phone rings off, then straight away, worst noise in the world, starts ringing again. It's even louder in my head, driving me fucking mad. I can't hardly just switch the moby off now, can I? — not after it's rung out. He knows it's on, doesn't he? Be like proper telling him to do one if I switch the phone off now. It rings off — starts ringing again, drill-drill-drill, screaming and banging round my head. Fuck it. Fuck them. Going to have to answer, aren't I? I make out like I've just run back to the car to answer the call, all exhausted and flustered:

'Yiss?'

'What kept you?'

'All right, Dara?'

'Need a little word.'

'Now?'

'Now.'

Fuck. Fuck it. Fuck them all.

'Where?'

'Usual.'

'I've got to see the big fella. Give us half an hour.'

'Ten minutes, Alfie. Get me?'

Line goes dead. For fuck's sake.

Shakespeare

I might have known. Of all the cops in all the world. Still. Needs must. May happen best not tell the ladies of my intentions, but Shakespeare going to need a showdown with Mac-See, soon as.

'Listen to me, Sagal. Will you stay here with Misha?'

She gives it her posh little laugh.

'I'm hardly going anywhere, am I?'

'Thank you.'

'That doesn't even come into it. They'll have been on my scent and after my blood too, as soon as they realised I was gone . . .'

'OK. Try not to worry. Shakespeare going to get you out of this, you hear? Just . . . sit tight. And look after each other. Yes?'

They nod. They terrified. Me too. But so help me, I'm going to deliver these girls out of this purgatory. Back to life, somehow – back to Freedom. I try to let them see in mine eyes that they could trust Shakespeare – that I will not let them down – but those poor girls are the living dead now. They know that the longer this go on, the more it likely going to end up bad. I gravely do not want to leave them here like this, but they isn't a moment to lose. Misha looking pensive, then she seem to make up her mind.

'Here.'

She holding out a scrap of paper – card maybe, no bigger than a Rizla packet. I take it.

'Una. She the other cop, right?'

'Kalan's handler. Everything went through her.'

'We could trust her?'

Misha thinking long and hard on this.

'I only met her a couple of times. Yes. Maybe. As much as we can trust anyone.'

I stow the number away. Suddenly Misha lurch forward and hold me close; hugging me, hard – and then she kiss me. I could die a happy man. For she, I would do so. I promise them I will not let them down, and take my leave. Come on, Evan. This a far, far better thing you do than you do most day. You *can* prevail, boy! You can overcome.

Hodge

One is suddenly conscious of the old headmaster's adage: 'This is going to hurt me more than it hurts you . . .'

So true, so true. What tone to strike? The evidence is damning, and yet . . . this is McCartney we're talking about here. I should have been at the ASO do half an hour ago, so one doesn't feel too cheap or cowardly taking a quick nip of Jura, then another small one for good measure. Get it over with, Hubert. Call the boy in and do what has to be done. I go to the door myself. He's sitting there, dripping wet, but it can't wash the guilt from his face. As soon as I open the door and he looks up at me, and gets to his feet all bristling and awkward, I know that I've got my man. He knows it too; tries for that stoic-but-hurt tone as I beckon him into the office.

'Got to say I'm intrigued, sir . . .'

I bet you are, Billy.

'Still – I'm sure that's why we're here, eh? I'm sure you're going to sit me right down and tell me what this is all about . . .'

He knows though, doesn't he? McCartney knows what this is about, all right. Still, one does as he asks, more or less. One finds it increasingly difficult to look him in the eye so I gesture for him to sit down, hang my head – for this truly does hurt – and I come straight out with it.

'I want you to cast your mind back to that time on the golf course, Billy . . .'

McCartney

What's he on about, 'that time on the golf course'? I wait for him to look up, but he carries on as though he's looking for something on his desk. Highly unusual – very, *very* unlike the Hodge not to look you in the eye. The big man is a stickler for those back-to-basics hardcore family values. The firm handshake. The no-frills, no-bull exposition of How It Is. And whether his message is palatable or no, Hodge always but always delivers it with an unblinking eye-lock. Here and now he is almost sheepish, though, ruffling through papers on his desk, trying to give out this impression of calculated distraction. I've seen it on just a handful of occasions before, once when he was having to 'let go' the good Diana, over the heinous matter of fiddling her expenses. I've never been on the receiving end, till now. Slowly, slowly, he raises his head and seeks me out. He clears his throat, hits me with the rheumy old eyes.

'Billy? That time on Tango . . .'

'Sir?'

'When we thought we had them. The Triangle . . .'

I feel myself tense up, and immediately try to fight it, stay loose. Suck it up, McCartney. Suck that rubbish up. I can't though. I can't just stand here and smile and pretend that never happened. It happened. *We* didn't nearly have them Hodge. *We* weren't even on the same page by the end, were we? *I* had them all wrapped up and ready to serve. I had them, there, trussed like turkeys, yet all I got back was not yet, wait, careful how you tread with the girl. And hallelujah, knock me down with a bleeding feather if those scurvy bastards didn't catch wind of the operation and make us look completely stupid. Correction – they didn't make *you* look daft, did they, Uncle Hodge? No, no, no! You, as ever, kept a keen, clean distance from anything too contaminating while Lanky Lance Campion laughed his way to the bank then did a moonlight flit, never to be seen again on the shores of the River Mersey. So how do we think he caught that wind, Chief Super? Which little birdy gave Lanky the whistle? Maybe we'll never know, what-what? Maybe we'll just never fucking know. Do I remember that time on the golf course!

'I remember it well.'

'I know you do. It hurt, hey?'

'It certainly wasn't easy, sir. All the work that had gone into it . . .'

'Mmm. Never easy, a disappointment like that . . .'

'No, sir. I won't deny it. It was a setback, for sure.'

'It was. Big job – came to nothing.'

He's looking me up and down now like it's *me* who's let *him* down. He clears his croaky throat again.

'How much did it hurt, Billy?'

'Sir?'

'How much did it hurt? My decision not to go ahead? Was that your waterline, Billy?'

He gives me the long, searching, questioning look.

'My what, sir?'

'When I put you on the back burner . . . were you disappointed enough to question this whole thing? This choice, this way of life . . .'

'In all sincerity, sir, I don't know what you're talking about . . .'

'I'm talking about the thing we've always done, Billy – the thing you and I have always agreed upon. I'm talking about beating the bad guys. Have you ever questioned that basic function we provide? Your own commitment, as a cop?'

Hodge is still giving me the intensive eye scrutiny. He taps his desk with the base of a sleek lacquered fountain pen.

'Did you question that commitment, Billy? Think, what's the bloody point?'

And with that, belatedly, the penny drops. I see where he's going with this. Well, fuck him. Fuck them. Fuck this fucking job.

'I did, sir. You know I did. Very much so.'

'Yes. How long were you away for?'

239

'Not long. A month or two.'

'Hmm . . .'

You can never quite tell with all his 'hmmms' and 'mmms' whether he's just clearing his raddled throat or making some deeply perceptive observation. The way he's looking at me now with his eyes all calculating and sly exudes some horrible pompous belief that he can suss things just by fucking looking at you. Can he fuck. *I* can. I know a wrong 'un at a hundred fucking paces! But Hodge? It's madness. It's laughable. He hasn't set foot out of that office of his for five years, unless it's to hack his way around a golf course or go for a long lunch at the Athenaeum. No doubt about it, though; the old bastard's got me down as bent. It's shining out of him, even if he won't come out and say it. I just stare back at him, and it all plays out again in lurid saturated hypercolour. The shrewd old eyes appraising me now belong to the same crazed face that looked up from the putt he was sizing as it dawned on him his subordinate was marching in on his sacred place. He shakes his head, chuckling bitterly, seemingly bemused by life itself.

'I don't know, Billy. I just don't know . . .'

Quite right, Mr Hodge. You don't know; you never did. You can look me up and down and all over but you do not, you will never *know*. The phone's vibrating in my pocket. I slip it out. Missed call. Soprano.

'Sir. You called me in as a matter of some urgency. Is that it, sir? Was this the thing you needed to discuss?'

'Somewhere you'd rather be?'

I muster all the gravitas I can.

'Just one or two pressing matters, sir. A brutal murder and a major shipment of narcotics – and a young girl at large, in fear of her life. But do carry on if there's something I can help you with . . .'

He rakes his eyes all over me. It's hard to tell now whether he's angry, or puzzled, or hurt – he just looks slightly confused.

'Nothing specific, Billy, no. I just wanted to see you . . .'

He goes to say something else, but shakes his head and starts reading some circular on his desk. The phone's klaxon goes now. New text message. I wait for Hodge to look up, but he's still rustling papers around. In spite of everything, I feel rude as I slip out the BlackBerry to read Gorton's SMS.

'Don't let me detain you, McCartney.'

I feel like punching him. I feel like killing him, the way he's sitting there, ignoring me – yet some deeply submerged sense of kinship keeps me there, wanting to believe we're still on the same team. He looks up.

'Just got this, sir. A witness has come forward. Saw the thing in the *Echo*.'

'A witness?'

I pull my phone out properly, read Soprano's message in full.

'A student from the flats by the park . . .'

This strikes a chord with him. He may well be staring at the wall away to the right, but he's sitting up straight, rotating the pen between finger and thumb, digesting every word.

'Wants to speak to us about what she saw . . .'

'Who is she? Is she going to be of any use?'

'That's what I need to establish, sir.'

Whatever boozy flush is left drains out from his face.

'Good, good. Very well . . .'

He gulps hard and begins shuffling papers again. He tries to sneak a little look up from his paperwork, check whether I'm still there. I send out the most resigned, disappointed look I can muster.

'I hope I was of some small assistance there, sir. Whatever it was that was so important . . .'

I turn to leave.

'Billy.'

I stop, but don't turn round.

'Everyone has their tipping point.'

He says it with a certain sadness. I nod once and carry on out of his office, more sure than I have ever been in my adult life that as soon as this one is laid to rest, I'm off. I'm out. If Hubert Hodge can think that of me after all the shit I have tolerated here, then that's me. Finito. They can stick it.

Hodge

I watch McCartney hunch against the rain as he steps into the car park and all I can think is that, once this week is over, I have merely two more weeks to endure. One has gone past caring. Truly – I am no longer even ambivalent. I'm numb to it – all of it. All this business with Billy – I just don't know any more. I really do not know what to do with the fellow. And there's Connolly – the very fact of having to deal on any level with the architect of so much disorder genuinely renders one nauseous. Add to that the way the Rozaki job has spiralled downwards from triumph to disaster, the scandal and compromise one has wreaked upon Gilroy and this matter with Lambert . . . it somehow all feels beyond one's control, suddenly. The whole caboodle leaves me cold.

I reach inside my top drawer – Hodge's treasure trove, keeper of so many secrets over the years – and my fingers jiggle for the trusty old servant who's served one so dutifully over the years. Three more functions, four at most if they spring a surprise on me, then I can put the old dependable out to grass too. I dig the sleek old dicky bow out of its padded satin case, flip my collars up and pad across to the mirror. I'm better out than in, all things considered. It's a different job, these days – different entirely to the one I set out to do. One started out with so much hope; such good intentions. That's all gone now. Those feelings, those aspirations . . . one so very rarely feels that any more. I'm glad my time here is nearly done. I take a good, long look at myself – tense, drained, no longer the man I was. Satisfied that my bowtie is damn near perfect, I phone down for the car.

McCartney

I zap the kart open, jump inside, jiggle the keys into the ignition. Whatever has gone down with Hodge, whoever has got to him, it's nothing to do with me. I can only affect the things I can affect. I call Soprano again, try to strike a diplomatic tone as I ask him, nicely, if he'll start the ball rolling with Sue Strong until I get there – and take Lucy Smithson with him.

'No can do on the latter, sir. Allerton's had to take her back.'

'Since when?'

'Since about an hour or so ago, sir. Been a couple of incidents locally. Short-staffed. You know the dance, sir . . .'

'Huh. No one said a thing to me. OK. Just hold the fort until I get there please, Tony. Low-key as you like. Yes?'

'Roger that, sir.'

I snap the phone away, start the engine, pull away. Although the rain has subsided there's a delicious squish as the tyres engage with the wet road surface. Eight minutes later I am being informed by a non-bearded case worker at Barton Lodge that no, I cannot have a quick word with Derek Lambert. I can have no words at all with Derek Lambert, in fact, because he is deceased.

Shakespeare

Never thought I'd see the day. Shakespeare in a public telephonic booth, copper's calling card 'twixt thumb and forefinger, contemplating a connection. Not even a phone box, incidentally. It not even red. Just a bubble on a post in the middle of the street with a telephone. Ah well – the hell with it. What needs, must. I punch in the requisite digits. I wait. Mac-See phone ring, but the man himself don't answer. I consider this to be very rude indeed and I leave him a message telling him just that.

'Mac-See. Why you don't answer your phone? You too busy? Got better thing to do? Or you too damn scared? Just . . . stop what you doing, yay? This about the thing we discussed, seen? Nothing can be more important than what I got to tell you. Not unless you out saving someone life right now as I speaking to you . . .'

I can't think what more to say, but I stay on the line anyway, and I glad I do so cos a splendid notion occurs to me, myself and I. From where I be here in Garston I can get to the Allerton police station in no time at all.

'Mac-See . . .'

I clear my throat for the gravitas of what is to follow.

'What I going to do is I going directly to Allerton Road constabulary, right now, get me? See if they can locate your good self. Should you intercept this message in the meantime . . . see you there, Mac-See. See you in Allerton Road presently. Soon come.'

I quite pleased with that; neat and to the point. Just a matter of waiting it out now. I still got some call credit left. I prise the folded-up phone number out of my hip pocket and ponder on the wisdom of calling up this Una who may or may not be a ally. In such circumstances I got to reflect that fortune favour the brave. I call she but another no-answer. These cops. Never change. Can't trust a single one of them.

McCartney

My mind is going like the bumper cars at Bognor, one thought colliding into the next before I can process it. Somewhere, within reach, is the truth. It's like the particles that whizz and whirr around your head the moment you turn off the bedside light. You know they're *there* but you just can't see them. You can't touch them. All you can do is sense them, out there, oscillating around your night-space, a thousand million specks whizzing away under their own random force. There is information in my subconscious here, there is truth — but the override that governs my animus won't reveal it. The details remain concealed.

I try to slow my reverberating mind to a stop. I sit in the kart and pinch my forehead. What is going on here? What is going on? Poor Lambert is at the core of this somehow. Think on it. *Think*. Lambert called; made you mad with his cryptic proclamations. Told you about the buzz-saw noise. Said it wasn't a chainsaw, it was *different*. Did you mention that to Hodge, Billy? Did you tell him what Lambert said? My head lurches. I did — I told Hodge about Lambert's call; the buzz-saw noise. He suddenly had to see me. About what? *Why* did he need to see me all of a sudden, right then, no alternative, no negotiation? Why did Hubert Hodge want me there on site, at that particular time — then have nothing in particular to say to me? Was I his alibi? If so, why? I need to speak to Gilroy, find out what he knows about Lambert's cause of death . . .

Phone goes. How I would love to just kill the engine, sit back and succumb to Satie. It's a 427 number. 427? Probably someone from the Residents' Association wanting me to weigh in for a new downpipe, or sign a petition to have the current gardeners sacked or some such life-or-death emergency that *absolutely cannot* wait till tomorrow. I'll let that one go on to answer, thank you very much.

I'll speak to Mal Gilroy, but I'm late for the meet with Tony Soprano at this new witness's place. Stalled at the Great George Street lights I decide to do a good thing – something that I *can* control. I turn *Fields of Fescue* down – 'Bowling Green', a classic if ever there was one – and I fish out the BB and dial her up. Four rings and we're straight on to answer.

'Smithson. DCI McCartney here. I was sorry to hear they'd had to call you back. Just wanted to say – it was good working with you. You did very well. Some other time, I hope. Over.'

I feel better for that. If I'd had a little more encouragement myself in those early days instead of being thrown to the hyenas, who knows how things might have panned out? I might, for one thing, have developed some basic human empathy; the ability to trust. Once upon a time it seemed normal that I was lonely – a loner. It all made sense. Not now it doesn't. Now even the job, my true love, is doing the dirty on me. So it goes, eh? *C'est la vie.* The lights blip on to green and I turn up 'Bowling Green' to a full-blast finale as I move back into the fray. I'll do what I always do when my world stops making sense. I dust myself down and I do the dance. I go on out there, out into the dark, to find the bad guys.

Manners

I can smell that this one's wrong the minute I step inside their gaff. Dara's perched on the corner of the desk with their kid's kipper on him – same serious, snarling look on him staring me in the eye like he's trying to see inside of me. Moz is sat off on the couch, reading the paper. Doesn't even look up when I come in, the ignorant twat. Dara gestures towards a chair. I sit.

'How long have we known each other, Alfie?'

I shrug. If I didn't know Dara as well as I do, and if I wasn't absolutely rock-solid certain that I've never even once let him down over all these years of toing and froing for them, I think my arse would've started twitching by now. The way the pair of them are looking at me, then each other — I'd be thinking it was game over. I've got nothing to worry about though, have I? I breeze right back at him.

'Years, isn't it, lad? Must be, what . . . got to be getting on for twenty years, eh?'

Dara nods. Shoots his brother another little look. Moz nods. Dara pushes himself off the desk, walks towards me, crouches so's he's at eye level with me. He just stares right into my eyes without blinking once. He stares at me for a good thirty seconds — which feels like a whole fucking night — then this sad look comes over his face.

'I'd like to think you trust me, Alfie.'

I nod. Not much else I can do, to be fair.

'I'd like to think you consider me a friend.'

'I do, kid. I like you.'

He does that half-sad smile again, gets to his feet. I get up too, but he signals for me to stay seated. He points a little remote control at the telly that I now see has a frozen image waiting to spring into action. He hits Play and there's my good self, looking well dodgy as I sit in some waiting room. A young girl comes in, in a towelling bathrobe.

'Hiya, Alfie, love. Sorry to have kept you waiting . . .'

'That's all right, darling. I'm sure you'll make it up to me . . .'

It's grainy but it's very obviously me. Our special feature presentation moves on. Alfie Manners, up to all kinds. Brasses. Cocaine. Unlicensed fights. Gentlemen's Evenings with strippers and roast swan. And in between each little clip, there's myself getting dropsies, left, right and centre. It's like a Goal of the Month of kickbacks, but I'm in every single shot. A grand here. A monkey there. Whichever kid they've brought in to put the thing together, he's had a bit of a laugh the way he's done this one jagged kind of sequence that's just my hand going in and out of the stash box, dead fast, but different jacket or shirt on each time. There's no doubt about it – I'm at it, big time. The little video ends with one I don't even remember, me off my cake, grinning into the camera, big mad cabbaged grin on me, leering like fucking Tony Montana, right up and into the camera's eye, going: 'I'm Alfie fucking Manners and I'll do what I want!'

Feel a bit of a quilt now, to be fair. I try to stay calm, see if I can smile my way out of it, but the truth is I'm flapping badly. I turn to Dara.

'What is this, kid? Is there some way I can help you boys?'

My face must be a picture. He clasps his hands together like he's still trying to make his mind up, or summon up the courage, whatever. Then he just comes out with it.

'I need you to kill somebody for me.'

He says it like he's asking me to make a parking ticket go away. Something like that. He's back crouching down now, all his weight on to the balls of his feet as he lines up his eye level with mine.

'Possibly more than one person. I've considered all the options, and all things taken into account, you are the only person who can provide this service for me. In recompense – and in full acknowledgement of your long and devoted service to myself and my family – we propose to pay you one hundred thousand pounds. You can inspect the money, and you can take it right now, if you wish . . .'

He looks to his brother and laughs – a really horrible, blood-chilling cackle.

'Don't worry . . . we know where you live.'

My heart's stopped here. I don't know what the fuck's going on. How have these got me pegged as someone who'll do someone in for money? He's talking again, but I can't hardly hear him because what I now realise, is – I'm thinking about it. I am actually taking this proposition fucking seriously and that scares the shit out of me. Now Moz is up, and even *he's* fucking smiling. This is fucked up. Proper. He puts one hand on my shoulder and talks in that horrible fucking cold, deadly voice of his.

'Alfie. We found out something today that hurt us greatly. Something you could not – or would not – uncover for us . . .'

'Moz –'

Hand goes up. Shut it.

'People seem to think we're nutters. Monsters. We're not. All we want is justice. An eye for an eye. We merely seek to do unto those who have hurt us what they have done unto ourselves. Kalan is dead, Alfie –'

'He's *dead*?'

Hand goes up again. Shut the fuck up.

'Yes. He's dead. And now we're calling upon you to take away the nearest and dearest of those who killed him . . .'

'Who?'

Swear to God, that's what comes out of my mouth. There's a hundred things I could have said; a hundred things I should have said – go and fucking do one, you pair a no-marks being one such reply – but my brain is frozen and my mind is locked and all I can say is: 'Who do you mean?'

'The Ibrahima girl. She has to go.'

'You're not telling me she –'

'You must shoot her, Alfie. You must kill her.'

'But –'

'No buts this time, Alfie. There is no choice in this. You *have* to find her . . .'

I must just be sitting there, staring at him, because the next thing this look comes over his face – pure, naked rage. He cracks my face with the back of his hand and walks off. Dara takes over.

'We know now why they're all so interested in Kavanagh.'

'Kavanagh?'

'Shakespeare.'

'Fuck's *that* loon got to do with anything?'

Dara's face goes all tight and distorted.

'Listen. Alfie. Shakespeare knows where that bitch is hiding out. Tail him, torture him, bribe him out of the fortune we've just given you . . . whatever it takes, you find that African bitch. And when you find her, you shoot her. Yes? Shoot her through the mouth. Him too, if he's stupid enough to hang around.'

He hands me a plastic bag, heavy, all taped up. I don't have to open it. I know what it is. I feel weird. Little bit faint, little bit dizzy, but mainly just . . . *weird*. Weird because, though I can't picture myself pulling the trigger, I already know for a nailed-on cert I'm going to do this. A hundred large – that's laughing money, that is. With that, my pension, bits and pieces I've stashed away – I can start living, at long last. Me and Marie and the girls can have a little taste of what these have been enjoying all these years. The good life. The best of fucking everything. Fuck it. I'll do it, all right. And I'll get away with it and all. Moz comes back and gives me a rucksack full of dough. Looks at me like I'm shit, turns on his heel and he's gone. Dara puts a hand on my shoulder.

'Best way, lad,' he says. 'Best all round.'

He waits for me to go so he can lock up the garage.

McCartney

Sue Strong turns out to be a medical student living on the top floor of a student house overlooking the park – or the trees, at least. From Sue's kitchen, where we now stand, the view extends to the gardens of neighbouring houses, and one long, ramshackle wooden fence which separates the gardens from the peripheries of Sefton Park. Sue is small, intense, bespectacled – a bit like the one with the bins from *Scooby-Doo*. Compared to a hundred per cent of all witnesses questioned, I have to say Ms Strong is absolutely pukka. Precise, consistent, very sure about her information, detailed and articulate in disseminating it. She was in this very kitchen, heating up a microwave meal around seven thirty on Tuesday evening. First thing that took her attention was the 'demented, terrified' shouting and screaming from one of the houses – she points down out of the window, and to her left. She described the screams as being 'like someone who was scared to death. It was absolute terror . . .' Sue looks out of the window to see what's occurring. Back door comes crashing open, lad tears out into the garden, got nothing but his boxer shorts on, running like mad, diving right through the bushes and hedges, even runs through this fish pond – Ms Strong goes as far as to surmise there weren't any fish in it, as she always had the impression it was 'stale, stagnant'. She says that a group of masked men then comes charging out after the lad – Kalan, obviously, though neither Ms Strong nor the hapless Tony Gorton has the foggiest that this is the case. Soprano interjects.

'How many men, Sue?'

She thinks on it. 'At least four of them. Maybe more. I . . .'

I give her the old understanding smile. 'That's fine, Sue. Four or so is very helpful . . .'

'Thanks. I must admit my first reaction was to duck down . . . stupid, I know.'

'Not at all. These were very violent men.'

'The shouting from them all . . . it was terrifying. I . . .' She's welling up a bit. 'I peeped back out and they were hitting him . . . I thought they were sticks at first, but as he was running away, I could see all these cuts on his back. They didn't stop, though. As the boy ran, they were all slashing and hacking at him with these, I don't know . . . swords or meat cleavers . . .'

'Would you recognise one if I were to show you some examples? The swords?'

'I think so. Will I have to?'

'We can't be sure yet, Sue. But please. Carry on. I can't tell you what excellent information this is.'

'The boy who was running away . . . he managed to get over the back fence. The park is on the other side. Well . . . the bit of scrubland that leads on to the ring road inside the park. You know . . .'

'The perimeter road. Yes . . .'

'But . . .' Her lip starts trembling, now. She fights hard to keep it all in. '. . . One of them grabbed his ankle. They kept hacking at his back, trying to drag him back down into the garden. His screams . . .'

She pulls her arms in tight across her chest, starts rocking on the balls of her feet.

'Sue – I'm sorry to have to ask you this . . . Did they . . .'
I try to find the form of words. No luck. Information is king, here – blunt is best. 'Did the gang hack his foot off?'

Good work, McCartney. Girl just breaks down crying.

'I-I-I . . . I don't know!'

'Is it a possibility? That they may . . .'

She's shaking her head, eyes all wide and scared.

'I don't think so. He-he-he . . . got away. At least . . .'

I make the appropriate face – carry on in your own good time. I'm not pushy, me. I'm sensitive.

'. . . I *thought* he'd got away, anyway. They didn't seem to go after him. There was a brief discussion at the bottom of the garden, but I couldn't hear anything at that point. I would have come forward, but . . .'

'It's perfectly understandable. You must have been terrified?'

'I thought they must have seen me.'

'Of course . . .'

She composes herself, looks up at the ceiling for strength.

'I called an ambulance . . .'

'Not the police?'

'Them too.' She realises; brief, guilty look as she corrects herself. 'You too . . .' She gives a nervous little laugh. 'I'm a medic – the ambulance was my first thought . . .'

'Quite right too. You said "at that point"?'

'I'm sorry?'

I refer to a notebook in which I have written absolutely nothing.

'Just now you mentioned that, once the men with the meat cleavers had given up their pursuit, they had a discussion or a debate, but you couldn't hear anything *at that point*. Does that mean you heard something later, perhaps . . .?'

'Yes. That's why I hid. The men came back to the house. They were literally standing *right there* . . .'

She points down out of the window and I humour her by looking out and nodding solemnly. I give her a little smile and nod for her to continue. She gulps and swallows and goes again.

'I think another two or three of them came out at that point and they started arguing among themselves and pushing each other . . .'

'What were they arguing about? Could you hear?'

'"*The girl!*" they kept saying. "*Where's the girl?*"'

Soprano gives me the look. I blank him.

'They were arguing about a girl?'

'I thought they were talking about me . . .'

She gives me this heartbreaking 'am I in trouble?' look. I try the smile, but I can picture how it looks. Forced. Unnatural. Sue Strong blows out through her cheeks.

'I just slid down on to the floor and tried not to make a sound.'

'What happened then? Did they go back inside?'

'Not at first, no. There was another voice, older, *really* loud, and he was shouting and bellowing, "Where is she? Where's Mica?" I think he said Mica. Couldn't be sure. He was irate. Really, really violently angry . . .'

'What did you do?'

She darts us a little look. Funny how people will always think they're in trouble, even when they've done nothing wrong.

'I just sat there, dead still. After about an hour I turned all the lights off and just curled up under my kitchen table for hours, until I was sure they'd gone. I haven't slept . . .'

As they all do, she starts crying. She mainly wants reassurance that she's going to be OK — not unreasonable given the fucking horrors she's seen. Tony Soprano steps forward with a mini-pack of Handy Andies — one thing he is always good for.

'There go, love. You have a good old cry if you want, girl. No one's watching . . .'

I shuffle my feet.

'Know what, Toe? We're as good as done here. Been a long day for everyone. You get off back to the family if you want . . .'

'You sure, boss? I don't mind staying . . .'

I give him an indulgent smile. He sneaks a sly look at his watch and nods his gratitude. Good. Now Tony gobshite Gorton's out of the way, I can get down to business. I lower my voice.

'Sue. I appreciate that you spent the remainder of the night under the table, in fear for your own safety, but . . . was there *anything*? I mean . . . did you *hear* anything, after that?'

She thinks about it, shakes her head. 'No. Not that I can remember . . .'

'OK. Thanks. That's fine. I'm going to leave you in peace now . . .'

That actually elicits a little smile. Wahey! I really am the cop who cares! I duck my head a little closer.

'Just, before I go . . . try to remember, Sue. Did you hear any, I don't know . . . was there a *buzzing* sound, maybe? Like . . .' I shrug and try to look as innocent as possible. '. . . was there any sound like someone was sawing trees down?'

For a moment she just stares at me like I'm mad, then her face goes all wonderstruck. She clamps a hand over her mouth.

'My God! *Yes!* Yes, there was. I remember thinking, at the time . . . I mean, thinking back, that was probably what finally persuaded me it was OK to come out . . .'

Her bat-like eyes are staring at me in wonder from behind those milk-bottle lenses.

'It was the *familiarity* of it . . . I'd know that noise anywhere!'

All of a sudden my soul begins to drain away. Where hope lay, there's a void. It's just like those other times, years ago – I am as nothing. All sound drops away, and all that's left is my pulse throbbing in my eardrums. Sue Strong is looking at me now, worried. She's scared again. I force myself out and back to the here and now.

'And what noise was that, exactly, Sue . . .'

She smiles at me for the first time.

'What I heard was the sound of the saws we use.'

I must still be staring at her. She looks nervous again, takes a step away and wraps her arms around her chest. I make a real effort to sound jaunty.

'Saws?'

'You know. For amputations . . .'

I just stand there and nod. Wild and disconnected thoughts

swirl just out of reach. I go after them, try to file things . . . try to make sense of it all. Sue Strong's voice cuts through my computations.

'I am going to be OK, aren't I?'

That, out of everything, is what finally snaps me out of my dream-daze. I'm back with her, trying to assure this brave volunteer that she did right in coming to us. So many people just lock themselves in, lock us out and let a case take its own course. Sue was one of the brave ones and now she's beginning to regret it.

'This was a targeted attack, Sue. A tragedy, it goes without saying, and a traumatic thing for anyone to have to witness, in any way, shape or form. But . . .'

I slide the card for Victim Support, which applies – or should apply – to witnesses of horror just as much as it does to victims and those close to them.

'. . . there genuinely . . . look at me, Sue.'

She forces a little smile from behind those outsized specs.

'There really is nothing for *you* to worry about here. The only link between yourself and what has taken place here is an accident of geography. This was the scene of the crime, but things have moved on now. I can absolutely assure you that those responsible have been and gone. They don't even know you exist. So . . . thank you once again for your help. Really – you have been incredibly useful. I may be in touch again but, for now, Sue, sleep well – everything is going to be fine.'

As she triple-locks her door behind me, the paucity of the promise I've just made her plays on my mind. We gave Kalan and Misha similar assurances, too – Hodge even more so than myself. We can't undo what resulted from that now – but maybe it's not too late to remind Chief Superintendent Hodge of his pledge to the many decent citizens whose lot it is to live and work in this unspeakable shithole that we are here to serve and protect them. Hodge may well crave the Hollywood finale but, in the meantime, in the real world there are bad men with machetes roaming these streets and it's down to us to stop them.

Shakespeare
I well recall the place. Too well. Look more like a library than a bridewell, but it's the nick all right, once they get you in here. Had me here two or three times; none of them resulting in a charge. I go inside, note that the duty sergeant clock me, ignore me, redouble his attempt to look busy and, after a pause, I clear my throat.

'Excuse me, officer. I'm here to locate . . .'
'Take a seat. With you as soon as possible.'

I sit myself down in this kind of bucket screwed on to a metal bar and await the arrival of the good McCartney. Good cop? Don't make me laugh!

McCartney
Soprano is already in his car, on the phone; ordering his takeaway, no doubt. *That's* why you'll always be a sergeant, Tony! You have no devotion, no dedication, no rage for right to prevail, come what may. You suffer none of the schisms I do, laying off one crime against another, plea-bargaining with myself as I try to justify the crimes I fight; the way I fight them. These are the moments, Tony, when your head is cracked with fatigue and compromise and once again you're asking what this is all about; why you *do* this; what it's for. Did I become a crime-fighter to prioritise? to juggle? to wriggle? to prize one scalp, one collar, ahead of another? I can't remember now. I barely even know why I *did* join up. I'm so tired and it's all so long ago. But you call it a

day, Tony Gorton. Off to bed with you. Sleep is for wimps.

My head is lurching as I wave Tony off, dislocated shards of ideas ricocheting round my brain. There's been a constant bombardment of facts and insinuations and considerations over the past few hours: Hodge trying to imply I'm at it; Lambert's sudden death; Sue Strong hearing the same noise as he did on the night of Kalan's murder. My head is shattered, though. I just can't put things together. I know there's a tensile thread linking all this, but *the* thing that keeps coming back to me is the image of Kalan in his boxer shorts, his life bled out of him just because . . . because what? Why is Kalan Rozaki no longer alive? Why is he a truncated corpse, lying incognito in the body bank? Why? Because we didn't get there in time? No. Because we took too long to sort out his immunity? In part. But the real reason that Kalan Rozaki is dead is that somebody killed him. On my patch, on my watch, an innocent young law student was butchered, and we haven't caught his killers yet. *That's* what matters here. That's *all* that matters here. We have a witness now. We have a witness and she heard a name. That's more than enough to start knocking doors down and making arrests – and that's exactly what I aim to do. Tonight.

Fuck the Rozakis and their drug juggernaut. Fuck all our side deals and compromise and trying to line this up so we skewer all our targets with one true arrow. As of now, I will not be a party to putting the brakes on justice, prizing one catch ahead of another for the sake of Hodge's pride and my obsession. A kid is dead and his killers are at large. I'm calling Hodge right now.

Smithson

I'm right by the copier. I know who he is before he tells Dooley his name. Even in his running gear – I presume this is Shakespeare's training attire — he looks like a funky Royal Tenenbaum in his bright red tracksuit and his natty little Moorish hat. Dooley just ignores him, tells him to sit down, but as soon as Kavanagh is out of sight he's straight out here and on the phone.

'Alfie? Guess who just walked in. Yep. Yep. Got you. Will do, lad.'

That bastard has basically cut me dead since I kicked up a fuss that first shift. He's got away with it, of course — said it was just a bit of banter. Told the rest of the station he was treating me as an equal — giving me as much stick as he'd give a bloke. Yeah? Really? Does he come up behind every bloke and put his arms round their waist? Does he breathe his horrible cancer breath all over them? Tell them they've got 'ten out of ten threepennies'? Does he? To people like Dooley, people like me will always be nothing. Girls on the force are either 'one of the lads', or they don't exist at all.

Whatever Dooley's conspiring there, I can't let it happen on my watch, under my nose. I have to get Evan Kavanagh's attention, warn him that Manners is on his way, but *how*? What to do? I finger my mobile in my pocket. McCartney's message is all very well and good, but he's the last person I'm going to call, isn't he? I crane my neck out to see what Kavanagh is doing. Shit. The old boy is just sitting there in his bright red tracksuit, taking his chances, waiting for law and order to take its natural course. I cannot just stand here and let this happen. To him. To me. There's a code I've signed up to here, and if I sit back and let Manners and bloody Dooley carve this up . . . No way, Welshie — no way in the world am I letting that happen. I really don't have any choice in the matter. I pull out my phone. One thing I *will* say for McCartney — the likes of myself . . . I'm not invisible to him. I'm not nothing.

McCartney

Hodge tries to sound affable, but his heart isn't in it.

'Billy. What now?'

There's the tinkle of glasses and a robust buzz of merriment in the background. I recall, now, he said he was headed for a function. There are only three words in his greeting, but you can hear his impatience and annoyance dripping through. There's fear, too – so I tell him what now. I tell him that, on the basis of Sue Strong's testimony and based on what we already know, I see no justification for delaying arrests any further. I tell him I want to bring in Misha's father and oldest brother for questioning.

'If you're not prepared to sanction this, sir . . . then it may well be time for me to stand down and pass the case to the Serious Crimes Squad.'

For a long time Hodge says nothing, then: 'Billy, trust me – I understand why you're saying this –'

'Good. So that's a green light, is it?'

He must think I'm wired up. I can hear the cogs of his mind working out the form of words least likely to incriminate him.

'Just give me a moment while I step outside, Bill . . .'

Another lengthy pause as I picture him knocking past chairs and tables on his way out. I can hear his wheezy, heavy breathing – then he's back, panting.

'Billy. You do appreciate the implications?' Panting like a thirsty dog, he is. He's had to walk all of twenty paces and he's done for. 'If we begin making arrests?'

'I fully understand the implications, sir.'

'Any remaining element of control we exercise –'

'Yes, sir. I'm fully aware that –'

He coughs and clears his throat simultaneously, talking right over my objections.

'Come and see me, Billy.'

'Sir?'

'Half an hour won't make a difference. Before we go steaming in with all guns blazing, let's just have a civilised look at this from every perspective. Yes?'

Slowly, slowly, I let the air out as I think it through.

'Where are you?'

'I have a room in the Hope Street Hotel. Walk straight past reception and take the lift to the penthouse suite. I'll be there in ten minutes.'

I kill the call and fire up the kart. This time of night I can be outside the hotel in five. Getting there early is key. It always is, always has been, always will be.

Shakespeare

Where the blessed heck is the man? I wait and wait, and still he don't come. Police cars and vans and sirens wailing all night, in and out, action time, over and over again, but no sign of McCartney. I go back up to the desk and wait patiently while the duty sergeant ignores me still.

'Officer? Excuse me . . .'

Nothing. I know him — know that face. Nightmare. He streaked and scarred with the thread veins and burst capsules from a lifetime's dissipation. Booze and backhanders, that his game.

Lady bustling round in the office out the back there. *Wild* red hair she got, man — I mean it *glowing* red, proper red, none of your ginger for she! I know this going to get the duty sergeant mad but needs must when a chap has plighted his troth to two damsels in distress. I raise one arm and waft it as innocent as I can.

'Madam? Excuse me?'

Now the duty officer look up, but the Little Mermaid has

appeared on the scene. He lookin' twitchy, but he don't say a word.

'May I help?'

I reach for my most reasonable tones.

'I hope so, madam. Mr . . . Detective McCartney. Do you happen to know if he got my message?'

Her face betray some kind of something. She shaking her head, mouthing the word 'No!' with a school-ma'am warning look. 'I have no idea.'

I lean my arms on the counter so I'm closer to her level.

'Just that he to call Shakespeare soon as can be . . .'

No doubt about it – the lady definitely know something. Her face positively rippling with nerves and doubt.

'I would greatly appreciate your help, officer. It really is most important. Is there any way at all you can get a message out . . .?'

The lady policeman acting mighty strange. She carry on shaking her head ever so slightly, so slight that you could hardly notice she moving her head at all, eyes all wide and warning like she telling me Shut Up, Evan. And then I know why. The duty sergeant has gone out back and he muttering and conniving with old ferret face himself, Alfie Manners, looking dreadful. He ducks his head around the doorway. His face is all washed out, worse than usual, even. For a second it seem like he's going to step into the little reception area but he suddenly starts to act like he all distracted. Takes one to know one is the saying and I know damn right that Manners up to something here, whistling and trying to seem like he looking for something important. I return myself to the redhead, try to keep my voice hush-hush.

'Should Mr McCartney return to base –'

She shaking her head, angry now, almost hissing at Shakespeare, she is.

'This *isn't* his base!'

OK. So it goes. I get it, lady. I get it. I nod, grimace, nod, and turn to exit. I know how this play – I'm on my own here. I'll walk back to the pub to make sure, but I know there'll be no show from Mac-See tonight. I'll think of something. Come hell or high water, old Evan going to make good on his promise to they girls. I going make it right for them, so help me. I going to deliver them, safe and sound. Just as I get to the steps, fire-hair lady appear at my side.

'Listen,' she whispers. 'That man in there . . .'

'The ignoramus on the till? Or Bad Manners his-self?'

She can't help herself. She smile, nice.

'You know him then?'

'Our paths have crossed.'

'OK. Good. He's been asking about you. Just . . . be careful, OK? Be aware –'

'I shall be mindful. What's your interest, PC –?'

I try to hit her with the old Shakespeare charm.

'I mean it! Be *really* careful!'

'Thank you, PC . . .'

'Smithson.'

I nod, smile again.

'Thanks, Miss Smithson. I mean it.'

'You're welcome.'

Girl look worried. She gradely nervous. I step up to she, try to seem as reasonable as can be.

'If you could possibly appraise Mr Mac-See of the situation . . .'

She all confused, now.

'McCartney,' I smile. She crack a little half-grin too. I hit she with my most meaningful doleful eyes.'It could be very, *very* important . . .'

Little Mermaid nods, just once, but I think she sincere. 'Thanks. I mean it.'

She nod again and gives me that half-a-smile. I turn and start into a steady jog. The Big Plan hasn't quite formed in mine elegant bonce just yet, but there's no harm giving Bad Manners the runaround in the meantime.

McCartney

I'm now well into the final quarter of another twenty-four-hour shift and I'm starting to feel it. Parked up in Hope Place and scanning the hotel through my wing mirror, my lids feel like they've had a lead coating. My eyeballs are tired and gritty, and a deep fatigue drifts through me. I'm just persuading myself that a five-minute disco nap will do me no end of good when the answerphone siren blares into life, jerking me out of my torpor. Good job. There's Hodge looking dodgy as hell, scanning the road up and down as he exits the Carriageworks eaterie. *He* came a long way then! Function in the Carriageworks and a nice cosy suite in the hotel next door. I take it receipts for same will be submitted to Merseyside Constabulary for speedy reimbursement of the sort one could never expect if it were, God forbid, an overtime chit or a claim for the six vile coffees I've drunk these past few hours in a dread effort to keep myself awake. I hop out and lock up, eager to surprise him.

It's well worth it. In classic fashion, just as the elevator doors are sliding closed I get my foot in and join old Hubert inside. He can't hide his shock – even though it's him who summoned me hither – and, enjoying the role play, I act like we're not acquainted, focus my eyes on the ascending numbers as they each light up. We get to the top floor and I stand back to let Hodge out. He harrumphs his way to his room, opens up and ushers me in. Nice. There's a little kitchen and dining area with a jaw-dropping view out over the Catholic cathedral.

'Don't get too excited,' mutters Hodge. 'I drank the fridge before I went out . . .'

'Anywhere nice?'

'Adequate. Supposed to be a fund-raiser – Association of Senior Officers thing . . .' He jerks his head in the vague direction of down below. 'Turned into a bit of a reunion for some of the old boys from next door . . .'

It takes me a second to twig that we are something like one hundred feet in the air, right above what used to be the Hope Street police station. How could I ever forget?

'Was Yards there?'

I've spat the question out before I can check myself.

'You knew Doug?'

'Knew? Is he no longer with us, sir?'

'Sadly not. Doug Yardley passed last year. Good man. Good cop.'

I'm shocked to hear about DI Yardley, but I can't share Hodge's assessment of the man. Another one bites the dust. May his type die for ever, too.

Hodge starts shuffling up polished wooden steps so steep they're almost a ladder. By the time he reaches the top he looks ready for collapse, but it's worth the hike. The entire wall is one huge sheet-glass window which Hodge slides back, letting in a blast of cold night air. He pads out on to the balcony, leans on the rampart and waits for me to join him. For a moment we just drink in the cityscape. Both cathedrals tower over the skyline, backlit in mellow amber and gold. The lights are shimmering all the way down to the docks and out on the river the tugboats blare. I turn and lean my back on the thick glass barrier, look up at the clear night sky. Hodge doesn't move.

'Billy, I . . .'

He just stops. Not a sound from him. I'm alert now. All

I can think is that this sheet of glass is all that's separating me from an elegant six-storey death tumble. I look at Hodge, composed. Deadly serious. I rock myself away from the edge and turn round again, resting my chin on my forearms. Hodge flicks me a look that's barely more than a blink, then sighs hard.

'Stop me at any point at all, Billy, but it's probably best I just talk . . .'

I nod. Hodge gives me one last wistful glance, then shifts back round so he's looking out over the city.

'Let's, I don't know . . . I was going to say let's start at the start, but I'm not really sure when the start is. But let's just go back to what we were discussing earlier . . . the Anglesey misunderstanding –'

'Misunderstanding?' My laugh echoes back into his cube-like chamber. 'Some misunderstanding!'

'Yes, yes . . . and, as ever, one can only apologise for the . . . *selective* information flow.'

He gives it one of his heaviest, most heartfelt sighs-out-loud and waves his hands in the air.

'One has only ever thought of the result, Billy. Perhaps rashly, perhaps unrealistically, I have always operated on a need-to-know basis. The less others knew, the better one could control an operation and navigate one's way through it. It's far from perfect, I know . . .'

He lays those mournful eyes on me.

'There have been times I wish I'd handled things differently . . .'

'Operation Tango being one such time?'

A deathly pause. He nods, once.

'Yes.'

My turn to nod. I feel sick.

'You'll recall I was playing golf that morning?'

I'm still haunted by the scenario, I want to tell him.

'You may also remember my golfing companion?'

'Yes. Mediterranean-looking guy . . .'

'That gentleman goes by the name of Theo Papadopoulos
— surname ring a bell?'

If I felt sick before, my head is now beginning to spin.

'Mello Pop? Melanie . . .'

'Her father was someone I'd known from my earliest days
. . . well . . . *here*.'

He gives it the expansive, sprinkling-seeds gesture, gesturing
all around with one hand. Who is he? John fucking Gielgud?
He allows himself a chuckle.

'Right there, actually. Theo had one of the cafes on
Hardman Street, you know? Open all hours for the boys in
blue . . .'

Spare us the All Our Yesterdays, I'm thinking. I really badly
need to grab some zeds if I'm going to be any good to anyone
here.

'Family lives over on the Wirral, these days — partly as a
result of . . .'

He sighs and shakes his head again, and this time turns and
faces me.

'Theo came to see me a few days before the operation was
due to strike. Remember?'

I don't recall any such thing, but I nod anyway. Where is
he going with this thing? Hodge pauses to make sure he has
my full and undivided attention. He's got me, all right. I barely
even blink.

'Theo Pop had been worried about Melanie for some time.
She'd begun consorting with her cousins — couple of tearaways
from the South End. You'll guess, straight away . . .'

He waits for me to fill in the missing name. I plug my
bottom lip out and shrug.

'No? Her cousins go by the name of Rozaki, Billy. Dara and Moz Rozaki are Theo's nephews by marriage. Annie Pop, Theo's good lady wife, was plain old Annie Rozaki when she first came to Liverpool in '79 . . .'

My eyes must be bulging with horror and surprise. Hodge sounds like he's enjoying himself.

'The Rozakis arrived with the first wave of Iranian asylum seekers . . .'

I can't control the little squeal of bitter amusement that escapes.

'The Rozakis are *Iranian*?'

Hodge gives it the knowing nod.

'Well – Iranian Kurds. The Ayatollah had it in for them too, you know. Liverpool's, if you like, *native* population may well have been on the decline by the early eighties, but by golly there was a definite influx too. Boat people, Iranians, Kurds, Somalis . . .'

I stifle a sneer. 'Kurds and Somalis, hey?'

Hodge nods. 'Indeed. Dara and Moz Rozaki are Annie Pop's nephews. They're her big brother's boys . . .' He lowers his voice. 'Kalan, too.'

I'm shaking my head slowly. Hodge grimaces.

'I know. So Melanie, who is already something of a wild child by this time, thinks her big cousins are just the coolest kids on the block . . .'

To my continued horror and amazement Hubert Hodge, sixty-five, is doing inverted commas with his forefingers as he says 'coolest kids'.

'She's out all hours, taking drugs, cutting school, completely out of control . . . well, you know this. And then Theo comes to see me and tells me he's found a gun in Melanie's wardrobe. A Glock 26 semi-automatic hand pistol, to be precise . . .'

I can't stop myself. I let out a long, slow whistle of admiration.

'Indeed. At that point one began a root-and-branch risk assessment of Operation Tango . . . You may recall I came to see you regarding precisely this?'

I shrug and shake my head. 'About a *gun?*'

Hodge smiles. 'Perhaps I was a little opaque in my phrasing on the night. I had no wish to —'

'Are you certain, sir?'

'Your, ah . . . *apartment* . . .' He allows himself a little chuckle. 'Funny how one always remembers the trivial details. The place you'd bought — it smelt of paint . . .'

His eyes seek mine, and all it comes back to me — the night Hodge called round, asking me, no, *warning* me to tread very carefully with 'the girl'. I thought he was threatening me, that night — warning me off.

'One had to take very seriously the prospect that Melanie Papadopoulos was setting herself up as some kind of teen killer.'

'Thanks for the warning, boss!'

'I *did*. I tried.'

Silence between us.

'There was only so much I could say . . .'

'I still don't understand, sir. How come you pulled the plug on Tango?'

More desperate sighs and grunts from Hodge.

'To cut a very long story extremely short — the morning of the golf course . . . *altercation* . . .'

'Sir?'

'Theo had been to see his daughter in hospital . . .'

'Hospital?'

The Hodge Hand is raised before I've even got the word out. Halt. Go no further. All in good time.

'Melanie was terrified. Told Theo he had to go to the police . . .'

'Go on . . .'

'Said this George Smallwood wretch was out of control . . .'

'Serious?'

Hodge nods gravely. 'He was planning a hit on Mikey Greene.'

'Jesus Christ . . .'

'That's what Theo told me. Not only that Greene was to be executed – he told me the identity of the hit man. Hit men.'

'The Rozaki boys?'

Hodge nods and grimaces. 'In one.'

'They were *kids* back then!'

'Natural-born killers, hey? Theo was petrified, of course. He'd seen trouble – which entrepreneur in Liverpool hasn't had a visit from the Chuckle Brothers? But this . . .'

'Nonetheless, sir – we had Lance Campion on toast!'

'Did we, though, Billy? Or was he being served to us on a silver salver, with all the trimmings? Think back, Billy. *Think!*'

He gives me one of his epic, tired-of-life sighs.

'What do we *know*? In situations like this it never hurts to pare back and pare back until we hit incontrovertible truth. No?'

'Sir?'

'Shall I start? Evan Kavanagh, if I remember correctly, was to introduce the bogus notes into Campion's system, yes?'

'Yes, sir. More importantly, the bags with the pin microphones . . .'

'Of course. So – as far as one is aware, this all came to pass. You yourself, Peters and Anderson were receiving the clearest indications possible that Campion was on the brink of a major drug deal. Their getaway driver, what's-his-name? Flynn?'

I nod.

'Micky Flynn tries to disable the Valley RAF surveillance helicopter. Now, the Lance Campion we all know would *not* go to the lengths of ramming the force's aerial surveillance if this job was not happening. As of 5 a.m. that morning, a major shipment of cocaine is about to leave Cobh. Operation Tango is most definitely *on* . . .'

He's exhausted himself. He pauses for breath, still the deathly expression in his eyes.

'Wind on to 9 a.m. – a mere four hours later. Theo Pop calls me, distraught, and *begs* me to meet up. Absolutely paranoid, he was. Thought he was being followed. He insisted upon meeting away from the city, in an open-air location . . .'

'The golf course . . .'

'The golf course. He was very, very scared. Melanie had been attacked in her cell . . .'

'Hence hospital,' I muse out loud, before I can stop myself.

Hodge nods. 'One of the inmates slashed her neck with a broken light bulb. This was no warning to Melanie – they went for her jugular. It was intended to be fatal. Her father was out of his mind with worry . . .'

'Naturally . . .'

'He told me that masked men had been round to the house, demanding to know the whereabouts of Georgie Smallwood. All this in the space of a few hours . . .'

I can't stifle the groan that escapes as it begins to dawn on me.

'The Triangle got wind of the switch? The counterfeit money?'

Hodge shrugs. 'One can only assume so. That, or they'd found out about the hit that Smallwood been planning . . .'

'Why didn't you *tell* me, sir? Why let me go through all that —'

Hodge's eyes bulge. 'Billy, for crying out loud . . . Theo was in the very act of telling me what he was telling me when you came charging across the fairways like a bloody . . .'

He points one gnarled finger at me.

'You helped me make up my mind, as it goes. When I told you Operation Tango was off, it was, quite literally, the latest news. Do you understand what I'm telling you, Billy?'

I do understand — or I'm beginning to. My brain is galloping here. Shit. It makes sense. It all makes horrible sense now. Lanky dropped off the face of the earth for six months after Tango, before returning to our attention with that gun fight in Amsterdam. He's never been back to Liverpool since. As for Georgie Smallwood — he was found in a shallow grave a few weeks after the great Anglesey oyster bust, in the Forest of Bowland. And Mikey Greene . . . if memory serves me, Mikey fell foul of the Brennan boys a long time ago. I find myself doing a Hodge, shaking my head in reluctant admiration. Never underestimate Lance Campion. Never imagine that he won't be one step ahead of us all. I try to stifle a laugh, but it splutters on through.

'It would have made life easier had you just told me what was going on, sir . . .'

'It would have made life easier if you'd been there to tell . . .'

And he's right, of course. I took my leave, as Hodge recommended that day — and then I took some more. Three months I was gone. I went out into the wilderness and took a step back, had a good long look at my life. I very nearly didn't come back at all. But I did, eventually — I came back. That time away from the job was the making of me. It was the making of Billy McCartney.

'So, OK — you knew it was a set-up —'

'Surmised the operation was doomed to failure —'

'You knew Anglesey was going to go wrong. How come we let Customs go charging in? Did their modesty not matter?'

He gives a strangulated chuckle. 'You flatter me, Billy.' He smiles — not unkindly. '*Of course* I told Peters and Anderson. D'you think I'm mad? I could hardly *stop* them, though, could I? Their decision to proceed was all their own. Peters, for one, was positively *gleeful*, having Tango all to himself. He could hardly wait!'

I realise I am still shaking my head, unsure what's being said here; unsure what to believe. Hodge turns his back to the city. Behind him, winking lights creep all the way out along the coastline. I badly want to trust Hodge, but my every instinct tells me he's reeling me in here. He smiles as though reading my thoughts.

'Billy — Theo was literally making his revelations as you came striding across the fairway! You would have been my first call — had you given me chance.' He ponders long and hard. 'I sometimes wonder whether you've ever forgiven me.'

'Sir?'

He gives me his 'I see inside your soul' look and proceeds to shock me to the core with his next offering.

Shakespeare

Any other set of circumstance and I've got to say this is some fun. I'm being as casual as you like as I go about my business — no way in the world would Bad Manners think I suss that he tailing me. So I'm in and out of every place I know he going to *hate*, man! I surprise the good ladies in All Nations who stay open late on a Thursday night to provide eyebrow weaves, fancy plaits and hair extensions for the weekend crowd. They surprised as hell see Shakespeare coming through the door for a casual chat, big smile on my face. They be even more surprised if they but know that Alfie Manners pacing up and down the Lane out there, seething. I wink at Althea and ask if any tea brewing but her think I'm after tail and chase me pronto, laughing all the time.

'Come back if you want me to do something with that beard of yours, man!'

I never look round once, just bounce around the barrio like I king of Lodge Lane. I pass by Sagal and Misha's shop without even so much as a sideways glance and I head straight on up to old Kebabish Original for some of their rightfully celebrated Chops Masala. Man, they grub so good in this place! Proper grilled lamb chops, real good meat, can see the chef prepare it all, fresh chillies, real spicy spice, right there in the open grillkitchen as you sit and wait. And what of Manners? Will he sit and wait? Will he thump! He got a real problem now, what to do around these parts while Shakespeare partake of his repast. How is Alfie going to play *that* one? Not that there no white faces round Lodge Lane – that far from being the case, thank you very glad. Just not much call for racist, violent, corrupt, volatile police persons round Granby ward as a general rule of thumb, and not much for them to do. I take my time chewing every little morsel of chilli, enjoy every little explosion and sensation in my mouth before deciding on where I'll take him next.

McCartney

Hodge turns to face the river, checks himself and swoops back round, hitting me with his yellowing old eyes.

'Terry Connolly tells me you're at it.'

'Me?'

I'll admit it – my response is pathetic. I'm like the kid in the front row at school who gets accused of pinching the girl sat next him. All wide-eyed and 'Who, Miss? Me, Miss?' I *know* Hodge has been harbouring doubts, but still, he's winded me with this one. I try again.

'So Top Cat's your trusted *confidant* now, is he?'

The hand again. Hodge and his damned 'halt right there' hand.

'I'll get to that. But let's just say . . . let's just assume we've been . . . *compromised* . . .'

It takes me a second or two to twig.

'No. Sir . . .'

Hodge nods, slowly, face full of ponderous significant thought.

'I'm afraid so, Billy. The Rozakis know.'

My guts drain right out of my backside. I always thought it was just a saying, but I go weak at the knees. If Hodge ever thought I was the leak then he knows better now. I have to sit down. If my face betrays a flake of how I'm feeling right now then Hubert Hodge will know my world has just caved in. My mind is going into shutdown. All I can envisage is a deep, cavernous hole.

'How? Who?'

Hodge is shaking his head. 'Connolly says it's come from inside. And before you say it — it isn't Manners. I'm certain of that . . .'

'With respect, sir, and I mean that, how can you possibly be certain of anything Connolly says — or anything whatsoever where Alfie Manners is concerned?'

'Because Alfie Manners works for me.'

I want to laugh, but nothing comes out. I can see my reflection in the glass door, my mouth hanging open.

'Manners?'

Hodge pushes his bulk up from the barrier and slowly, deliberately, begins walking towards me. He's a big man

– must have been strong, powerful in his day. He's getting on now, but from the look in his eye he can still summon up some righteous anger when the situation calls for it.

'Come here, Billy.'

My head is spinning. Hodge has got me here. Trapped on his roof, hundreds of feet above the place where I started out. All his men down below, drinking his good health. He's bigger than me; older, but much more powerful. I take a step away from him, and a step backwards, then another. I come up against the thick, cold glass of his apartment wall. Hodge holds outs a hand.

'Billy . . .'

Manners

I never set out to be a Bad Cop. Who does? You do this job because you want to make a difference. You want to do your bit. But you've got not the faintest slight idea of what it's all about – the reality of the job, day in, day out – until you start working these streets for real. Everything is stacked against you, right from the start. The odds don't bear thinking about, but no one really wants to know. It's just – go out there and fucking get them. The way I've gone – that just creeps up on you. I honest to God did not mean it to go that way – any of it. It starts out as nothing then, next thing, you've took a drink off one of them or they've kept a gaff open late for you. You can't help it – you think to yourself, yeah, he's not so bad, him, after all. For a wrong 'un, he's all right. Then there's a bit of freelance they need, bit of security, cash in hand. Upstairs starts clamping down on overtime and exies, making it harder to make a living, and harder to do the job we want to do and it just goes from there, doesn't it? You start asking yourself who the real baddies are. The ones you're knocking around with – they don't seem so bad at all, next to your

Hubert Hodge and the likes. Oh aye, Hodge is in there, balls-deep with the best of them — all kinds of think tanks with fucking Tom, Dick and Harry, all his fucking junkets on exies while we can't even get a sign-off for overtime when something meaty comes on top. Before you know it, you've lost all sight of what it was you signed up for in the first place. I'm not proud of it. It is what it is. But I never set out to be this way, I swear to God.

McCartney

I laugh and shake my head, still reeling from Hodge's confession — if you can call it that. That's exactly what it felt like, though. This was Hubert Hodge making peace with himself.

'Anything else to report, while we're clearing the air, sir?'

The Hodge manages a rueful grin himself.

'That's everything, Billy.'

We've been in here half an hour and the revelations just kept coming and coming. I'm punch-drunk, here. Hodge checks his watch and heaves his bulk up from the deep leather couch.

'I'd better pop back down there, I suppose. Boys'll be wondering what's happened to me.'

He gestures around the suite, cold as an ice cube with the veranda door still open.

'Feel free to stay as long as you want. I doubt I'll be coming back . . .'

And with that he clears his throat to let me know the hard part is over, grips the polished wooden banister and clunks noisily down the stairs. I hear the swoosh of the door as it vacuum-seals behind him. I stretch out on the couch, stare up at the brilliant white ceiling and try to make sense of Hodge's revelations. After Chinatown, in all the fallout from what Hodge calls 'The Vine Affair', DC Alfred Manners and his colleague DC Kieran Dooley were both suspended pending a full internal investigation into allegations of corruption, brutality and links to local crime families. A month or two later, Hodge himself suffered a nervous breakdown. No explanation was given for his absence but, after six months away from Merseyside, DCI Douglas Yardley was appointed as Acting Superintendent, a position that, without any great song and dance, became permanent until his own health issues cut short his career in 1996. One of the first things 'Yards' did back in '84 was to apply for the reinstatement of Manners and Dooley, successfully arguing that there was insufficient evidence against either of these upstanding officers, both of whom had served under Yardley previously, with great distinction.

When Hodge returned to Liverpool — which he confessed, at one point in the conversation, had become a 'mission' — after a lengthy stint and exceptional results in Northumbria, and a short, unhappy stint on the Isle of Man — one of the first things *he* did was to make certain Alfie Manners understood the lie of the land. Hodge recognised there was scant chance of his bombing Manners out of the force without it looking like a witch-hunt; equally he was all too well aware that the leopard would never change its spots. So he made plain to Alfie that he, Hubert Hodge, expected regular and reliable information from Manners's impeccable 'sources'. For Manners, it has been a game of brinksmanship ever since, trying to work between the lines and stay in the game long enough to collect his pension. I almost feel sorry for the despicable snake.

'*That's everything, Billy,*' Hodge told me. But it isn't, is it, Hubert? Those particles are oscillating again, closer this time, close enough to see but not quite close enough to touch. What are you not telling me, Hodge? What are you protecting so doggedly — or who? I push myself up off the sofa and let myself out.

Manners

If I ever had any doubts about seeing this thing out then the last hour's set me straight. I'm sat in the bagwash like some fucking doley, reading the *Sport* and trying my best not to look like Job, when two deadheads both try to pull into the same parking spec at the same time. Telling it how it is by the way, every cunt thinks they're in a fucking gangster film, these days. Every prick in a 4x4 thinks they can have a fight, and that's just the birds. These two are in those horrible fucking tanks they all drive, blacked-out windows, exhausts the size of missile launchers, and they both dive for the same parking spec resulting in a minor prang. There's no damage but the two musclemen can't be seen to be losing face so the next thing they're rolling over and over in the gutter, ripping their designer strides to shreds; one's got his thumb in the other's eye socket, the other's trying to bite his fucking nose off. Telling you, how the fuck do you police *that*? Why would anyone want to? Let the pair of bell-ends tear lumps out of each other, far as I'm concerned.

I fold my paper under my arm and mosey over to the curry gaff's window and wait for the sooty to look up so's I can give him the evils. He don't look up. He's that hungry all's he can see is the bone he's picking dry. Take your time, Sambo. I've got all fucking night. You're *my* meal ticket, you are.

McCartney

I'm about to pull out into Hope Street but the indicator — loud and clunky at the best of times, though nothing like this — comes thumping through my head like it's wired directly to my eardrums. Bang-click-bang-click-bang! I lean my head back, breathe hard. The road lights are tripping out into freakish blurred streaks and trails like those city-at-night photos where they overexpose the neon and the headlights of whizzing taxi cabs. I'm going under – absolutely flailing. I haven't eaten. I haven't slept. I have no choice, though. I have to keep going, keep going . . .

I have a choice. I pull the kart over, check around and about and open up the boot. I ease the leather wallet out from its lair, get back in and prepare a shot. I sit back and do the job quickly, feel it rush through me. Better. Better. I look at the spent works and think about the newly deceased Lambert. A smackhead, no less – but somebody's son. I'm overcome with a sudden need to speak with my old man. It's a nap he's going to be fast asleep by now, but I spark up a carlota and dial. His voice on the answerphone makes me smile. I wait for my cue.

'Hiya, Dad. It's me. Just wanted to say . . .'

I don't really know what I wanted to say. I'm feeling weak and tearful and I badly want to see him – to hold him, close, while we still have each other.

'Just that I will be back this weekend . . .'

I pause and try to stem the onrush of emotion that's coursing through me out of nowhere.

'Come hell or high water, Father, I shall be there. Can't wait to see you, old fella.'

Pause. Long toke on the little cigar.

'I love you.'

Kill call, sit back, finish cigar. OK. OK. One step at a time. I lean my head back into the soft leather and blink away the sleep that strokes and soothes my aching eyeballs. Rewind, Billy, rewind . . . Lambert's call. Yes – Sue Strong heard the same thing that Lambert did. Shit. Lambert. Anything suspicious about his death and I'll have no choice but to question the Hodge himself. First thing tomorrow I'll call Gilroy. But then, Eureka! From the mere act of switching my thoughts back to Gilroy, there it is all of a sudden – the thing that has been eluding me. The thing that I knew was out there; the thread that ties all these strands together; the thing my dog-tired mind kept hiding from me these last few days and nights surges forth and reveals itself, at last! As soon as my mind factors Gilroy in, the image flashes back. Gilroy in the back of the meat wagon. I never did get round to asking him about that . . .

'*You boys drag me out of bed at all hours of the night . . .*'

I'm very near giggling as I do a left at St Anthony de Padua's and try to remember which of these rambling mansions is Mal's. Whatever separates Me, McCartney, from the subconscious engine that owns me and drives me on, my abject, my absolute fatigue has closed that gap and brought myself and my alter ego back together. There's no other way of explaining it. These notions, newly thought, these ideas that have just now filtered through and come to rest in the foreground of my attention – they've been there all along. The things I now know, I have known all along. Suddenly they're here, at last – processed; complete. I have engaged with the notion and given it form. And now I'm pulling up outside Malcolm's house, hiccuping silently, just like I used to in my nervous, childish excitement at school-work suddenly and unexpectedly making sense. I'm laughing inside because, as of five minutes ago, I've worked out Malcolm Gilroy's role in all this. I bang my head on the wheel in admiration, get out and crunch along Mal's drive, honed for confrontation, maybe, and confirmation – definitely.

* * *

Malcolm looks tiny now, sitting erect and frightened in the exquisite, threadbare old armchair in the corner of their living room. I remain standing. I'm a little harsh on him, if I'm honest about it, but I'm dog-tired, and right now I just need to *know*.

'Why were you there in person the other night, Mal? You're long past having to cart the cadaver back yourself, aren't you?'

'Why was I where?'

'Mal. Come on. I can see it in your eyes. You *want* to tell me . . .'

'Tell you? Come to the point, will you, Billy! Tell you what?'

'You want to tell me about the saw, Malcolm? Was that your idea, or Hodge's?'

He just stares at me, boggle-eyed. There's a hiss and a shake of the head and he slumps down low in his seat. He presses his forefingers to his temples, and then out it comes, the joyous tumult, the catharsis of confession. Gilroy is almost in tears here.

'All I agreed to do was help him get the body away from there, and get it, you know . . . hidden.'

'So what happened?'

'Ask Hodge!'

He covers his face with his hands; begins slowly, slowly shaking his head.

'By the time I got there . . . I don't know. I swear to you, Billy, there's only Hodge could even get me to contemplate *that* . . .'

'Let's start at the start, shall we? What Hodge got you to contemplate was that, in order to disguise Kalan's identity for the next few crucial days, you should use your surgical tools to remove all the usual signifiers. Yes?'

Mal just looks stunned. He's pale, frightened, completely washed out. He nods. I blow out my cheeks in amazement.

'That's pretty extreme.'

'Believe me — I didn't like it one little bit.'

'Wouldn't it have been . . . I mean, allowing you felt it was the only way . . . couldn't you have done it back at the mortuary?'

'What? With all the CCTV? All sorts of jobsworths around waving their forms for you to fill in? Hi, can you just log this one in so I can cart it off down the corridor and mutilate it beyond all recognition!' He lets out a bitter snort. 'Hodge was insistent it had to be there and then — absolute Code Red. He even wanted me to inject the poor kid with morphine — make it look like a drug slaying . . .'

Part of me is impressed; mostly, I'm appalled. However Gilroy wants to dress it up, he's part of this conspiracy. Him and Hodge cooked this up before they even thought of calling me. Wonder if Una knew? Mal buries his head in his hands. His wife hovers at the door, anxious, unsure whether to come into the room. I smile as warmly as I'm able and beckon her in.

'We're very nearly done, Mrs G. My apologies once again for having to disturb you.'

She shuffles over to Malcolm, stands behind the chair. He reaches out and finds her hand, squeezes it tight. I'm strangely moved at the sight. I'll never have that.

'Will I be charged?'

I do my very, very best to look aghast.

'*No!* Don't be foolish, Malcolm . . . what possible purpose —'

'I think I'd like it on record, though. Just in case . . .'

I take a step towards him and rest my hand on his shoulder.

'We can talk about that some other time, hey? Let the dust settle, first. Just one thing I need you to do for me before I let you good people get back to bed . . .'

'Sure. Anything at all . . .'

His servitude makes me feel grubby; unworthy. I know where this is all leading, and it doesn't feel good. I need to know, though. I have to know if Hodge has done for Lambert, too.

'You're a gentleman. OK. If you could just put in a call and find whoever logged a kid found dead this evening, Barton Lodge hostel . . . Name of Derek Lambert?'

No phone call is going to be necessary. You can see it in Mal's face. He's done that one himself.

'Yeah, yeah – very straightforward, that. Been a few of them, all down to the same batch . . .'

'Batch? What batch?'

He shrugs, as though it's common knowledge.

'There's been four addicts died in the last twenty-four hours. Overdose, every one. Three more in hospital. Unusually pure grade of heroin in circulation. We're working with the agencies . . .'

I tune out for a second. A bad batch? Why am I always the last to know these things?! I am dragged, kicking and screaming, back to horrible reality when Gilroy says:

'Alfie Manners phoned that one in . . .'

'Lambert?'

'Pretty sure. Yeah.'

I squeeze his shoulder again, apologise to Mrs Gilroy and stumble back out to the kart. Right then. Right. So the moment I left his office, Hodge called in Alfie Manners – *Manners* – to take care of Derek Lambert? This all suddenly becomes so much easier. Everything is clear. Everything, now, is simple. I've been a Hodge man for so long. I owe him so much. But this has killed me. It's killed McCartney. We'll clear this up as best as we're able, then, tomorrow if I'm lucky, I can supply the *coup de grâce*. Sorry, Mr Hodge, sir, but I think a certain William A. McCartney is going to beat you to that curtain call now.

*   *   *

284

I sit out there behind the wheel, stunned, unable to move. From deep down within I feel an upsurging desire to laugh – but it doesn't come. That strange impulse comes instead, the indefinable motor that pushes you on to take the next step. I pull out my phone and scroll the missed calls. I dial up my voicemail. The 427 comes as a surprise. It was Shakespeare calling from a phone box, telling me he's heading for Allerton nick. That was hours ago. Won't be there now. I'm thinking I could perhaps call Smithson, when there she is. Next message. Timed at 10.11 p.m.

'Sir. Don't know what to say, really. Don't know whether this is appropriate. Sorry if I . . .'

She breaks off. Come on, Lucy! Say it! Whatever it is, say it!

'Just . . . that guy Evan Kavanagh came in, asking for you. I was trying to . . . anyway, doesn't matter . . . I managed to warn him.'

She sounds *so* young.

'Thing is, DI Manners showed up. Tried on his irresistible charm . . .'

'*Irresistible*'. Love it! She snorts in derision.

'He asked me lots of questions in that way he does. Sleazy, you know? I didn't tell him anything. Anyway, sir. Just thought you should know. Please let me know if there's anything I can to do to help . . .'

She tails off and that's that; and that's me, back in the game. Whatever queer adrenalin fires us cops and drives us on and over the line, something massive just kicked in. Forget your Alfie Manners and your Hodge by the way. This is for all the regular cops who do what they do because it's in them. Because it's Right. This one's for you, Lucy Smithson – a damned good cop. McCartney's back in the kart and I'm gunning through every which one-way, no-entry and backstreet I know, trying to beat the clock.

Shakespeare

Well I never. The man himself. Wonders will never cease. I pad downstairs to let him in. Anyone else, you'd feel sorry for him. He look shattered. Even by Mac-See standards of no-expression pale face, the man looks all in. I open up.

'Better late than never, I dare say.'

He far from being his usual bristling superior self, but he still can't take a hit from myself.

'I came literally as soon as I got your message, Evan.'

Oh. It 'Evan' now, is it? Well. Not quite a admission of guilt, much less an apology, but still – Mac-See in humble mode a step in the right direction.

'Come on up.'

'Thanks.'

He follow me up to my quarters.

'Tea?'

'Don't suppose you could rustle up a coffee?'

'Sure. Blue Mountain OK for you? Got a nice mellow Nicaraguan if that too rich for you blood . . .'

He thinking I make some kind of joke here.

'Honestly, don't go to any trouble. Instant is fine.'

'Instant I can't do. But I got all the gubbins here if you want a cup you could taste.'

'Really? Then yes. Thanks. A very strong coffee would be just excellent. Thank you.'

I can see myself make that 'what got into *him*?' face as I pass the glass door into my little kitchenette. What happenin', man? McCartney almost human here. I grind the beans and get the old Alessi furkling. Ploop . . . ploop . . . ploop. A watch-pot never boil. I go back in, sit with Mac-See.

'I been trying to reach you . . .'

'So I gather. What's up?'

'I been playing hide-and-seek. With Bad Manners.'

He smile at me. I never seen this bastard smile once – never.

'I take it you kept him at bay?'

I shake my head to myself, stand up.

'Half. Last time I see him he pacing Lodge Lane looking like he could kill some cat. Sugar?'

'Normally? No. But tonight . . . anything to keep me awake.'

I wink at him.

'For the purposes of this tape-recording, Mr Kavanagh is not in the habit of substance abuse and had no illegal pick-me-ups for the officer in question . . .'

Now the bastard laughing! Dear Lord above. Wonders really will not cease. I go through, get the coffees.

Manners

I'm just sat here in the passenger seat, staring at the rucksack like it's going to go up in a puff of smoke if I let go of it for one second. Berghaus, I notice for the first time. Neat little logo tucked just under the side flap. A hundred and five large, they've give me. Twenty-one stacks of five grand. They're so fucking brewstered they've give us an extra five key and they don't even know it. Sickening, that. Just plain wrong to be that rich you don't miss five grand. What I want to do here is take that fucking rucksack back and tell the pair of them to stick it. I won't though, will I? I'm never going to do that. Too far gone, aren't I? You travel so far in the one direction, there's no going back.

Shakespeare

Still can't be sure. With any cop you know not to trust them, and with McCartney? That would have to be a double no. And yet, and yet . . . he saying all the right things. Lot of what he telling me, he just couldn't know this shit if he weren't on the level.

'Look, Evan, I'm not completely stupid, yeah? I know how this thing works. Where the boys in blue are concerned, it's three wise monkeys . . .'

He standing up now, pacing around the room.

'Just – I am genuinely fearful for that girl. She may well be a witness to a murder – a slaughter. She may unwittingly have a connection to a major, major crime family. For all I know she's already been hunted down and murdered, because – let's have this right, shall we? – the people who are after Misha want her dead. End of story.'

Now he stopped gradely still, piercing me with them ice-cold eyes he have. I wish he wouldn't do that. Make old Evan feel he back in trouble. Reminds me Mac-See just a cop. I drop my head down between my knees, staring at the floor.

'Evan. Look. Please. If you *do* know anything about Misha Ibrahima's whereabouts . . .'

There he go again. Talking like Lawman. Talking down at we miserable wretches. 'If you *do* know anything about where-abouts . . .'

He a *cop*, for crying out loud! How can a man like me ever trust a man like he?

'It is of paramount importance – *absolutely* paramount importance – that you consider sharing that information with me . . .'

'Excuse me – share with you? Mac-See? The cop who on my tail day after day, year after year. The cop who, above all, is a Cop. For real. For ever. You a Lifer, Mac-See, just like I am. But we on other sides of the tracks. I so-so sorry about this, Mac-See . . . but I just can't do it. I can't trust you. I can't . . .

'Whatever you're thinking my game is here, my motives, whatever . . .'

Jesus, man! Will you stop it? Have some dignity, will you?

And he do – he stop right in the middle of whatever he was going to say and I swear as I stand here, he starting to cry. The cynical, snidey career cop that is McCartney going to pieces here in front of old Evan and he fighting now not to proper break down. He gulping hard and pinching his nose and he takes a big gulp of breath and tries his fiercest stare on me again.

'Evan. This is not you and me. Us and Them. The Law and the Lads. My sole concern, I swear to you, is the well-being of one very young, very frightened, very vulnerable young lady who may well be hunted down and hacked to death in the same way her lover was. I simply can't have that on my conscience. Can you?'

He can see I starting to wobble here, and he moves in for the kill. He looking me up and down like he not sure, but then he comes right out with it.

'You have a conscience, Evan. I know you do . . .'

He take a step closer.

'You still think about her sometimes, don't you? Melanie. Little Mello Pop, and how she betrayed you with Georgie Smallwood . . .'

'Mac-See, I think it high time you –'

'That's why you told Lanky, isn't it, Evan? You stewed and you stewed and you just couldn't have it –'

'Couldn't have it that Shakespeare at beck and call of you filth, no!'

McCartney shaking his head all sad.

'No, Evan. I don't think that was it –'

'Yes, McCartney. Yes it was. What you take Evan Portius Kavanagh for? Someone for sale? Someone sell his soul?'

Mac-See don't say nothing. Just look at me, like I a very bad man indeed. He snap himself out of it and go to leave.

'Fair enough. I can't argue with that. In its own twisted

way, it's a principled stand and, whether you believe me or not, Evan – whether it means a thing to you, and I sincerely doubt it does – I have always had you down as a man of principle. That's why I'd hoped you might help me find Misha . . .'

The fella's good. He very near got me. I admit it – I know what happen to Melanie Pop. I hear all about it, how they try to whack her in her cell. How she lose pints and pints of blood. I know even more. I know she a medic these days – one of the girls living over there nowaday say she swear Mello stitch her finger back when the dog took a funny turn and go for she. Little Mello Pop, a surgeon! That was very glad tidings for Shakespeare because, truth be told, I have buried all memory of my Melanie and our love to the very far-flung recesses of mine recall. I know I did her wrong. McCartney know that too. He taking his leave now. He stops by the stair door.

'I wish you well, Evan. No hard feelings. I'm going to find that kid if it's the last thing I do . . .' He pause like he some great orator. 'And, once I've done that, I'm out of here.'

'Ha! Happy holidays. It's all right for some . . .'

'No. No holiday. I'm leaving the city. Leaving the job.'

He smile again. Real smile. He actually look human on it, this time.

'That a promise, Mac-See? Maybe let a chap carry your bags to the station . . .'

He start laughing, proper rolling guffaws of laughter and then he standing there crying real tears. I go to him, hold out my hand to shake.

'No hard feelings either, Mac-See. But you know I could never trust a cop.'

McCartney

Hours after her call, I still can't sleep. I'm splayed out on the floor staring out at a hazy moon that hangs low in the sky.

'I know everything. It's all in hand.'

All she'll tell me now is she's got Shakespeare onside. She's lying low. I'm to meet her first thing tomorrow. I'd expected some sense of closure; if not elation then satisfaction, and an appreciation that everything, now, could be laid to be rest. Yet it came at such cost; such a price. I seek out my works, ready for tomorrow's early start. That's another thing that'll be going too. No more needle. No more fixing up McCartney.

It's past three when I finally hit the sack, yet for all that every flinching sinew of me is crying out for rest I cannot close down. I lie here and stare at the ceiling, willing sleep upon me. I try to name and picture every lag I've ever nicked, but my motor keeps on turning over, no matter what I try. I try telling myself to stop thinking. I try to think about sleep itself, the very act of nodding off. It will not come. Each and every time, my foremost preoccupations jolt me back to a realisation that I'm still awake, and my mind bucks back into action, conned into a sense of having just woken from sleep. I'm alert again, now, and there's nothing I can do about that.

I return to my earlier conviction that this grand finale tomorrow will be McCartney's last ride. The Lone Ranger, galloping through the lawless highways and byways to put the bad men down, guns blazing left and right as they continue to come at him – he'll be no more, that superhero. He can lay that gun down for good. The mask can, at last, come off.

I groan in desperate weary anguish, knowing that without sleep, none of this can come to pass. I think of Dad, again. Those first few months when the penny finally dropped with him that he would never walk again, he was beyond reach;

beyond help. Two or three times that I know of, he tried to end it all. There were doubtless other attempts too. Virginia couldn't hack it – the screaming in his sleep, the mood swings, her role as nursemaid to a man cut down and enfeebled. Yet when she left, it was as though Dad was reborn. It was like he'd dragged himself out of one long nightmare and was so elated to find it was all a horrible dream that it gave him a new lease of life. I would push him along the prom and he would just drink in the fresh sea air and tell me he was blessed.

'I know who I am,' he would say. 'And everyone else knows, too. That *means* something. I've made my own mark, no matter how small. When people think about me or talk about me they know, without question, who I am and what I stand for. They can think of me and say, without any shadow of a doubt, Harry would *never* have done that. I may have been simple, love, but I was reliable. I stood for something.'

I did, too, and I think this is what hurts more than anything. Hodge judged me by his own standards. He let the idea seep through his mind that Billy McCartney could be a bad apple. I can't stand that thought. How could anyone think that of me?

My head is throbbing with a leaden fatigue. My very consciousness is hurting like hell, yet it's too late, now, to do a pill. First thing tomorrow I'm wrapping this up, all of it – and there'll be no hangovers of any sort to impede the day of reckoning, least of all the gorgeous, leaden fog of a zopiclone morning-after.

I did, too, and I get out of bed and look out of the attic window, out over the dark, dead city that has somehow become my home. I stand there for an eternity, staring out, seeing nothing but darkness. I shuffle across to the far wall where my records are all stacked up. I'm in the S box, thinking I should slip Satie on, lie back in tranquil, exquisite misery and drift away on dreams and splintered memories of that one brief time of bliss, when I see her looking up at me. Patti Scialfa, *Play It As It Lays*. I smile to myself. This was meant to be. I slide Patti into the tray and skip on to 'Town Called Heartbreak'. I catch sight of myself in the mirror – a fraud. A freak. I really need a shave. I dance, slowly, feeling every sinew of the song as the tears run freely down my lonely, unloved face. Fuck you, Liverpool. Fuck you, Billy McCartney. Who were you trying to kid?

First light, new mood. The streaky dawn casts shafts of light across the attic floor and with it comes, at last, a surge of well-being. It is upon me now; one of these hugely significant days we cops live our lives for. Days like this are few and far between and, speaking for McCartney, there have been few bigger. *Carpe diem* is the motto, but never has it carried such enormity.

Una is there in the layby – an excellent start as all she would commit to on the phone last night was 'the place'. I'm relieved that I guessed the right one. She checks left, right, front and behind as she crosses the park's peripheral road and jumps in the front seat.

'So. Evan Kavanagh called last night . . . He said you'd not long left.'

Ten minutes later, the plan is in place and this smile just will not leave my face.

Hodge

It would appear McCartney has me over something of a barrel with the Gilroy capitulation. Clearly one can pull rank on him and sideline him altogether but with what he knows for sure – and what else he might surmise – one doesn't wish to be alienating the McCartneys of this world at this delicate juncture. Connolly's not happy about it but he doesn't exactly have much to bargain with, himself. We await McCartney's arrival and, as ever, he is punctual to the minute and immaculately dressed. He sets down a tray of drinks.

'Thanks for agreeing to come in, Terry,' he breezes.

'Well, it's in my best interests, isn't it?'

Connolly casts a glance at myself for a second, then darts a little smile at McCartney.

'I presume we *are* here to agree the terms of my . . . cooperation?'

'We are, Terry. We are here for precisely that,' beams McCartney. The fellow's near demented with happiness. He cannot stop smiling. 'Tea with two I believe, isn't it?'

Connolly nods. McCartney slides a mug across the table.

'Sir. Black coffee?'

I don't like it. McCartney's too jaunty here – far too sure of himself.

'Excellent,' smirks Connolly. 'Should I not have Prendergast here?'

McCartney's all wide-eyed and innocent.

'Oh, by all means. If you feel you'd like to have your lawyer present . . .'

'I didn't say that. I just . . . if we're cutting a deal?'

'We are?'

Connolly looks panicked now. I clap my hands together.

'Can we just get on with this, please?

McCartney meets my eyeline full on and smiles right into my face.

'By all means. So . . .'

He sits down, all ardent eye contact, then, without looking away for a second, he takes a slug of his coffee. Automatically, Connolly and myself do likewise. He beams at us like some born-again religious nutter and leans forward till his nose is almost touching TC's face.

'Mr Connolly. As I've already indicated to Mr Hodge here, I'm acquainted with a former officer you may recall. It's some time ago . . .'

'Really.'

In Connolly's shoes, I wouldn't go for that approach. There's something about McCartney here . . . he's got the bit between his teeth. Connolly's not taking it seriously enough. He's slouched down, pretending to be bored, but McCartney knows he's got him.

'Yes, Terry. Really. Let me refresh your memory . . .'

He pulls out a photograph. I recognise her straight away.

'Her name is Harriet Vine. Most people called her Hattie. Name ring a bell?'

'Should it?'

'It ought to. You ought both to remember her. On what turned out to be her final day's service here in Liverpool back in 1984, Hattie was raped in the cellar of a Chinatown restaurant. You were there that night, Terry . . .'

I watch Connolly carefully. His eyes flicker briefly, but nothing more. Time for me to remind them both who's boss here.

'McCartney, what has this to do with anything —'

Cheeky bugger tries to silence me with a hand. I see now he's wearing plastic gloves. Interesting.

'All in good time, sir. As I've just mentioned, I knew Hattie Vine. I knew her well. I know she'd be gratified — vindicated, one might venture — if her attacker were, finally, to be brought to book . . .'

'Why now, all of a sudden?'

'Good question, sir. If you were to ask Vine herself she'd doubtless merely say the timing was right, somehow. Maybe she feels, I don't know . . .'

He gives me a curious, somewhat malicious smile.

'Maybe Vine would feel that there was nothing to lose now? But if it's me you're asking, I'd say it's no different to any other job. It's all down to quality of evidence, sir. It's down to *proof* . . .'

'McCartney . . .'

'Three little letters, sir. D. N. A. Something we didn't have at our disposal back in the day . . .'

He stands up, ambles over to this end of the table and casually collects the cups. *Now* one comprehends the latex gloves. For a second, I'm chuckling inside as he bags the coffee mugs and puts them to one side, still in view. Connolly is drained of all colour. One almost feels sorry for him. McCartney turns his chair the wrong way round and sits with his arms dangling over its back now, like he's some high-powered investigator, interrogating *me*.

'I've asked you both in for this little chat, because somebody in this room perpetrated that awful crime —'

'McCARTNEY!!'

I'm out of my seat before I know it, pointing right in his face. He just smiles, indicates that I should sit.

'Sir, please, if you will. This is of the utmost importance . . .'

To one's own amazement, one finds oneself complying. I seat myself and McCartney continues.

'From what Vine recalls, the assailant had to be around five feet six in height. His knees dug into the backs of her legs at a point that would indicate he was, well, diminutive in stature . . .'

I sit back and observe Connolly as he scoops the sweat from his brow. McCartney turns towards me, face triumphant.

'So, sir — my sincerest apologies for my insistence on your being here to witness Connolly's confession . . .'

'Confession!'

Connolly's up out of *his* seat now, all affronted. McCartney's right in his face.

'Sit the fuck down and let me cut to the chase, Connolly. *Top Cat . . .'*

He hisses that nickname with all the contempt he can muster, making it, and Terence, sound extremely silly, all of a sudden. Top Cat. Connolly looks anything but, right now.

'Listen to me, Connolly, and understand this. You will be going to jail soon, for a very, very long time . . .'

Connolly's standing there, eyeing me wildly, looking for some kind of reassurance.

'No matter what the boss here may have told you to the contrary, CPS intends to prosecute you for your involvement in the import and distribution . . .'

TC bounds over to me now, standing behind me as though I'll protect him from the bullies.

'All right, all right, enough of this shite —'

'I'd advise you to sit, Terry —'

'I want my lawyer here. Now.'

McCartney just smiles at him again.

'Of course. I'll see to it right away. While I'm gone, I just want you to ponder a notion if you will — all in your own good time, of course . . .'

For once, TC is lost for words.

'Like I say, Terry — you're going down. You will very likely die behind bars. So what you need to consider now is how you want to be perceived by your fellow inmates — and how you want you want to be remembered by your own family, by the criminal community you hold so dear —'

'Hold it, hold it . . . you going to just sit there and let him spout this crap, Hubert —'

'Hubert, is it? Nice. So my question is this, Terry – do you want to go down as a cheeky, opportunistic, "if I didn't do it some other cowboy would" drug dealer?'

McCartney gives it five seconds for dramatic impact, then:

'Or do you want to go down as a nonce?'

That, I have to say, has Connolly floored.

'Do you want the world to know you're a rapist, Terry?'

Connolly eyes up the coffee cups as though he's considering one last crazy lunge for them, then you can literally see the fight fizzle out of him. He sits back down, arms spread out and face down on the table in front of him, and he lets out this long, awful, desperate groan. One simply cannot feel anything approaching sympathy for a committed outlaw such as Connolly, but suffice to say one can physically experience the dismay he now radiates. It has all gone desperately, horribly wrong for Terence Connolly – his daughter, his empire, his liberty . . . all gone. What is, no doubt, even worse for someone like Connolly is that this is all way beyond his control now, too. McCartney and I exchange a look. He shrugs. After about a minute, Connolly resurfaces.

'Come on then. What do you want?'

McCartney smiles again.

'Good. Excellent. We want what we always want. We want the truth.'

'The bird won't press charges?'

'That's correct, Terry.'

'Definitely?'

'If your information turns out to be reliable, I assure you that the Chinatown incident will rest on file, never to be reopened.'

He thinks it over. I'm about to say something when McCartney claps his hands together, even louder than before. I hate to say it, but I think he got that hideous affectation from myself.

'So. OK. There's another reason I wanted Mr Hodge here today, Terry . . . I'm given to understand you've intimated to the Chief Super that one of the families concerned in the supply of narcotics and munitions in this city may have breached force security?'

'If you're saying what I think you're saying the answer's yes. They're into you.'

'And you're saying that I'm the leak?'

He hangs his head. That's not Top Cat sitting there. That's a spent and broken old man. A has-been.

'I didn't say that —'

I'm up and at him.

'Whoa-whoa-whoa . . . hold on, Connolly . . .'

He smiles up at me.

'It's Connolly now, is it?'

'It always was.'

I let this sink in with him.

'Did you or did you not tell me the Rozakis were getting their information from McCartney?'

He sits up straight and faces me now. He means to enjoy this bit.

'I did not, sir.' He seems emphatically sure of that.

'Oh?'

'No. I asked you how many people knew what was going down, and you drew your own conclusions . . .'

Connolly points at me — one manicured finger.

'What did I say to you, Hubert? Human error. No?'

McCartney's back swinging punches.

'I don't think rape comes into that category, does it, Connolly?'

Connolly wants to snap back, but you can see it in his eyes. He has nothing. He's a goner. McCartney's nose is almost touching TC's face.

'Let's stop fucking about here, shall we? When does the gear come in? I want dates, names, times, locations, everything. Shoot.'

The pair of them are just eyeballing each other now. Top Cat's first to crack – he just starts laughing, and doesn't stop. It builds and builds and builds until he's almost hysterical. Eventually he's able breathe long enough to speak.

'You really are one clueless pair of dickheads, aren't you?'

McCartney says nothing. Just waits. Connolly shakes his head very slowly, stifling the laughter as he speaks.

'The gear's already here, soft lad. Come in through Harwich last Sunday – not that you thick bastards would ever have known . . .'

He starts welling up.

'Useless fucking Pakis never even cut the shite, did they? Lazy bastards just pressed it and whacked it out. Surely even you no-marks must know there's near perfect smack doing the rounds? Bagheads going down like flies all over the show.'

He's shaking his head again, slowly, sadly.

'That's what killed my little girl. That's why I want those bastards hung . . .'

It's embarrassing. One of Liverpool's most notorious villains is now sobbing freely, his lip trembling as he hangs his head low. With the necessary self-censure, I now understand why Top Cat was so insistent McCartney did not attend our recent briefings. McCartney would have seen through Connolly a mile off – making out he was prepared to give us the relevant information in exchange for his own freedom. Ha! And all that time he was preparing his own little exit strategy while the drugs were already here. McCartney moves his chair that little bit closer to Top Cat and, after a second's pause for thought, he takes his hand.

'Terry . . . the drugs that killed your daughter. The drugs that have killed half a dozen kids this week alone. What . . .'

He hesitates. Might be for effect. Never know with McCartney. You just never know. He gives TC's hand a little squeeze.

'What else can you tell us about those drugs?'

'It's fucking *them*, isn't it? Them Kurdish scumbags! I don't give a fuck what happens to myself. Get those fucking Rozaki no-marks and string the bastards up.'

'We'll get them, Terry. We just need a little more help, if you can.'

Connolly's stopped his snuffling now. He's just staring at the same spot on the table.

'Go 'ead. Ask us whatever.'

McCartney clears his throat, shoots me another quick look. He's excited. Like myself, he can smell the breakthrough.

'Where are the drugs now?'

Connolly remains silent for an eternity.

'Terry? Where are the drugs?'

One would hate to imagine what train of thought is playing across Connolly's mind – let alone the images accompanying them. He lets out one long, cathartic sigh and mutters, almost inaudibly, 'It's all at Bobby's.'

McCartney leans right into him.

'Bobby's? Who's Bobby?'

Connolly stares at him like he's mad.

'Bobby, you tit! Bobby Kelly.'

McCartney looks as though he's going to faint. Connolly holds out his wrists melodramatically, symbolic acceptance that, for him, the game is up.

'The gear's at Bobby's yard.'

McCartney stands up, his face perfectly expressionless. Then he smiles, like he's suddenly seen the light. We all have. I arrange for Connolly to be taken down, and McCartney and I get right into our plan of action re the Rozaki and Ibrahim arrests, along with my crowning glory – the raid on Bobby

Kelly's timber yard. I could hug McCartney. I really could hug him.

Shakespeare

The hell he expect me to get cats from? Cats and dogs – the hell he even on about, anyway? I going to go along with it, because the girl got no other choices, but for crying out loud – kill a fox? Why? Even by a copper's standard, the man half sick.

Manners

Aye aye. Mayday Mayday. Careless talk costs lives, McCartney, lad. See you on the other side, divvy. Here we go, then. Tell you something for nothing, lad, once this is all done and dusted, first thing Alfie's getting himself is a proper set of wheels. Feel ashamed going after McCartney in a fucking Vauxy, even if it was made on the banks of the royal-blue Mersey.

He swerves right into Devonshire, then left on to Eggy Road. There's Cheers on the left – used to be. Little dance studio now. Picture of innocence. Wonder if the kids in there now know what went down there before it was all pink tutus and *Britain's Got No Talent* wannabes? Used to get a late drink in Cheers, back in the day. All changed now. Everything's changed. Thank God it's fucking Friday, Alfie lad. Thank God you're offski.

I feel the gun in my pocket. McCartney's heading full tilt towards Speke. I follow as best I can.

Now then, now then . . . Indicating right just before St Mary's. There's fuck all down there. Used to be a thriving docks, Garston. All closed down now that, far as I know. I can't exactly follow him down there. There's fuck-all traffic, just the one muddy track leading to a dead end where the port used to be. He'll suss us right away; best I can do now is stow the car and follow the useless twat on foot. Not like he can go anywhere, is it?

McCartney

I pull the kart in on the left, before the road track trails off into a quagmire. I park up behind a stack of rusting container crates and just sit there for a moment, scoping it all out. Shakespeare described Misha's hideout to Una in great detail but, precise as he was or tried to be, there are two dozen containers here that could match that description. I rack my brains and circle three hundred and sixty degrees, searching for a clue. He told her he'd scrambled past a big stretch of water, so I head down to the dock to my right.

There's a huge, cavernous, dilapidated frame of a landing shed, completely out of sorts next to the noble solidity of the sandstone wharf. The water itself is perfectly still and almost overlapping the dock walls, so high is its level. There's a rusting old container right at the water's edge, still branded with the vivid bright yellow of the Geest banana logo. I sense ghosts everywhere, relics of times and mores gone by.

The moment I get past the dock itself, I know I've found the right place. Although it's surrounded by other similar containers, there can be no mistaking the one that's being used. There is a deep, curving rut where the door has been dragged open and shut, carving its signature in the soggy earth. There are other signs too – footprints, fresh orange peel, things most people wouldn't pick up on, but to me, it's clear as can be that this red metal box is where she's hiding out. I approach very slowly, releasing the safety catch of the Glock in my pocket. Now we'll see if you can ever trust a copper, old Shakey my friend.

Manners

Lost him for a second there, but I sees him now on the other side of the wrecked shipyard. Got to hand it to the old weirdo, he moves fast for a fella his age. Our age. I ducks down and scrabbles along down the side track, trying to keep him in sight without the bastard sussing me. I just want to be certain where he's gone and where she's hiding, then it's just a case of waiting it out. Soon as he's out of the picture I can move in and get the job done.

I pops my head back up, give it the full scan, left and right. Lost him again. He was over by that stack of old steel containers, then whoosh! Gone. I scope all round again. No one. Nothing. It's grey and overcast and the viz is not so good. Suddenly, this doesn't feel right. What if McCartney's seen me? What if he's doubled back round? I hunch my shoulders and feel for the pistol, bricking it all of a sudden. I try to calm myself down, think it through. I've done fuck all yet. I can walk away from this, make a call . . . just back the fuck right away from them two lunatics. Then again – a hundred large. I could always deny it, try to keep the wedge, but would you want the fucking hassle? Fuck it. Do the fucking thing, Alfie – in and out. I pulls the gun out, put my finger on the trigger, trying to bring up a image of all that dough in the Berghaus. This is it, Alfie lad . . . once you've thought the thought, you've as good as done the deed, anyways. What I'm thinking is that I am already halfway to fucking hell and I may as well damn myself good style, when suddenly:

WHANG! BANG! BANG!

Three fucking explosions that sound like they've gone off inside my own fucking skull it's that near, and that fucking loud. Jesus Christ! I completely shit, there – did not know what was going on. Still half in shock now; my head's ringing. I duck back down behind the container and crawl on hands and knees as far as I can away from the shooting. Fuck getting muddy – I'm more bothered about getting out. Whatever's gone on down there, whatever McCartney's got himself into, I know better than to call it in. Thing like that, it'll call itself in. Proper. No way someone hasn't heard that, and no way yours truly is going to be found anywhere near the smoking gun.

I stow myself in a little alcove underneath a stack of crates and I sit there and wait. Sure enough, the sirens come. I crane my head out. Paramedics. Bobbies'll be along any minute too. Nailed on. I'm all of a sudden very glad I'm not out here on my tod. I gets myself up and out of the little hidey-hole, and I try to inch closer and see what I can see. Can't get the clearest view of it, but there's a stretcher getting taken back into the ambulance. I'm trying to get myself up on to this kind of mini-crate when suddenly my heart plummets stone dead with that nervous, anxious joy you get sometimes. Fear. Anxiety. Anticipation. Excitement. I strain my eyes to make sure. They've covered her up and that, so obviously she's gone – but it's got to be her. There's a slim, brown arm trailing down from that stretcher, and what is pure heaven here is that she's game, set and match and it is fuck all to do with DI Alfie M. Can I fly it with the Brothers Grimm? Fucking right I can! All's they wanted was the girl gone, and that, to me, looks like she's well past her sell-by date. I gets my phone out, set focus and snap a beauty of the stretcher getting took back to the ambulance, girl's arm clearly visible. One-o-five kay for fuck all, man. Result.

The paramedics' siren screams out again and the ambulance is skidding its way back through the mudbath to the unmade road out of there. I gives them five and let them go, then – and I'll admit, I'm shitting it, here – I makes my way over to the container where the shooting come from. Red steel box.

Poor girl's coffin, that, kidda. I hold my breath and force myself in there. Blood all over the fucking walls. Mattress all splattered too. I starts snapping away for more proof, just so Moz and Dara can't get weird on us. There's always something that sets you off at a scene of crime like this, and when I sees her teddy bear with her blood streaked across him I pure can't help myself. I'm gone.

When I pulls myself together, I phone Dara and tells him what's gone down.

'You're sure she's gone?' he goes. No tone in the voice. Business, business, business.

'Finito, lad. Got photies and everything.'

Long pause from him. Says nothing at all, until I'm starting to think the line's gone dead, then he just goes:

'Come to Bobby's.'

Puts the phone down, end of conversation. Telling you – world's fucked up.

McCartney

I observe Manners sneaking back out of the container, more furtive than a kid in an orchard, and I watch him all the way back up the track to his car before I stow the binoculars. Funny how he actually moves like a rodent too. I make my way back to my beautiful old Merc, start her up and make the short drive to the landfill site we identified. The ambulance is already in situ. I tap on the back door and Una opens up.

'Best get rid of these, hey?' she goes, holding her nose and making a face.

I nod. She hands me one of the thick industrial bin bags and jumps down with the other. We drag the cadavers over to the landfill and heave the bin bags over the edge into that vast, disgusting sump. Mine tears as it tumbles to a stop – red, bloody guts tumbling out, then the serene, slender head of the fox. Shakespeare did well. Two cats and a fox, pinned to the container's walls and ready for me to shoot at close range. Enough blood to fool a fool like Manners. I bound back into the ambulance.

'OK, everybody. All clear.'

There's a good-humoured groaning as the blankets come off and Evan, Misha and her sister Sagal sit up.

'Couldn't have stand that for much longer, Mac-See,' grins Evan.

Sagal has a protective arm around her sister, who just looks lost. She's hardly with us at all, poor kid.

'What now?' says Sagal.

I explain what now – that it's up to Misha and Sagal. We've created a workable exit strategy, should they so choose. Where the girls take it in legal terms is a matter for their own reflection – especially young Misha, should she decide to give evidence. Only she can prove irrefutably who was involved in the attack on Kalan. It's her own family she'll be putting away here, and McCartney will be long gone by the time it comes to court. If it *goes* to court.

She's safe, anyway, and that was always my overriding priority. For myself, it's a quick coffee now and a dash across town to witness the *pièce de résistance*. The troops will have been briefed by now and well on their way to Kelly's yard. Ever the nobleman, I've handed the collar to the Hodge – how could I not – but I badly want to be there to see this one go down. I make one more phone call – to Barnaby Giles. A promise is a promise, after all. No matter what the provocation, one has to stand for something.

Hodge

Dog & Gun. Never was a district so aptly named as this nasty little ghetto off the East Lancs Road. Wedged in the miserable no-man's-land between Croxteth and Gilmoss, what's left of Dog & Gun is little more than a bookies, a Boozebuster, the wretched estate itself and a clutch of middling businesses, clinging on, one imagines, for the grants, the incentives and the excellent access to the main motorway networks. That's what's in it for Kelly. M57, M62, M6, all just a stone's throw away. He can ship the stuff in and trundle it right out again, all under the emerald-green livery of his timber trucks. I'll confess to a level of surprise and no little embarrassment that we didn't think to knock on his door before now, but the good news is our ground troops confirm there are substantial quantities of drugs still on site there, and all the main players are gathered for tea and crumpets. I shall relish the look on their faces as we make our presence known. And on a purely personal level, I'll be fascinated to see with my own mince pies just exactly how these cowboys conceal their consignments. I've seen some ingenious methods over the years and I have to say my curiosity almost matches my hunger to lock these bastards up and throw away the flaming key. Ideally, McCartney would be here to enjoy the entertainment, the crowning moment of our dogged – occasionally, admittedly, somewhat ragged – pursuit of these villains. But we've got them now, and the moment the rear exit routes are sealed off we're going in, whether McCartney makes it here or not.

Hello, hello, hello, though – what's all this? Surely that's not DI Alfred Manners zooming in through the main gates? I tend to think it is. Which, on the one hand, rather puts the cat among the pigeons in terms of our timing . . . we're not quite ready to go yet. But on the other hand, it does somewhat hand us that final scalp on something of a silver salver. Oh, McCartney, McCartney – wherefore art thou? You really should be here for this! I can't risk the moment over a point of sentiment, though. Everything's in place now and we're good to go. I engage my walkie-talkie, take a deep breath and utter the words of destiny.

'All units stand by. Over.'

I'll admit to a moment's pause – not for the drama but because, atypically for myself, I am suddenly completely and utterly choked. I'm barely able to force out the appropriate command, and find myself settling for a muted: 'Let's go.'

And that's it. I listen to the hiss and crackle of numerous 'go-go-go's and wait for the beginning of the end of all this. I sit back and watch as the boys in blue – and high-visibility yellowish-green – go steaming in and I rest my head backwards and wait for my tears to pass.

McCartney

It seems I missed the Rozaki boys being dragged kicking, literally, and screaming to the meat wagons. I missed Alfie Manners, by all accounts shocked silent, absolutely stunned as he, too, was led away. A large sum of cash was retrieved from his vehicle and the word back from the labs is that the first few bundles of banknotes are contaminated with gack and smack, and there are still another seventeen wads of dosh to analyse. Alfie has some explaining to do.

As I get there and join Hodge at his vantage point, I see Bobby Kelly's fat head being coaxed downwards into the back of a Special Response vehicle. He is wearing a shiny black shirt, tucked into what I can only describe as waiters' trousers. The only part of the spectacle I witness in full and awful cop-vision is the distressing sight of Kylene Kelly, my little Dolly Parton clone, flinging herself upon an arresting officer, spitting and scratching and hurling the most inelegant invective at the poor sap. I sigh and shake my head at Hodge, who simply turns and walks back to his vehicle. He's left me with little choice but to step down there and calm Mrs Kelly myself. If she's there, then she's a suspect.

I take my time ambling into the main forecourt of Kelly's yard, anticipating the moment when she clocks me; the initial confusion, the recognition, the penny finally and horridly dropping for her. I know exactly how this will play. Somehow Kylene Kelly, up to her eyes in complicity, guilt and connivance, will turn herself into a victim here. In this city of denial, Kylene will not allow the notion that she deserves what she's getting – what she's about to get. She will simply not accept that we have her and her fella bang to rights for crimes knowingly and cynically committed. She will instantaneously switch to full-on siege mode, with herself as the betrayed, and good old McCartney playing the classic Bad Cop. Her face will cloud over, then twitch with vituperative malice as she twigs that the guy in the suit, the cop coming towards her to take her down once smiled at her, socially, after hours – the ultimate and unpardonable sin in this twisted, tainted, infernal hellhole of a city.

'You go the Nugget,' she'll be muttering to herself. 'You go the Nugget and you never said fuck all about what you do . . .'

I pause two yards from her, and offer up a smile of true regret. She looks me in the eye and tries to spit in my face, but her effort falls some way short. I see a jubilant Barnaby Giles heading towards me, smiling. From out of nowhere, Hodge arrives to supply the necessary *mots justes*. Doubtless he'll head down the Athenaeum after this, and break out that bottle of Cheval Blanc. It's a matter of mild regret that DCI William A. McCartney will not be there to help him sip its velvet splendour. McCartney has left the building. McCartney has left the Pool. I miss the cursed place already.

* * *

Yesterday was another marathon session – multiple interviews, applications for extended detentions and slowly, slowly, the first confessions and charges. I was at it and at them until past 2 a.m., yet I feel bright today – livelier and lighter of step than I have done in weeks. I'm not tied to any specific time, but I want to surprise Dad by getting there before teatime, get us both out in the fresh air for a good old walk along the seafront before a damn good supper in the Ship. I can taste it already – Freddy's succulent gammon and pineapple washed down with a pint of Palmer's Dorset Gold. I can honestly say that I haven't felt this kind of excitement in ages – that innocent, giddy, childlike anticipation of good times ahead. I love my old man and I relish the time I spend with him and all of sudden I'm wishing the next few hours away and wishing I was there on the prom with him. Virginia? That's another story. I might get in touch if I decide to stay on a while, but I'd only be doing it for him.

I have to look my best for Dad – always. Every time, the moment I walk in through the door, he'll look me up and down like I'm on inspection. But in spite of the severity of the job in hand, I'm in and out of Alternatives in no time at all. Natalie knows exactly what I need and, checking myself again in the kart's mirror, I've got to say she's excelled herself. All this test I've been shooting and the twenty-hour shifts and yet more shots to get me through these last few sleepless days – it's all taken its toll. I've had stubble like Desperate Dan, but Natalie in her peerless brilliance has stripped me bare. Smooth as a grape, I am – not a trace.

I sit for a moment in this crinkled old soft leather car seat then I start up the kart. Deer Tick comes on. I settle back, try to enjoy the drive back down south. It's one of the things Dad's drummed into me – try not to be always looking forward to the pudding and the After Eight mints; make the most of what's on your plate right now. Nonetheless, I am what I am – a brooder – and in no time at all I'm thinking back to him. To them.

We'd only been there just over a year. It was always Mum's dream to move to Devon or Cornwall, but when the chance came up of a sub-post office so close to the seafront in Swanage, she just begged Dad to go for it. Dorset was close enough to Devon and she wouldn't take no for an answer. So Dad spoke with his Super, tied up his pension and retirement benefits and departed the Leicestershire Constabulary a few months shy of thirty years' service. They had me late – never thought they could have kids – so, for me, the move down south was a complete adventure. New town, new school – I could almost reinvent myself. 'Goodbye Dear Friend' comes on. I turn it up.

I remember the morning it happened as clearly as if it were happening right now. I wish I could erase it or suppress it, but it never goes away. It haunts me. It inspires me. We were upstairs having breakfast when there's a knocking at the main door. They were clever – it wasn't an aggressive or intrusive knock; it was familiar, almost friendly. One of those tap-tap-tap-tap rhythms your own postman would use. Dad opened up expecting an early delivery and was immediately bundled into the back room by two men in balaclavas. I'd got halfway downstairs to help him unpack and lay out whatever had been sent – stamps; Premium Bonds; tax discs for cars were my favourite. The robbers were too fully immersed in the moment to look up, but I saw the whole thing. Dad toughing it out, bluffing that we had no safe. The robbers getting more and more angry.

'Open the safe!'

Just three words, but they froze me dead. My heart stopped, I swear. I was there, but I was paralysed. Helpless. Useless.

'Open the fucken' safe, you prick!'

Scousers.

They hit him, but Dad was having none of it. Laughed at them and told them they had less than thirty seconds to run. Told them he'd already hit the alarm under the counter. One of them started to drag the other one out, but the accomplice just stayed where he was, like he'd fallen into a trance. Then slowly, oh-so slowly, he raised his sawn-off shotgun and rested it on his right forearm, closed his left eye and aimed at Dad's face. That's when I jolted back out of my rigid terror. I screamed and launched myself down the stairs. The gun went off. The robbers fled. Dad was shot right through the pelvis. One minute he's Dad – the next he's in a wheelchair. Your life can change in a second, just like that. Mine, too. Up until then I wanted to drive a juggernaut. From that moment on, I wanted to be a cop.

We're enjoying the silence. The sea breeze, though strong, is warm for this time of year. I like the sensation as it bristles through my scalp and whips up between my legs. As we approach the junction with Station Road, I brace myself. I never enjoy this part of the ritual, but I know it gives Dad some strange kind of comfort. We go through the same routine, every time I come back. I park him up outside the Spar shop where our little post office used to be, and I sit on the bench and wait while he stares and thinks and runs things over in his mind. In a moment we'll be on our way again, off to the Ship where Dad will thrill to my latest heroics. I'll have to take my time and stop repeatedly as I explain, again, who Moz Rozaki is and how he's related to Theo Pop. But he'll love it. He'll love the fact that his little girl is out there, doing what I do to make this sordid world a less bad place for people like my dad.

He lets me know he's done, for now. I step over and release the brake, turn him back round. He reaches back over his shoulder for my hand, squeezes it and keeps hold of it.

'I hope you'll pop round and see your mother while you're home?'

I don't answer.

'Hattie?'

I ruffle what there is of his hair through his tweed cap. 'We'll see.'

'She misses you, you know. You shouldn't be so harsh on her.'

'Fine, Pater. I shall do, then. For you.'

I lean forward so the wind can't muffle the levity in my voice.

'For you I shall endure Virginia's icy welcome.'

'She's your mother, love.'

I squeeze his hand and very slowly let it go as I begin pushing again. We trundle on in happy silence.